Dear Readers:

There's nothing quite like taking a vacation with your best friends: the spring break getaway on a student budget, the rowdy bachelorette party in your twenties . . . and decades later, the revitalizing divorce trip.

Bad Tourists taps into the thrill and comfort of going away with the women who know you the best. The first ones you call when you fall in love, or when you can't make it out of bed.

Darcy, Kate, and Camilla are a trio of close-knit friends in their forties who are treating themselves to an extravagant retreat—paid for by Darcy's hard-won divorce settlement—at the remote and luxurious Sapphire Island Resort in the Maldives. They're grown women, and they want a real vacation; they've earned it. With private villas perched over the ocean, breathtaking views in every direction, and spa amenities you can only fantasize about, the resort is the perfect place for the trio to unwind, reset, and embrace a fresh new chapter in midlife.

So why can't they relax? It could be the menacing emails from Darcy's ex-husband. Or the bruised face of their new friend, Jade, a young newlywed staying at the resort on her honeymoon. Or the looming anniversary of the night that left Kate traumatized by survivor's guilt for the past twenty years. The tension escalates when the body of a resort guest washes up on the beach, igniting wild suspicions and reckless confrontations that explode into a jaw-dropping and unforgettable final act.

Bad Tourists is Caro Carver's first entry into the world of women's suspense thrillers, and her first work under a new pen name. (First of many!) She set out to write an irresistible story that combines female friendship and murderously menopausal women with a new take on a classic vacation thriller narrative and an oh-so delicious twist.

We don't immediately know why Kate, Camilla, and Darcy are friends—it's a bombshell when we discover just what ties them together, and I was utterly hooked from that point on. This propulsive read is impossible to put down, whether you're lounging in an armchair for a staycation or turning the pages in a beach chair and looking over your shoulder at the other tourists. We may not have a new season of *White Lotus* in 2024—but we will have *Bad Tourists*.

Yours,

Carolyn

Carolyn Kelly

Carolyn Kelly | Associate Editor | carolyn.kelly@simonandschuster.com

ALSO BY CARO CARVER

BAD TOURISTS

CARO CARVER

AVID READER PRESS

NEW YORK LONDON TORONTO SYDNEY NEW DELHI

Avid Reader Press
An Imprint of Simon & Schuster, LLC
1230 Avenue of the Americas
New York, NY 10020

This book is a work of fiction. Any references to historical events, real people, or real places are used fictitiously. Other names, characters, places, and events are products of the author's imagination, and any resemblance to actual events or places or persons, living or dead, is entirely coincidental.

First Avid Reader Press hardcover edition July 2024

AVID READER PRESS and colophon are trademarks of Simon & Schuster, LLC

Simon & Schuster: Celebrating 100 Years of Publishing in 2024

For information about special discounts for bulk purchases, please contact Simon & Schuster Special Sales at 1-866-506-1949 or business@simonandschuster.com.

The Simon & Schuster Speakers Bureau can bring authors to your live event. For more information or to book an event contact the Simon & Schuster Speakers Bureau at 1-866-248-3049 or visit our website at www.simonspeakers.com.

Interior design by Carly Loman

Manufactured in the United States of America

10 9 8 7 6 5 4 3 2 1

Library of Congress Cataloging-in-Publication Data

ISBN 978-1-6680-5884-8
ISBN 978-1-6680-5886-2 (ebook)

Dedicated to Alice Lutyens, agent and friend

Tyger Tyger, burning bright,
In the forests of the night;
What immortal hand or eye,
Could frame thy fearful symmetry?

—WILLIAM BLAKE, "THE TYGER" *(1794)*

WE'LL BEGIN WITH THE INDIAN Ocean. Night has transformed its ultramarine waters to shades of bruise, a navy lick shimmering with the reflections of a billion dead things. Stars, in other words, for dead things can also be beautiful.

Like the body in the water, bleeding into the reef. Even in death, the man is beautiful—especially so, his black hair visited by yellow and silver fish, severed tissues billowing in the current, as though he were an oceanic element. A rare anemone. Everything is more graceful underwater. Even murder is a ballet.

Night brings predators here. There won't be much left by morning, the human distinction of his corpse erased. Unsuspecting resort guests might take a kayak out, its fiberglass belly slicing over a dark secret.

I relish the thought of that. The drama that lies in the possibility of discovery. It's a gift of sorts, a sudden treasure I can reward myself with again and again.

All it takes is the flick of a knife.

PART ONE

Dover, England
September 10, 2001

SHE'S THE LAST GUEST TO check in.

It's after midnight. The field trip starts at six in the morning. She'd planned to be in bed long before now to be fresh for their dig. To make Professor Berry proud.

Everything went wrong tonight. First she lost her student rail card, then the train was delayed, and then the taxi driver took her to a different Spinnaker—Spinnaker House on the other side of the city. Absolute chaos.

Spinnaker Guesthouse—the place she is actually booked into—is a detached Victorian house in the middle of nowhere, at the wrong end of an industrial estate. No corner shops nearby, very few streetlights. Everything looks worse at night, she thinks, hefting her backpack up the steps to the front door. Where's the bell? It's dark inside. She'll need to wake the owner, who'll probably give her shit for being so late.

But no—the front door is ajar, and she spots a faint light from an interior door that leads to the small reception office. She pads quietly inside, relieved to see an older man at the desk, mid-fifties, the age of her dad.

"Sorry," she whispers. "The taxi took me to the wrong place."

He smiles but doesn't say anything, pushing a clipboard across the desk. "This you?" he says. She looks over a list of names. Hers is the only one without a tick, and she nods, watching him place one against it.

The man is standing in a weird pose, his right hand pushed into a stiff jeans pocket. And the way he's smiling at her without saying anything . . . it's odd, like a kind of frozen grimace.

"Can I have my room key?" she says finally.

He turns, unhooks a key from a panel, and hands it to her. The tag reads ROOM THREE.

"Thanks."

She turns and heads back into the hallway and up the stairs to a dark landing lined with doors. Room three is the one closest to her, its brass number glinting in a wisp of light.

The room is basic and smells of weed, but she doesn't care—the bed feels delicious when she falls on to it. She doesn't undress, doesn't set her alarm.

SHE WAKES WITH A JOLT. What time is it? Her watch reads a quarter to six. She's stupid, so stupid, for not setting her alarm, but lucky that she's managed to avoid sleeping in. Just. This trip has been circled on the flip calendar in her student bedsit since the last academic term.

She washes her face, brushes her teeth. She rubs a roll-on deodorant under her arms, changes her socks and pants. Outside it's still dark, but she feels better for having slept.

Her stomach rumbles. Professor Berry said he'd take them to get coffee and croissants at a cafe by the site before they start.

She throws her toiletries bag and underwear into her backpack, gives herself a last once-over in the bathroom mirror, fixing a blue hair into place and wiping sleep from her eyes. Then she opens the bedroom door and heads onto the landing.

No sign of anyone. The waiting area in the small reception office is empty, no sign of the creepy guy from last night.

Five minutes to six.

She had expected to see Professor Berry waiting downstairs, eager to set off, or maybe Bao, a fellow postgrad whom she knows is also staying at this guesthouse. A dozen of the other postgrads are staying at a different place, due to this one being fully booked. The minibus should be here, too. Where is everyone?

Panic grips her—what if this is also the wrong guesthouse, too? Last night was such a fiasco, it wouldn't surprise her.

She sets down her backpack and heads back upstairs, hoping to find someone she recognizes, someone she can ask.

But the place is silent as a grave.

She notices that the door to room four is slightly open. Perhaps she could glance inside, see if she can spot someone she knows. She knocks.

"Hello?"

Through the opening she can see a backpack and a familiar pair of brown hiking boots neatly placed beside it. This is Professor Berry's room. A moment of relief: she's in the right place.

"Professor Berry, are you in there?"

She risks a glance around the corner of the door, and what she sees is so confusing, so wrong, that she staggers backward, winded and choking as though someone has struck her, hard, right in the solar plexus.

Her beloved professor is lying on the bed in a glossy pool of blood, his legs folded awkwardly beneath him, his eyes wide and staring. She rushes to him, her brain wheeling. *How does CPR work? Should I check his pulse?*

"Professor Berry," she pants. "Professor Berry!"

But then she sees the gash across his throat, a deep slit above his pajama top, a dark hollow where his left eye should be. Blood the color of plums congealed there.

She screams and lurches away, unable to comprehend what she's seeing. "Help me!" she screams. "Someone! Help!"

No one answers. She stumbles blindly along the hallway, her mind lurching. One of the other doors is open and she falls against it.

Inside the room, she begins to plead with the man in the bed to help her. He's asleep, she thinks, burgundy covers drawn up to his throat. But above the headboard is a long smear of red, like a marking from the Old Testament. She approaches, whimpering, resisting the voice in her head that shouts at her to get out. The curtains are open, the window overlooking gray squares of empty industrial lots. The stranger in the bed wears a grimace, the sheets sopping with his blood.

IN THE ENSUING YEARS, SHE'LL tell a jury, then a psychologist, how she ran outside and fell to her knees on the pavement, vomiting. How the minibus arrived, the driver finding her howling on the ground. He thought she was having a fit.

In the back of the ambulance, she shook in giant, uncontrollable spasms as she watched body bag after body bag being carried down the steps of the guesthouse.

Six people murdered in cold blood by the man at reception with the smile that raised the hairs on the back of her neck.

The one who let her live.

TWENTY-TWO YEARS LATER

1

DARCY

She's dreading leaving the boys.

Nine days away from them. The longest *ever*. Charlie isn't speaking to her, either, which makes leaving even more difficult. What if he doesn't say goodbye? He's twelve, and Marsha said her boy was the same at that age. If the newborn stage was tough, parenting a tween feels like masochism, and it's especially tough now that she's divorced. Last year Charlie was still giving her cuddles and telling her he loved her. But he's always looked up to Jacob, his father. He looks like Jacob, too, his clone: that same intellectual forehead, same feathery blond hair, and deep-set blue eyes. When Charlie took a lead role in the school play, she offered to help him prepare. She loved theater as a teenager, excelled at it. But her attempts to help backfired, and now he isn't speaking to her.

Through the bedroom window Darcy sees the metal gates fold open, a black car gliding up the driveway, and takes a deep breath.

"He's here, Marsha," she calls to her babysitter, who is downstairs with the children.

"Right, come on, boys," she hears Marsha say. "Let's say goodbye to Mommy."

Darcy's suitcases are in the hall already, but she spends another few moments scanning the room in case she has missed something. Of course, she hasn't missed anything—this is Darcy, Queen of the Lists, and she's already checked her Maldives list a dozen times over—but nerves are kicking in, drawing a cloud over her brain. She inspects herself in the mirror, tugs a strand of freshly dyed chestnut-brown hair over her ear. She frets for a moment about the shade of pink the manicurist painted her nails—it's so bright, not the sort of shade she imagined wearing at forty-one years old. Camilla had encouraged her to go for acrylics with some kind of nail art—miniature cacti or llamas, for God's sake. She wasn't sure if Camilla was pulling her leg. The pink was already outside her comfort zone. For the flight, she's picked a knee-length cotton day dress from Boden—navy with a white scalloped hem—and matching navy espadrilles, a delicate gold chain at her neck. No makeup. Darcy never has any time for that, what with running around after three boys.

She deserves this trip. God knows she deserves it.

She heads down to the entrance hall, where Ben and Ed, seven and nine years old, respectively, are standing like two little soldiers against the radiator, waiting for her as Marsha suggested.

"Thanks for babysitting at short notice," she tells Marsha. She's a woman in her sixties whose own children have flown the nest. She looks after the boys sometimes when Darcy is at meetings.

Marsha gives her a kind smile. "Pleased to help."

"Jacob will pick them up at six, but any problems, just make sure to call me."

"Darcy, I'll be fine," Marsha says warmly. "Make sure you enjoy yourself. You deserve it."

She smiles at Marsha and touches her on the shoulder.

The boys look crestfallen as she bends down to them.

"'Bye, Mommy," Ben says. "Will you call us?"

She touches his face. "Of course I will. You be good for Marsha, OK?" Then, turning to the doorway where a sliver of Charlie's body is visible: "Love you, Charlie."

No answer. She takes a step toward him, but the door closes with a bang in her face. She sighs and glances at Marsha, who gives her a sympathetic smile.

"Have a great time," Marsha tells her as she heads to the taxi. "And try not to worry. Everyone will be *fine*."

Heathrow sits just thirteen miles away, but traffic is usually bad, and she pulls out her phone to check if there are any messages from Camilla and Kate. Nothing from Kate, but one message from Camilla, with the usual stream of emojis:

At Terminal 5—buying gin! 🍸 📷 🍸 💄 ✈ See you outside Pret?

She feels her heart lift. It'll be worth it, this trip. Sometimes you have to remind yourself why you're doing something to push away all the mom guilt.

This is her divorce trip, the mother of all celebrations to herald the end of a terrifying custody battle and a full-scale war to ensure she received the financial recompense that she deserved. Jacob's business specializes in artificial-intelligence software, and he's made a fortune at it. Darcy helped him set it up. She did his books in the beginning, wrote emails, proofread his contracts, drafted project bids. She never thought to ask for a slice of the company. She assumed her marriage was a done deal. The only contract she needed.

It's also the anniversary week of a devastating moment in her life, one that changed her for ever.

The cab driver takes her bags, and she waves at Marsha, Ed, and Ben, a tear in her eye.

"Sorry," she says to the taxi driver, plucking a tissue from the box between them. "First time leaving them."

And then they're off, the house and her three boys behind her.

What was it the lady at the counseling place told her? *Not my circus, not my monkeys.* It was a mantra Darcy was to repeat whenever she found her thoughts flinging back to her marriage, to the old life. One of the wonderful things about the otherwise unfortunate business of divorce was all the freedom she now had, all the *autonomy*.

She tried to focus her mind on that. Autonomy, power, independence . . . The thing is, she isn't bothered about those things. They're important to people like Camilla and Kate. Darcy, however, thrived on being the figurehead of her family, the one who found keys, made meals, washed clothes, removed splinters, cut toenails, endured sports day. Two years in a row, she'd stayed up all night to make costumes for World Book

Day. From scratch. Jacob didn't even know how to work the dishwasher, for God's sake. Darcy was the captain, a full-time wife and mother, the CEO of their family—and she did it well.

And now, it's all gone. She has sacrificed her body, her career, her time, and her identity, for—what? Her roles as chair of the parents' committee at her children's school and elected parents' representative for both their swimming and football clubs gave her enormous pride. But her reputation had been blighted by gossip when Jacob left her, and she had ended up stepping down from her positions, citing "lack of time" to save face. The real reason was shame. She couldn't bear to be treated differently, with pity. Her dignity erased.

Everything in Darcy's life had been ordered with the kind of precision that would have pleased her navy lieutenant father, had he lived long enough to see it. She had thought she and Jacob were happy as a result of her efforts. But a lipstick smear on a shirt collar blew it all to shit.

She's reduced to a cliché. Spiraling like a condom wrapper in the tumble dryer. For the first time in many years, she feels an old itch under her skin, demanding to be scratched.

Heathrow is dizzying and chaotic, travelers bustling past, knocking into her. She feels flustered, irritated, until a voice calls her name from behind.

"Darcy?"

She turns to see Camilla waving at her, wearing a floppy fedora with an orange ribbon. She's had hair extensions put in since they last met, twelve inches of glossy black curls tumbling down from either side of her hat. She's wearing an orange silk dress—no bra—a mass of gold necklaces, heeled sandals. Her chest and arms ripple with muscles, and her shoulders glisten, round and solid. Darcy feels instantly frumpy in her presence.

"Camilla," Darcy says, squeezing her tight. Camilla always smells and looks gorgeous. She steps back and looks Darcy over, her dark eyes twinkling. Camilla is of Filipino heritage, though she was born and raised in Cambridge.

"You ready for this?" she asks.

Darcy lifts her eyes to Camilla's. The nerves she felt a moment ago dissipate, and she gives an assured nod of her head. Her phone pings with a flight notification.

"Ready."

2

KATE

NOW

Kate reckons she's the most reluctant person ever to go to the Maldives.

Sand, sun, sea and sweat—the four most repulsive *s*'s she can think of. Also, salad and syringe. She doesn't like either of those, and sex . . . actually, it's been so long that she doesn't have an opinion on it any more.

She pops another Jaffa Cake into her mouth and eyes the black square of the flight information display suspended in the middle of the concourse. It's like an object of deep time, she thinks, a lump of gneiss streaked with white minerals. Her eyes track to the flashing red digits at the left of the screen. She springs to her feet—the red numbers mean her gate is closing. How could it have happened so quickly?

She hefts her backpack on to her shoulders and lumbers toward the signs that tell her gates 11–23 are to the left. By the time she reaches the left-hand corridor she's swimming in sweat, dismayed to find that it's about a mile long. Where is the fucking gate?

Kate drives her legs forward, inner thighs chafing uncomfortably, a sharp pain blooming in her lungs. She keeps her eyes down, avoiding the stares from other passengers. Finally, a sign appears—GATE 22. Still running, she rummages in the side pocket of her backpack for her passport and boarding pass, thrusting them at the desk agent.

"On you go," the woman says, and Kate feels her knees almost give.

By the time she finds her seat on the plane, she's wheezing and red-faced, and too knackered to care who sees.

She takes her seat, wincing at the small space she must squeeze herself into—and between two strangers. She thinks of her favorite armchair, roomy and comfortable, in the front window of her home in Carmarthenshire. It's a rustic cottage that she's sweetened over the years with hanging baskets and a lot of hard labor in the front and back gardens. Last year, she painted the door and window frames sage green. Mrs Williams down the lane painted her garden gate a similar color not long after. Kate, a trendsetter! She's not one for fashion, or trendsetting for that matter, but she takes pride in her cottage. It's where she works, plays, and rests. She has absolutely zero desire to go anywhere else.

She looks down at the ground as it falls away from the plane, the streets and houses of Cardiff diminishing into little dots along the Welsh landscape. She could have hopped on the train to Heathrow and flown with Darcy and Camilla, but she's relieved not to have to sit for ten hours next to Camilla. Camilla exists on chia seeds and air, has strong opinions about macros. Kate has nothing against anyone who wants to spend two hours a day strengthening their core, but Camilla likes to lecture everyone else about the importance of it. And given that Kate hasn't seen or felt her core since 1992, she's glad of the chance to avoid that.

The seat belt sign flicks off. With a sigh, she reaches for her backpack beneath her seat and pulls out her laptop.

Kate is a ghostwriter. Her latest project involves working with Niall Hardman, a soccer player from the noughties who has decided to bless mankind with his literary talents in the form of a series of crime novels. The first is about a psychopathic serial killer, which has required extensive research on her part into the mind of a psychopath. As per her previous clients, the idea is that Niall provides the basic outline of a story, and she the finished book. But Niall's ideas are secondhand drivel, and his ideological leaning is, to put it mildly, *on the old-fashioned side*, so Kate has had a hard time trying to nail down a decent plot. Worse, Niall is convinced that he's a storytelling maestro, and that Kate's role in the process is merely to transcribe his terrible plots word for word, like a typist. She's avoided using the term *misogynistic* when discussing his plotlines, which has taken great diplomacy. When she attempted to point out that some readers might find his female body count problematic, he suggested that she "wasn't much of a writer."

"Aren't you supposed to shape the story around my plotline?" he said over a Zoom call.

"To a degree," Arthur chipped in. Arthur is Kate's agent, and a friend. "Why don't you leave the twists and turns up to Kate? That's why you hired her, isn't it?"

Niall fell silent, chewing the skin around his fingernails, revealing a heavily tattooed hand. Later emails from his agent indicated that he'd felt "pushed out of the process," but she couldn't give two figs about how Niall felt. She has written for plenty of celebrities, and their theatrics didn't faze her. Niall caved in the end, as she knew he would.

Secretly, though, she's been putting off writing Niall's book, and she's working on her own novel, now, under a pseudonym. She hasn't even told Arthur. No psychopaths in this one. It's about a young girl who goes on a solo journey to a remote wilderness and makes peace with the monsters of her past. It will be the first novel she publishes as her own work, after over fifteen years of writing. It feels nerve-racking, and lately she's considered giving up the idea entirely. She earns a decent living from ghostwriting, so why create more work for herself?

But it's not about the money. It's about . . . something she can't put her finger on.

Kate opens up the document with the new novel, then closes it. She's almost finished, but she can't face it. Instead, she brings up the pdf brochure Darcy sent her about the resort in the Maldives. It looks amazing, no doubt about it. It's situated on a talc-white island amid a pristine turquoise ocean. There are images of colorful reefs and dolphins, people relaxing on sun loungers or massage beds, getting black stuff rubbed onto their backs. Pictures of people snorkeling and doing lots of sporty things. Pictures of cocktails, and artful food.

Kate tries to summon some enthusiasm, to feel grateful for what is undoubtedly a once-in-a-lifetime opportunity. Darcy has paid for it all out of her divorce settlement; Kate clocked the price when the QR code brought up her booking—fifty grand. *Fifty grand* for three people to go on a nine-day holiday. Yes, it was a last-minute thing, booked less than two weeks ago, but Kate's Carmarthenshire cottage cost fifty grand, and she'd had to take out a twenty-five-year mortgage.

Nine days she'll be at the resort, celebrating Darcy's divorce from Jacob with all the cocktails and spa treatments and sunshine she can manage. She likes the idea of a cocktail, but indoors, perhaps beside an open fire, curled up on an armchair instead of a sun lounger. With her laptop, or a book. And maybe a steaming pot of tea instead of a cocktail.

Why anyone would want to sit on a beach all day is beyond her.

But this trip is about much, much more than sitting on a beach.

She must remember that.

3

KATE

Kate lands at Malé in good spirits. The connecting flight from Amsterdam was on a much larger plane, and Darcy had booked her into first class, which was an utter delight. Kate had a cubicle all to herself and a seat that folded out into a bed at the press of a button. She had her own TV, minibar, and goose-down duvet, and the food was exquisite. She wrote and slept for the whole journey and barely noticed the time passing.

And now, she's here.

"You're under arrest," a voice says behind her. Kate freezes. She spins around and finds Darcy there, her face in a wide grin and her arms outspread. Kate wraps her arms around her and squeezes her tight.

"Oh, it's so good to see you!" she says. It's been seven months since they were together, though they've had plenty of Zoom calls. But only now can she see the full toll of Darcy's divorce; she's a good bit thinner, the bones of her face pronounced, a strain in her eyes that wasn't there last time they met. A screen shows a fraction of reality, Kate realizes.

"Hello, gorgeous," Camilla says, her arms flung out. Camilla's hugs are weird, the kind that feel as though she doesn't want to touch you any more than she needs to. But despite herself, Kate is glad to see Camilla, too. Nobody but Camilla ever calls her "gorgeous," "babe," or—on occasion—"sugar tits."

"Do we get a taxi to the hotel?" Kate asks as they head out of the terminal.

"Seaplane," Darcy says, nodding toward a fleet of small planes parked on the far side of the building. Kate registers the size of the aircraft, the rickety propellers and the steps that creak under her feet, and doesn't feel as nervous as she ordinarily would. Probably for the best.

And as they soar over a sapphire ocean, drifting toward the palm-tree paradise that is their resort, Kate's mind turns to the past. Small things, nothing traumatic, not yet—a pair of jeans she loved, two palm trees embroidered on the back pocket. She wore those jeans to death in her early twenties, back when she wore such things as jeans. She thinks of kneeling in the dirt, running a paintbrush gently across stone, sweeping the past away grain by grain. She thinks of Professor Berry, the way his eyes crinkled when he spoke, a triad of lines forming deep in the skin. He came alive when they were on a site, a different energy coursing through his body. An energy she wanted to possess.

She watches Darcy and Camilla on the seat opposite, their faces turned to the window as the plane veers toward a white strip on the island.

"We're all agreed," Camilla says. "No emails. Yes?"

"Yes," Kate and Darcy echo.

"Good." Camilla pulls a folded wad of paper from her Chanel handbag. "I've got our itinerary all planned."

"Itinerary?" Darcy says with a nervous laugh, glancing at Kate.

Camilla hands out sheets—stapled at the top, Kate notices—to the others. "Turns out there's a proper way to *do* a divorce trip, so I felt it only right to follow the rules. Don't worry, nothing too taxing. Well, aside from the fire walk, but we can discuss that."

"What's a fire walk?" Kate asks, scanning the sheets. Camilla has made a table on each page with the days clearly marked out, the weather report added in, and a lengthy description of each activity typed in Times New Roman.

"It's hot coals, isn't it?" Darcy says, a little stunned. She looks from Camilla to Kate for confirmation. "That's what a fire walk is, right?"

Kate is appalled. Walking across hot coals?

"Is there also a public stoning?" Kate asks mildly. "Perhaps some flogging?"

"Don't panic," Camilla says, laughing. "We don't *have* to do the fire walk. All optional, just ideas. A fire walk is a rite-of-passage kind of thing, so I thought it'd be fitting for a divorce trip, yeah?"

"Hasn't she already done the hot coals bit during the divorce, metaphorically speaking?" Kate asks.

Darcy smiles. "I'll think about the fire walk. What else is on here? Oh, a champagne party on a private sandbank? That sounds nice, doesn't it, Kate?"

The fire walk idea has made Kate suspicious of pretty much everything on the itinerary. "What's a private sandbank, exactly?"

"It's actually a tiny island in the middle of the Indian Ocean," Camilla says.

"Aren't we already going to a tiny island in the middle of the Indian Ocean?" Kate asks.

"Well, a small island, yes. The sandbank excursion is where they take us out on a speedboat and drop us off at an island that's literally just sand. They set up a picnic blanket and some fairy lights and we have champagne under the stars."

"Oooh," Darcy says. "That sounds amazing."

Kate can't bring herself to fake a look of delight. Her mind is turning quickly to the range of disasters folded inside that idea. The planet's melting under their feet, global warming wiping out ancient glaciers and seaside towns. In twenty years, the Maldives probably won't exist, swallowed by the rising seas. She foresees the speedboat breaking down, a rogue wave crashing over the sandbank. Sharks.

"Are there sharks in the Maldives?" she finds herself asking, and is perplexed when both Camilla and Darcy break into laughter.

"You won't be eaten by a shark, lovely," Camilla says soothingly, but her tone only makes Kate bristle. How does Camilla know she won't be eaten by a shark? Is she a psychic now, as well as a Pilates guru and social media influencer?

"There are hammerheads," Darcy says. "Nurse sharks on the reef, but they've no teeth. No great whites or anything like that. I checked."

Kate runs her eyes down the list. "Paddleboarding? What's that?"

"Ah, so that's *loads* of fun," Camilla says, the words making Kate's heart sink. "A paddleboard is basically a big surfboard that floats on the ocean. You sit or stand on it."

Kate stares at her, waiting for more. "Why?"

"Because . . . it's fun?" Camilla says, visibly restraining herself from showing how confused she is by Kate's question. "There is also plenty of time built into the schedule for relaxing, so don't worry about that. I'm not here to punish you both. And this itinerary *is* just a suggestion. It's your trip, Darcy, love. So you call the shots, OK?"

"I like the sound of a manta ray adventure," Darcy says.

"Oh *yes*," Camilla says, flipping over to sheet five. "That's my favorite too. This one involves our own personal scuba instructor. He—or she—takes us out on a speedboat to the spot with all the manta rays and we get to swim with them. Incredible, right?"

"*Incredible*," Kate says, making her finest effort not to sound sarcastic, so she's puzzled when both Darcy and Camilla start laughing again.

"What?" she says.

Darcy reaches out to squeeze her hand. "Oh, Kate," she says. "I'm so glad you're here."

Kate smiles, feeling momentarily useless in the face of Camilla's itinerary. Camilla has been divorced several times; Kate has never been married, has no idea about divorce. She has nothing to offer Darcy in terms of understanding what she's going through, or what to do about it. And she isn't of the inclination to pretend otherwise.

The plane starts its descent to the resort, which is on a larger island connected to a smaller one with a long meandering wooden causeway. She can make out rows of overwater huts on the edge of the larger island, a bushy green midsection indicating a hell of a lot of tropical trees. Trees mean bugs. Thank God she packed an assortment of bug sprays. She registers how isolated they'll be out here, no islands or ships nearby. No hospitals or emergency services.

But . . . . she'll have actual peace and quiet. Lovely food. Writing time. Camilla and Darcy can go walk on hot coals until the cows come home.

Perhaps the isolation isn't a bad thing.

4

KATE

The seaplane lands, and Kate finds herself drawn in by the postcard-perfect view that greets her at ground level. Such purity in those shades of blue! The plane door is opened, and just feet away from the small ladder is a vast sea that gently sways in warm gradients: turquoise, cerulean, lapis. The tide that nudges up to her feet is clear as glass, and along the creamy sand red hermit crabs scuttle about. A few islands are visible on the horizon. Emerald Island, home to the smaller sister resort, sits about a quarter of a mile to the west, a bank of palm trees as green as its name.

A large black bird shoots out of the trees behind, but when it swoops by she realizes it's not a bird at all, but a bat with a furry brown body and leathery wings.

A group of staff uniformed in black trousers and white tunics with SAPPHIRE ISLAND RESORT & SPA embroidered on them in gold wait in a row by the pier to welcome them.

The heat is astonishing, a wall of it blasting into Kate's face, as though she's opened the door of her oven while roasting a side of beef. She's been here two minutes and is already damp with sweat.

A woman approaches, dressed in the resort uniform, carrying a gleaming silver tray stacked with three glasses of something that looks like champagne. Cripes, any more fizz and Kate will fall over. But she drinks hers anyway, right as she spies her luggage being whisked away on the back of a tricycle. She should probably have invested in nicer luggage, she thinks. Her ancient Samsonite case looks tatty next to Camilla's gold-handled Louis Vuittons.

One of the men steps forward, introducing himself as Rafi. He's an older gentleman with a kind face and a gracious manner, his tunic slightly stretched at the belly.

"Miss Kate, I will be your butler while you stay at Sapphire Island. Anything you desire, you must tell me, OK?"

Kate is quite taken aback. A *butler*? She glances at Camilla, who is having a similar conversation with another gentleman. It seems they all have butlers. Good grief.

"Thank you," she says, but already she feels queasy at the imperialist echoes of having this man at her beck and call.

Darcy comes from money, and Kate often finds herself confronting long-established prejudices that she knows have no place in her friendship with Darcy and Camilla. Even now, when she's in a place as idyllic as this, all of it paid for by Darcy, Kate can easily recall the sting of poverty shame. Memories of going to school hungry; tatty, oversize hand-me-downs; of a teacher asking in concerned tones about "the situation at home." She worries she hasn't packed appropriate clothing. No, not worries—she knows she hasn't. There is nothing in her wardrobe that would be suitable for a night of champagne on a private sandbank. Come to think of it, she doesn't even know what kind of outfit *would* be appropriate for something like that, or where she'd begin to look for one.

Perhaps she should have asked Camilla for advice. At the very least, she should have ironed.

Rafi invites them to climb into a golf cart, and they huddle up close together, knees to chests, as he drives them through a miniature jungle of sandy paths toward their accommodations. Everyone is barefoot here. There are wooden signs to things like SERENITY SPA and PEACE DEN, jewellike glimpses of the main restaurant, of a smaller, more intimate bistro, and of enclosed beaches through the trees. Rafi shows them the meeting place for excursions, like the manta ray adventure or the turtle cruise. He points out the bar, which is on the edge of the island and housed under a large white pergola, an assortment of chairs and tables gathered by a crystalline pool.

A woman's high-pitched shriek breaks the calm, a man's voice shouting something in a language that Kate can't place. German, or perhaps Dutch—she isn't sure.

"What's going on?" Darcy asks Rafi, and as they pass by a break in the trees Kate spots a couple of guests on a beach, screaming at uniformed staff. A boat pulls up to the jetty, the word POLICE written across the side.

"Sometimes we have visitors from the Emerald Island Resort," Rafi says. "And sometimes they are problematic."

"God, an arrest?" Camilla says with interest, lifting her phone to film it. "How exciting."

"It doesn't happen very often," Rafi says with a smile.

"Can I ask a favor, Rafi?" Camilla says then. "I teach Pilates, and I emailed a few days ago to offer a free Pilates class to the guests. Do you think you could follow up on that? I wouldn't charge anything so long as I can stream it to my socials."

Rafi gives a gracious nod. "I will speak to the manager."

"Thanks."

Kate watches as Camilla lifts her phone again to photograph the scenery before pulling her and Darcy in for a selfie. Camilla sticks her tongue out as though she's having a dental examination; Kate attempts to smile but looks like she's sucked a lemon. She notices Camilla editing her out of the picture before posting it to her Instagram page.

In a few minutes, they arrive at a row of overwater huts.

She knew they were all getting individual villas instead of sharing, but she assumed this was because the beach huts were too small for all three women to stay in one comfortably. Not so: the villas that seemed shedlike from the plane are positively enormous.

Outside the sixth villa, Rafi hands each of them a key card. "Your room key," he says. "You are our guest at villa two," he tells Kate. "Miss Darcy, you are at villa six, and Miss Camilla, villa four."

"What time is it now?" Darcy asks, once Rafi heads off in the golf cart.

Camilla checks her phone. "In Maldivian time? Just after half eight in the morning."

"Let's meet up for drinks?" Darcy says. "That'll give us time to freshen up. Maybe have a nap."

KATE PRESSES HER KEY CARD against the digital panel on the wooden door of the villa. The door springs open with a whirr. Inside, she finds soaring ceilings with wooden beams, an open-plan living room with soft white linens and macramé wall art, a ceramic sculpture of a dolphin on a side table. Upstairs, the master bedroom contains a four-poster bed draped with mosquito netting and sprinkled with rose petals. A monstrous TV, walk-in wardrobes, and a glass wall that parts seamlessly at the touch of a button, opening out on to the ocean.

She steps out onto the balcony and pauses for a moment, breathing in the warm, salty air.

"Kate!"

Darcy waves excitedly from the balcony of her villa to the right.

"This is stunning!" Kate calls back.

Darcy raises a glass of champagne and laughs in agreement.

Turning back to the vast spread of silky ocean before her, Kate holds her smile, forcing herself to lower her shoulders. But beneath her delight is the feeling she can't get rid of, twisting away in her gut now that she's here.

It's fear.

5

JADE

I scan the room before I sit upright in bed. Rob's not here. I hold my breath, listening hard to pick up any sign of him behind the closed door of the bathroom. On the bedside table, bright sunlight falls on something metallic—his platinum wedding band, just five days out of its velvet box. He's probably at the gym.

I tiptoe to the bathroom, just in case. My little gecko friend is there, sitting on my makeup bag. A long tail lies across my toothbrush.

A small eye tracks me as I stand before the washbasin, looking over the bruise that's darkening beneath my left eyebrow.

I feel like I'm in a nightmare, like I've stepped inside a parallel universe.

Two years. That's how long Rob and I had been together before it started. We'd just gotten engaged, and he'd thrown a massive party with all our friends to celebrate. Oh my God, I felt like the luckiest girl in the world.

Two nights later, Rob got in a mood about something and started asking me about a guy I'd been chatting with at the party. I had literally no idea who he was talking about. He kept on about it, badgering me. I was just home from work, exhausted after a long shift. I hadn't even had time for lunch. I was rummaging in the cupboard, trying to find some pasta or something, as Rob hadn't bothered to cook. He came up to me as I turned on the gas cooktop, his face close to mine. I remember flinching at his expression—it didn't look like him at all. It was like someone pretending to be my fiancé, my lush boyfriend. The one everyone said I was lucky to have.

He started pointing in my face, then dug a finger into the top of my arm, between my shoulder and chest. It really hurt, and I lurched away. "Hey!" I shouted. "Rob, for fuck's sake!"

And then he hit me. An open hand that he brought quickly across my face.

It was a soft slap, not hard enough to knock me over or anything. But I reeled at the fact of it, the words *Rob has just slapped me* running through my mind.

He apologized immediately, and I watched as the strange imposter seemed to melt away from him, returning the man I loved. He said he was having a bad time at work. I knew he was. It all made sense. Rob would never hit me, not intentionally. He'd snapped. He didn't mean it.

Eight months passed. We planned the wedding. Rob went all out, insisting that we have the kind of wedding I'd always dreamed of. And the honeymoon, too—I'd have been happy with a few days in Crete. But then Rob's nephew got married, and the newlyweds went to the Maldives for their honeymoon.

Rob started telling everyone we were going to the Maldives for our honeymoon, too, before we'd even discussed it. I knew he'd inherited a bit of cash when his mom died, but I thought we'd put that toward buying a house. No, he said. We had the rest of our lives to do boring stuff like that.

The day we booked the honeymoon, he pulled my hair. The imposter was back—I could see it on his face, smell him on the wind. I remember how I felt strangely unnerved the minute I got home, as though the air carried an invisible code that I could decipher.

Rob asked me if I'd gotten the confirmation email about the booking for the Maldives. I said I had. And this I remember—I opened a packet of potato chips, because I hadn't time for lunch again, and asked him if he'd booked the right date. I asked this because the wedding venue— Lindhurst Hall—had queried the wedding date we wanted, which was the second, and asked if we could do the third. We both kept mixing up the dates as a result, and I worried that we might have accidentally booked the honeymoon before the bloody wedding.

I saw his eyes harden. I'd only asked him if he'd booked the right date. But he slapped the packet out of my hands, sending a shower of chips to the floor.

"Rob!" I shouted, throwing him a bewildered look before bending to pick them up. As I lowered myself, he grabbed a fistful of my hair, pulling me to my feet with a yell. I turned to him, horrified, and saw the rage in his eyes. He let go and stormed off.

Again, the imposter fled, and the man I loved returned, brimming with mortification and apologies. It seemed so genuine, so plausible. And the thought of losing him was devastating.

I was excited for our wedding, seriously. But I also had this weird feeling in my chest.

The year turned, and Rob was his old self: funny, kind, sexy. No way does he look forty-one. Anyway, I was determined to make our wedding special. I planned it all myself. Reception menu, dress fittings, cake tastings. Seating arrangements to ensure estranged relatives weren't in speaking distance.

The night before our wedding, Rob hit me with a closed fist.

It wasn't hard enough to knock me down. But it was a punch, and it hurt. It left a mark that grows uglier by the hour.

I'd heard about other women getting punched and secretly judged them when they didn't pack their bags and leave. But this isn't the same. Every relationship is different, right? He apologized; the stress of wedding planning was driving him insane. Our budget was blown, since we'd chosen the Maldives over a few days in Crete. I considered mentioning that the Maldives honeymoon and the big fat wedding were his idea, but thought better of it. After all, he was ashamed of his behavior, was eternally in my debt—but now that I look back on it, I see that his apology had something new about it. An extra quality.

Blame, just a hint of it.

He *was* sorry, but I had used a tone, and that had made him snap.

I pushed the blame to the back of my mind and told myself never to use a "tone" with him again.

I was causing this. I was the one screwing up our relationship.

Instead of walking down the aisle crying tears of joy, I walked toward my hubby-to-be worrying that I hadn't applied enough makeup to hide the bruise he'd left on my face. When I said "I do," I felt numb. When I signed the register, I wanted to vomit.

It's so hot here, ninety degrees, 80 percent humidity. But I feel cold inside, the numbness that crept in just days ago now reaching my bones.

I brush my teeth, then slip out of the lace negligée I bought for our wedding night and back into my bikini. Here, concealing the bruise with makeup is pointless—it just slides off. At the airport, I bought sunglasses and a beach hat with a wide brim. That should cover my eye. If anyone does ask, I'll tell them I whacked my face on a cupboard door.

From somewhere in the villa comes a knocking sound, as though someone's trying to get my attention. I freeze, listening hard for the heavy footsteps that announce Rob. In a matter of seconds I realize it isn't him—I've dialed in to his every movement, now, can read his mood from a mile off. No, whoever is inside the villa is not Rob. Maybe it's Devaj, our butler.

"Hello?" I call out. "I don't need any new towels, thanks."

"Oh, sorry," a voice says. An English accent. I look out of the bedroom door over the mezzanine. A woman in an orange dress is standing there, a Chanel bag held at her side.

"Sorry," she says again, looking up at me. "I must have the wrong villa."

She pulls out some paperwork to check, and I throw on my robe to head downstairs.

"Do you need help finding your villa?" I ask gently.

She studies her paperwork. "I'm in villa number four." She rakes her eyes over me, and I flinch. "What number is this?"

"Villa three."

"Oh God, I'm sorry. My key card worked, though—"

"That's fine. Don't worry about it, really. I mustn't have locked the door properly."

I ask her if she wants me to show her where her villa is and she says no, she doesn't need me to go to any trouble, but I insist. I like the way she's dressed, so stylish. She's about my mum's age but she's slaying in those gold sandals and the floaty orange dress.

We head outside to the wooden causeway, and I walk with her along to the next villa on the left.

"You been here long?" she asks.

"Three days. Ten days left."

The woman smiles. "You liking it?"

"It's nice."

"Where're you from?"

"South London," I tell her. "Though Liverpool originally. Most of the other guests are from Germany and Spain." I don't know what else to say. "Are you on your honeymoon?"

She gives a loud, filthy laugh. "Oh, *no*," she says. "I'm here on a divorce trip. There's three of us, celebrating my friend's divorce."

I raise my eyebrows. What a weird thing to celebrate. To each their own, I guess.

"What about you?" she says, and I see her eyes settling on the bruise above my left eye. "Holiday?"

"Honeymoon." I reach up self-consciously to flatten my fringe over my forehead. Wrong move—she clocks it.

"Looks like you hit your head," she says.

"Had a fight with a cupboard door," I say, the words rolling easily off my tongue. She nods, but I'm not sure she's convinced. I glance nervously behind me in case Rob's heading back from the gym.

"Anyway," I say, nodding at the villa we've arrived at, "this is number four."

"I'm Camilla," she says, extending a hand, and I shake it. "It was nice to meet you."

"Jade. You too."

"Have a drink with us later, won't you?" she says, opening the door.

I feel myself blush, flattered that someone so confident and stylish is interested in me. "I'd love to."

6

JACOB

NOW

Back in London, Jacob isn't celebrating his divorce. Instead, he's sweating bullets. The analytics appendix at the back of the document in front of him doesn't make sense. He has looked it over several times and still something isn't right. Dembe, their new partnerships officer and also his new girlfriend, stands at the front of the meeting room presenting the two packages they'll be pitching to equity investors in a week's time. She notices that he's distracted and pauses, causing his business partner, Kabir, to give him a nudge.

"You OK?"

Jacob looks up. "Uh, yeah. Sorry."

Dembe nods and clicks through to the next slide, a bracingly sci-fi background with a smiling woman in the middle.

"In an increasingly time-poor society, the complexity of the contract process is detrimental to customer satisfaction and business development. Our contract management software offers Shelley, a friendly AI assistant designed to empower users by extracting key information in seconds—"

"I'm sorry," Jacob says suddenly, rising from his seat. "I have to—"

"Mate," Kabir says, watching Jacob squeeze past, headed for the exit, "the meeting's next Thursday."

Jacob opens the door and glances back. "I'll get Sam to debrief me."

And then he walks out, striding down the hallway. He pulls off his tie and runs a hand through his silvering hair before bursting into the smaller office next to his, where his assistant, Sam, sits at his desk.

"Can you take over for me in the meeting room, please? I need notes to follow up on."

Sam nods and rises quickly, spotting the urgency on his boss's face.

In his office, Jacob is too agitated to sit down. He paces, palm to brow and face aglow with sweat, reading and rereading the meeting reports on the software package. Yes, he sees it, he's sure, now he's alone—there has been a security infraction on the Shelley program. It's such a small detail, so easy to overlook, but it's there, and he can't for the life of him figure out how it didn't trigger any of their alarms.

Shit. He stands by his desk, his heart racing. Last night he did coke for the first time in months, and he's feeling it today. He's forty-five, in good shape, but his rib cage feels like it's in a vise and his heart is beating wildly, even now that he has forced himself to stop pacing.

A knock on the door. He glances up, his jaw slack. It's Sam.

"They've rescheduled the meeting," Sam says, adjusting his glasses. A wary look. "Can I get you anything?"

Jacob shakes his head, conscious that he probably seems like he's having a breakdown. "Actually, yes. Come in. Close the door."

Sam looks alarmed but does as he's told. Jacob shows him the analytics that are bothering him, the times and dates that make no sense.

"Can you pull the data on these?" he asks, taking out a pen from his shirt pocket and circling the ones in question. "Usernames, location, ISP. Whatever you can get a hold of."

Sam studies the appendix. "When do you need this by?"

"Yesterday."

A moment of hesitation. "OK."

As Sam heads back into his office, Jacob considers that he has only himself to blame for this particular intrusion. God knows he's tried to hold it together lately, keep up appearances, but the collapse of a marriage is no easy thing to manage. The logistical impact is endless. Darcy, off to the Maldives, has left him with the boys the very week he needs to concentrate, and the babysitter can only stay until six o'clock. This hack could be costly. He fears it might reveal a vulnerability in the exact same software they're about to pitch to investors.

Shit.

His brain spins in multiple directions at once, trying to deduce the reasons for the infringement, the cause, and—better yet—the solution. Last time they had a security violation, it ended up being a rival company, someone he had worked with years before. He had wanted to pay the guy off, but Kabir got the police involved. It turned out that the law hadn't caught up yet, and so the guy walked free. The software was essentially binned.

He won't let that happen again.

"I have something," Sam's voice says. He looks up, realizing that he has sat down, put his tie back on. Sam is staring at him, and it's raining outside. It was sunny before. When did it start raining?

"I managed to pull out a couple of usernames and email addresses," Sam says. "They're probably not what you're looking for—"

"Give it here," Jacob says, tearing the sheet of paper out of Sam's hands.

He looks it over, his eyes widening when he sees the names.

"Fuck," he says.

7

CAMILLA

Camilla watches Jade walk back to her villa. *Quite a nasty shiner*, she thinks, recalling the times in the past when she used the same excuse. A cupboard. How unoriginal. But on her *honeymoon*? The husband must be a nasty bastard. Poor thing. And so young, a mere wisp of a girl. She can't be more than twenty-three, a little older than Camilla's daughter, Natasha, though nowhere near as ballsy, as acidic. Camilla makes a mental note to keep an eye out for Jade, make sure she's all right.

She crosses the threshold of her villa with a sigh of pleasure. This is one of those rare occasions when the website photographs don't do the venue justice. She marvels that she has this whole place to herself, this huge villa right over the ocean, with the designer ceiling fans suspended from the beams like miniature aircraft, the marble sinks with pricey brass fittings, and the generous glass aperture in the living-room floor revealing colorful fish. It's all right up her alley.

She hangs her hat on a hook by the front door, then climbs the stairs and looks over the bathroom. A deep slipper-bath in the center of the room, atop marble tiles. That'll do nicely. She imagines the kind of Instagram content she can produce here. She's been meaning to post more images of relaxation to break up the workout videos—too much of the same stuff costs her followers, so she's started posting pictures of meals, her garden, even her sofa. Interesting how sometimes those pictures get more responses than even her best workouts. A photo of her in the bath should go down well.

In the corner of the bathroom is a brass waterfall shower with a slim glass divide, a long counter with two sinks and a welcome basket brimming with expensive lotions and gels. A vase of fresh white lilies, a built-in cabinet with plush white towels. She sighs again. It's heavenly. Better yet, she has some peace and quiet.

She strides across the wooden floor of the mezzanine, glancing down at the living room below. She shudders—she can't look down from a height without imagining someone's head splitting open like a melon. It's a consequence of too much cannabis, or perhaps unresolved trauma, though ironically the cannabis was intended to resolve the trauma. *C'est la vie.*

At the far end of the corridor, a balcony is perched on the corner of the villa. With her phone, she snaps an image and posts it to her Instagram Stories with a link to the location, then WhatsApps the same image to Natasha. An instant later, a message pings back:

Nice.

My full-day didn't show.

Natasha means that a client who has booked a full-day tattoo session didn't turn up. They'll forfeit a deposit, but that'll cover the rental space at the studio and her travel. A day's wages lost. She messages Natasha back.

How much did you lose? x

Why?

Tell me and I'll put the money in your account x

You don't have to do that, Mum. I'm a grown-up now, remember? ☺

I want to.

sigh 450

Camilla opens her bank app and deposits the money in Natasha's account.

Done. Love you xx

Love you too, Mum. Next time you want a tattoo, it's on me xo

Camilla is tenderhearted when it comes to Natasha. The result of Camilla's first marriage, she lives in a tiny flat in London with her partner, Sîan, and their bulldog, Clio. Natasha is a twenty-year-old tattoo artist and has zero interest in Pilates, though she has the perfect, willowy form that Camilla has spent years trying to achieve. Natasha was into dancing as a teenager but gave it up abruptly one day, to Camilla's dismay. Camilla hasn't a single tattoo; Natasha has over a dozen, one of her arms completely covered in daffodils, octopus tentacles, and a portrait of Nefertiti. She has a ram's skull on her chest, thick black horns curling across her skin. She has long red hair, moss-green eyes, and pale skin with freckles, barely a trace of her Filipino ancestry visible in her coloring. Natasha can't fathom why Camilla gets Botox; Camilla can't fathom why Natasha insists on piercing every orifice.

They adore each other.

Camilla looks over the al fresco dining area with its round birchwood table and chairs, frayed-edged parasol, four fake trees in large gold pots. It's a lot like the patio area she recently had built outside her house in Berkshire. She's lived there three years now, and it almost feels like home. She's a restless soul, preferring to move around. There's nothing like the feeling of a new home to create a sense that you're moving forward in life. At forty-nine, Camilla isn't sure she'll ever feel like she's *arrived* at whatever it is she's moving toward. Perhaps she'll know it when she sees it. So far, three husbands have failed to assist in that journey, and even the success of her Pilates business hasn't quite hit the spot.

Heading to the bedroom, she checks the responses to her post. Fifty likes and several comments, a handful of personal messages asking questions. Good.

She grew her Instagram account over a couple of years, building her coaching business off the back of it. She has a training academy now, all self-employed coaches who assist others with fitness and health goals. She doesn't do much one-to-one work anymore, and she misses it. Having seven thousand people like and comment on a post is great, but it comes with downsides. Trolling, mostly, people posting the most hideously personal comments. Lately, she has found it exhausting. A comment about her face the other day made her cry. Why does she bother reading the comments? She knows by now that it's stupid to do so. But she's only human, still invested in her business.

Her body is stiff after the flight, particularly that last, cramped journey on the seaplane. She slips off her sandals and stands by the long mirror in the bedroom, tucking her pelvis under and releasing several times, drawing in her abs. Then she bends forward, pressing her palms into the floor, and breathes deeply, before sitting down, cross-legged, working out the tenderness in her tailbone.

She only lasts so long before she opens her inbox. A flicker of guilt—she was the one to stipulate that this trip be email-free—but she does run an online business; foolish, really, to think she could go a whole nine days without so much as scanning her inbox. She resolves to only check once a day. Maybe twice.

There are a handful of messages, one from her virtual personal assistant, a couple of reminders about the Pilates conference she's going to in Mexico in November. But her eyes settle on one in particular, and she has to do a double take. The sender's name is Jacob Levitt.

Darcy's ex-husband.

From: j.levitt@immersiveAI.com
To: Camilla_papaki1973@gmail.com

Camilla,

I need to speak with you urgently. I think you know what it's about.

Thanks, Jacob

She reads the message four times before setting the phone down and staring out of the window. She's heard plenty about Jacob but has never met him. Why the fuck is he emailing her? And that second line—*I think you know what it's about.*

She starts to compose a reply, then stops. She's short-tempered, especially after a long-haul flight, but past experience—or rather, her daughter—has taught her that she should probably hold off.

She sits on the plush sofa and glares at the message, realizing that she's in a bit of a pickle. Whether she likes it or not, she finds herself in the position of potentially ruining the holiday that Darcy has looked forward to, the one she so rightly deserves, because if she tells Darcy about this, Darcy will get upset all over again, fretting about what her ex is playing at by emailing her friends. But if Camilla doesn't tell her, it might end up looking like she's keeping secrets from Darcy.

Oh *God.*

Camilla finds herself tempted to dial the mobile number at the bottom of the email, just to see what Jacob will say. His divorce from Darcy is finalized, so what can he gain from bothering them? But that's the thing with bastards like Jacob—they don't act rationally. Camilla has had a lifetime's experience of bastards. They just want to sabotage everything and everyone around them for the hell of it.

That's exactly why Jacob has sent the email, she decides. He can do nothing now, so he wants to ruin their lovely holiday, just like he wrecked his marriage. She trots off a deflective reply and clicks out of her inbox, chiding herself for having checked her email in the first place.

That'll teach her, she thinks. That'll teach her for breaking her own rules.

8

DARCY

She's late, which she hates. Darcy is never late, not even on holiday, but she must be more exhausted than she realized because she slept straight through the alarm she set for half twelve, which is when she was meant to meet Camilla and Kate for drinks. That plan was probably a bit too optimistic, given they've all had such a long journey. She's heard about what happens to your body when you don't have to be up at dawn for work or small children—it forces you to sleep, compensating for all the rest you've missed out on.

And the heat! God, it's intense. She loves it, and the way the water sparkles everywhere the eye falls, palm trees towering above, much larger than any she's seen before. The resort is like a miniature jungle, a vast green canopy of tropical leaves. Small paths stream away to various buildings. She walks across the wooden causeway, where the gym sits to the left, a white building with ice-cold air-con. To the right, an old swimming pool. She plans to use it while she's here. And why not? She's started training again. She came fifth in the under-eighteen British Swimming Championships many years ago. Five miles was easy for her. Now she finds a hundred laps hard going, has to use the loo halfway through, on account of how crap her pelvic floor is after the kids. The joys of getting older. But her arms are still toned, the cap of a defined deltoid visible at the opening of her kaftan. She put on a slick of red-tinted ChapStick, and the gold bracelets she bought just for this trip. She's glad she got her nails done, now. They seemed garish back in London, but they're perfect out here, where the light sharpens all the colors. She reminds herself to tell

Camilla how grateful she is for pushing her into it. Sometimes you need friends who see through your own bullshit, right?

She heads back, following the path that forks off to the restaurant, where breakfast, lunch, and dinner are served in a buffet that extends across three different rooms, one entirely dedicated to salads. More tables on the deck outside, by the ocean, restaurant staff shifting chairs.

"Darcy!"

An arm is waving from the outdoor pool, where a row of sun loungers faces the ocean. She recognizes Camilla's hat and walks toward her. Kate is there, too, and there's another girl, seated beside Camilla. She looks young, early twenties, wearing a white string bikini, slender, undimpled limbs fake-tanned to an almost grubby bronze. She has a lip piercing, and her black sunglasses take up half her face. Icy-blond, ruler-straight hair with a long fringe, and her nails are acrylics, like Darcy's, though sharp as claws, with a French polish and diamanté nail art. Darcy's nails look tame in comparison.

"Sorry, girls," Darcy says. "I overslept."

"We thought maybe you were shagging a handsome stranger," Camilla says, shielding her eyes.

"We *hoped* you were," Kate says. "Not that we don't enjoy your company."

Darcy watches Camilla and Kate and smiles to herself—you couldn't find two more opposite women if you tried. Camilla wouldn't look out of place in a magazine, a long string bean in a red bikini with gold clasps, red lipstick, glossy black hair, microbladed eyebrows, every part of her body cinched and shimmering. Kate is sweating under a strange bucket hat that has been badly creased in her luggage. She looks flustered, strands of gray hair sticking to her cheeks and her pale legs bent at angles on the sun lounger. She's wearing a heavy green dress, no nail polish, no makeup. Her hands are swollen and her cheeks flushed, and Darcy wonders for a few seconds what she's doing with that towel, moving it strategically around herself—ah yes, she's using it to conceal the parts of her body she feels awkward about. Poor Kate.

She sits down on the sun lounger beside the new girl and smiles at her. "Hi," she says. "I'm Darcy."

"This is Jade," Camilla says, leaning forward. "She's from London. She's staying in the villa next to mine."

"Hiya," Jade says. "Camilla was telling me all about you."

"Lies, all of it," Darcy says, lifting the bottle of sunscreen on the table next to her, and Jade laughs. "That's not a London accent, though?"

"I'm from Liverpool originally," Jade says. "I moved to London a couple of years ago."

"Nice," Darcy says. "Whereabouts in London?"

"Stockwell. It's not that bad, actually. Where are you from?"

"Dudley, originally, though we're in Richmond now."

"Posh," Jade observes.

"*This* place is posh," Camilla tells Jade. "Therefore, by extension, so are you."

Jade beams.

"Cocktail or wine?" Kate asks Darcy.

"Ooh, what are you having?" Darcy asks, eyeing the gorgeous drink on Kate's side table—a tall glass filled with something yellow, an elaborate skewer garnish of watermelon, mango, and dragon-fruit balls.

"A peach Bellini mocktail," Kate says, craning her neck to get the server's attention so Darcy can order one.

"I can get it," Darcy says, jumping up to head to the bar. "Anyone else want anything?"

"Jamie from *Outlander*," Camilla says. "Preferably naked. *Je suis prest*, baby."

"I'll take another Negroni," Jade says.

"Could you ask if they have any fans?" Kate says. "Perimenopause and sun don't mix very well, I'm afraid."

Darcy orders two peach Bellini mocktails and a Negroni at the bar, and a tall glass of water. She's drained from the plane journey, and from worrying about her boys and whether or not she packed sunblock. She is olive-skinned and doesn't tend to burn, but she has several large moles on her shoulders that the kaftan doesn't cover, and you never know. Skin cancer's so prevalent these days. It's not worth getting a tan, even though Jacob used to compliment her when she returned from their holidays looking golden, her tan bringing out the fiery hues in her hazel eyes.

She lifts the tray of drinks and heads back.

"Oh," she says, as soon as she reaches her sun lounger. "Sorry, Kate. I forgot to get you a fan."

"It's fine," Kate says, wafting herself with a napkin. "I think I packed one."

"We could go into the pool," Camilla says. "Much cooler there."

"No, thanks," Kate says, spreading the towel across her legs.

"You on HRT yet?" Camilla asks Kate, while Jade looks on, both curious and shy.

Kate pulls a face. "The GP says my bloods are fine. He recommended cold medicine and sent me on my way."

"*Cold medicine*?" Camilla exclaims. "Not even proper sleeping pills?"

"Nope."

"Ugh, I *told you* to go to a private clinic. I've brought my estrogen pump if you want to give it a go?"

Darcy notices Jade looking disorientated by the turn of conversation. "Have you been here long?" she asks her, steering the subject on to better terrain.

"Just a few days. I'm here with my fiancé . . . I mean, my husband."

"Ah," Darcy says, grinning. "Freshly wed. This is your honeymoon, I take it?"

Jade nods, smiling. She glances away, and Darcy notices something beneath the girl's sunglasses. A purple bruise around her eye. Ouch. She decides not to pry.

"Can you recommend any excursions?" Darcy asks her. "We fancied doing the manta ray trip."

"We did the dolphin trip on our first day," Jade says. "I love dolphins. Rob's big on exercise, though, so he's either in the gym or swimming. He finds it hard to sit still."

She sounds apologetic. Darcy nods and smiles, flicking her eyes to Camilla. She's certain Camilla has already clocked the bruise.

"Is the dolphin trip on tonight?" Kate asks. "I fancy doing that."

"I thought you were against excursions?" Camilla answers.

"I'm not *against* them," Kate says. "I wasn't keen on dying, that was my point."

"Dying?" Jade asks, amused.

"You have to understand—Kate's a control freak," Camilla tells Jade.

"I am *not* a control freak—" Kate counters.

"—so because I planned some fun activities, she got huffy about it —"

"Walking over burning coals," Kate says loudly, "hardly sounds like *fun*."

Jade scrunches up her face. "To be fair, I wasn't keen on that one, either."

Kate is vindicated. "You see? A sane woman, at last."

Camilla flicks her long hair over her shoulder archly. "Change doesn't happen in your comfort zone, love."

"Who said I want to change?" Kate says, winking at Jade.

"Shut it, you two," Darcy says, shielding her eyes from the sun. "You bicker like an old married couple."

"Did you have a traditional wedding?" Kate asks Jade. "Or did you do something more . . . elopey?"

"'Elopey'?" Camilla repeats with a laugh.

"I've never been married," Kate explains to Jade. "And the last wedding I went to was in 2003, so I've no idea what the done thing is anymore."

"We had a massive wedding," Jade says with a grin. "At Lindhurst Hall? Both Rob and I are only children, so our families wanted something special. And after Covid, we thought, *Fuck it*."

The trio make noises of understanding.

"Very sweet of you," Camilla says. "To think of your parents like that."

"It was Rob's idea," she says. "Nothing like a big wedding to bring lots of family together, yeah?"

"Quite the opposite, in my experience," Camilla says with a frown. "A fight broke out at my first wedding."

"A *fight*?" Jade says, drawing a hand to her mouth.

Camilla nods, smiling. "Between two of the bridesmaids. A cousin and a family friend. Proper fisticuffs. Dresses torn, hair ripped out. Madness."

"The photographs must have been something," Kate says, and Camilla laughs ruefully.

"Oh, a complete train wreck," she says. "Mother-in-law in tears, bride looking daggers at the bridesmaids, both bloodied and bruised. Groom so drunk he can't stand." She shrugs. "Standard."

"What on earth were they fighting about?" Darcy asks.

"I think one of them was cheating with the other's boyfriend," Camilla says. "I can't remember which one it was. We're talking a quarter of a century ago, here."

"You don't look old enough to have been married that long ago," Jade says sweetly, and Camilla reaches out with a mock sob and hugs her.

"Darling," she says theatrically, "you're my new bestie."

"It's the Botox," Kate says, rubbing a fresh layer of sunscreen into her freckled arms.

"And this is why you and I don't see eye to eye, Kate, darling," Camilla says, flicking her hair in irritation.

"Just over here keeping it real," Kate says, which is such an un-Kate thing to say it makes Darcy laugh out loud.

"What was your dress like?" Darcy asks Jade, trying to keep the tone light.

"Oh, it was lush," Jade says. "Off-the-shoulder, right? A pearl bodice, ivory satin skirt with a short train. Classy. I didn't wear a veil. Just white roses pinned into my hair. I wore it in a long plait, like Elsa. You know, out of *Frozen*." Her eyes slide to Darcy, and she looks apologetic. "I feel awful for talking about all this," she says. "Given that you're here after a divorce."

"Oh God, no," Darcy says. "Please don't feel bad. I'm glad I'm divorced, honestly. It was a long time coming."

"Glad?" Jade repeats. "Was he bad to you?"

Darcy shrugs. "Well, if you call having multiple affairs being bad to someone, then yes."

"I'm sorry," Jade says.

Darcy finds her skin prickling, the shame of it still in her body. "Oh, it's hardly your fault."

"Jacob is a grade-A bastard," Camilla offers, and Darcy makes a noise of disagreement.

"You're saying he wasn't?" Kate asks, sitting forward.

Darcy considers this, faltering. The conversation is getting a little deeper than she intended. "Oh, I think people are more complex than that is all. He changed once his company took off."

Jade looks interested now. "What does he work in?"

"He runs a tech company. Artificial intelligence."

Jade gasps. "I've seen loads about that on the news lately. People are frightened, aren't they?"

Darcy rolls her eyes. "It's all hogwash. Fake news."

Kate takes off her sunglasses. "You think so?"

"Well, yes, there are reasons that AI can be a bad thing," Darcy says, "but most of the fearmongering is just corporations trying to fudge the markets."

"Oh, I don't know about that," Kate says. "I reckon there's more than a grain of truth behind the fear. What about those driverless cars that crashed into people?"

"I read something the other day about this AI chatbot for mental illness that encouraged people to attempt suicide," Camilla offers.

"Bloody hell," Darcy says.

Camilla nods at Kate. "And what about the AI that writes stuff? You'll be out of a job soon, babe. The robots will be writing *all* the novels, mark my words."

Kate takes that in. "You don't think a robot can teach downward dog?"

"That's yoga," Camilla says, sipping her drink.

"Pilates, then," Kate sniffs. "Pretty sure *your* job's the one in jeopardy."

"Ladies, play nice," Darcy says, softening the tone.

Jade looks like she doesn't know what to make of all this. "How long were you married?" she asks Darcy after a few moments.

"Fifteen years."

"Wow," Jade says. "That's a long time. You must have been quite young, like me."

"I was twenty-six," Darcy says wistfully. "He was my first real love."

"I'm twenty-three," Jade says. "Rob's forty-one. Everyone comments on it."

The others make noises of disapproval.

"It's no one's business," Kate says.

"Oh, I think you can know if someone is your person," Darcy tells Jade reassuringly. "Age is just a number, right?"

"It'll be my eighteenth wedding anniversary in December," Camilla says.

"What's your secret?" Jade asks.

"I think neither of us can be bothered getting divorced, to be honest," Camilla says, which makes Jade laugh. "Too much hassle. And we do like each other, Bernie and I. Maybe more like brother and sister, now. We have kind of a silent open-marriage arrangement."

"A silent open marriage?" Kate says. "Is that a fancy way of saying you both have affairs?"

Camilla shrugs. "Bernie watches these ASMR videos when he's feeling stressed. Rugs being cleaned. Vets gouging nails out of cows' hooves. I thought he was bonkers but then I found myself watching them, too. Surprisingly soothing."

"What has that got to do with anything?" Darcy asks, laughing.

"Hmm?" Camilla says. "Oh, I mean you impact on each other without even realizing it. Your lives become so intertwined that it's difficult to disentangle, even if you want to."

"It wasn't difficult at all for Jacob," Darcy says flatly.

"Shit," Camilla says, sitting upright. "Sorry, Darcy. I didn't mean to be insensitive."

Darcy raises her glass and offers a brave smile. "It's why we're here, remember? To celebrate. Here's to a new chapter for me *and* Jade."

"Cheers," they all say, clinking their glasses.

"Gouging nails out of cows' hooves is soothing?" Kate asks.

"Honestly, it is," Camilla says. "I'll WhatsApp you a link. You tell me I'm wrong."

"So where is he, then?" Kate asks Jade, setting her glass on the table next to the lounger. "Your new hubby?"

"He's at the gym," Jade says. "He's training for the Battersea Park Marathon."

"That's soon, isn't it?" Darcy asks. "Third week of October?"

Jade nods. "Just over six weeks. He ran the half-marathon last year. This is his first full marathon. I can't even run a mile, never mind twenty-six of them."

Her face falls suddenly, and Darcy tracks her gaze to a figure walking toward them. A dark-haired man, significantly older than Jade. He could be her father, Darcy thinks. He's about five-foot-nine, a brick shithouse compared to his wife, but with the same rust-colored tan. His muscular arms and chest are covered in tattoos, a large one of a bare-breasted mermaid on his left arm.

She spots the tattoo of the tiger on his neck, and her stomach spasms. His eyes slide to hers and she looks quickly away, a sudden heat rising in her throat.

"Rob," Jade says as he approaches. Darcy watches fear skid across her face, an involuntary reflex that she moves swiftly to hide with a smile. "This is Camilla, Kate and . . ."

She's so flustered that she's forgotten Darcy's name. "Darcy," Darcy offers, smiling up at him. "How do you do?"

He grins at the women. He's handsome, and his manner toward Jade is affectionate, if not a little rough, plucking up her hand and pressing it against his lips. Darcy watches him closely, trying to figure out if he's the cause of the bruise on Jade's face. "I was worried," he tells Jade, "when I found you weren't in the villa."

"Oh," she says. "Sorry. I was just—"

"I can see you're having fun with some new friends." His eyes rest on Darcy. It's hard to tell in the glare of the sun, but for a moment he does a double take, as though he recognizes her.

Jade rises. "I'll come back. . . ."

"No, no," he says, backing away. "Take your time. Nice to see you having fun."

With a wink, he slings his towel over his shoulder, walking toward the villas. Jade hesitates, visibly weighing something up in her mind. Finally, she turns. "Sorry, girls," she says. "I'll catch up with you later, yeah?"

"Of course," Camilla says, raising her drink.

"We'll be here all week," Kate adds.

Darcy says nothing, watching the desperate way Jade runs after Rob. She thinks of her younger self, the way she ran after her love, too.

The things she would have done differently, if she'd known then what she knows now.

9

KATE

First real love?

She can't get Darcy's comment out of her head. Why would she say Jacob was her first love?

Back in her villa, she thinks of Elijah, Darcy's real first love. The boy whose death has overshadowed the rest of Darcy's life, including her marriage to Jacob. Elijah Morrison was just nineteen when he died, a handsome soccer player, in his second year of a chemical engineering degree at Exeter University. Darcy said she had never stopped loving him, and that she realized she had never loved Jacob. Kate knows Darcy isn't the sort of person to say such things lightly.

She's obviously reading way too much into it, she tells herself, but she can't let it go. Darcy has told her so much about that chapter of her life, about Elijah, that it's almost as though she's lived it.

THE NEXT MORNING, SHE SLEEPS in past breakfast, enjoying a coffee on her balcony while she writes in her notebook. Ideas for her novel are beginning to prickle in her mind, a plot twist ascending from the silt of memory.

At ten, she puts a clean dress over her swimsuit, then heads to the spa. Darcy and Camilla are waiting in the lobby already, surrounded by potted orchids and statues of Buddha.

"Babe," Camilla says when she takes the seat next to her, "you all right?"

"Missed you at breakfast, Kate," Darcy says gently. "Did you sleep well?"

"I slept fine," Kate says, fanning herself. "Just my arthritis is acting up. I'll be fine."

"Oh no," Darcy says. "It'll be the heat. It's aggravated your joints, hasn't it?"

Kate nods reluctantly. "Bloody perimenopause. Cold in here, though."

"I'm getting my estrogen gel," Camilla says, rising. "Seriously, I had the same thing and it worked within days—"

Kate pulls her back down. "I'm fine," she says.

"Thank God for air-con," Darcy says. "And a massage should help the symptoms."

"I'm not sure," Kate says. "I've never actually had a massage."

Darcy reaches for the treatment menus on the coffee table. "Maybe avoid the strenuous ones," she tells Kate, drawing a finger down the menu. "What about this one? The Frangipani Cocoon? 'A nourishing wrap that helps you relax while mood-altering oils work their magic.'"

"Jesus Christ," Camilla says. "'Mood-altering'? Maybe this place is a front for drug runners. I bet magic mushrooms would help a *ton*, Katie baby."

"At this point," Kate groans, rubbing her elbow, "I'll give anything a try."

"Oh, before I forget," Camilla says, flicking a long strand of black hair over her shoulder, "I was thinking we could do the dolphin cruise tonight."

Darcy shrugs. "Sure."

"Maybe," Kate says, less enthusiastic. "How long does it last?"

"I think it's an hour," Camilla says. "And it's not exactly taxing. You just sit on the boat and look over the edge at the dolphins while drinking cocktails."

"I think that would be nice. Though I might stay away from the cocktails."

"Good idea," Darcy says. "That breakfast prosecco really went to my head."

Camilla rolls her eyes. "Lightweights."

"Should we invite Jade?" Kate says, spotting her through the glass wall to their right.

"There's the husband," Darcy says, as Rob passes by. He's dressed in a short-sleeved shirt open at the neck, tight red shorts. He lays an arm across Jade's shoulders, pulling her to him.

"She's so jumpy around him," Kate observes.

Camilla nods. "My guess is he's beating the shit out of her."

"God," Darcy says sadly. "Hopefully not? I mean, it's their honeymoon. . . ."

"Hope all you like," Camilla says. "Her body language is screaming it."

"Wouldn't she have stood him up at the altar if that was the case?" Kate says. "I mean, why would someone go through with it if they're being battered?"

"There are a *thousand* reasons why someone would marry someone who's beating them," Camilla says, a little too loudly. Darcy nudges her, telling her to shush.

"Which are?" Kate asks.

"Well, it's like being on a burning train that's steaming along the track at a hundred miles an hour," Camilla says. "You could jump, couldn't you? Or is it perhaps too scary, the thought of jumping from a train going so fast?"

The spa manager, Chinda, greets them with a bow, and asks for their chosen treatments.

"Deep tissue," Camilla says.

"We're both getting the Frangipani Cocoon," Darcy says, indicating Kate.

With another bow, Chinda invites them to follow her to an inner courtyard, a large lily pond with fountains pouring delicately, a stone bridge leading to another building. Inside, they find a darkened room lit softly by candles. Soothing music plays from a speaker, and three massage beds are set out side by side.

Chinda nods at the disposable knickers on the beds and towels they can use for modesty.

Camilla's the first to strip, tossing off her kaftan and bikini with zero hesitation. "Shit," she says. "I forgot to bring a hair elastic."

"Here," Darcy says, taking one off her wrist. "I always keep a spare."

Kate slips out of her clothes awkwardly before scooting herself onto the table and covering herself with the towel. Finally, three female masseuses appear, each taking her position at the head of a table.

Kate's head is throbbing, her muscles aching in that familiar way that feels like she's been trampled by elephants. She wonders if she should call it quits and go to fetch her medication. But the masseuse has started, quietly rubbing a fragrant oil into her back, asking in soothing tones if the pressure is all right. It feels nice. Kate lies perfectly still as the woman massages her arms, her shoulders, her calves, then her scalp. Slowly, the pain in her limbs subsides. Perhaps she should have tried massage before now.

"Turn over, please," Kate's masseuse says, and she lies on her back, feeling the warm pressure of a hotel towel wrapped around her, then another.

"Now, you relax," a voice says, and the three masseuses leave the room, closing the door.

"I forgot to ask," Camilla says then, shattering the quiet. "How was Charlie when you left, Darcy?"

Silence. Kate turns her head to see if Darcy's all right. She hears a whimper and realizes that Darcy is crying.

"Darcy?" she says.

"Oh, *Darcy*," Camilla says, jerking upright. "Me and my stupid mouth."

Kate manages to get off the table, cocoon of towels held in place with a firm grip, and plucks up a box of tissues for Darcy. She reaches down and gives her a hug.

"Sorry," Darcy says, dabbing her eyes. "I'd hoped Charlie would start talking to me before I left. But . . ." She trails off. "Sorry. I didn't mean to ruin our spa day."

"Don't apologize," Kate says soothingly, squeezing Darcy's hand. "You're not ruining anything."

"You love your boys," Camilla says, and Darcy nods.

"More than anything."

"You know, when Natasha was Charlie's age," Camilla says, "she bloody hated my guts for a while. Nothing to do with a divorce. Just . . . being a teenager and deciding that I was the devil. And do you know what I did?"

"What?" Darcy says weakly.

"Exactly what you're doing now. I cried, I felt guilty, I thought she'd hate me forever. Nothing worked, and I mean *nothing*."

Kate frowns. Camilla isn't the most tactful woman alive, but this doesn't sound very comforting.

"And then what happened?" Kate prompts.

"She got over it," Camilla says. "As soon as she turned sixteen, *bing*! Like a light bulb. Whatever had come over her seemed to fade away."

"He'll come round," Kate tells Darcy.

"Do you think so?" Darcy says. "It just feels like five minutes ago he was a tiny baby and now he loathes me."

"Honestly, teenage hormones are the worst," Camilla says. "The years between eleven and sixteen are a bastard."

Darcy laughs, then throws them both a tearful smile. "You two," she says, "are bloody brilliant. I'm so glad you're here."

Kate feels Darcy take her hand in hers, and the sensation sends shivers up her arm. It has been so long since someone held her hand. Two years ago she didn't know either Darcy or Camilla existed, and now they're close friends.

Funny how quickly things can change. Sometimes for the better.

10

KATE

She took a seat near the window of the cafe. It was February, and heavy rain had transformed London, disorientating her.

She wished she'd asked them to come to her cottage.

"Ready to order?" The waitress's question gave Kate a start. She realized she'd been staring at the menu for about five minutes without actually seeing a word.

"I'm waiting on a couple of people," she said.

The waitress nodded and left to serve another table. Kate picked at her nails, glancing at the entrance. Camilla and Darcy were both nice people, she reminded herself. Camilla was a famous Pilates instructor with a hundred thousand followers on Instagram. Darcy was married to a tech millionaire and lived in a mansion in Richmond. Neither of them was her usual sort of person.

A woman stood in the doorway of the cafe, looking around. She had chestnut-brown hair cropped just above her jaw and tucked behind her ears, and she wore a practical puffer jacket and trainers. It was Darcy. Kate waved at her, and Darcy headed over.

"Kate," she said, smiling, and there followed an awkward moment when they weren't sure whether to hug or shake hands. Eventually Darcy leaned in for an air-kiss, then stood back to survey Kate.

"People always look different in the flesh, don't they?" she said.

Kate touched her hair self-consciously. "Yes, they do."

"It's the environment," Darcy said, signaling the cafe. "I'm used to seeing you on-screen with the sketch of Skara Brae in the background."

"Ah, you recognized it," Kate said, brightening. "Not a lot of people know what it is, much less what Skara Brae is."

"We've been to it, actually," Darcy said. "Jacob's ancestors are from Orkney, so we made a family trip up there a few summers ago."

Another woman approached, shaking her coat off.

"Ladies," she said, opening her arms for a hug. This was Camilla— tall, slim, raven-haired, an expensive silk shirt open to her cleavage, black leather trousers, a handful of gold necklaces gleaming on golden skin.

She embraced Darcy, then Kate, who suddenly felt wildly under-dressed, Camilla's expensive perfume sending her olfactory nerve hay-wire. Camilla's presence had electrified the cafe, and Kate caught other customers glancing over at their table. *They're wondering*, she thought, *what on earth someone like Camilla is doing sitting at a table with some-one like me.* And Darcy—she looked like she'd just come straight from a charity cake sale to raise funds for the school play. The three of them made an odd group.

"Well," Darcy said with a warm smile. "Here we are."

"Here we are," Kate agreed, her heart racing.

SHE HAD WHATSAPPED AND ZOOMED Camilla and Darcy before, but meeting for the very first time in the flesh, here in this unfamiliar cafe . . . it was surprisingly emotional. She looked at Camilla and saw she was wringing her hands. Clearly, she wasn't the only one who was nervous.

"This feels very strange," Kate offered, allowing herself to say it aloud. Then, seeing Darcy's face fall: "Lovely, but strange."

"It is lovely," Darcy said, tension running through her voice and bur-ied in her smile. "I know you said you wanted to meet to discuss some-thing, Camilla, but really I'm just glad to meet you both in person."

"I don't know about you," Camilla said, finally hiding her hands under the table, "but I'm bloody starving. Have we ordered?"

"Not yet," Kate said. "I wanted to wait until you both got here."

Camilla made a show of glancing over at the waitress, leaning forward to catch her eye. The waitress saw and returned.

"I'll have the chia pudding and an oat latté, please," Camilla said.

"I'll have the same," Kate said, curious about what a chia pudding was.

"The avocado toast," Darcy said. "Please."

The waitress vanished into the kitchen, and the conversation moved to their respective journeys to the cafe, the way this part of London had changed, the weather. Darcy was the first to break into laughter, then Camilla, though she quickly reached for the napkin on the table to dab her eyes. Kate realized she was suddenly overcome with emotion.

"Oh, darling," Darcy soothed, rubbing Camilla's back.

"I'm fine," she said. "Sorry. It's just . . ." She blew her nose, silenced by fresh tears. "This is all just so . . . I thought I'd be over it by now. But . . ."

"It's not every day you meet two other people who have been through the same thing you have," Kate offered.

THEY HAD, AFTER ALL, BEEN affected by the killings at the Spinnaker Guesthouse just as much as she had, with Darcy losing a boyfriend and Camilla losing a brother to the man who'd let Kate live. The massacre she had survived as a postgraduate student was one of the most heinous events in twenty-first-century Britain that no one had heard of, on account of its proximity to 9/11. The day after she woke to find she had slept in a building full of bloodied corpses, the Twin Towers collapsed, and the world was forever changed. Every camera and microphone turned to New York, diminishing what media coverage might have been given to the guesthouse massacre.

She kept her eyes on the table in front of her, steadying herself. She felt close to Camilla and Darcy, much closer than if their friendship had been forged in ordinary circumstances. They had a trauma bond—the uniquely intimate connection that tethers you to other people who have experienced trauma like yours.

KATE'S BIRTH NAME WAS BRIONY Conley; during the trial, she had changed it to Kate Miller. A common name, shared with thousands of women around the world. A first step into obscurity.

But some people had remembered who she once was.

In 2021, Camilla had set up a private Facebook group for the victims' families. Darcy's first love, Elijah, had also been a victim, and she was an admin of the group. Though they had not spoken at the trial, they had remembered her, and when Darcy's message pinged into her inbox, Kate had felt a torrent of emotions. Gradually, through a series of faltering messages, she had felt as though she was finding her way out of the desert.

"I'll be honest," Camilla said, turning her phone to silent, "I'm really glad to meet you both today, really I am. But I didn't sleep at all last night."

Darcy nodded sympathetically. "Nerves?"

"I kept hearing my brother's last words to me," Camilla explained. "I spent a decade in therapy to *stop* hearing that phone call."

"What phone call?" Kate asked, cocking her head.

Camilla glanced from her to Darcy. "You don't remember? From the trial?"

Darcy and Kate shook their heads.

Camilla blew out her cheeks. "Cameron rang me that night. Right before he was killed . . ."

"What did he say?" Kate asked, her heart beginning to thud.

"He said he'd heard a shout in the room next to him. When he went out into the hallway and saw the door was open, he leaned in to check and he found that the man had been stabbed. Blood all over the bed-sheets." Camilla paused, righting herself.

"It was Elijah he found," Darcy said quietly. "Wasn't it?"

Camilla nodded and squeezed Darcy's hand. "It was. He was gone by that point. Cam ran back into his room and, well, we'll never know why, but instead of calling the police, he called me."

Camilla explained in strained tones that Cameron had recently turned his life around, taken a job at a builder's firm in Dover. He had been staying at the guesthouse for a week, just a few feet away from Kate.

"He said he didn't know what to do," Camilla continued, a tremor in her voice. "He said it was dark and he couldn't find his way out. I'd no idea he was even in the country. I asked him for the address but there was a crash, as though he'd dropped the phone. And then . . . the sound of him crying out. And I felt it, too, a strange sharp pain in my ribs." She twisted and pointed at her lower back, showing them the spot. "When it passed, I knew he was gone. I *knew* it."

KATE FELT AS THOUGH SHE wanted to be sick. This had all happened right before she checked into the guesthouse, and Camilla's report of it took her straight back to the days of the trial, when she had sat, rigid with fear and astonishment and nameless emotions, learning of the lives that had ended so violently, corpses lying in the rooms next to her while she slept. Years of insomnia had followed. Years of feeling guilty for surviving when six strangers did not.

"The investigation was a disgrace," Kate heard herself say then. Darcy and Camilla nodded in bitter agreement. "You know, I heard on the radio recently about a study that was carried out on survivors and their well-being. Guess what the most important route to recovery is?"

Darcy shrugged. "Having supportive friends and family?"

Kate shook her head. "Justice. Not family, not an apology, not financial compensation. When the victim of a crime feels that justice has been served, that the scales have been properly balanced, they can begin to heal."

Camilla took a deep breath. "Well, that must explain why I'm still so fucked up after Cameron's murder, then."

Darcy nodded in sad agreement. "My marriage is over."

"Oh God," Kate said. "Darcy, I'm so sorry."

She shrugged. "He was unfaithful. But they say it takes two, and maybe they're right. Maybe I messed it up. I never got over Elijah. My first love. Still, I tried to make it work with Jacob. I suppose I thought time would fix it. For the kids, you know."

"Time fixes nothing," Camilla said bitterly. "The only thing that works is *action*. It's why I set up that Facebook group for the families of the victims. I wanted to see if anyone else felt like the investigation was a shitshow."

The day after the massacre, a bloodstained Hugh Fraser had walked into a police station and confessed to the murders. Even so, a senseless tangential inquiry had been opened to explore whether the slain owner of the guesthouse, Mike Rotzien, had had anything to do with the killings, due to his criminal record.

September 11 had affected the media coverage. What attention the guesthouse killings did receive was wildly confused, a chaotic investigation spilling out on to broadsheets in the form of misinformation. A radio station reported that the killings happened in Dorset instead of Dover. A news report speculated that the murders were related to drugs, obviously on the back of the protracted inquiry into Rotzien's criminal past. And according to more than one newspaper, Briony Conley had not even survived, but was listed among the victims.

Reading about her own death had prompted Kate to start writing, burying herself in stories, as though to retell her own.

"I always, *always* go by my gut instinct," Camilla said, punctuating her words with her nails on the table. "And my gut has always told me that there was more to that night than Hugh Fraser going on a rampage."

Kate froze then, as she always did when she heard or read the name of the Spinnaker murderer. Fraser, a fifty-eight-year-old pedophile with a hideous past. The man who had checked her in that night, the creepy vibe he had emitted from the reception desk. In court, he had looked pathetic—hunched over and thin, his skin yellowing, coughing into a hanky. He had shown no remorse for his crimes. His motive, according to the judge, was a diagnosis of terminal cancer. She recalled the way he had smiled at her that night in the darkness.

"I don't believe Fraser was the only killer," Camilla said.

Darcy's mouth fell open. She turned to Kate, then back to Camilla. "What?"

"A couple of years ago, I remembered something really bloody important," Camilla continued. "Something I *forgot* when the police interviewed me back in 2001."

"What was it?" Kate asked, her stomach twisting sharply.

"When Cam rang me," Camilla said, "I looked at the clock by my bed. It was one of the first things I said to him. 'Jesus Christ, Cam, it's midnight; some of us have work in the morning. . . .' It was one of those digital clocks. It said it was three minutes after midnight."

Kate thought back to the trial. Fraser had gone to a corner shop a quarter of a mile from the Spinnaker Guesthouse. He was gone between five minutes to midnight and sixteen minutes past.

"Cameron died at six minutes past twelve," Camilla said, pronouncing the numbers crisply. "Which means that Fraser wasn't the one who killed him."

Kate and Darcy stared at her, taking this in.

"Can you be sure?" Kate said. "I mean, it's so close, isn't it, the timing. Difficult to get it exact . . ."

"I am *sure*," Camilla said, her dark eyes blazing. "I even went to the police about it."

"And what happened?" Darcy asked.

A muscle moved in Camilla's face. "Well, they told me to fuck off, didn't they? Not literally. They humored me for a bit, took a few notes. I even got my hopes up." She scoffed. "But then they told me there was no reopening the case. Fraser confessed, forensic evidence backed it up, and the case was closed. And I had no proof, did I? I couldn't get the phone records twenty years after the fact." She paused, then, swallowing back a bitter memory. "The police asked why I didn't mention it at the time. I told them that I was too busy grieving. I hate myself for not remembering it sooner."

"You shouldn't hate yourself," Darcy said quietly.

"Why not?" Camilla said archly. "Maybe the trial would have gone differently if I'd remembered earlier." She turned to Kate. "And this is where your study is all wrong. Justice doesn't matter to me. It doesn't matter to me that Fraser got handed six life sentences. The fact was that I was on the phone to Cam at the moment of his death, exactly six minutes after midnight, and there was a guy who said he'd sold a pasta salad and two cans of Coke to Fraser at exactly that time. Why buy two Coke cans at the shop?"

"Because he was thirsty?" Kate asked.

"Why not a large bottle?" Camilla added.

"Well, did the shopkeeper have any proof? Or was it just his word?"

"It was his word. He remembered. And it suggests that Hugh wasn't alone, doesn't it?" Camilla said. "And anyway, this guy was dying of cancer. We all saw him at the trial. He could barely lift an arm above his head. How did he have the physical capacity to kill six people?"

"He killed them when they were asleep," Kate said, her mind racing.

"Not Cam," Camilla said. "He was on the phone to me, remember? My brother was working as a builder, could run six miles without breaking a sweat, and you're telling me that Fraser tackled him?" She shook her head.

"I've been getting roses from a mystery sender," Kate said then. She drew a nervous breath, cautious. "I've never told anyone this, except for the police. But . . . every year, on the anniversary, someone's been sending me six red roses. One for each victim."

"Oh God," Camilla said.

"Did the police not find out who it was?" Darcy asked.

Kate shook her head and took another breath. "No. They won't investigate unless it contains a threat."

"And you've been getting them every year?" Camilla asked. "Like, still?"

Kate nodded, feeling sick at the thought of it.

"Jesus Christ," Darcy said.

"Lot of nutjobs out there," Camilla said darkly.

"It probably is someone with a morbid interest in the case," Kate said, wrenching herself together, "but at the back of my mind, I've sometimes wondered—or feared—if maybe it's someone with more than an interest. Someone who was involved."

The group fell silent, contemplating that.

"I've been contacted by a journalist, Motsi Sibanda," Camilla said then. "She ran a story on the killings a couple of months ago, just a small piece."

"She contacted me, too," Kate said. Then, guardedly: "I pulled out of the interview."

"How come?" Camilla said, and Kate lowered her eyes.

"It was just after Christmas. I was going through a hard time."

Camilla either didn't care that Kate's voice was laced with emotion or didn't hear it. "Did she contact you, Darcy?"

Darcy shook her head. "Maybe she was only interested in talking to relatives. I'm sure she spoke to Elijah's parents."

"Well, his parents died years ago, didn't they?" Camilla said.

"Of course," Darcy said, tutting at her mistake. "I was thinking of the families of the girls that died, too . . ."

"Bao and Chan-Juan," Kate added.

"Bao and Chan-Juan's families are still in China and don't speak English," Camilla said. "Then there's Mike Rotzien's family, but they're not interested, and the professor didn't have any family. . . ."

"Professor Berry," Kate supplied.

"Right. So really, it's just us three who are the most invested in reopening the case."

"That's quite a responsibility," Darcy said with a sigh.

"Motsi got the go-ahead for another piece," Camilla said, leaning forward. "A full-page report this time. So much more page space, more detail. She said she wants to take her time with it, make sure she speaks to the relatives of the victims to get a sense of both the aftermath of the trial and the months before the massacre." She looked over at Kate and Darcy, noticing the color rising to their cheeks. "And get this—she wants to look deeper into Fraser's past. Talk to people who knew him. Talk to his victims, his family."

"Why would she want to do that?" Darcy said, recoiling.

"I told her things I remembered," she said. "From the phone call."

"What did she say?" Darcy said. "I mean, is there even a chance it could all be reinvestigated?"

"Well, we all know the guesthouse has been knocked down," Kate said. "So they couldn't conduct another forensic investigation . . ."

"There's this newfangled technology now," Camilla said. "Motsi wants an independent inquiry into how the case was handled. But I want to go a step further." She held them both in a meaningful look. "I want the case reopened. No more bullshit. No more wondering and gaslighting and telling myself, *No, no, no, they put the killer behind bars. . . .*"

"I understand," Kate said. "But . . . are you sure you're not just frustrated by the lack of media attention? I know I was. I mean, I didn't *want* photographers in my face, and I certainly didn't want to speak to the press about it. But I always felt sorry for the victims' loved ones. For *you* . . ."

Darcy nodded in agreement. "It was appalling, really. Just . . . nothing. Barely anything on the news. As if it never happened."

Camilla shook her head, dismissing the idea that her feelings were driven by frustration. "I know it's a risk. I know I might push for this and find that Fraser *did* act alone that night. But my gut says . . . he didn't. Motsi says forensic technology is light-years away now from what it was in 2001. If we push hard enough, we can get them to reexamine the evidence."

THERE WAS A LONG, PREGNANT silence as the women took in the possibility that Camilla's hunch might be correct. It was one thing to meet, nearly twenty-two years after the horrifying event that had upended their lives and marked them in myriad ways. But to bring together the lingering despair that the handling of the killings by the police and by the media had bestowed on them . . . It felt like they had created a phoenix that was about to burst from the ashes. Back then, they had been young women, tender saplings quivering in the winds of unthinkable tragedy. Darcy had been the youngest of them, just nineteen. Camilla had been twenty-seven, Kate twenty-four. But now they were in their prime, fierce, wise, and bloodied. Menopausal, wholly themselves, done with all the bullshit. In other words, they were ready for war.

"There *is* something that has never sat right with me," Kate heard herself say. "And until now, I've never spoken it aloud."

"Go on," Darcy said encouragingly.

"It was day before Fraser died. You'll probably recall that he mentioned the massacre."

Camilla nodded. She remembered.

"He'd not spoken about it the whole time he was in prison," Kate continued, "but this day, he did. It was one of the last things he said. He told one of the guards, 'I saved her, you know. There could have been seven of them.'"

Darcy nodded. "He meant you, didn't he?"

"He did. But he said, 'I saved her,' and that always struck me."

"Didn't he mean that he let you live?" Camilla said, glancing from Darcy to Kate. "That's what he told the police when they arrested him, right?"

"Yes," Kate said. "But all the way through the trial, Fraser said that he *spared* me. This time, he said he *saved* me. The wording is different."

"I think you're right," Camilla said, after a moment's consideration. "There is a difference in those two statements. I mean, you're the writer, here. You pay attention to these sorts of things."

Kate felt so relieved she wanted to slide off her chair and under the table. Oh, how she had wrestled with her own doubts! The trial had been brief, with the facts lined up very neatly: Hugh Fraser had slaughtered everyone in the building but her. The next morning, he'd walked to the police station and confessed. No motive, other than what he called "a moment of madness."

But Fraser's story kept changing. Details about how he'd killed the victims and in what order. He claimed to have blacked out, blamed his shifting memories on the cancer that killed him just a month into his prison sentence.

"I think we should hire a private detective," Darcy said quietly. "If the police won't take our concerns seriously, we should just do it ourselves. *Action*, like you said, Camilla. Get the facts."

Camilla threw her hands up. "Exactly."

Kate began to cry then, relief and terror and guilt and all the years of looking over her shoulder crashing down on her. For a moment, she wanted to tell Darcy and Camilla to leave it alone, to let the past be. Leave her to her stories and her cats and her identity as Kate Miller.

Let Briony Conley stay in the past, with her beloved professor.

But then Darcy reached out and squeezed her hand, her eyes filled with determination. "You leave it with me. We'll find someone really good, and they'll get our answers. I promise."

"Justice," Kate said, turning to Darcy. "That's what I want. Not just answers."

Camilla nodded. "Me too."

11

JADE

Rob's at the gym again, and I'm on edge. I can tell Rob doesn't like me talking to Darcy, Camilla, and Kate. Maybe it's because they're so much older, more his age than mine. God, I don't know. With hindsight, it's probably a bit selfish of me. We're on honeymoon in the Maldives—we should be gazing into each other's eyes, not hanging out with strangers.

I've sat on the settee for an hour now, trying to read a magazine. I thought about texting Annabella, or even calling her. I picked up my phone and looked at her number for ages. She blocked me about six months ago, when I didn't go on the trip for her twenty-fifth. She wanted a group of us to go to Barcelona, told me months in advance so I could save for it, and I was all up for it until Rob said he'd arranged for us to take his nana to Peterborough that weekend to see her other grandkids. I'd not met his stepbrothers, and I knew his family meant the world to him. So I told Anna I couldn't go.

But he'd not said anything about us going that *exact* weekend until I said I was going to Barcelona. I'd even booked my flight and paid for the hotel. Lily and Olu were sharing, and I was sharing with Anna. Anyway, he was so upset about it, especially since his nana had been poorly. He said it was important that we go because he had a feeling she wasn't going to last much longer.

I botched it. I kept hoping that Rob would change his mind, or that he wouldn't get the weekend off work, but that didn't happen. As far as he was concerned, we were going that weekend to Peterborough. What could I say? No matter what I did, I was going to upset someone.

I said nothing to Anna until the night before, and I was a legit coward about it. I should have gone to see her and told her face-to-face that I wasn't going to Barcelona. But I didn't—I sent her a text message.

She lost it with me. Said I was selfish, that I'd *changed*. It stung, coming from her. I've not heard a word from her since. She didn't come to my hen party, or my wedding. I've known her and Olu since I was five, when we all went to dance class together. And now they've blocked me.

But I miss them, I really do. I seem to have pushed so many of my friends away, without meaning to. My family, too—it's been so long since I spent any time with them. Rob is all I have left. And I don't want to be on my own.

I get up and decide to set the room up a bit, make it romantic for when Rob comes back. We told the staff that we were here for our honeymoon, so they strung fairy lights around the big window of the living room and scattered rose petals on the bed. So sweet of them.

I turn the lights off and fold the glass doors back so we can look out over the ocean, then take a bottle of sparkling elderflower out of the cooler and set it on the table with a couple of glasses. I want to put Rob in a good mood. He's only drinking alcohol in the evenings to watch his calorie intake. I could feel his mood turning when I was sitting by the pool with those women. He says he just wants quality time with me, that I'm always putting him second. I did work overtime leading up to the wedding, to make sure we could afford everything and that I was paying my fair share. We were like ships in the night. I've tried so, so hard not to put him second.

The front door creaks open, and I jump. Rob appears in the hallway. He's showered and changed—he must have done it at the gym. He glances at me, then at the fairy lights.

"Looks nice," he says.

My shoulders lower. "You like it?"

He sees the bottle of elderflower and the wineglasses, then grins at me. I try to read his face, but I can't. I don't know why. Maybe it's because we've both been working so hard and been so preoccupied by the wedding that we don't know each other anymore.

Or maybe it's because he smiled just like that before he punched me in the face.

I watch as he slips his shoes off and sets them neatly by the front door, then clicks it shut, turning the lock. My eye still feels tender. Almost a week ago, now.

We've still not talked about that night. I know he was nervous and stressed. Weddings really aren't for the people getting married—at least, ours wasn't. It felt like a whole thing, this big production instead of an intimate celebration of two people in love. I knew how much it meant to him to bring everyone together like that.

"Have you eaten?" I ask.

He nods. "I was starving after the gym. You?"

I shake my head. "I wasn't sure where you'd gone. Didn't you get my text messages?"

"I'd have messaged you back if I had," he says. "You know that."

I serve my meekest smile. "You want a drink?"

He crosses the room, a hand in his pocket, the other at his chin. He's mulling something over. When we got together, we always spoke our minds. The old me would have asked him what was wrong, and he'd have said something like, *Babe, I'm worried about this*, or, *I was thinking we should* . . . But now the question stops in my mouth. I don't know what's safe to ask.

He walks slowly toward me, then opens the bottle of elderflower fizz and pours us both a drink. He hands one to me, and I take it, watching him carefully.

"I wanted to talk to you about something," he says.

"Yeah?"

He's still standing. I'm sitting in one of the armchairs, unsure whether I should stand or stay sitting. Is this about the bruise on my eye, the one he won't look at? Maybe he wants to apologize.

"Let's go to the balcony," he says. "Come on. We'll talk while looking out over the ocean."

For a moment, the old Rob is back, in his eyes, in his smile. Phew. What a relief.

I follow him up to the balcony, listening as he tells me about his afternoon at the gym—he ran the full marathon in four hours, his best time ever, but he's still trying to get it under that.

"That's amazing," I say.

He turns and looks me in the eye, and I feel something twist in the pit of my stomach. Was my tone wrong? Did I sound sarcastic? The old me would have cracked a joke, said something like, *For God's sake, Rob, a tortoise could have run that in four hours*. And the old Rob would have laughed. But when I speak to him now, I weigh up every single word in case it's offensive in some way, in case my tone might trigger a row. I sound like a robot.

And I feel like he knows it.

He sits down on the wooden lounger on the balcony, and I sit in the one beside him. For a long time, he simply sips his fizz, looking out at the ocean. I do the same: sit with my glass in my hands and my knees together, staring out to sea. Waiting for him to speak.

"I want us to try for a baby," he says finally.

He turns to meet my gaze, but I don't manage to fake a happy reaction.

"No?" he says, clocking the fear that's sprung onto my face. "You don't want to have a baby with me?"

"No, I do . . ." I say, trying hard to look excited or happy. Why won't my face work?

He turns his full body to me, cocking his head as though he can see my thoughts. "I think we should try straightaway."

"Now?" I say, too loud. "You mean . . . on this holiday?"

"Yeah, why not? I'm not getting any younger. Nana might live to see our first child."

I think back to Nana. Fit as a fiddle, that woman. Treats Rob like he's still ten years old. She legit raised him, which is why she babies him. She's eighty-seven, uses a walking stick to get about. But otherwise, she's as sharp as a tack and nowhere near as ill as Rob makes her out to be. She was the center of attention at our wedding.

"You came off the pill last month," he says. Then, suspicious: "Didn't you?"

"Yeah." I remember it with a sick feeling. I was getting migraines, my vision all smashed up and the right side of my head feeling like it had been bashed in. Some days the pain of it made me puke. The GP made me come off the pill right away and get an IUD. My appointment for the IUD fitting isn't for another six weeks, so in the meantime we've been using condoms.

"We could start trying tonight, if you wanted," he says, when I don't add anything else. "It can take years to conceive, can't it?"

It can also take moments, I think. My mum fell pregnant with me the first time she slept with my dad. My grandma was super fertile, too. I realize in one horrifying moment that the absolute last thing I want right now is to fall pregnant with Rob's baby.

But he rises to his feet, beaming with joy, and takes the drink from my hand. Then he sets it on the ground and leads me back into the bedroom. I still haven't agreed to this. He cups my breast with one hand.

"God, Jade," he says with a shudder. "I never thought I'd marry such a beautiful woman."

He kisses me, removing my panties with his free hand. For a moment, all the tenderness is exactly like the old Rob. His brown eyes lock with mine, and there's a look there I recognize: the way he used to look at me.

But it fades as quickly as it appeared. He lays me back on the bed and pushes inside me. No condom. I look around the room, focusing on the mosquito net around the bed, the drone of the air-conditioning, the white-framed watercolor of a boat on the far wall. I wish I could get on a boat. But where would I go?

I think of what Dad said on the morning of my wedding. *Last chance to back out.* I looked at him and gave a nervous laugh, expecting him to say he was joking. But he didn't.

As usual, the sex doesn't last long. I see Rob's expression change, the familiar gasp, then wait for him to roll over. I head to the bathroom quickly, letting it all fall out into the toilet bowl. *Hopefully*, I think with a shiver. *Hopefully, it didn't reach far enough.*

By the time I get back into bed, he's fast asleep.

And I still haven't said yes.

12

KATE

The boat for the dolphin cruise is at the port at the top end of the island. The heat of the day has cooled, now that the sun is lowering, and a reviving breeze lifts from the sea. A boatman invites Kate, Camilla, and Darcy to climb the ladder at the side of the boat to the rooftop, and, after a bit of a wrangle with the narrow steps, Kate finds herself watching the islands that appear in the far distance and the fish that move like shadows in the water below.

There are eight guests up there, five on either side, seated on padded mats on the wooden roof, small bottles of wine and soft drinks sitting in ice buckets in the center. Darcy and Camilla are sitting side by side, deep in conversation; to Kate's left a couple lie facing each other, and opposite them is another couple in their seventies. A retirement holiday, she thinks. She and the man to her right make eye contact.

He leans forward on to his knees, reaching for an ice bucket. Plucking out a bottle of white wine, he turns to Kate.

"What would you like?"

She smiles at him, noticing a thick accent, Spanish or Italian—she can't place it exactly. Even so, he spoke English to her. "A Coke, please."

He passes her a bottle of Coke, then a plastic cup from a stack beside the bucket.

"Cheers."

"*Salud.*"

He pours the contents of his wine bottle into the cup. "You don't drink?" he asks.

"Only very occasionally," she says. "Since I turned forty, alcohol tends to give me restless legs. Do you know what that is?"

"You mean 'itchy feet,' like you are bored and seeking adventure?"

She smiles and shakes her head. "It's a condition. Restless legs syndrome. It makes you feel like bugs are creeping beneath your skin."

He grimaces. "Oof. I'm sorry to hear that. Yes, very smart to avoid alcohol, in that case."

He's older than her, mid-to-late fifties, attractive in a world-weary way. Salted sideburns and quiff, the rest of it jet-black. Heavy brows, sharp cheekbones, dark-brown eyes that don't miss a beat. He wears a white linen shirt and khaki shorts with flip-flops, has inordinately hairy legs. She immediately likes him. Consideration for strangers goes a long way with Kate. That, and his eyes have yet to fall to her breasts.

"Have you been to the sister resort?" he asks, nodding at the island they're passing.

"No, not yet," Kate says.

"It's identical to this one," he says. "But good to kayak across to. Only twenty minutes. The water is so clear you can see all the way to the bottom. You can rent a glass-bottomed kayak. The reef is beautiful."

"Are you holidaying alone?" she asks.

"I'm with my nephew," he says. "Salvador. He's eighteen, just graduated from high school, so I brought him here to celebrate. But unfortunately, boat trips like this don't interest him."

She laughs. "Teenagers, eh?"

"If someone had offered to take me on a boat trip in the Indian Ocean to see dolphins at his age, I'd have ripped their arm off," he says, and she laughs. "But he has TikTok, or whatever it is, so dolphins do not matter." He sips his wine. "And what about you? A holiday for one?"

"I'm with a couple of friends," she says, nodding at Darcy and Camilla opposite. "Darcy's just got divorced. We're celebrating."

He nods, understanding. "Congratulations. Divorce can certainly be a good thing. Especially if no children are involved."

"Well, children were involved, sadly," she says.

"The divorce was not her decision?"

Kate shakes her head and smiles. "No. Not at all."

He processes that. "I'm Antoni," he says then. "A pleasure to make your acquaintance."

"Kate. Likewise."

"You're English?"

She nods. "And you?"

"Catalan."

"Oh," she says, her interested piqued. "I've been to Barcelona a few times. Do you live there?"

"Not quite. Girona. Salvador is planning to attend university in Barcelona, however."

"Nice. What will he study?"

"Archaeology," he says. "A strange subject nowadays, I grant you. But his passion is for old things—"

"Not a strange subject at all," Kate interjects. "I've been to the Altamira cave."

"You have? Oh, this is Salvador's favorite place in the whole world. A cave with paintings inside, yes?"

She nods, enjoying the chance to chat about something she adores for a change. "From the Stone Age. An eight-year-old girl discovered that cave, did you know that?"

"This I did not know."

"But sadly, you can't go inside the actual cave unless you're a special visitor. And even then, you must wear a biohazard suit."

He studies her with a smile. "But you—you've been inside? The real cave, not the replica?"

She reddens. "Oh, many years ago. It was a very special moment."

"I shall tell Salvador," he says sincerely. Then, leaning into her: "He might want to touch you, given that you've been inside that cave."

Kate tilts her head back and laughs. "He can have a lock of my hair. Though to be honest, the replica's every bit as good."

"So, you're an archaeologist?" he says, sipping his wine. "This is what you do for a career?"

She hesitates, struck by how difficult it is to say that she isn't. "I'm a writer."

"A writer? For newspapers, or . . . ?"

"For other people," she says enigmatically. "I'm a ghostwriter. I write novels that other people claim they've written."

Antoni looks puzzled for a long moment, until a voice breaks into his thoughts.

"I see you took the last wine," the voice says accusingly. Kate looks up to see Camilla on all fours, studying the contents of the drinks buckets. She lifts her head and glares at Antoni, who studies the cup of wine in his hand.

"The last one?"

Camilla plucks the other bottles from the ice buckets in mock disappointment. "Coke, Coke, Fanta, Sprite . . ."

"Here," Antoni says, passing her his cup. "You can have the rest of mine. I only drank a little. . . ."

Camilla gives a laugh and waves it away. "No, you can keep your germs, thank you very much."

"My germs are all very healthy and strong, I promise," Antoni says, continuing to hold the cup out to her. Kate smiles, noticing how riled Camilla is becoming.

"You could have the plague for all I know," Camilla shoots back. "I don't even know who you are—"

"Antoni Caballé, born October twelfth, nineteen sixty-four," Antoni rattles off loudly. "I'm a dance instructor from Girona."

Kate is amused. She risks a glance at Camilla, who is rolling her eyes with her whole body. Antoni seems unfazed. He extends his other hand to Camilla. "And you are?"

"Unimpressed," Camilla says, turning her back to him to lie on her belly, her knees bent. Antoni looks at Kate with a shrug.

"I tried," he says lightly.

A clamor from the lower deck alerts them, and the boat slows. "Oh no," Kate says, fanning herself. "Is it engine trouble?"

"Dolphins," Antoni says. He points over the side, and she turns to see the slick, bullet-gray bodies arcing through the waves. They're beautiful, a big pod of them. Golden light spirals over the curves they cut through the water and the spray flinging up, diaphanous in the low sun. As the boat picks up speed, the dolphins move faster, impossibly fast, the boatman clapping to draw them close.

As the dolphins gather near, Kate worries they're too close to the boat, that the engine will cut into their skin. She rises to her feet, troubled. Everyone around her is clapping now, calling to the dolphins. She glances behind, noticing some of the pod trailing in the white furl that the boat is plowing through the sea. What if they get caught in the engine? What if the blades of the propeller slice into their beautiful skin, cutting them up? She can't help the direction of her thoughts, spinning quickly to unfathomable scenes of blood and bodies.

Her mind plunges underwater, seeing the scene from beneath the boat: the churn of the engine, the screams of the pod, babies lost in a cloud of red. . . .

Her skin goes cold, a storm gathering at lightning speed in her brain, her throat tightening. Her heart rate has gone through the roof, and she feels so dizzy she can barely answer when Antoni and then Camilla are suddenly leaning over her, asking what's wrong.

She's conscious that she's sitting down again, her legs straight out in front of her, palms pressed to her eyes. Her face is crumpled, tears streaming down her cheeks, and it's hideous—she hates crying in front of *anyone*, never mind complete strangers, but she can't stop. The air won't reach her lungs, and no matter how hard she tries to suck it in, she can't control it, can't make the panting stop.

The clapping has stopped, the boat's engine cuts out, and all eyes are on her. *What's happened? Is it a heart attack? Should we call a doctor?*

Someone offers a drink of water, but she can't take it.

She can't breathe.

The scene that plays out in her mind is more colorful than the one on the boat, more real, too—bodies and blood everywhere. Not dolphins, now. People.

"Kate? What's the matter, darling?"

Darcy is there, kneeling in front of her. Someone is asking if anyone on the boat has medical expertise.

She sees Professor Berry on the bed in the hotel room, his head turned and his mouth open as though he wants to tell her something. She sees the awful stillness of his chest, the way his legs have folded beneath him. You could never lie like that for long, not without getting a cramp in your leg. There's a dark stain at the crotch of his khaki trousers from where he pissed himself. The glint of his wedding ring beneath bright red blood. The deep cut two inches above his collarbone, two flaps of skin like a snarling mouth.

"Breathe, Kate," someone says. "You need to breathe!"

The crushing sensation in her chest is rising now, the edges of her vision starting to blur. Professor Berry's eyes are fixed on her.

I'm so sorry, she thinks, squeezing her eyes tightly shut. *I'm so sorry.*

13

CAMILLA

Camilla's brain feels like scrambled eggs.

She pours a glass of wine with one hand, not stopping until the glass is full, then turns and studies the scene behind her: Darcy, Antoni, and a shaken-looking Kate sitting in the living room of Kate's villa.

The twenty-second anniversary of the Spinnaker massacre is two days away, and now this. It feels like someone is taking a cheese grater to her nerves. She would kill for a joint right now.

After Kate took ill on the boat they turned straight around and brought everyone back to the island. They were a good hour away from the resort by then, and that hour felt like an eternity. Kate was still hyperventilating, and Camilla and Darcy looked at each other in terror. What the hell were they going to do? Was she having a heart attack? Camilla's mind raced ahead to all worst-case scenarios. Who the fuck was Kate's next of kin? She's estranged from her parents, and she has no spouse or siblings. So who would they contact? What happens if someone dies overseas? Would they have to arrange flights home immediately? How bad would it look if they simply stayed on for the rest of the holiday?

The boatman called the resort's first-aid unit, who were waiting for them when they arrived at the jetty. Antoni, the guy Kate had been talking to, helped get her off the boat. Camilla assisted on Kate's left, Antoni on her right, and they pulled her to her feet. Darcy guided her down the stairs from the roof, placing her feet gently onto the steps. The first-aid unit had a stretcher set up, and they helped Kate lie down on it. And then, after she was wheeled off, the rest of the group sobered up.

Nobody knew what had happened. One minute Kate was standing

at the side of the roof, enjoying the dolphins. The next she was on the ground, trembling and gasping for breath. Camilla's head is thrumming, and she's agitated. Goddammit.

She thinks back to the email from Jacob. Maybe she should have called him back, asked him what it was about. No, for God's sake. That has nothing to do with what happened to Kate. The medic said it was a panic attack—a bloody panic attack, which, ironically, Camilla is experiencing right now, because she had thought Kate was dying and didn't have a clue what she was meant to do to help.

As Kate was wheeled to the first-aid unit, Antoni had walked alongside Darcy and Camilla as they followed, not sure what to expect. "I feel responsible," he said, in a way that suggested he wasn't responsible at all, but felt helpless, just like Camilla and Darcy.

Once Kate had been treated, the medic took them on a golf cart to Kate's villa, and now they're all in here—Darcy, Camilla, Kate, and the man, Antoni, who felt responsible for her panic attack.

"Sorry for all the fuss," Kate says, clutching a glass of water in an armchair by the macramé wall hanging. She looks pale, her face drawn.

"Oh God, don't be sorry!" Darcy says.

"I am," Kate says quietly, sinking back into the chair. Perhaps it was just the heat, or perimenopause, or the fact that the anniversary is in two days' time. *Yes*, Camilla thinks grimly. *Probably that.*

The second week of September is hell week, as far as Camilla is concerned. When Darcy announced she was going somewhere fabulous to celebrate her divorce and asked Kate and Camilla to come along, Camilla didn't want to protest too much, but when Darcy said the best time for her was slap bang in the week of the anniversary . . . well, it was almost a deal breaker. Camilla usually spends the anniversary under a duvet, the door locked and the curtains drawn, stoned out of her mind.

Darcy had said it was a good idea, that being together in a gorgeous place on the anniversary of the event that tied the three of them together would be healing.

Like fuck it is, Camilla thinks bitterly. And here is the proof—Kate, looking like a battered cabbage.

"We're just glad you're alive, sugar tits," Camilla says dryly, which makes Kate laugh. It's a lovely sound. But then the room falls silent, and Camilla glances at Antoni again, wishing he would just piss off. She's not at all convinced that a man would be so worried for the well-being of a complete stranger that he'd be content to sit indoors asking concerned questions instead of enjoying the resort.

"Did I hear you're a dance instructor, Antoni?" Darcy asks then. She's sitting on the sofa next to him.

"Yes," he says. "I teach at the dance school in Girona. Our students perform all over the world."

"Wow," Darcy says. "Have you always danced?"

He nods. "I performed flamenco for many years. I worked on some films, actually, teaching the actors how to do this dance."

"That's impressive," Camilla says, her interest piqued at the mention of dance. "What films?"

She sits in the armchair opposite Kate, spilling wine on herself.

"A *Mission Impossible* film with Tom Cruise," he says, his voice growing softer. She can tell he doesn't like talking about himself. Or maybe he's feigning modesty. "Another one with the man from *Bill & Ted . . .*"

"Keanu Reeves?" Darcy says, and he nods.

"Crikey," Camilla says, eyeing him anew. "Bloody famous, you are. We should be getting your autograph."

"Anyway, enough about me," he says, looking at Kate. "If it's OK to ask, how are you feeling now, Kate?"

"I think the Valium has done the trick," she says with a weak smile. "A good night's sleep will also help, I think."

He nods. "I have had many of these so-called panic attacks, so I was very concerned. They are not minor things, not at all. They usually have triggers."

"What sort of triggers?" Darcy asks.

Antoni shrugs. "It can be anything. A sound, a smell, the feeling of something you touch . . ."

Darcy turns to Kate. "Do you think you know what triggered yours?"

Camilla watches Kate intently, wondering if she should head off a potential re-triggering. Surely Darcy knows what caused Kate's panic attack? She just needs to look at a calendar.

"Maybe the heat," Camilla says then, and Kate nods.

"Yes, the heat. The heat."

It's clear to Camilla that she doesn't want to talk about it, not yet.

"If I can do anything, please let me know," Antoni says in a smooth Catalonian drawl. "If you want to talk, I can also listen. I know all about this kind of illness. It took many years for me to stop having these attacks."

"I've never had a panic attack—not that I know of, anyway," Darcy says.

"Oh, if you've had one, you know," Antoni says with a rueful laugh.

"Do you know why you started having them?" Camilla asks Antoni, interested. It's unusual for her to encounter a man so open about his own feelings, and she's intrigued.

"I do," he says. "And if you would prefer me not to share in case it might trigger you again, Kate, please tell me."

She shakes her head and murmurs that it's fine.

"My wife and I were in a car accident," he says. "It was fifteen years ago. The car rolled down a steep mountainside, both of us inside. We were trapped. When the car stopped, I could not get out, nor could my wife. Eventually the emergency services came and cut us out. She did not survive."

"Oh my God," Camilla says, and she feels a sting of remorse for how she snapped at him on the boat.

"Terrible," Darcy says, pressing a hand to her mouth.

He takes a deep breath. "The physical injuries healed in about a year. But the injuries in my mind and my heart took much, much longer. At first, I thought I was going crazy. I mourned my wife, of course. But then this thing happened, the attacks. Something would happen and it felt like I was in the car again, trapped inside. I could not get out. I would shake and cry, like Kate did."

"Sounds like PTSD," Camilla says, and he nods.

"Exactly."

There's a moment of silence when everyone takes that in. Kate stifles a yawn, and Antoni sets down his glass and makes to leave.

"This is a good sign," he tells Kate. "The adrenal gland has stopped shooting neurotransmitters through your bloodstream, and now you are tired, which means your body is ready to recover. I will go. But please, call me if I can be a help in any way."

He gives Kate a nod, and she looks up at him with a small smile. "Thank you," she says.

Darcy rises to her feet, murmuring words of thanks to Antoni and closing the door behind him when he leaves. Then she turns, folding her arms. The three of them are alone at last. Camilla's agitation has shifted down a few gears, and now she feels like she could sleep for a week.

"Shall I stay?" Darcy says.

"I don't mind," Camilla offers, glancing at Kate. "Kate, do you have a preference?"

"Neither of you needs to stay over," she says. "I'm fine, really."

"You don't look fine," Camilla says.

"Cam," says Darcy, a warning tone in her voice.

Camilla feels like she's had her wrist slapped. "What? I don't mean that she looks awful . . ."

"Thanks," Kate says with a little laugh.

"If you'd rather we didn't stay, I understand," Darcy tells Kate. "You just gave us quite a fright, that's all."

"It was out of the blue for me, too," Kate says.

Darcy passes Kate her mobile phone, setting it on the seat next to her. "You text us if you need anything," she says. "*Anything*."

"I will."

14

DARCY

It's Saturday, and she's awake early. Even when jet-lagged, Darcy likes to be up with the sunrise, making sure she starts the day right. A cup of coffee, some stretching, then she'll head to the gym. It's disappointingly small, the gym, with only two treadmills. She runs outdoors at home, but it's already eighty-six degrees, even at six in the morning, and she doesn't fancy running on sand.

She checks her phone for messages from the boys. Marsha has sent an update about what the boys did at school, what they ate, what time Jacob came to take them to his for the week. They coparent like this, one week at hers, the next at Jacob's. She still isn't used to the arrangement, nor to the unfairness that is only seeing her children for half the year because her husband decided to shag half the country. Whoever said *all's fair in love and war* clearly never experienced divorce.

Ed and Ben have sent cute little notes from Marsha's phone, including a video message telling her how much they love and miss her. Nothing from Charlie, who has his own phone. She sends two messages back to Marsha, both addressed to Ed and Ben, and another one to Charlie.

She throws the phone down and sighs. Yet another curveball from the wilderness of parenthood. Tantrums, she can deal with. Sleep deprivation—she's got all the T-shirts for that one. But stonewalling? She loathes it. Her mother was excellent at it, and it drove Darcy bats. Darcy was like her father, an open book, naturally inclined to share, talk things through. Volatile, too, until she learned to control it. Ah, genetics. How much of parenting involves dealing with your parents all over again in the form of your children's behavior. Echoes of the past, both the good and the bad.

Everything is different when it involves your own children. She has no idea—not a single clue—how to handle this one. And least of all from the other side of the world.

Maybe the time away will be good for Charlie, she thinks. Maybe he'll come round once he realizes how much he misses her.

A small part of her is worried, though—what if he doesn't? What if this is as good as it gets?

A red number thirteen sits at the corner of her WhatsApp icon, and she clicks on it, expecting to see a stream of messages from her parents' group. The thread is about the dates for parents' evening, and she scrolls through it, her heart sinking. Usually she's tagged into such questions, because everyone knows she's on it, that Darcy's *always* on top of these things. School trips? She has every single date in her calendar, along with payment info and details about suitable clothing. But this is another consequence of the divorce—because she only has the boys every other week, she's no longer the source of wisdom, the go-to Queen of School Knowledge. It has affected her other WhatsApp groups, too, the ones that have devolved into discussions about recipes and air-fryer tips, and the one about environmental sustainability. Darcy has a talent for repurposing furniture, but her wisdom is called upon less and less. No friendly messages either, asking about her divorce trip.

It irks her. Secretly, she liked the role she had acquired among her peers. Darcy, Queen of Upcycling! It seemed to work better when she was married and a full-time mum. She suspects that people avoid divorced people—particularly divorced women—as though being cheated on is contagious.

To hell with them, she thinks, tossing her phone into a bag.

She gets up, brushes her teeth, pulls her hair back into a stubby ponytail, and throws on her gym gear. Thank God she brought shorts instead of leggings—the humidity would cause chafing.

The gym attendant is there already, handsome, young, muscular. She feels the first stirring of something that has lain dormant for years—sexual attraction. A reminder that she has a libido. Perhaps she should take Camilla's advice and shag everything with a pulse. There has not been another man since Jacob. Not since their first date seventeen years ago. She's not built to be unfaithful. She can be selfish, has dealt many blows below the belt during a row, and Charlie's stonewalling definitely comes from her side of the family. But infidelity is not in her genes. Once she's with someone, that's it.

"Good morning," she says to the attendant. A boy, really. In his early twenties. She feels so old now, when she considers she could essentially be a mother to a man this age. It makes her nostalgic for her own twenties, when she and everyone her age was breathtakingly gorgeous and didn't know it. Completely oblivious to the staggering beauty of youth that was dripping away from them with every minute.

The place is all hers. She's glad she got up early. She hates gyms, both because of the inevitable germ bath that accompanies a visit to one and because of the idea that she has to work out in full view of strangers. But this one is empty, with the exception of the hot adolescent who is staring at his mobile phone by the water cooler.

She places her water bottle in the cupholder of the treadmill, then walks for five minutes to warm up her muscles. She used to be able to plow straight into a jog, but nowadays her calf muscles scream for days if she doesn't take time to stretch and warm up properly.

She's only beginning to jog when she hears the door open, a man's voice greeting the attendant. A few moments later, a figure appears on the treadmill next to her.

Her stomach drops. It's Rob, Jade's husband. He meets her gaze, his dark eyes locking with hers. No nod or smile, no acknowledgment.

She turns away before anything slides into her expression, her eyes fixed on the numbers on the treadmill screen.

Rob walks for thirty seconds before powering the treadmill into a sprint. Nine miles an hour. Her dial reads 6.6 miles an hour. She pushes the PLUS button to increase her speed, Rob's thick legs pounding quickly next to her, his arms swinging. A moment later, he increases his speed, and she increases hers. It's a game, she thinks, a silent competition, and she isn't sure why. He puffs and grunts as he pushes himself harder and harder, sprinting so fast the whole treadmill is moving. The door opens again, and from the corner of her eye she sees the attendant leaving.

Shit, she thinks. The withdrawal of the third person in the gym is like a new chemical being thrown into a pot, altering the balance. Her irritation turns quickly to vulnerability. The gym is made of glass, but you can only see out from the inside, not in from the outside. The glass panel in front of her shows only the palm trees and the sauna. No sign of anyone nearby.

She slows down the speed on her dashboard to a fast walk. Part of her desperately wants to head back to the villa, and she's furious with the attendant for leaving like that, is already scripting a complaint in her head. *To the management: at no times should gym users be left unattended* . . . Another part of her hates that she's doing what all women do when confronted with an aggressive male, which is back down, seek the escape route, mentally prepare to knee an attacker in the bollocks. It's exhausting, living with the undercurrent of threat because of your gender. She was secretly glad when she had sons; so little had changed for women that she dreaded raising girls, dreaded the thought of preparing them for a world that makes being a woman so bloody difficult.

She stays on the treadmill, eyes straight ahead, playing Rob at his game. She can see him glancing over at her. He's in touching distance, the treadmills set ridiculously close together on account of how tiny the gym is. Not exactly Covid-friendly. She mind-scripts another complaint to the resort management.

Rob slows down to match her speed. His head is firmly turned toward her now.

"Where do I know you from?" he says.

"Hmmm?" she turns her head and smiles mildly, as though she's only just realized that he's there. God, she wishes she'd brought earbuds.

"I said, where do I know you from?" he says, his lips curled into a sneer.

"Oh," she says. "We met the day before yesterday. I was chatting with your wife by the pool."

"Nah," he says. "I don't mean then. We've met somewhere before, haven't we?"

She gives a laugh that comes out far more shrilly than she intended. "I don't think so."

He keeps staring. "I have this gift," he says. "Terrible with names, never forget a face."

"Really?"

"Have you heard of that test you can do online? Super recognizers?"

She shakes her head, but she has.

"I'm in the top five percent."

She watches the window in front of her, not to avoid his gaze but because she can see the door of the gym in its reflection. She's watching out for the attendant, or another guest, because her nerves are jangling, all her female instincts on full alert. The problem with the gym being in a whole other part of the resort is that Rob could bludgeon her with a dumbbell and she'd be dead before anyone knew it.

She hits the red STOP button on her treadmill and feigns tiredness, like she feigned it so many times when she could read Jacob's desire for sex in his gestures, in his increased tenderness toward her. She gives a slight sigh, raises a hand to rub imaginary bleariness from an eye, takes a long drink from her water bottle. She steps down casually from the treadmill and dabs her brow with a towel, heading toward the door.

When she steps outside, she hastens along the track toward the wooden causeway. She's careful not to look as though she's running away, but lengthens her stride, her pulse quickening. A voice in her head tells her she's overreacting. So what if this man came into the gym and ran beside her? So what if he said he knew her? That kind of report would make any resort manager dismiss her out of turn.

But when she glances back, she sees the gym door swing open, Rob's powerful form lurching out. She sees him glance to his left, then to his right. He sees her and starts running.

Oh God.

She moves faster, light on her feet. She feels the causeway beneath the soles of her trainers, but she's still a good four hundred yards away from her villa. No one is around. A bird with a long, pointed beak skitters across the path in front of her, and bats lift off from the trees into the blue morning sky. *Keep calm*, she thinks, but it's useless. Her heart is jackhammering in her throat, and recognizing how freaked out she is by Rob striding quickly behind only serves to make her fear worse.

The long sway of villas is in sight. She spies someone sitting on their upper balcony, with a good view of her and Rob, and breathes easier.

"Good morning," she calls up, pointedly. The man looks down, confused, and waves. She waves back, arm high, signaling to Rob that they have an audience now. When she glances back, Rob has slowed to a walk, studying his mobile phone. Apparently oblivious to her.

At the door of her villa, she lunges for the handle, relief swamping her. But it's locked. *Shit.* She pats her pockets for the key. Where is it?

"Looking for this?" a voice says.

She jumps a little at the sight of Rob standing right behind her, grinning. He holds a key card out to her. She reaches for it, but he swipes it away.

"Say please," he says.

She reels at the arrogance of it. Then, relenting: "Give me the card."

"'Give me the card, *please*,'" he urges.

"Fuck off," she snarls, and his grin widens.

"That'll do," he says, handing it over. She snaps it from his fingers and presses it against the door, pushing down the handle and stepping into the villa.

"It'll come to me," he says.

"What will?" she says, turning angrily to face him.

"Where I know you from," he says.

Darcy quickly shuts the door.

15

CAMILLA

NOW

"You're going to draw your abdominal muscles right in, as though there's an elastic band tugging your navel to your spine."

Camilla is leading a sunrise Pilates class on the wooden half-moon platform on the far end of the island, overlooking the ocean. A domed roof provides shade for the group of seventeen, the high ceiling lending the space a sacred quality. Not yet 7 a.m. and it's already eighty-six degrees, but the sea breeze is drifting inside the space. Camilla's phone is propped on a tripod nearby, capturing the class live for Instagram, where another eighty-four participants from around the world follow along. The scene is idyllic—swaying palm trees, the gentle wash of the ocean all around them, Camilla looks fresh-faced in a white yoga outfit, her black hair pinned up in a bun, though her signature gold hoops are still in place. She's always calm when she teaches Pilates, and when she practises; the fluidity of the movements switches off the part of her brain that is, as her husband, Bernie, likes to say, always gearing up for a fight.

"Now, gently raise your legs up at a forty-five-degree angle, pointing your toes at the sky. Try and keep the knees soft while maintaining straight legs. You're using your abdominals here to hold the pose." She scoops in her belly, then lifts up her arms. "Keep legs and arms nice and straight without locking your knees or elbows."

She glances over at the guests while holding the pose, still as a rock. She's a bit annoyed that Darcy and Kate didn't join in. But she recognizes a couple of faces—Antoni is at the back of the group, and Jade is in the third row, sunlight falling on her blond hair. She is the only participant under forty, and the only guest to wear a bikini with a sarong instead of workout gear. The gentleman next to her wearing a red bandana has yet to turn his eyes to Camilla, preferring instead to study Jade, his eyes glued to her chest. If Jade notices, she doesn't let on, her gaze on Camilla.

"Hold it for thirty seconds," Camilla says. "If you need to lower your legs, that's fine, but maintain the contraction in your abdominal wall. Think of yourself as holding a beach ball between your feet and your hands. That's it."

Several guests topple over, and someone farts.

"That was not me," Antoni announces, laughter rippling throughout the group. Camilla smiles at him, hiding her displeasure at the break in the serenity. Hopefully the camera didn't pick that up. Antoni is the only guest able to follow along properly, and she's glad that he showed up this morning. Several guests won't stop yawning. Maybe it was a bad idea to do an Instagram Live. She makes a mental note—do another Live instruction for her followers tomorrow morning, without the guests. The yawning is starting to grate.

"Now, holding that position, let's lift our hands up and down, as though we're sitting in a puddle and beating the water."

She notices Antoni getting up. "Apologies," he says, heading up the platform. "The sun is in my eyes."

She nods approvingly, and he relocates next to Jade, squeezing in between her and Red Bandana Man.

"And now we'll just move our hands beneath our knees and gently rock like a ball," she says, smiling a little at the visible displeasure creeping onto Red Bandana Man's face. "Let the lower back touch the mat first, then the middle, then your shoulders. Then slowly up again, controlling the movement."

She rises to help one of the older participants return from his backward motion, pressing her hand gently on the man's spine to guide him up from the roll. He struggles. Christ, the man has no core strength. *This* is why people need Pilates, she thinks.

"That's it." She beams, striding back to the front. "Now, with your legs on the ground in front of you, you're going to stretch your arms out at either side, turning from the waist. Again, use the core to help you rotate. Slowly, slowly. Good."

For a moment, the class seems to have gotten it, rotating in one motion, like synchronized puppets. She tells them to lift their legs and hold again before pumping their arms up and down.

She turns to the camera, beaming. "How are all my followers at home doing? Remember to always engage the core. Try and think of yourself sitting in a puddle, slapping the water with the palms of your hands."

"Why would we be sitting in a puddle?" a voice says. She turns to see that another guest has joined the class, despite it being half over. It's Jade's husband, Rob.

"Welcome," Camilla says, stretching her face into a wide smile.

He stands against a pillar in the middle of the space, next to Jade, one leg crossed over the other, arms folded. A dark look on his face.

"Please, join us," Camilla says, holding out her hand to invite him to sit down. He shakes his head and holds up a hand as if to say, *I'm good.* She frowns. Is he really just going to stand there, watching over his wife like he's her bloody bodyguard?

Apparently, he is. He keeps his head turned to Jade, who smiles up at him uneasily.

"Up on our feet for this next one," Camilla says. "You'll need a bit of space, so spread out just a little. That's it."

The crowd shuffles outward, Red Bandana Man finding himself in touching distance of Rob.

"Right hand behind the head," Camilla says, demonstrating, "left leg to the side, and we're just going to tap the toe of that leg on the ground before lifting it upward, left knee to right elbow. Like this."

She performs the move very slowly, explaining the little muscle in the right side that people want to feel with this move.

"Good!" she says, clapping. "We'll do ten of these before moving to the other side."

Some participants are unsteady, but after a moment or two most of them begin to synchronize the movement.

"Now the other side. Right leg, this time, and left elbow."

Jade wobbles on this one, almost toppling over. Antoni is there to catch her, and she rights herself.

"Are you all right?" he says, a hand still pressed flat on her stomach, the other on her back. Camilla notices Rob unfold his arms, his face dropping. The tension is immediately palpable.

"I'm fine," Jade tells Antoni.

Antoni holds his hands on her body a second longer, as though to make sure she isn't about to topple, but Rob is having none of it.

"Hey!"

A booming voice, echoing off the domed roof. Everyone's head turns to him, then several turn to Camilla. She smiles, as though this is all part of the routine. Jade's face is tight, her eyes fixed on Rob. Antoni holds his hands up as if to say, *No big deal*, and resumes the movement. Jade leaves the group apologetically to approach Rob, full of appeasement. She takes his hand and presses it to her cheek as though consoling a child. Camilla sighs angrily to herself. Another forty-year-old toddler. So insecure he can't even let her attend a bloody Pilates class.

"All right," Camilla says in an upbeat tone, clapping her hands. "This next move is *really* spicy."

She shows them how to curtsy, one leg behind the standing leg, lowering and rising, hands on the hips. Jade and Rob are still standing at the side of the space having a heated conversation, and although she can't hear what they're saying, the drama is drawing the participants' attention away from her. She imagines people online watching this unfold, a lovers' tiff upsetting the professional, calming atmosphere she prides herself on creating. Not at all the way she wanted her first Instagram Live from the Maldives to go.

Bloody men.

AFTER THE CLASS, CAMILLA CHATS briefly with the participants, giving advice on how to alleviate their sore backs or sort out that nasty pinch in their shoulder. A normal part of teaching. Some promise to follow her online, which makes her happy.

Back in her villa, she showers, makes coffee, texts Darcy and Kate the same message.

Morning! How are you feeling? xx

Her phone dings, and she lifts it, expecting a reply from Darcy. But it's an email notification. Another message from Jacob Levitt.

From: j.levitt@immersiveAI.com
To: Camilla_papaki1973@gmail.com

I need to speak to you about Adrian Clifton. My number below—call anytime.

Jacob

She stares at the message for a long moment, reading it slowly and carefully, as though the words are some kind of code. How does Jacob know about Adrian Clifton?

Did Darcy tell him?

They swore, all of them, that they would never mention Adrian to anyone else.

And Jacob is the very last person she'd expect Darcy to tell.

Her hands shaking, she selects "filters" from the menu and searches for a way to block Jacob's email. She begins to enter his address, then falters. Perhaps she ought to call him.

Her uncertainty is overwhelming. She is seized by blind panic, trying to work out Jacob's meaning, his strategy.

Why would he ask about Adrian Clifton?

16

KATE

Kate heads downstairs, yawning. Another morning of radiant sunshine. She *wants* to love it, but she suspects she is irrevocably a creature of the dark, a night owl, born to burrow into earthen spaces by tree roots. Perhaps she might ask her butler for a fan to keep cool, and a blanket, for comfort. She misses her cats, the nubs of their noses against her cheek at dawn, a velvety coil at her feet.

She heads to the kitchen to make a pot of tea, then reverses course, drawn by something that doesn't look right. The villa door is open. Just a little, about an inch, a fresh breeze spiraling in from the sea. She approaches it, confused. How long has it been open? Did she leave it like this? Her heart begins to pound, and she wonders if someone has come inside during the night. Panic is beginning to rise again.

She reaches for the phone and presses the button that summons her butler.

"Hello, Rafi? Yes, Kate Miller here, in villa two. I think my door might be broken. Could you come and take a look?"

Ten minutes later, Rafi is there with a younger colleague.

"These are new digital locks," he says, wiggling the handle. "Sometimes a little temperamental."

"Can it be fixed?" she asks, still talking down the fear that rose up in her before. PTSD is a difficult thing to explain to people, and it's exhausting, carrying so much anxiety. The constant mental sorting of rational from irrational fear. Fear can save your life, but it can also drive you mad.

"Yes," Rafi says, adamant. "But if you are worried, I can move you to a different villa?"

She watches the younger man work the digital locking system, closing the door tight, a red light on the panel confirming that it has finally locked.

"It's fine," she says. "As long as it's fixed, I'm happy with that."

"I'll give you a new key card," he says. "And if it bothers you a moment longer, just let me know. It is not a problem to change villas."

"Thank you," she says. "Perhaps I might ask for a little favor?"

He nods, glad to help. "Of course."

"Perhaps I might get an extra air-cooling unit? And a woolen blanket? As heavy as you can find."

He doesn't blink at this strange request, probably a first. "Do you need anything else? I could bring you breakfast?"

She goes to say no, it's fine, but stops herself. *Yes, why not?* she thinks. Her default setting is to say no to any offers of help, that she's fine, even when she's not.

"I'd love breakfast," she says.

He produces a folded leaflet from his pocket and hands it to her. It's a menu. "Just tell me what you'd like."

He and the younger man head off, her choices selected, and she looks down from the deck at the water below. She feels fragile this morning, still wary of another panic attack. It just leaps on you, she thinks. One minute you're completely fine, chatting with people, having a drink, and the next you're ambushed by an invisible assailant, one that lives secretly in your own brain. She hasn't had a panic attack for well over a decade. That took years of therapy, as well as antidepressants, which she still takes. Maybe they're wearing off. Maybe she needs a higher dose.

Inside, her phone is buzzing. She lifts it and sees it's a message from Darcy, sent to both her and Camilla.

Rob followed me back from the gym this morning.

Before she can reply, a response from Camilla pops up.

What??! What happened?

Darcy fires back a reply.

He didn't attack me, but he was pretty threatening.

Kate studies the words on the screen, recalling the rough way that Rob gripped Jade's hand by the pool, crushing her delicate fingers against his lips. Kate doesn't usually like to judge character based on appearances. Rob stands out, certainly, with his swagger, his tattoos, eyes like knives. It's Jade that makes her worry. She's twenty years younger, a young woman. Could pass for his daughter instead of his wife. Walking around with an awful bruise over her eye. Kate tries to imagine Jade's wedding day with that bruise. The whispers. She remembers how skittish she became when Rob approached.

Kate sends a reply.

Shall we come over?

Darcy:

Thanks, loves. Going to have a nap. Meet at 12?

Kate:

See you at 12. Meantime, call us if anything happens.

The door opens downstairs; Rafi has returned with a tray of food that she can smell all the way from her bedroom.

"Here we are," he says, presenting her with a glorious full English, along with a bowl of porridge topped with banana and honey. An Americano, a tall glass of water, and a glass of freshly squeezed orange juice. "You want it on the balcony? I'll carry it upstairs."

"Yes, thank you," she says, and she follows as he takes it up the stairs and along the hallway to the dining area outside.

"Rafi," she says. "Could I ask a question?"

He removes the items from the tray and lifts it to take it back to the kitchen. "Of course."

"Well, it's about another guest," she says, feeling awkward. "In villa three. An Englishman named Rob. Have you come across him?"

Rafi thinks. "I think I have seen him. Very strong. Black hair. Tattoos."

"That sounds like him. He has a tattoo of a tiger on his neck."

Rafi nods. "Yes, I have seen him."

She pauses, trying to word her question the right way. "My friend had a run-in with this man earlier. Do you know how we might report him to the island management?"

"A run-in?" Rafi asks, confused.

"A kind of . . . confrontation," she says. "I'm just concerned, really. What happens here on the island if a guest causes trouble with others?"

Rafi considers this gravely. "I will speak to the resort manager."

"Please don't mention names just yet," she says. "And if you hear anything about this man, would you let me know?"

He nods, his expression full of sincerity. "You have my word."

SHE TURNS TO HER BREAKFAST as he makes his way back downstairs and out of the front door. Despite how beautifully it's presented, she has little appetite for it, only managing half the coffee and a corner of buttered toast. She has a clearer sense now of the events that preceded her panic attack, a loose chain that begins to reveal a pattern: Rob's snarling tiger tattoo on his neck, the lips folded. Then the dolphins. Somehow, these two scenes tugged the memory of finding Professor Berry in the guesthouse to the front of her mind. Funny how memory works according to its own logic, that a tiger tattoo could put her in mind of that terrible moment. The cut at the professor's neck had seemed to snarl at her, the two folds of skin created by a blade. A half-second that expanded into an eternity, in which she felt she would be next.

It's not real, she reminds herself, trying to summon the words she was to say when anxiety got the better of her. *I am here, I smell the seawater, I can feel the wood under my toes, I can taste the coffee on my lips.*

The mantra is only mildly effective. She looks down at the waves, suddenly desperate for an intervention. A shock of cold water might help to rinse out the memories that have crawled out of their hiding places.

IN HER BEDROOM, SHE PULLS out her new swimsuit from the top drawer, looking it over. Nothing spectacular about it, certainly nothing sexy. She bought it at the supermarket on a whim. Plain black, sensible straps, and, what's more, it fits. She pulls off the tags, tugs it on, and pins her hair up before slathering on sunscreen. Rafi left her a snorkel mask and flippers in the hallway. She'll avoid the flippers, but the snorkel mask seems practical.

Lowering herself carefully down the ladder attached to the side of the balcony, she heads to the lower deck, and from there into the water. It's not stinging cold, as she'd expected, having only known British seas. This water is warm as a bath. It's beautiful, and a very effective distraction.

She slips the snorkel mask on. It's one of those full-face ones, no sticking anything in her mouth. A plastic transparent lens covers her eyes, mouth, and nose, providing her with a better chance to see the reef.

Gingerly, she pushes her face beneath the surface, curious. Instantly the world below is revealed: dozens of striped fish, unfazed by her presence, moving easily beside her. The reef is otherworldly, majestic. She recognizes the coral that looks like the tool she uses to clean her dishes, rubbery fronds poking up from the ocean floor. There is coral that looks like horns, another huge one that looks like a brain, and plenty of the type that looks like broccoli, housing smaller fish that seek refuge in flashes of blue and orange.

It takes a minute or two to get used to the snorkel, or to trust that she really can breathe underwater, so long as she keeps the tube that sticks up like an antenna above the surface. There are cool patches in the water, which feel gorgeous, and she stays there for a moment, enjoying a brief respite from the pounding heat. Deeper in the shadows, she makes out a larger shape among the fish—a turtle. She watches, excited as a child to see it here—not in an aquarium or pet shop, but in its natural habitat. It's an unspeakable privilege, she thinks, to encounter such things as this, unplanned, without compromising the creature in any way. Well, except for the plastic in the ocean, in everyone's bloodstream. But she's seen no plastic out here, not even in the restaurant—all water is served in glass bottles with swing-top silicone seals. No litter anywhere; even the leaves from the trees are carefully raked from the sand and disposed of before the guests start to file out to breakfast.

There is damage here, though—the reef is vibrant in parts and dead in others, bioluminescent coral flickering its gas-blue flame beside what looks like stone, the living coral cheek-to-jowl with the dead. This is certainly not the Technicolor kind of reef she's seen in the documentaries of Jacques Cousteau and David Attenborough, but then, this is just the house reef. Perhaps the more colorful, rainbowlike reefs are farther out to sea. She moves a little farther on through the water, toward the parts where the reef fans outward. The fish are more plentiful there, too, shoals of powder-blue surgeonfish glinting near flat coral that spreads out toward her in large terraces, like aquatic fungi.

The turtle sweeps past her, sun rays picking out the small round eyes and pointed beak, the lovely mosaic of its shell.

It darts away, spooked by a sudden flurry of water behind Kate. As she turns her head in the direction of the spinning water, a black oar slices through the surface, brushing past her head. A flash of orange above tells her she's in the path of a kayak. She can't make out which way it's heading. Another oar beats down, and another. Her head rings.

The only safe option seems to be to plunge underwater, out of reach.

17

DARCY

NOW

Darcy's brushing her teeth when she hears a knock on the door of her villa. A moment later, her phone shows a message from Camilla, telling her she's downstairs.

"I knew you wouldn't be able to sleep," Camilla says when she lets her in. "How are you? Tell me what happened?"

"So, I went to the gym," Darcy says, heading through to the kitchen. She spits and rinses her teeth in the sink before turning to Camilla. "And Rob came in and started running on the treadmill right next to me. He starts doing this childish thing of . . . I don't know . . . racing me." She bites her lip, not wanting to mention how *she* raced *him*, and she definitely doesn't want to mention the part about him claiming to recognize her.

"And then the gym attendant left," she says. "So there was just me and him in the place, right next to each other. I got this weird feeling. . . . No one was around. . . ."

Camilla nods, folding her arms. "And so you left."

"Right. I was only about a hundred yards or so up the path when I turned and saw him behind me. I kept walking, and when I got to the villa, he said I'd dropped my key card."

They stare at each other in silence, each registering the other's concern.

"He turned up at my Pilates class this morning," Camilla says. "He must have come straight after he saw you. Macho dickhead."

Darcy's mouth falls open. "What did he do?"

"Oh, you know. Struts up right next to his wife like he's Tyson Fury, then yells at that Spanish guy when he tried to stop her from falling over."

"God," Darcy says.

"Do you think he took your key card on purpose?" Camilla asks.

Darcy shrugs. "I don't know. It all just felt deliberately intimidating."

Camilla nods, her mouth in a thin line, and Darcy senses she can tell she's holding something back. For a moment, she feels transparent. As if she's revealing too much.

"I need to ask you something," Camilla says then. *I was right*, Darcy thinks. Camilla can read her. She knows there's something more.

Darcy nods, shifting her weight on to her other foot. "OK."

Camilla looks down, suddenly wary. "Did you say anything to Jacob about Adrian Clifton?"

Darcy is silent, weighing up the question. Why is Camilla asking this?

"No," she says, and it's true—she never breathed a word. "We promised, remember? Right at the start, we said—"

"I know," Camilla says, wearily. "Look. I need us all to be honest with each other. The three of us. There can be no secrets. Not now."

Darcy nods. "Of course not."

"We have to trust each other a thousand percent," Camilla continues.

"I never said anything to Jacob about Adrian," Darcy repeats. She watches Camilla closely, spotting the conflict on her face. "Did Jacob contact you?"

Now it's Camilla's turn to hesitate. Darcy sees it all—indecision writ on Camilla's face: whether or not to tell the truth, despite what she's just said about trusting each other.

"Yes, Jacob contacted me."

Darcy draws a sharp breath. "What?"

"I have no idea how he got my email," Camilla says quickly.

A million questions are spiraling in Darcy's mind. What is Jacob playing at? And how come Camilla even checked her email after expressly forbidding everyone from using it?

"And what did he say?"

"He said he wanted to talk to me. I figured he was just trying to, you know, mess up our trip, cause whatever havoc he could. So I didn't say anything because I knew you'd worry. But then he emailed again, asking about Adrian Clifton."

"Asking about Adrian Clifton?" Darcy repeats, checking to see that she's got the wording right. "What exactly did he say?"

Camilla takes her phone out of her kaftan pocket and scrolls frantically. "I can never remember the exact wording of things. . . ."

"Can I see the messages?" Darcy asks.

"I think I deleted them," Camilla says. "I was angry."

Darcy can't hide how shocked she is, and Camilla's face falls.

"I didn't say anything because I didn't want to worry you," she says sheepishly. "You deserve this holiday. That's why he's doing it. Right? He threw that bloody custody petition at you right before you left. It was shut down. He's out of ammo. So now he's trying anything he can to spoil your trip."

"Right," Darcy says. She feels betrayed all over again, the extent of Jacob's deception falling on her like a shower of bricks. The vein above her left eye has started to pulse, the distant rumble of a migraine.

"But if you didn't tell Jacob about Adrian," Camilla says, a new thought crossing her face, "then who did?"

"Have you mentioned Adrian to anyone?" Darcy asks, rubbing her forehead.

Camilla shakes her head firmly. "Just as we agreed. Not a single word."

Darcy puts her hands to her face, relieved. At least that's something.

"Do you think Kate might have said something?" Camilla says in a low voice.

Darcy clicks her tongue against her teeth. "I honestly have no idea."

"Either way," Camilla begins, and Darcy knows exactly what she's going to say. "It's not good that he knows about Adrian, is it?"

"No," Darcy says, pressing the tips of her fingers to her lips. "It's not good at all."

18

JADE

"What the fuck are you doing?"

Rob is yelling at me as I step out of the kayak, sliding my oar into the seat hole. "Jade!"

I don't have time to explain. I plunge feetfirst into the water, in front of the rest of the group who are kayaking, and dive down, searching for the person I spotted snorkeling just a moment before. I had just said to Rob that I thought someone was swimming out there, despite this being the no-swimming zone of the resort. "That's their problem, isn't it?" he snapped, and the next thing I knew I'd struck something with my oar, a snorkel mask floating quickly to the surface.

Shit.

I'm not a strong swimmer, but I'm not thinking of that. I'm thinking of how I might just have killed someone and sent them to the bottom of the Indian Ocean. My eyes are stinging from the salty water as I look around, a trail of bubbles obscuring my vision. In the shadows I spot a white limb.

As I move toward the figure, I see it's Kate. Oh, shit—*she*'s the one I struck with my oar. And worse, she isn't moving. She's just suspended in the water, her arms like a puppet's, slowly sinking.

For a moment, my heart stops. I have no idea how to save a drowning person. I might have killed Kate already.

I kick my legs and push forward, grabbing Kate's arm. It feels like hours pass as I tug her to the surface, finally moving beneath her to shove her upward to the light.

At the surface, the group of kayakers have gotten into the water to help. I'm trembling now, the shock of what has just happened settling in fast.

"We need to get both of them out," a man says.

A German couple manage to pull Kate on to their kayak, where she promptly vomits. *Where's Rob?* I think, just as I hear his voice.

"That's my wife," he tells someone. He's still sitting in his kayak. *Coward*, I think. Finally, he paddles up to me, extending a hand, like John Wayne offering to rescue an injured cowboy by tossing him onto the back of his horse.

I probably shouldn't, but I shake my head, refusing him.

"Don't be daft, Jade," Rob says firmly. "We need to get you back to land."

BACK IN THE FIRST-AID UNIT, it appears the staff already know Kate.

"Back so soon?" one of them says with a grin.

"I like it so much here, I just had to come back," Kate says weakly. Rob makes a fuss over me, helping me onto the bed on the other side of the small room.

I grimace. None of his lavish gestures are sincere, though I wish they were. He's performing a big show, the chivalrous knight pouring kindness on his damsel. *And the Oscar for Best Actor goes to . . . Rob Marlowe!*

"We'd a bit of a kerfuffle out in the no-swim zone," Rob tells the medic, Emir, who places a blanket over me, and one over Kate. "I think this one got hit on the head with an oar."

"The name's Kate," Kate mutters angrily from the bed. "My head is fine. I swallowed a good bit of seawater, but I vomited back there, so I should be all right."

Emir looks amused. "Vomiting? This is a remedy?"

"Well, I'm breathing, aren't I?" Kate says.

"This is good," Emir says, checking her pupils for dilation. "But if you swallowed a lot of seawater, we need to keep you hydrated. So, we'll tell the chef to cut all sodium from your meals. You need to stay inside for a day or two with lots of fluids." He opens a wall cabinet and pulls out a long row of white boxes. "Also, antibiotics."

"What for?" Kate asks.

"The sea contains bacteria. Some of those bacteria will respond to antibiotics, some will not. Let's hope you only swallowed the kind that does, eh?"

He sets a box down and washes his hands in the sink behind him. "You hit your head, too?"

"I think I struck her with my oar," I tell him.

"Not really," Kate says. "I felt it nudge me, so I tried to get out of the way."

Emir stands behind Kate, inspecting her head for injuries. "Does it hurt here?" he asks.

"A little," Kate says.

"What about here?"

"No."

He moves to me, checking my vitals. "Did you also swallow seawater?"

"Not really," I say.

"You weren't swimming?"

"I was kayaking, but then I spotted a snorkeler in trouble, so I dived in."

"You didn't know about the no-swim zone?" Emir asks Kate.

"Evidently not," she says.

"You could have been killed," Rob says, and I roll my eyes. "Any farther out and you'd have been in the jet-ski zone."

"That's helpful, thank you," Kate says dryly.

"Shall I take my wife back to the villa?" Rob asks.

"Which lady is your wife?" Emir asks, and Rob looks at him as if he's lost his mind.

"*This* one," he says, nodding at me.

"Both women should stay in the unit for at least an hour," Emir says. "For observation."

Rob shifts his feet, and I can tell he can't stand the thought of being in this place for that long. A phone rings on a counter on the other side of the room, and Emir moves to answer it.

"Why don't you go for a swim?" I tell Rob gently. "Come back in an hour?"

He eyes me, suspicious. "If you're sure."

I squeeze his hand and smile bravely, the rescued damsel paying her knight for his courage by urging him on to conquer another day. When I hear his footsteps trail off into the distance, I breathe a sigh of relief and turn to Kate.

"I'm really, really sorry."

Kate glances at me. "Now, now," she says, adopting a matronly tone. "No need for apologies. I was the one swimming in the no-swim zone."

"I only saw you at the last minute," I say. "We were trying to synchronize our rowing but I kept knocking into Rob's oar. I should have looked where I was going."

"Touché," Kate says. "So much for it being a big ocean."

19

JACOB

God, he wishes he had trained as a software engineer. He has a first-class honors degree in computer science, but given that it's from 1999, he might as well have studied dentistry.

It's Saturday morning. He has five days to work out the kinks in this software product. It would be much faster if one of the QA guys could do it, but Jacob needs to keep this under wraps for now. He sent an email to his girlfriend of two months, Dembe, carefully worded—he doesn't want this to get back to Kabir. He asked her for instructions to run another security audit. She suggested penetration tests, which he has done, both black- and white-box tests.

So far, everything seems to be fine. His biggest worry was command injection. Seeking investment for an AI product riddled with bugs would be disastrous.

Jacob can't deny that this is all his own fault. Given his state of mind lately, it's possible that the analytics problems aren't indicative of vulnerability, not at the level of coding or hacking.

He might just be making this problem bigger than it really is.

Even so, the email addresses that Sam produced shouldn't be anywhere near his product. And then there's a name in there that he doesn't recognize—Adrian Clifton. A Google search has yielded no clues. Who is this guy? Why is there no email address for him? Jacob needs to dig deeper. He was shocked when he recognized the names of the users associated with the hack. Camilla Papaki and Kate Miller. Friends of bloody Darcy's. He's heard her mention them in passing.

Camilla's response to his email about it was abrupt. *Fuck off*. Nice.

Not the kind of woman he ever expected Darcy to be associating with. Did they access the software at Darcy's home, on her computer? Or is she part of this? She knows about the investment meeting. She knows how important this product is.

She helped him grow the company. He managed to get her to sign over most of her shares, leaving her with much less in the divorce settlement than she might have had. Perhaps this is payback.

Perhaps it's paranoia.

He pours himself another cup of coffee from the French press on his desk and decides to keep pushing. The last thing he needs is the investment to fall through because of a tiny software hole he can't find. Adrian Clifton is the missing piece of the puzzle, here. He writes the name down on the desk notepad and circles it.

"Dad?"

Jacob looks up from his desk in the small room at the top of his house. His oldest boy, Charlie, stands in the doorway. He's wearing his pajamas and his hair is ruffled.

He gives Charlie a nod. "You OK, son?"

"Can I come in?" the boy asks.

Jacob gives a sigh. He could really do without being interrupted just now. "Sure. What can I help you with?"

Charlie approaches warily and flops down in the armchair beside the desk. He's getting tall, Jacob can see that. The same look in his eye that Jacob has in his old school photos from this age. Stubbornness, rebelliousness. The thought occurs to him that Charlie might be doing drugs, and he feels nauseous.

"What's your new girlfriend like?" Charlie asks. "Dembe?"

"Oh," Jacob says. "She's nice. She has a daughter. Jasmine. I haven't met her yet."

"Will we get to meet her?"

"Well, yes. I think so."

"Will she be a good stepmom?"

Jacob gives a nervous laugh. He likes Dembe very much, surprisingly so. "What's all this about, then?"

Charlie drops his eyes to his hands. "Have you talked to the solicitor about the custody?"

Jacob thinks. "Uh, not yet."

Charlie meets his eye. "Why not?"

"Well, living with me full-time is a big deal. I thought we'd see how it goes."

"I thought you asked for full custody," Charlie says, and Jacob looks away. The bid for full custody was his lawyer's idea. He dropped it shortly after, settling for joint custody.

"Charlie. Look, I do want you. But your mum . . . she'll be upset."

"I don't care," Charlie says.

Jacob pauses, considering his words. Charlie's a good boy, and he's not given to disliking people. He used to be such a mummy's boy, just like his younger brothers. Jacob never imagined any of the children choosing to live with him after the divorce. It was after that trip Darcy took him on that Charlie got really angsty. The theater weekend. He contemplates whether he should press Charlie a little more, but bites it back. Charlie withdraws under scrutiny.

"I want to be sure this is really what you want, son," Jacob says.

"It is," Charlie says, his face tilted up at Jacob. "It is."

Jacob sighs. "OK. I'll email my lawyer tonight."

"Ben and Ed want to live here, too."

Jacob gives another nervous laugh. "They do?"

Charlie nods. "I think it would be good. It's closer to our school here. The rooms are bigger."

"Uh, we'll have to see," Jacob says, scratching his beard. He needs to shave. "Go on to bed, now."

Charlie seems pleased, the corners of his mouth threatening to lift upward for the first time in weeks. "Remember I told you about Lennie Aspey?" he says.

"The boy who was bullying you?"

Charlie nods.

"I thought he stopped bullying you," Jacob says.

"He did. Mum intervened."

Jacob raises his eyebrows. "That's good, right?"

Charlie looks like he wants to say more, but Jacob needs to wrap this up quickly. He has work to do.

"Off to bed," he says. "It's late."

"What's that?" Charlie asks, spotting the notepad on his desk, with the name *Adrian Clifton* written in capitals and circled several times.

"Oh," Jacob says. "Nobody. Just someone I work with."

Charlie's eyes are wide. "I need to show you something. Stay here."

Jacob watches as he darts out of the room, returning a minute later with a small piece of paper, torn from a larger sheet.

"Here," Charlie says, handing him the piece of paper.

Jacob takes it, opens it. There is a row of eleven numbers, which he deduces to be a mobile phone number. On the other side, he finds *ADRIAN* written in Darcy's handwriting.

"What is this?" he says, looking up sharply.

Charlie looks bashful now. "I saw this film the other day. About a spy. He had this secret phone and—"

"Charlie," Jacob says, his voice a little loud, "what is this?"

Charlie hesitates. "I found a phone in Mum's wardrobe at home. It was like the secret phone in the film."

Jacob narrows his eyes, trying to work out what his son is saying. "A secret phone?"

Charlie nods. "It wasn't an iPhone. Just one of those cheap ones like she got me when I went to camp."

"How do you know it was secret?"

"I saw her," he says. "She was using it. And then I saw her hide it from me and the boys. So later, I went and looked for it. But I couldn't find it."

Jacob turns his body all the way around now, facing his son. "OK. And?"

"I found this piece of paper in her drawer, tucked away. I thought it might be important."

Jacob looks down at the phone number, his mind spinning. "OK. Well, thank you."

Charlie smiles, pleased to have done something he considers to be useful. Jacob watches him slink out of the room, perplexed. It's a bit strange, the way Charlie wants to live with him. A hassle, in more ways than one. But he feels flattered. Darcy has always been there for the boys, he knows that.

Turning back to the computer, he sees Kate Miller's email address on the screen.

He begins to type a message.

20

DARCY

NOW

She arrives at the restaurant early, while the staff are still lighting table candles and setting out the buffet dishes. Darcy is wearing a white cheese-cloth maxi-dress, her hair pinned back, and she decided to add a red hibiscus just above her ear. Not one she picked, but one she found on the path on the way here, a fallen bloom. It seems fitting.

Fifteen minutes to six, the sun setting in a glorious blaze of apricot and bronze light splashed across a vivid blue sky, silhouetted figures by the tide taking photographs of it on their phones.

It's the anniversary of the massacre tomorrow, the date rolling to the front of her mind. September is also the month of her wedding anniversary, and for the first time it fills her with sadness instead of pride.

She watches dinner guests begin to arrive and settle at the tables, wondering for a moment if their lives have ever been unhooked and sent into a tailspin like hers. Her presence here in this luminous place feels suddenly shameful and desperate. She has always known that living involves performance, but the role of dumped ex-wife isn't one she ever wanted to play. Jacob was a sure bet, loyal, from a family of stalwarts. Until her dying day, Darcy will swear that it was the success of Jacob's company—the company *she* helped him build—that made him vain, selfish, and, ultimately, unfaithful.

Even so, Darcy's so-called new chapter feels increasingly like the dupe version of a clean slate. A grubby, cracked slate, with an acute loss of purpose.

With a frustrated sigh, she pulls out her phone and decides to call her sons. It's Saturday afternoon back home, and she knows that Jacob has asked Marsha to babysit until six, despite it being the weekend. Jacob has a Big Week at work, but this is laughable—*every* week at work for Jacob has been big for the past sixteen years. He's a born workaholic.

She calls Marsha and asks to speak to the boys.

"Here is Ben," Marsha tells her, and Darcy's heart pangs at the sound of her boys' voices in the background, their happy squeals.

"Mummy! Mummy!" Ben says excitedly, his mouth far too close to the speaker.

"Hi, Benny Ben," she says. "I miss you."

"Mummy, can I ask you something?" Ben says.

"Of course."

"Ed says if you poo in someone's bum it'll come out their mouth! Is that true?"

She pulls away from the phone in disgust. "What? No. Darling . . . ?"

"Are you *sure*, Mummy?"

"Yes, I'm sure. . . . Ben? Hello?"

He's gone. In the background she can hear him tell his brother, "I told you, it won't come out their mouth!" A few moments later, Marsha comes on the phone again.

"Sorry about that," Marsha says. "They're busy playing."

"What about Ed?" Darcy asks. "Or Charlie?"

She hears Marsha call through the house for Ed, then, when he doesn't answer, Charlie.

"They're playing with their water guns in the garden," Marsha says. "Gorgeous day here. Are you having a lovely time?"

"We are, thank you."

"I'll have the boys call you, perhaps when they've settled down a little."

"Great, thanks."

She hangs up and swipes to her WhatsApp, finding Charlie's number, suddenly full of longing for the days when the boys were small. When Charlie would hold her hand everywhere they walked and Ben and Ed would kiss each other. Adorable. Her WhatsApp messages to Charlie from a year ago contain heart emojis and silly GIFs. Lots of messages from her telling him to brush his teeth. Jacob never bothers to check when they stay at his. He'll happily send the boys to school with odd socks and unironed shirts, earwax dribbling onto their collars. They probably exist on hot dogs and ice cream as his place, too, not a vegetable in sight. She makes a mental note to order children's multivitamins, the good ones, and have them sent to Jacob's address, with strict instructions for the boys to take them when they stay.

She texts a long WhatsApp message to Charlie.

Charlie darling! I hope you're having a wonderful time. I miss you so. It's beautiful here, you'd love the ocean and the little hermit crabs. I saw dolphins yesterday and thought of you. They were quite big and super fast! Perhaps when I come back we can plan a Mummy and Charlie date? We could go to the movies and then get a milkshake, how does that sound? Love you lots xxx

Tears prick her eyes, the boys' voices in the background of the phone call echoing in her ears. They don't miss her. No matter how hard she worked, no matter how much time she dedicated to caring for them, they have always looked up to their father. It's how they're wired.

It's how she is wired, too. An invisible line connecting her to her father. Nothing he did or said created it, or affected it—it was just there.

She flicks to her photos, to the recent ones of the boys. A photo of the three of them, taken just this summer in the back garden. All shirtless, their arms around each other. Three versions of Jacob. Big, gap-toothed smiles, sun-pinked skin, floppy blond hair, and blue eyes. Not a trace of her dark hair and hazel eyes.

A text flashes up from Charlie, and she clicks on it eagerly.

LEAVE ME ALONE! I HATE YOU!!!

She stares at the message, not breathing. A voice in her head tells her that he's only twelve, only a boy. His anger comes from her. Hot as a furnace, terrifying when allowed to simmer, no outlet, no escape valve.

But she has never been on the receiving end of it, until now. Her eyes brim with hot tears, but as a waiter approaches, she swipes them quickly away.

"Can I get you a drink, ma'am?"

"Uh, yes, please," she says, plucking up the menu. "I'll have a glass of red wine, thank you."

She holds the smile in place as the waiter heads off to get her drink, though it falters when she spies Rob strutting through the restaurant in a striped shirt with short sleeves and a pair of chino shorts, his sunglasses still in place despite being indoors. Jade follows behind, in a pastel-pink fitted dress under a black kaftan. They sit three tables across from Darcy's right, a tall artificial cypress tree serving to hide her. A mirrored wall panel ahead provides a reflection of them, and she watches as they sit for a moment without speaking. Jade is studying her phone while Rob watches the chefs in the buffet area, drumming his fingers on the table impatiently.

She thinks about Kate in the first-aid unit, nursing her head. Thank God it wasn't any worse. They could have had a death on their hands. She shudders at the thought. Strange, too, that Rob was involved in that incident, after this morning's episode in the gym. Did he plan it, she wonders? The timing is interesting. Everyone made a fuss about how Kate went into the no-swim zone. But surely *someone* in the group of kayakers must have spotted her before they collided? And it was Rob and Jade's kayak that collided with her.

He's bad news. She knew it the moment she first laid eyes on him.

She knows *him*.

She thinks of leopards moving through grass, head, neck, and spine rod-straight as they creep forward, eyes locked on their prey. It's how she feels when she looks at Rob. Brimming with rage. Years of it, channeled now toward this man in a volcanic simmering. She knows men like Rob, what they can do, and what they can get away with.

Of course, he recognized her, but she finds she doesn't care as perhaps she should. In fact, her hunch was right—she *wants* him to recognize her. The tiger must surely relish the moment when its prey finally sees it, terror flashing brightly in its eyes. To be feared is to be powerful. Who would think that the wholesome mum with the sensible haircut and the wet wipes in her handbag would be a vessel of violence beneath all that chair-of-the-PTA charm?

She'll pick her moment to tell Kate and Camilla. She has a plan in mind, a dark plan. She's not sure if the other two will be up for it. But if it comes together, everything will be right again. Her purpose secured.

She wanted to ask Kate whether she had spoken to Jacob. Whether she had told him about Adrian Clifton. The thought of it sends a chill up her spine. If Jacob knows . . . what then?

"Evening," Camilla says, shimmering in a turquoise dress covered with sequins, her black hair styled in tousled waves.

Darcy snaps out of her reverie, glancing up at Camilla with a smile. "You look stunning. Like a mermaid."

"Really?" Camilla says, disappointed. "A mermaid? I was going for Monica Bellucci."

Darcy doesn't know who that is. "Well, you look very nice."

"I'll take that," Camilla says.

Kate arrives and sits down next to Darcy. "Are you all right?" she asks, eyeing Darcy carefully.

"Fine," Darcy says, stretching her mouth into a wide smile. "Absolutely fine."

The waiter approaches then, carrying Darcy's glass of wine on a silver tray. He sets it in front of her. "Oh, I'll have one of those, too," Camilla tells him.

Darcy feels the hairs on the back of her neck stand up. From the corner of her eye, she can see in the mirrored wall panel that Rob is staring right at her, his shoulders turned in her direction. She flicks her eyes up, pretending to be reaching across the table for the salt, and sees that he is actually looking past her. His expression is alarming—he looks angry, his mouth creased in a snarl. She tries to turn without drawing suspicion, but she guesses that Rob is too distracted by whoever is behind her to really pay any attention.

She follows his eyeline to her left. At the row of silver buffet dishes, Antoni is standing, his hand on a woman's back. It's Jade.

Oh God, Darcy thinks, quickly registering Rob's reaction to this.

When she turns back, Antoni has removed his hand, his conversation with Jade apparently over. But then he seems to recall something else, something of vital importance, and he leans in once more, laughing, bending close to whisper something in her ear, his arm drifting across her shoulder.

Rob erupts out of his chair, storming toward Jade and Antoni. Jade sees, her eyes like saucers, fear laid naked on her face, but Antoni is caught up in whatever he is telling her, still amused and gesticulating with a free hand before turning back to the buffet. *Oh shit*, Darcy thinks, clocking the look on both Camilla's and Kate's faces as they track Rob striding through the tables, his face purple with fury and his fists clenched at his sides.

A waiter carrying a tray full of drinks spots Rob and tries to intervene.

"Sir?" he says, panicked. "Sir?" He holds up a hand to stop Rob from barging into the buffet, but Rob sweeps the waiter out of his way and the man falls, drinks and tray landing on the tiles with a loud crash, a slash of red wine flinging across a woman's dress.

"Jesus Christ," Kate whispers, rising up out of her seat to observe the skirmish.

"He's going to kill him, I think," Darcy says.

Camilla holds her phone up high to film it, gleeful. "Ten quid says he drowns him in the veggie curry."

Rob towers over Jade, who has her hands pressed to his chest, mouthing words of appeasement and apology. Two other waiters step forward to assuage him, but he pushes them aside and strides down the buffet section, where Antoni is chatting to the chef at the pancake stand. The atmosphere in the restaurant is charged with anticipation and unease, the other diners watching through the glass partition as Antoni turns around to find Rob in his face.

"You want to fuck my wife, is that it?" Rob yells, grabbing fistfuls of Antoni's shirt and dragging him close. Behind Rob, Jade is nailed to the spot, hands cupped to her mouth.

Darcy watches silently as Antoni attempts to prise Rob's hands off his clothing, reasoning with him. Rob lets go and pushes him away with disgust, and Darcy's mind flips forward—she waits, breathless and expectant, for Rob to slug Antoni. His right arm is rotating back, his fist bunched. Antoni looks so slight compared to him, old and easily crushed.

She sees the waiters react to this climax, three of them risking another plea with Rob to return to his table. One puts a hand on his arm, the right one that's twitching for a powerful blow, and he explodes.

"Get off me!" he yells, shoving the waiter away. The waiter is a young man, but tall and muscular. He staggers backward, sending a pot of red sauce spewing over his shirt like blood.

A murmur spills out from the tables as Rob turns on his heel, sweeping a box of cutlery to the floor. The ring of metal against tile is brittle and sharp in Darcy's ears. She watches, riveted, as he storms through the restaurant to the exit. Jade follows quickly, hunched and ashen-faced.

The restaurant holds its breath for a few seconds beyond Rob's exit before bursting into chatter.

"What the fuck was that?" Camilla says, breaking the silence at their table.

"I honestly thought he was going to kill him," Darcy says.

"We should go after her," Kate says, scanning through the window to catch sight of Jade.

"Absolute pond scum," Camilla says with a sneer, putting her phone away. "Shameful. Making a scene in a place like this."

Darcy watches as a fresh group of resort staff clamor around Antoni. The young, brawny waiter whom Rob shoved into the red sauce is attempting to wipe the sticky residue from his uniform with a tea towel, with little success. Another has fetched a bottle of wine for Antoni's table, an ostensible attempt to make amends, while two members of staff in different uniforms—from the management team, Darcy reckons—corral him with apologies. Antoni smiles and brushes off the fuss, pausing at tables to chat with the diners who want to check on him.

Kate pulls out her phone and begins to text.

"Are you messaging Jade?" Darcy asks.

"Yes," Kate says, without looking up. "I'll ask if I can catch up with her later. See if she's all right."

"Later might be too late," Darcy says.

"Do you think we should go after her? Knock on the door of the villa?"

"I say leave them be," Camilla says. "Rob's so volatile that it's likely to make things worse if we intervene."

Darcy watches her, then Kate, who appears to be torn between racing after Jade and staying put.

You need to tell them, she tells herself. *Now more than ever.*

21

CAMILLA

NOW

What a fucking day.

Camilla sits alone in the bar area, having said good night to both Kate and Darcy. It's just past nine. She can't face going back to her room. The anniversary of the Spinnaker killings is just hours away now. She's on her fourth cocktail—a piña colada with a flamboyant garnish and a sugar-rimmed glass—and quite prepared to keep drinking so long as it keeps the knot in her stomach from getting any worse. In fact, she might just keep drinking until she passes out. Darcy and Kate will understand, surely, if she doesn't appear tomorrow morning. But better to pass out in her villa than here in public view.

She's just getting up to leave when a figure appears next to her.

"Good evening. May I join you?"

She looks up to see Antoni, who is accompanied by a lanky, square-jawed eighteen-year-old with liquid brown eyes.

"Antoni," he says, putting his hand to his chest. "In case you'd forgotten. And this is my nephew, Salvador."

She smiles. "No, I hadn't forgotten. Sharp as a tack, that's me." She shoots a tipsy grin at Salvador. "Evening."

She sits back down in her chair, the idea of being alone suddenly unappealing. Antoni turns to the young man and says something in Spanish. Salvador nods, responding, though she has no idea what he's saying, with the exception of "*sí, sí*," which she understands as "yes, yes."

"Salvador doesn't speak English," Antoni explains. "He's going to have a drink with a girl he met earlier."

Salvador smiles awkwardly at Camilla and lifts a hand in farewell. "*Mucho gusto.*"

"*Mucho gusto,*" Camilla says, raising her glass and spilling a little of its contents as Salvador departs toward a younger woman sitting expectantly at the bar.

Antoni takes the seat opposite Camilla, and she can tell he's stone-cold sober. He's smartly dressed: a crisp linen shirt, open enough at the neck to reveal chest hair. Strong arms, too, the hint of a pronounced bicep at the sleeve hem.

"Antoni," she says, quickly remembering the fray at dinnertime. "God, that was crazy earlier. Rob, I mean."

He nods. "*Sí,* he was very angry. His young wife was upset, too. I was trying to give her some advice for the Pilates move you showed us. But . . ." He tuts, shakes his head. "Her husband is a *torracollons.*"

She gives a loud laugh. "A what?"

"A ball ache."

"Maybe you can teach me some Spanish swear words," she says, raising her glass.

"Catalonian," he says.

"Is that another word for ball ache?"

"Yes and no," he says. "It's my nationality. I'm from Catalonia."

She realizes her error and laughs again, her head flung back, drawing looks from the guests nearby.

"How is Kate?" he asks.

"She's fine," she lies. "Absolutely fine."

"That's good to hear. I was worried."

She fakes a smile, slighted by the assumption that he's only here to ask about bloody Kate. "I'll pass on your good wishes, shall I?"

"What are you drinking?" he asks.

"My sorrows."

His expression changes, his eyes moving across her. "Ah, that's not so good. Have they a more cheerful cocktail?"

She glances behind him. They're sitting in the bar, rattan chairs and tables spread out beneath a straw roof, the light murmur of jazz music from speakers overhead. Candles glimmering in glass jars, the night sky filled with stars.

She nods at the waiter, who approaches their table with a tray.

"A piña colada for my friend Antoni," she says.

"Certainly. And for you?"

"I'll have one too."

The waiter vanishes toward the bar. She drains the rest of her glass.

"I heard about Kate," Antoni says. "Another accident."

"She's lucky is what she is," Camilla says, her tone more spiteful than she intended. "Went swimming with the kayaks and paddleboards. Took an oar to the head. But she's fine."

He nods, his fingers laced. "That's good. Not good she took an oar to the head, of course. But I'm glad she's all right." A smile, his eyes lightly scanning her. "I find holidays can be a double-edged sword."

She cocks her head. "How so?"

"Well, the opportunity to rest is wonderful, is it not? But also, we put so much pressure on ourselves to make sure we enjoy every second. And sometimes a vacation allows the mind to unwind a little bit too much. We have all this time to think about the good, and the not-so-good."

She runs her eyes over him, impressed. He's deep, this guy. "I know. Some of us work, work, work just to keep ourselves from thinking too hard; otherwise we might go mad."

"Exactly. Vacations are not to be taken lightly. They can be *dangerous*." His voice deepens on the word *dangerous*, and he laughs, but she hears the truth in his tone.

"I haven't taken a holiday in about twelve years," she says. "I've gone abroad, sure, but it's always a working holiday."

His smile fades as he realizes she's confiding in him. "I'm sorry to hear that."

"I get scared if I've got too much time to sit around and think."

He cocks his head, trying to work out what she means. "Why scared?"

She shrugs, flicking a long strand of black hair over her shoulder. "I don't know. Fear makes no sense, does it? I keep thinking about my daughter, Natasha. She's perfectly fine, by the way, but I worry."

"Fear is fear."

"I suppose. I just . . . I don't know what I'd do if I lost her too." Her throat tightens. "I don't think I'd survive it."

He hears the catch in her voice and leans forward, placing his hand gently on hers. The feel of his hand jolts her, sobering her a little. She stares down at it; the sensation of a warm touch, of someone's hand on hers, is something she hasn't felt in a long time.

"Tomorrow's the anniversary of . . . losing my twin brother," she says, hesitating on the word *losing*. "It's always a hard time of year for me."

"Losing a twin must feel like losing a part of yourself," Antoni says softly.

The waiter appears before she can answer, setting down the cocktails on the table in front of them. Camilla doesn't lift her eyes from Antoni. She is either blind drunk or spellbound by this man and his soft manner, the kind and eloquent way he approaches delicate subjects, like her brother's death. Like grief.

And she realizes, in a way that makes her wonder why and how she has lived the last two decades *not* realizing it, that her entire adult life has been defined by grief. That she has made every single decision as a direct result of the night her brother was murdered.

"Tell me," Antoni says, "what was your brother's name?"

"Cameron," she says, feeling the heaviness in her blood when she says it aloud. She rarely says his name, though sometimes she says it just to keep him alive. It's something she wonders about recommending to bereavement counselors: *Tell people to say the names of the dead out loud.* The silence surrounding a name is the keenest way to kill them all over again, she thinks.

"What about your wife?" she says. "What was her name?"

Antoni pulls out a packet of roll-up cigarettes from a pocket. "You don't mind if I smoke?"

"No."

He lights one, his face relaxing as he takes a slow, luxuriant drag. "Estella. Estella de Quirós."

"Was she a dancer, too?"

He nods, smiling. "Much, much better than me. As a teenager she was told she could never have children, and this propelled her in a way to do something that the women in her family did not have the chance to do. Also, she was gifted, and a hard worker."

She raises her glass. "To brilliant, hardworking, gifted people who are no longer with us."

Antoni raises his. "*Salud.*"

He drinks, then sets his glass down, enjoying his cigarette. "What about your brother? Were you close?"

She shudders, hearing Cameron's voice in her mind. That last, terrifying phone call. So many hours of therapy over the years, trying to process it.

"Cameron and I were born six minutes apart," she says. "Both of us black-haired Filipino kids, the only Filipinos in our tiny little town. We clung to each other. But the, we drifted as teenagers. By the time we hit our twenties, he and I were on completely different levels. We weren't on good terms when he died."

She tells him, the words flowing out of her in an unstoppable babble, of how Cameron had fallen in with the wrong crowd in his teens, and instead of growing out of it he had become more and more embroiled. He had been a talented guitar player, was set to make a career as a musician. His descent was the climax of a horror movie in slow motion: the drugs, the jail time, the beatings inside prison, the thefts from their parents to support his addiction.

He started playing guitar again, then had a baby with a girlfriend, which offered their parents a glimmer of hope—perhaps this new child would make him turn over a new leaf. And perhaps they'd be able to see their grandchild.

Neither was to happen: Cam screwed it up, as he did everything else. The girlfriend refused access, worried that Cam would use in front of the kid. Their parents never so much as met their grandchild, a little girl. She must be in her mid-twenties now.

But that last phone call . . . *I think someone's here. . . . What do I do?*

Antoni's hand brushes against hers, bringing her back—where? She looks around, the alcohol making the air fuzzy, the ground shifting a little. Ah yes, she's in the bar, in the resort, in the Maldives. She's forty-nine. Twenty-two years have passed since Cam's death. And yet, time does nothing, heals nothing. The past is stunningly present, all the time.

HE SUGGESTS THEY TAKE A walk along the beach, which is lit up by neon lights that change color, flickering across the dark waves.

"He called *me* that night," she tells Antoni as they stroll slowly along the shore. "Not his girlfriend, not our parents, not any of his friends. He knew he was going to die, and he was terrified. We hadn't spoken in four years, not a single word. And despite everything that had happened, despite the lies and all the times he'd stolen from me, I was the one he trusted above everyone else." She swallows hard, her insides turning cold. "And there was nothing, absolutely nothing that I could do but listen to him die."

Antoni fixes his dark gaze on her for a long time while she toes the tide, feeling the horror of that night all over again, hearing Cameron's voice, the fear in it.

"I'm sorry about your brother," Antoni says.

She nods. "I'd envisaged it so many times. Getting a call from a hospital somewhere. The police turning up on my parents' doorstep to say he'd been found dead with a needle in his arm. But he'd cleaned up, seemed to be sticking to the program. Our expectations were *very* low. He was working for a building firm in Dover, had to stay for a few weeks." She sighs, her eyes tracking a shape in the water close by. "He was murdered. Nothing to do with drugs or gangs. Just some random attack."

Antoni looks pained, but then, this is why she never tells anyone about the nature of Cameron's death. If it ever comes up, she tends to say he died in a car accident. Murder raises too many questions, requires too much explanation. And some people have accused her of making it up.

"What about the killer?" Antoni says, reining his shock back in. He's too cool a customer to be flabbergasted, even in the face of news like this, which she likes. "Was he prosecuted?"

Antoni passes her his cigarette, and she takes a long drag, lifting the hem of her dress as the tide rushes in. Too late—her dress is soaked.

"He died in prison," she says, moving to dry sand.

Antoni follows, contemplative. "But he still took your brother. It doesn't matter that justice was done."

She gives a bitter laugh. "*Justice.* Such a small word for such a torrent of bullshit." Antoni laughs brightly, making her own laugh change key. She stares into his face. He's the same height as her, perhaps an inch taller, and she enjoys the way he looks at her. Or maybe it's the drink talking. Either way: he has such kindness, such depth of character in his face, and it occurs to her how underrated those things really are.

Who knew? All this time she sought out complicated, entitled, and often perverse men with bizarre fetishes, assuming they were the ones who were intelligent and sexy. An unfortunate combination. But here she is with a seemingly uncomplicated and straightforward man with kind brown eyes, and she is reeled right in.

He steps forward, a hand reaching to move her head gently toward his, and kisses her, a slow, achingly passionate kiss that melts all the irritation and bitterness away.

"Sorry if I was a bitch to you," she says softly when they separate.

He shrugs it off, lacing his fingers slowly between hers. "I saw straight through it."

And he kisses her again.

22

KATE

NOW

It's just past ten at night, and she's waiting at the jetty for Jade, as per their text messages. It's still beautifully warm, the night sky shimmering with galaxies, but she hugs herself out of worry. The way Rob pounded across the restaurant . . . it was so aggressive, like a bull to a red rag. After dinner, she walked past Jade's villa several times to check that she was all right, but there was no sound from inside, and she didn't want to knock.

Floodlights illuminate long shadows moving through the water below the jetty. Sharks, she thinks, coming out to feed.

She checks her phone quickly, in case Jade has texted to cancel. No new texts, but there's a new email in her inbox from Jacob Levitt.

Darcy's ex-husband.

Her heart racing, she opens it quickly, half-expecting it to be one of those spam messages asking for money or nudes. It isn't, but the content is no less confusing.

From: j.levitt@immersiveAI.com
To: katetheconstantwriter@oncloud.ws

Dear Kate,

I appreciate you're on holiday but I'm writing with regard to a software issue at my company. In particular, I want to get some information about Adrian Clifton. Could you email or call me at the number below as soon as you can?

Thanks, Jacob

She stares at the message, her mind spinning. A software issue? Why is Adrian Clifton mentioned? Did Darcy tell him?

And how the hell did he get her personal email address?

She reads it again, and again, before quickly responding.

From: katetheconstantwriter@oncloud.ws
To: j.levitt@immersiveAI.com

Dear Jacob,

I'm a bit alarmed by this email. Can you clarify, please, what you mean by "software issue," and what information you think I can provide about Adrian Clifton?

Best,
Kate

Footsteps sound behind her, and with a sigh of relief she sees Jade's slender form moving along the path. She has changed into a simple white bikini set and pink sarong. Quickly, Kate puts her phone in her pocket, forcing her shock at the email to the back of her mind.

"Hi," Jade says. "Rob's asleep."

"Good," Kate says with a smile. She had worried that Jade would turn up bruised and battered, but there's no sign of fresh injuries, at least not anywhere visible. "Shall we walk and talk?"

They walk along the beach on the east side of the island in silence, glancing at the resort on the other side of the lagoon, where a platform is illuminated by a purple light. Kate doesn't want to dive into questions, but rather lets Jade walk with her, letting her know she's not alone. Allowing her the space to share if she wants.

"It started about a year ago," Jade says, once they've moved far away from the villas. "It seemed like an accident, at first."

"What did?" Kate asks.

Jade stops and looks out over the lagoon, holding her arms across herself. "He . . . hit me. A total one-off, never-happen-again kind of thing. And then it *did* happen again, but it was months later. And then again, and again."

That bastard, Kate thinks. She feels so very sorry for Jade, but it's more than that—she sees exactly where Jade is headed if she doesn't do something.

They walk slowly, toeing the tide, pausing when a loud cheer arises from the restaurant in the distance. A celebration—exactly what they should be doing.

"Do you have family you can turn to?" Kate asks gently.

Jade shakes her head. "Not really. Everyone thinks Rob's amazing. He could charm the horns off a bull. They'd say I'm making it all up."

"Because he's older?" Kate asks, and Jade nods.

"I'm just a nail technician," Jade says, though she sounds like she is mimicking someone who has previously mocked her. "My dad's a recovering alcoholic. He loves me, I know he does, but I know exactly what he'd say if I told him the truth about Rob." She sighs. "It's complicated."

"Family always is," Kate says knowingly.

"Mom has her own thing going on," Jade says, hoisting her sarong up around her knees. "As far as she's concerned, I should be grateful someone like Rob wants to give me the time of day."

"What about friends?" Kate asks. "Anyone you can maybe stay with for a while?"

Jade looks deflated. "I moved to London to be with Rob," she says. "I haven't made any new friends there yet. I mean, there's the girls at work, but we're not besties. Rob always wants me to spend my free time with him. I did have a best friend back home, but she's not speaking to me now. I've managed to push everyone away."

They walk in silence for a few moments. Jade is skittish, jumping at the slightest sound.

"I want to tell you something," Kate says. "But if I do, I need you to promise you'll keep it entirely to yourself."

Jade nods. "I promise."

"When I was about your age, I experienced something that changed the course of my life," she says carefully.

"Were you married?"

"No. I was a student at the time, studying for a master's degree in archaeology at Leeds University. I'd won a scholarship. It was a huge deal for me. It was an escape route from my family, you see. As part of the degree, I was to go on a field trip to a site in Dover. There were fourteen of us. The night before, we all had to stay in hotels in the area. Me and a couple of others stayed in a guesthouse on the edge of the town." She draws a breath, remembering it sharply, bright as the day it happened. "My taxi driver got lost, I'd been delayed on the train, so by the time I checked in it was just after midnight."

Kate tells her, in broken, stuttering fragments, about the man at the reception desk, about waking the next morning, finding Professor Berry. About racing for help, but finding that every single guest had been murdered.

Jade stops walking, her mouth open in horror. They stand by the very top of the island where darkness falls on both their faces, deepening the hollows of Jade's eyes, and for a moment she looks cadaverous.

"You slept in that guesthouse," Jade says slowly, visibly shaken by what Kate has just shared. "And all those other people . . . they were already dead?"

Kate nods, feeling a familiar kick of fear in the pit of her stomach.

"Oh my God," Jade says. "Kate . . . I mean . . . that's horrific. I can't even . . . Did they . . . did they ever find who did it?"

"Oh yes," Kate says. "It was the man who checked me in. He was a sex offender."

Jade is still gobsmacked. "But, why? Why would someone do that? Kill people in their beds?"

Kate shrugs. "Nobody really knows. They say he just snapped. He's dead now."

"Shit," Jade says, her voice a little louder. Suddenly she grabs Kate's arm, as though realizing something even more terrifying. "Wait. Why didn't he stab *you*?"

Kate thinks back to the trial. Long, surreal days in that small courtroom, watching the hunched figure in a cheap suit on the stand, coughing into a tissue.

"He could have, if he'd wanted to. He had the key to my room. A psychologist said that he allowed me to live because he wanted me to spend the rest of my days knowing that every breath I drew and every thought I had was enabled by him."

Jade narrows her eyes. "That's evil."

Kate nods. "It is." She stoops to pick up a pretty white shell, thumbing the smooth inner part. She feels glad, as always, for the years that are between her and that night. For the small ways they've eroded the horror of it, just enough to allow her to cope.

"It's been over twenty years," Kate says. "The anniversary of it is tomorrow, in fact. Most of the time, I feel like I'm over it. I'm happy. I've had a nice life. I could have been murdered, like the rest of them."

THEY TURN AND HEAD BACK along the beach in a pensive, troubled silence.

"Like I said," Kate says after a while, "it changed everything. And it's made me realize that life is short." She stops and looks at the shell in her hand before pressing it into Jade's.

"You need to act quickly," she tells her. "If you hesitate any longer, it may cost you your life."

Jade nods, but she looks terrified.

"I don't know where I'd go," she says. "I don't have anyone other than Rob. I pushed everyone away. My salary goes into a joint account. Rob put a tracking app on my phone. He can see everything I do."

"I have a small savings account," Kate says, gauging Jade's reaction.

Jade looks surprised, her eyebrows raised. Her mouth opens, but she seems too stunned to speak.

"It's not much," Kate adds. "But it'll be enough to get you out of there, a few months' rent somewhere else."

Jade looks away, her hands clasped together. "I don't know what to say."

"You should take it," Kate urges. Then, with a sharp breath: "Before it's too late."

23

JADE

Kate heads back to her villa. I tell her good night before heading in the opposite direction toward the small island over the bridge.

Oh my God, my head is absolutely banging. Kate's story is so messed up. And the idea that the man who killed all those people let her live so she'd know that every breath she took was enabled by him. How twisted is that? How did she even carry on after something like that? And yet Kate had the kindness to offer me money to escape. I could tell she was genuine. But, *fuck*. Yes, she survived, but her life must have been so hard after all that. Waking up in a shitty guesthouse to find everyone had been slaughtered . . .

I need to walk to stop my brain from spinning, from imagining what Kate saw. But also it's like she's cracked open the prison bars, showing me a way out. For the first time in ages, I felt less alone when I spoke to her. Like I wasn't the only one with problems. Being here was actually making me even more miserable, and not just because of the situation with Rob. Everyone in the Maldives looks so bloody happy, radiant with bliss. And in the meantime, I'm over here, drowning in broad daylight.

I head through the trees, cutting away from the sand path in case Rob comes out looking for me. People are still sitting at candlelit tables on the beach enjoying supper, a string of fairy lights set up by the waiters to make it romantic. So many couples here, honeymooning. They look so happy. Maybe Rob and I look happy, too, from the outside.

I used to think it was cute that Rob asked so many questions about the people I spoke to. *Who was that? What did they say? And what did you say?* I thought it was because he cared. Now I know it's because he has to control everything. I guess I always knew that, but what I'm learning fast is that control isn't love.

Kate's right. I do need to act quickly. But I'm scared, too, because when we were kayaking, I told him to change direction. I saw someone was snorkeling just ahead of us and he was in the front seat, steering the kayak. But he kept paddling toward her, even turning us to go right in her path.

I didn't tell Kate that. What would she think? That he tried to hurt her on purpose? He had no reason to.

But then, he has no reason to hurt me, either. And it doesn't stop him, does it?

I turn left and see a light illuminating a doorway. The sign on it says SAUNA, and when I duck inside, there are male and female sections. Relief floods me. A moment of respite.

I strip down to my bikini. There's a woman in the small room. She looks up and smiles, and I recognize her. It's Darcy.

"Hi," I say. "You can't sleep either, I take it?"

She smiles and sighs. "I'm hoping the heat will help reset my body clock. Hey, are you OK? I was worried about you after what happened in the restaurant."

I nod, sitting down next her. "Yes, thanks. Rob was just a bit worked up."

"What are your plans for tomorrow?" Darcy asks. "No more kayaking, I bet?"

I laugh. "Maybe we'll go to the sandbank. I've heard it's nice."

She brightens. "Oh yes, Camilla mentioned that. I think I'll try it."

I nod, trying to muster up enthusiasm, but my mind keeps turning back to Kate's offer. I mean, I barely know her. And I don't like borrowing from anyone. But I'm desperate.

I clasp my hands against my stomach, praying I'm not pregnant. Rob's sudden decision to have a baby is strange. I feel like there's more to it than him actually wanting to be a father. I mean, we talked about starting a family, but we always said we'd wait until we'd bought our own place. I only get statutory maternity leave. We can't pay rent on just one wage.

But I'm too scared to say all this. He'll accuse me of not loving him, of stringing him along with false promises only to disappoint him.

"Jade?"

I look up at Darcy. I don't know how long I've been sitting here. Tears are rolling down my face. Darcy moves closer to me and touches my arm.

"What's happened?"

Her face is full of concern, but I can't say it. I can't even begin to tell her everything that's going on.

"Can I ask you something?" I say.

"Of course."

"Do you think someone can love another person enough to change?"

She looks surprised. "Yes," she says, and I feel so relieved I want to cry. Darcy is older than me, almost twice my age. She would know these things. "And no," she says, and my heart sinks. "It depends. People *can* change, but a lot of the time, they don't." She smiles sadly. "Does that help?"

I nod, hiding my dismay.

"When I was very young," she says then, turning to me, "I was deeply in love with someone. And I believed I could change him. I really, really believed that our love could transcend all the habits and beliefs that hold us back, you know? I honestly thought that if I loved him enough, I could make him what and who I wanted him to be."

I scan her face, feeling a bit better. It's like she understands what I mean.

"And did you?"

She hesitates, her eyes fixed on me. "No. And I was foolish for believing I could."

She rubs my back, and I try not to burst into tears again.

I wanted her to say yes. I wanted her to tell me I have another way out.

24

CAMILLA

SIX MONTHS AGO

She waited until the front door clicked shut behind Bernie before opening the lid of her laptop. *Meeting with friends for a drink, my arse*, she thought. Camilla wished he'd just be honest about it. Just say, *Look, I'm having an affair with Lucia. I still like you, and I like living here together, but I want to shag Lucia sometimes.*

She was of a mind these days that maybe some relationships worked better when they were open. She and Bernie had been married for almost two decades, and it worked well, apart from the sex bit. They weren't interested in each other that way, hadn't been for years. Fond of each other, but not in love.

She hadn't told Bernie about Darcy and Kate, about the Zoom meetings they'd been having. She had told him about Cameron, that he was murdered in a massacre back in 2001. Like everyone else, Bernie was astonished he'd never heard of it.

"A *massacre*? Here, in England?"

Camilla had showed him the newspaper reports. There were many of them, but she explained that the day after the guesthouse killings, two planes had crashed into the Twin Towers in Manhattan. Social media, smartphones . . . they didn't exist. The massacre went under the radar.

It had its benefits: the families of the victims were spared some of the intrusions that tend to accompany highly publicized trials. The police had their man, a fifty-eight-year-old pedophile named Hugh Fraser, and he was dead after serving just a month of his sentence.

Natasha knew a little more about Cameron's death. When Natasha was born, Camilla decided she didn't want her to grow up not knowing Cameron. It was unthinkable to her; he was Natasha's uncle, and she would know him every bit as well as though he were still alive.

So Camilla told Natasha about Motsi, and about setting up the Facebook group. She told her that she had become friends with Kate, the sole survivor, and Darcy, who was as grief-stricken as Camilla and felt so passionately about the Facebook page that she'd asked to be an admin. But Camilla didn't want her daughter to know that they were going back over the case, that they suspected someone was still out there who might have been involved in the killings. And she didn't tell her about Adrian. This omission was more out of protection than anything else. Camilla knew they were drifting toward potentially dangerous territory. They were searching for someone who had played a part in the violent murders of six people. Was she up for it? She didn't quite know.

But then her mind turned to that terrible night, her phone ringing, her brother's voice. The terror in it . . .

The guy next door . . . he's . . . he's been stabbed. . . . I don't know what to do. . . .

Camilla opened her Zoom app and joined the meeting. In a moment, Kate and Darcy appeared on her screen, both in their usual spots: Kate at her dining table, a picture of an old ruin behind her; Darcy in her study, a floor-to-ceiling oak bookcase in the background. Very cultured. Camilla owned a single shelf of books, all of them about Pilates. She much preferred exercise to reading.

"Evening, all," Kate said. One of her cats, the white Persian named Agatha, cruised across the screen. Hitchcock, the small black one, spread along the top of Kate's chair.

"Evening," Darcy said.

"Darcy, how you feeling, love?" Camilla asked.

Darcy gave an uncertain nod of her head. "I've definitely had better weeks."

"You're near the end, now," Kate said encouragingly. She and Camilla had both received WhatsApp updates about Darcy's divorce. Jacob would only communicate with her now through his solicitor, even over minor things.

"He's contesting spousal support again," Darcy said weakly. "I'm thinking of selling the house."

"God, no," Camilla said.

"Didn't he want you to sell the house originally?" Kate asked, and Darcy nodded. She reached for a tissue, growing upset.

"I told him it was unfair to the boys," she said. "This is hard enough on them without losing the place they grew up in. Ben and Ed were born in the front room, for God's sake. Jacob relented, but now he's giving me no choice. The solicitor's fees are astronomical. . . ."

"Darcy . . ." Camilla said, soothingly.

Darcy recovered and braved a smile. "Anyway, that's not why we're meeting, is it? Sorry . . ."

"No need to apologize," Camilla said. "He's putting you through the mill."

"Are you sure you want to do this today, Darcy?" Kate asked, and Camilla rolled her eyes.

"Yes, definitely," Darcy said. "I told Adrian to log on at ten past, just to give us time to chat beforehand."

"Oh, here he is now," she said then. In the fourth square, a man's face came into view. He was sitting in an office with a black filing cabinet behind him, a wall unit filled with plants and books. Adrian wore glasses and was bald, and his nose appeared to have been broken. She could see the collar of a navy polo shirt, white stubble, and ear hair. He struck Camilla as being in his mid-to-late sixties. Retired. A shaving cut below his jaw. Single, then.

"Hello," he said. "Can you hear me?"

"We can, Adrian," Kate said. "Lovely to meet you at last."

"So, we have Kate, Camilla, and Darcy," he said, reading the names on the screen. A London accent, Camilla thought, though he could be dialing in from anywhere. "How are you all doing?"

"I'm good, thanks," Camilla said.

"Well, this is quite a different kind of investigation," Adrian said. "Quite . . . traumatic, I'm assuming."

"Very," Camilla said sharply. "Darcy tells us you used to be a detective sergeant with the Metropolitan Police?"

Adrian nodded. "Thirty years. I served as an IO—that's an investigating officer—a homicide family liaison officer and a case officer during twelve years on the Met's Specialist Crime and Operations Command, dealing with high-profile murders in London."

"Impressive," Kate said.

"And you've been doing private investigating for twelve years?" Camilla asked tentatively.

"Yes," Adrian said with a proud grin. "Your case is quite unusual, but it has similar elements to other cases I've worked on in the past."

Camilla felt a weight lift from her shoulders. She had worried that the case had too many moving parts, that it was too long ago for anyone to tackle. But Adrian sounded confident, and capable.

"I've started making inquiries into the original canvassing operation," he said. "I can see it was quite thin on the ground."

"It was pathetic," Camilla said, and he chuckled.

"The main thing I want to focus on in the first phase of this investigation is who was in the area that night. What CCTV footage was gathered. And I'd really like to find a way to look into the forensic analysis."

"How easy will that be?" Kate asked. She sounded skeptical.

Adrian weighed it up, pursing his lips. "Under the Freedom of Information Act, I should be able to get most of it."

"Most of it?" Camilla asked. "What do you mean?"

"If they lock certain files, it'll take a bit more work. But leave it with me. I think your main goal is to gather enough evidence to persuade the police to open the case, correct?"

"Correct," the three of them said in unison. Camilla felt her heart pound. The thought that this might be possible, that the light of truth might finally fall on her brother's murder . . . it made her well up.

"You know, Adrian," she found herself saying, "even if it turns out that Fraser was the only killer, I'll be fine with it."

He nodded. "I see."

"For my part, I just want to know what really happened. I want to know that the investigation has been done thoroughly, with care."

"You didn't get the sense that the original investigation was comprehensive, I take it?"

She shook her head, noticing that Darcy and Kate were doing the same.

"No. Absolutely not," Kate said.

"Well, the timing is a bit unfortunate," Adrian said. "I'll bet that 9/11 resulted in most of the uniformed officers in Dover being sent to patrol the ports. Counterterrorism was a priority, as you can imagine. So if the police already had someone confessing to the murders . . ."

He trailed off, but Camilla understood. She blew out her cheeks, frustrated all over again.

"But not to worry," Adrian said. "I think I have everything I need. It will take about six to eight months, I believe."

"Six to eight months!" Camilla exclaimed.

"This is a big case," he said. "I promise to get in touch if anything comes up sooner."

"Thank you," Camilla said before logging off. She leaned her forehead to the desk, feeling her body shake with adrenaline. So many emotions still buried under the skin.

But, for the first time in a long while, there was something else stirring there.

A fragment of hope.

25

CAMILLA

Camilla wakes to the sound of the air-conditioning whirring above the wardrobes, the mosquito nets around her bed billowing softly. Light swells in the room, a celestial ray spilling through a gap in the blinds.

The night before returns to her in a warm rush. God, that was one hell of a shag. Three shags, actually, and they were more than shags. It was the first intense, actual lovemaking session she can remember for . . . years. Camilla's wary of one-night stands now, after a few encounters with men who seemed decent but turned out to be outright weirdos in the bedroom, but she's been on edge about this trip, and Antoni was there at the right time. A delicious distraction.

Antoni is a handsome man, but it was only when he removed his clothes that she really believed he was a professional dancer. What a body! And what a lover . . . They tried everything, all inhibitions flung to the wind. From behind, on the dining table, her in the highest heels she could find in her suitcase. On the stairs, in the shower . . .

To think it all started in such a somber fashion. They'd walked along the beach and talked about her brother. Antoni had told her about his dead wife, Estella, and they'd wept a little together. Quite a different kind of one-night stand. She usually makes a point of *not* talking about her brother, not thinking about him, if she can help it, but she ended up spilling her guts to Antoni. She's in a different place, far from home, slightly jet-lagged, so she feels undone by the memories that keep rising up in her, like the ice caps melting and releasing ancient toxins into the air.

And all the questions about Cameron's death that have never been answered.

She and Antoni planned to have breakfast together this morning, and she liked his company. She liked *him*. But he's not in the bed, nor is he downstairs in the kitchen, or in the shower. Usually, she's the first to slip away the morning after, or, if she's at home, she pretends to be asleep until the guy takes the hint and leaves. Now, though, she finds she's disappointed that Antoni has gone, that he snuck out before she woke up.

She stands in the living room, nothing but a bedsheet wrapped around her, feeling confused. Oh God. How stupid of her. The dead wife, the commiseration . . . it was all a tactic, then. No depth or meaning to it, as she'd supposed. She gives a sigh, regretting it all. Most of all, she regrets sharing so much.

The rest of her time here is going to be awkward, she thinks. She'll have to avoid him, which is easier said than done on an island the size of a soccer field.

She catches sight of something on the side table, a small black object. A phone. Not hers, and when she lifts it up the screen flashes up a picture of Antoni and his nephew. Her heart leaps. He wouldn't have left his phone if he intended not to come back, right?

She feels a breeze from somewhere, glances up toward it. It's coming from the French doors that lead to the outside dining area on the balcony. With a start, she thinks perhaps Antoni is out there, waiting for her. Why didn't she check sooner?

She heads out to the dining table, noticing that things have been rearranged since she was last out here—the day she arrived, she thinks. The centrepiece on the table has been slid to the side and the ashtray moved a few inches toward the lip of the table, as though someone has sat here to have a smoke. There are only a few tiny crumbs of ash in the tray, too, as though the smoker had tossed the rest.

So he's been here this morning. But where is he now?

She looks down the ladder that leads from the side of the balcony to the lower deck, and from there to the ocean. Perhaps he's gone for a swim.

A mark on the pale white wood of the deck below draws her attention, and she stares, trying to figure it out. It looks red, glossy, but it could just be the sun reflecting color in a puddle. It's too bright to tell. Her heart racing, she steps on to the ladder and quickly moves down to the ground-floor deck to get a closer look. The front window of the living room catches her reflection as she pads toward the mark that sits close to the edge, where seawater laps and a school of dark fish billows in the translucent waves.

She stares at the spot, but it's gone now, a wave having lifted above the deck and washed it clean. Camilla scans the sea, her thoughts racing. Is she seeing things now, or was it a splash of blood? Did Antoni go swimming and hit his head? The ladder is stainless steel. She looks over it, both sections: the one that leads straight into the water from the lower deck and the section that attaches upward to the balcony above. Nothing.

Keep calm, she thinks. *No one has drowned.* The realization that today is the anniversary hits her like a rock. That'll be why she thought she saw blood. Old trauma rising up to play tricks.

NONETHELESS, CAMILLA PLUCKS UP ANTONI'S phone and heads quickly to his villa. After a few knocks, someone stirs behind the door. It's Antoni's nephew, Salvador, dressed only in a pair of pajama shorts. He stares at her, clearly just out of bed. She remembers he doesn't speak English.

"Is Antoni here?" she says, enunciating the words in case he might suddenly grasp her meaning.

"Antoni?" he says, glancing at the phone in her hand. He turns and shouts into the villa: "Antoni!"

No answer. He turns and says something in Spanish which she presumes means *he's not here.*

"OK, it's just . . . I have his phone."

He nods, reaching out to take it, and for a moment she pulls away, inexplicably reluctant to give it back. He eyes her, uncertainly. He doesn't seem worried about his uncle, and it occurs to her that Antoni probably does this sort of thing all the time.

She makes the sign of a phone with her fingers against her head.

"Will you tell Antoni to phone me?" she says, and he nods. More Spanish. God, she wishes she'd learned it.

Salvador closes the door and she steps away, deciding to head to the restaurant for breakfast. No doubt she'll find Antoni there, and she'll bump into Kate and Darcy, who'll help take her mind off her brother.

ANTONI ISN'T AT BREAKFAST, AND nor are Kate and Darcy. Camilla browses the bread baskets, the yogurts and cereals, and decides she's not hungry. She plucks a glass bottle of water from the counter and opens it, relieving her thirst as she glances over to the row of wooden loungers by the outdoor pool. She does a lap of the island, resolving that it will kill two birds with one stone—she'll get her steps in while keeping an eye out for Antoni—and when he doesn't appear, she determines that Salvador was probably covering for him. Poor guy must have slunk back to his villa, only to leave his phone behind. Well, if that's the case, she's fine with it. But that mark on her deck . . . she can't get it out of her mind.

She heads to the main office. She reckons she'll feel better if she tells someone about it. Stop her from ruminating and overthinking.

The main office is a small white building by the jetty, where the colorful boats that take guests out on excursions are moored. Inside, a blast of air-con brings relief from the sun, and she eyes the woman at the desk, who is wearing a white hijab that matches her uniform. Camilla clocks her name badge. Nura, the resort manager. She remembers her from the restaurant, apologizing to Antoni after Rob's tantrum.

"Hello," Camilla says, giving a small bow. "I wondered if I could report something? An accident, perhaps."

Nura stops writing in her ledger and watches Camilla with a furrowed brow.

"An accident?"

"Well, maybe."

Nura gestures at the chair in front of the desk and Camilla sits down, feeling flustered and self-conscious.

"I spotted something on the deck, outside my villa," she says. "I think it might have been blood."

"Blood?" Nura says, straightening. "Which villa was this?"

"Number four," Camilla says, almost wishing she hadn't bothered coming in. It's not like she saw anyone getting injured. If it turns out to be some spilled food, she will be mortified. "I mean, I think it was blood. Just on the side of the deck. But it's gone now." She thinks she must sound completely mad.

"Was it your blood?"

Camilla shakes her head, and when it throbs she realizes she's still wobbly after drinking last night. "No. And I didn't see anyone get injured. I just thought I should report it, in case . . ." She bites her lip, falling silent. She feels stupid for reporting it. She's hungover, and it's the anniversary of her brother's murder. She's ragged with emotion.

She stands abruptly, feeling her mood crumble, and Nura looks even more puzzled.

"Sorry," Camilla says, and Nura rises, too. It crosses Camilla's mind that she's much too fragile to be thinking clearly. She'll have a nap, that's what she'll do. It's what she does most years on the anniversary. She usually puts her out-of-office on and stays in bed, with weed or a large bottle of vodka.

"Thank you for telling me," Nura says then. "We'll check out the villa." Camilla nods, feeling a little less embarrassed.

"It's probably nothing," she says, and Nura throws her a gracious smile and a polite nod.

IT'S JUST AFTER TEN IN the morning. Camilla moves slowly past Antoni's villa, glancing up at the balcony, then out at the handful of kayakers a little way off the shore. It's the Italian family, the ones with the adorable four-year-old that Camilla has spotted in the restaurant, a little girl with the most beautiful Italian accent. *Non voglio, Mamma! Non voglio!*

No sign of Antoni.

She stands outside the villa for a moment, wondering if she should risk disturbing Salvador again and harassing him in a language he doesn't understand.

Ordinarily she wouldn't have a problem harassing anyone, but today is different. A protective skin has been removed from her, and she feels raw and fragile. She can't face Antoni opening the door and being awkward over her presence, as though she's chasing him.

Not when the wounds of grief have reopened.

She knocks on the door of Darcy's villa, but there's no answer. She tries Kate. No answer, but the door is open, and she steps inside.

"Kate?"

"In here."

She follows Kate's voice to the dining room. There's a note of distress in it. *What now?* she thinks.

"Morning, darling," Camilla calls, spotting Kate by the dining table. "Shall we get some breakfast?"

But as she moves closer, she sees Kate is rigid, a hand pressed to her mouth, staring down in horror at something on the table. Camilla follows Kate's gaze to see a bouquet of long-stemmed roses, wrapped in white tissue paper and tied with twine. Such a gorgeous bouquet. The roses are bloodred. But Kate looks horrified.

"What's happened?" Camilla asks, looking again at the bouquet, scanning it for a note or some clue as to the sender. "Kate, what's wrong?"

"They've found me," Kate whispers. "Even here, they've found me."

PART TWO

MANTA RAYS. THEY GLIDE THROUGH the water like magic carpets, or angels, beings of a different world. They are shy and gentle despite their size. I reach to touch one and find that its white underside is soft as butter, and remember it has no bones. For a moment I am mesmerized by this fact. Now that I see them, I can't help but imagine slicing one up, a creature so enormous without so much as a cuneiform holding it together, the strong spine, long as a ladder, flexing without a single vertebra.

The gills especially are beautifully skeletal, like ribs. They spiral, a crowd of thirty or so, as though performing a dance. The mouths held open in a frozen scream.

The tail, though, is a strange product of evolution—whip-thin, seemingly pointless. I'm reminded of their cousin, the stingray, with a tail that acts as a dagger.

Contrary to its name, the stingray *stabs* its enemies. And, unlike its cousin's, its tail is a dazzling display of evolution's efficacy, a serrated barb containing venom.

Much better.

I watch the graceful manta rays fly into the blue distance.

How difficult it can be to tell innocent and villain apart.

26

CAMILLA

NOW

Camilla stands in the dining room of Kate's villa, confusion beating off her in waves. She looks down at the slim bouquet of sumptuous red roses on the table, six velvety blooms the size of fists at the end of three-foot-long stems.

"What's going on?" she asks Kate, who has a hand clasped to her mouth as though she's going to be sick. "Kate?"

"I told them, I always told them," Kate says, the words spilling out of her mouth in a tearful, whispered jumble. "I said someone was watching me but they never listened, they never . . ."

She's hyperventilating again, but Camilla is prepared this time. *Not another bloody panic attack*, she thinks. No way is Kate going to the first-aid unit a third time.

Camilla places her hands on Kate's shoulders and steers her away from the roses to the living room of her villa, setting her down on the sofa.

"Right," she says firmly, kneeling in front of her. "Start at the beginning. What happened? Did someone come here this morning? Who brought the roses?"

Kate is trembling, still struggling to breathe, and Camilla is frustrated. She wants to get back outside and walk around the island until she finds Antoni.

"Kate," she says loudly. "Katie baby." She snaps her fingers in Kate's face, trying to bring her back. Kate's eyes focus on her. "There we go," she says. "That's it, lovely. Keep looking at me, that's it. Repeat after me:

'I am safe. I am not in any danger. I am here, right now, safe in my lovely villa in the Maldives with Camilla. . . .'"

Kate tries to say the words, but her voice falters to a whisper. Her cheeks are flushed, and she closes her eyes, her hands balling into fists.

"No," Camilla snaps. "Focus, lovely. Stay with me, here. I'm here with you, OK?" It's not working as she'd hoped. She looks around, sees the wine cooler, and pulls out a bottle of Moët. "When in Rome, right?" She pours two glasses and hands one to Kate.

"It's the anniversary today," Kate says, her voice a whisper.

Camilla nods, her stomach churning. "I know. Twenty-two years."

Tears brim in Kate's eyes. Camilla rubs her back.

"Remember I told you about the roses?" Kate says, swiping tears from her cheeks.

Camilla pauses, studying Kate's face. "Told me *what* about the roses?"

Kate gasps for breath, trying her best to rally. "Every year for twenty-two years now, someone has sent me six roses." She sets her glass down too roughly. "For the six people murdered in the guesthouse."

Camilla remembers Kate mentioning it in the cafe when they first met. She turns her eyes to the bouquet in the dining room, as though seeing it anew.

"I thought I'd escape it this year," Kate says, trembling as though she's freezing cold. "They've only ever been sent to my home address."

"Who brought you the roses?"

"They were delivered. My butler, Rafi, brought them."

"Did you ask them who sent them?"

Kate shook her head wearily. "They won't know. Believe me, I've tried. . . ."

"They'll tell *me*," Camilla says, glancing around for the landline. "I'll call reception. . . ."

"Don't you think I've tried to find out?" Kate says. "This has been going on for twenty-two years, Camilla. *Twenty-two years*."

Camilla softens, aware that Kate is on the verge of hysteria. "Did you tell the police?" she asks.

"Yes!" Kate says, apoplectic. "Years ago. I begged them to look into it. They said it was probably someone who felt sorry for me." She gives a rueful laugh.

"You should have said before," Camilla says. "Adrian Clifton could have looked into it."

Kate makes a noise of frustration, pressing her hands to her eyes. "I emailed Adrian about it. He never came back to me."

"He still can," Camilla says. "We'll ask him again. It'll stop, I promise."

"I've just . . . felt watched," Kate says wearily. "All this time. I'm so angry. I don't have privacy. What if they're here, on the island?"

Camilla paces, wringing her hands. She thinks of the red mark she saw on her deck and draws a slow breath. Could it have been blood? Antoni's blood? She thinks of Jacob's emails. Could the roses be connected to those?

"Whoever sent them," Camilla says, turning back to Kate, "I bet you anything they're not on the island. They'll have found out where you are and then sent them. Probably some pathetic man-child festering in his mum's spare room in Swindon."

Kate is starting to shake again, her breaths shuddering as though she's about to pass out. Camilla starts to feel frantic. She raises a hand to slap Kate out of it but falters. Violence is probably not the best way to help someone in the throes of PTSD.

"Piss kink!" she yells at Kate. "Piss kink! Say it!"

Kate looks at her as though she's lost her mind. "What?"

"Piss kink!"

"What the hell is a piss kink?"

"Just say it. It'll help snap you out of the panic attack."

"Kiss pink . . . I mean, p-piss kink!"

"Again!"

"*What* is a kiss pink?"

"Piss kink, love, piss kink. Like, you know, a golden shower."

Kate pulls a face of disgust. "Oh God."

"Shout it!"

"Piss kink!"

"You feel better now?"

Kate takes a deep breath, then another, and nods, a little dazed. *Good*, Camilla thinks. *At least she can breathe.* Camilla climbs up on to the seat next to her, worn out from the adrenaline rush, while Kate leans her head on her shoulder.

"How hard is it to trace a bunch of roses, honestly?" Camilla says. "Look, I'll go and talk to the resort manager, OK? We'll get to the bottom of this."

27

CHARLIE

"Charlie, come *on*," Jacob says. But Charlie shakes his head and folds his arms.

They're at the swimming pool for the boys' swimming lesson, Ben and Ed already in the water with the coach and the rest of the group. Charlie is a poor swimmer, which is why he's still taking lessons.

The other parents are staring. Charlie feels like he might cry, so he shuts down, refusing to talk, despite how angry his father is growing. Jacob bends down to him.

"What the hell is going on?" he snaps. "This is your swimming lesson, Charlie. You're meant to get in the pool."

Charlie knows that, but he won't. He starts to head toward the changing room, but Jacob growls at him.

"Sit down," he says. "Here. *Now*."

He points at the seat next to him alongside the pool. Charlie looks up at him, sullen, and acquiesces. He is dressed in a swimming top and shorts, but he sits down as instructed, secretly glad that his father has relented.

"Just tell me the reason you won't get in," Jacob says after a few moments. "I have work I need to do and now you're acting like a bloody toddler. At least do me the courtesy of explaining why."

Charlie bites his lip. "Mum," he mumbles after a moment.

"Mum?" Jacob repeats. He scoffs. "You won't go into the water because of your mother? For God's sake, Charlie. I've emailed the lawyer like you asked. I've told you we can push for full custody. What more do you want?"

Even though he can tell his dad is furious, Charlie bites his lip and refuses to answer. And when his dad returns to his emails with a frustrated sigh, Charlie lowers his shoulders and swallows hard. He thinks back to that horrible holiday, over two years ago now, when he first saw something was wrong between his parents.

THEY WERE IN THE SOUTH of France during the Easter break when his mum wept openly one day, outdoors. Charlie was shocked. He'd never seen an adult cry in public like that. They were walking along the beach, past the parasols and the twinkling ocean, and his mum had tears running down her face. He looked to his dad, his mouth open to ask him why Mum was crying, but his dad's face was like stone. They'd had an argument.

Later that night he'd heard raised voices from his parents' bedroom in the villa. He'd tiptoed out into the hall and pressed his ear against the door. He could hear his father pleading, asking his mother to come away from the window.

"You don't want to do this!" he screamed, and Charlie's heart began to pound because he'd never heard his dad sound so scared. "Think of the boys, Darcy. Come on, now. Take my hand."

Charlie listened hard for his mother's response, but there wasn't one, just a banging noise. The sound of the window shutters against the wall.

"I'm calling the police if you don't come down," his dad said.

"Fucking call them, then!" his mother shrieked, and it was so loud and so unlike his mum that he felt tears of shock prick his eyes. He lurched away from the door, suddenly scared. He didn't feel like a big boy, now. Not like a ten-year-old. Something was wrong with his mum, and even though he couldn't see what was happening, he knew it was very, very bad.

The room had fallen silent.

Gingerly, Charlie moved to press his ear against the wood of the door again, listening. His dad was talking very softly.

"Come on," he was saying. "You'll hurt yourself if you're not careful, and we don't want that."

"Take it back," his mum snapped. "Say you didn't mean it!"

Charlie held his breath, wishing hard for his dad to take whatever it was right back, make his mum stop sounding like that.

"There, now," his dad was saying. "There we go." He sounded strained, as though he was lifting something heavy. There was another sound—of the shutters being closed and locked.

His mum began to cry. No, not cry—not like the silent crying on the beach. Now she was wailing like she was heartbroken, like a baby. Charlie started to cry, too, his hand against his mouth, his whole body shaking. He didn't know what had happened in that room but it was scary. Neither of his parents sounded like themselves.

He'd watched them both very carefully the next day, constantly on the verge of begging them not to do whatever they'd done in that room ever again. His mum wore dark sunglasses all day, even indoors, and didn't say very much. His dad's face kept sliding into a frown, and even when Ben and Ed told jokes, it was as if he was faking a smile.

Eighteen months later, their parents sat the boys down one afternoon after school and told them they had news.

"What's the news?" Ed asked them.

Dad and Mum were pointedly not looking at each other.

"Your mother and I are going to live in different houses," his dad said. "My new house is going to be just around the corner—"

"A mile away," his mum interjected.

"Still very close," his dad said. He paused to arrange a big smile on his face. Charlie watched his mum look up at his dad, her chin tilted. She looked angry, even though she was smiling.

There was a big pause, as though the room was holding its breath. "Why?" Ben asked then.

His dad took a breath and pressed his hands together. "Remember when Leo's mum and dad separated?" he said. "It'll be like that. You'll have bedrooms in both houses. Two Christmases, two sets of holidays."

"Do you hate Mummy?" Ben said.

"I very much do not hate Mummy," his dad said. Charlie looked at his mother. Her eyes were on her lap now.

"Why are you going to live somewhere else, then?" Ed asked, and his dad looked flustered again, running his hand through his hair in that way he did when things weren't going to plan.

"Look, it's early days," his dad said. "For now, we're just trying out this new situation, OK? And we're going to make it as pleasant as possible for everyone." He looked over at their mother, finally, as though pleading for her support.

Charlie felt his stomach twist. It wasn't just that his parents were separating—three of his friends' parents were separated and it didn't seem a bad thing—but more the way his mum looked, ashen and rigid, like she had been blown up and was struggling to hold herself together so she didn't crumble into pieces.

A SHRIEK FROM THE POOL brings him back to the present with a jolt. He watches his brothers and the instructor as they go through the swimming lesson, his father next to him, typing email after email on his phone. Charlie doesn't get into the pool. He can't.

It's time to leave. He watches Ed and Ben climb out of the pool, snapping their goggles over their heads. His dad gets up from his seat and turns to him.

"We're going to talk about this," he says. "You're going to tell me what's going on."

28

KATE

NOW

Kate steps into the bathroom and runs the cold tap, watching a small dribble of blood pour from the gash on her hand into the basin. The roses cut her, the sharp, unyielding thorns plucking at the soft skin of her lunar mount when she stuffed them into the bin.

A notification pings on her phone, the sound like the chirp of a baby bird. She lifts the device, noticing at once the name of Darcy's ex-husband on the screen. Jacob Levitt, emailing again.

From: j.levitt@immersiveAI.com
To: katetheconstantwriter@oncloud.ws

Dear Kate,

Thanks for your response. I'm concerned that you and Adrian Clifton have been involved in a security breach of some software that I've developed. Perhaps this has been done without your knowledge. . . . Perhaps Darcy hired him? I have a possible phone number for him— 07011 213012. Do you recognize it?

Either way, I will need to get to the bottom of it as quickly as possible.

Thanks
Jacob

She clicks out of her inbox without responding, annoyed that she bothered reading it. Another email from Darcy's ex is the very last thing she needs right now.

Darcy swore, right at the beginning, that Adrian would be their secret. Just the three of them. A week after that first, fateful meeting in the cafe, Darcy had FaceTimed her and Camilla.

"I've found someone," she said. "An old school friend works for the Met. He recommended a guy who has set up a private investigation practice after retiring. Adrian Clifton."

Kate deliberately kept her expectations low. The massacre was such a long time ago. Even if anything was to come of their hunch that Fraser wasn't the only killer, any evidence to prove it was unlikely to be found. And at the back of her mind, she began to doubt her feelings. Fraser had taken the easy way out, after all. Effectively, he served a month in prison—a single month for killing six people. Yes, he died of cancer, but that wasn't justice, was it? It was illness, which afflicted good people, too.

No, justice hadn't been served. And perhaps that was the driving force behind their hunch—perhaps they *wanted* there to be a second killer, someone who would serve the sentence that Hugh never had to endure. And she could get the satisfaction of showing them that she had lived her life.

If you could call this living.

She hears the front door open, the whirr of her room card. Camilla has returned, looking hopeful. She left earlier to ask Nura, the resort manager, about the delivery of the roses, and the confidence in her step makes Kate perk up. She throws on her kimono and puts her phone in her pocket. Maybe, just maybe, Camilla has had some luck.

"I've got it," Camilla says, her face flushed with pride. She opens the Notes app on her phone and shows Kate what she has written down. "Robin Y. Ceylon. Ring any bells?"

Kate shakes her head. The excitement that fired up when she saw Camilla returning feels hollow.

"No address, but I'm working on it," Camilla continues, typing the name into the search bar on her Facebook app. "You leave it to me, Katie baby, I'll find this bastard. . . ."

Kate presses her hands to her face. "It's an anagram," she says weakly.

Camilla looks up from her phone. "What?"

"The letters spell Briony Conley. My real name."

Camilla holds the phone closer to her eyes, studying the name she wrote down in excitement. "How do you know?" she says.

"It's been the same each time, every single year. Yoni Le Corbyn. Robyn Y. Nicole. Byron I. Ceylon." She sighs. "It's a game. A sick, twisted game."

She watches Camilla's face fall, knows intimately the feeling that's written all over it—why would someone do this?

"I paid her," Camilla says. "A hundred quid."

"Shit. I'm sorry."

Camilla pinches the fold of skin between her eyes. "What about the payment details for the flowers? Surely we can trace the card. . . ."

"It's usually a prepaid debit card," Kate says. "Or PayPal. Anyone can set one of those up, especially nowadays. Very hard to find the source when it's a virtual account."

"What about Adrian?" Camilla says. "We could ask him to look into it? I bet you he'd be able to find it."

Kate sighs. She's already emailed Adrian Clifton about it, to no avail. Perhaps he only works for Darcy, since she contracted him. But then, Jacob just sent her Adrian's number. . . .

"Hang on a moment," she tells Camilla, plucking her phone from her pocket. She taps the screen, deciding to ring Adrian and ask for his help directly.

29

DARCY

NOW

From: a.wallis@wallisbennett.com
Cc: k.moko@wallisbennett.com
To: darcy_levitt@redmail.com

Hi Darcy

I understand what you're saying, but as the court has issued a notice of proceedings there's not a lot we can do. When you return from the Maldives we can talk more about gathering evidence to refute your ex-husband's claims in relation to his petition for full custody. The court will be invested in which parent the boys prefer to live with, and they will also want to know about your relationship with your sons.

In the meantime, please make a note of the court hearing on October 24 at noon.

Best,
Anthea Wallis (she/her/hers)
Partner, Head of Divorce, Family, Finance & Children
for and on behalf of Wallis Bennett LLP, Solicitors

Darcy stares at the email on her phone, her heart sinking. She knew Jacob would do something while she was gone. *Your ex-husband's claims . . .*

They will also want to know about your relationship with your sons.

Given that Charlie hates her guts, this isn't going to go well.

He looks up to his father. Jacob will have stirred him up, found a way to get Charlie on his side. With tweens, it comes down to which parent allows the most screen time, or which parent will allow them to download Snapchat. She was vehemently against it: no social media until he's at least the legal age. And then she found he had Snapchat, TikTok, and Instagram already on his bloody phone, as well as a few others she'd never heard of—Swipr, Yubo, Wizz. It's a bloody jungle for parents, now.

God only knows what kind of stuff he's been watching, or who he's been in touch with.

She made Charlie delete the apps off his phone, and he threw a tantrum.

What the court will hear, though, is that she's a bad mother. She's too strict, doesn't respect boundaries. Kids are so informed these days. Just the other week, she told Ed he couldn't have chocolate cereal until the weekend. "That's child abuse!" he shouted.

And then there was the trip she took Charlie on to prepare him for his performance in the school play. God, how it backfired.

She exits her inbox and dials Jacob's number. He answers on the fifth ring, sounding like she's just woken him up.

"For Christ's sake," he says. "It's the crack of dawn—"

"Why are you doing this?" she demands, no time to butter him up.

"It's too early for this, Darcy. We'll discuss it in court."

"No," she snaps. "I don't want to discuss it further in court. I want to discuss it now. I want to understand why you would do this to our *children*."

"Like I said," Jacob says, "we will discuss this at the appropriate time and place."

"You want to annihilate my reputation, is that it?" she says, her voice wobbling. "You want to destroy my life? Tell me, Jacob. What have I done that makes you hate me so much?"

He sighs. "I don't hate you, Darcy. . . ."

"Then, why do this? Why deprive the boys of their mother?"

He pauses. "Because Charlie asked me to."

She swallows, hard. "You're lying."

"I'm not. And it's interesting to hear you accuse *me* of lying, Darcy."

"What the hell does that mean?"

"Look, Charlie doesn't want to live with you. And I want Ed and Ben to live with me, too. It's unfair to separate them."

She draws a sharp breath, bile rising up her throat. This isn't about their children. This is about control.

"Who told you about Adrian Clifton, Jacob?"

"It doesn't matter who," he says. "Why don't you tell me what he's been doing with my software, Darcy? Or do I have to ask through a lawyer?"

"What are you talking about?"

"A lawyer it is."

He hangs up. She stares at the phone and sobs. *It's over*, she thinks. Everything in her sphere has been set up for the boys, her whole life arranged around theirs. Jacob is charismatic, commanding: he'll win this case, she knows it.

Somewhere in the villa, another phone rings. She looks at the phone in her hand for a few moments in confusion, until she remembers that she brought her other one. But that phone shouldn't be ringing.

She hurries up the stairs, listening closely. Where the hell did she put it? She's sure she unpacked it. She goes into the bedroom and scans the space, but it's difficult to follow the ringing sound. It's *in* here, but she can't pinpoint where. . . . She tries her empty suitcases, zipped up and placed neatly inside the wardrobe beneath her dresses, then the chest of drawers.

Third drawer down, the ringing stops. She pauses and holds her breath, looks at the dressing table, at her toiletry bags. There, in the zip pocket of the little Orla Kiely bag containing holiday-size shower wash and period pads, is the tiny little black rectangle of her burner phone.

She takes it out and hits BACK to see who called her. It's a mobile number from the UK, beginning +44. The last three digits are 606. She calls it back, holding her breath as it rings. On the sixth ring, someone answers.

"Hello?"

She knows that voice. Darcy freezes, then quickly ends the call. She slumps back and runs her hands through her hair, reeling.

Why the living fuck would Kate be phoning this number?

30

JADE

I stir, and for a moment I feel peaceful, happy. I was dreaming about me and Rob, back when we first moved in together. We were back in that tiny flat, the one we rented in Bow for those first six months, with rats chewing their way through the skirting boards. In the dream we were building a set of bunk beds together, all the pieces laid out on the bedroom floor, and I was so excited, because I'd never been in a relationship this serious, not one where we moved in together. Rob kept calling me "wifey," and each time he did, it was like someone turning on a light inside.

That part was pure memory.

I turn over and blink, this fucked-up situation returning to me like an ice-cold shower. The restaurant. Rob's fury afterward. Accusing me of flirting with Antoni. Pulling my hair.

But now Rob is lying on the other side of the bed, his eyes on me, the anger gone from his face. He's naked, and rock hard. He reaches across to me and takes my hand, placing it on his penis. He moans, then reaches out for my breasts. I'm not wearing a nightie, just black lace panties, and he takes those off, rolling over on top of me. He kisses me and spends a long time sucking my nipples. I used to love this. Sex with Rob used to be amazing, but I know what's next. He won't wear a condom.

He's inside me, now, thrusting and grunting, his head in the pillow next to me. I feel nothing but fear. Perhaps, if I time it right, I can push him out . . . But too late—he blares in ecstasy, thudding into me. I want to get up and run to the bathroom, but he stays inside me, lowering himself onto his elbows and kissing me.

"Want to go again?" he says.

I force a smile. "You usually can't."

His face changes, and I backpedal.

"I mean, yes," I say. "Let's go again."

He turns me over, taking me from behind. I can't believe this. We've not had sex twice in a row in years. He asks me to tell him how much I want it, and I repeat it through gritted teeth, all while counting how many days I'm into my cycle.

To think I was thrilled when my period finished the week before our wedding. That means I am smack bang in the middle. I am ovulating.

Afterward, I resist hurling myself across the room to the en suite, and force a smile.

"Do you think we did it?" he says, stroking my face. "Do you feel I impregnated you?"

I shrug. "I don't know," I say. "Maybe."

Oh God.

"I've heard it works better if you lie for twenty minutes or so with your hips in the air," he says, getting up. "Try it."

I blink. "That's just an old wives' tale."

"Worth a shot, isn't it?" he says. "Wouldn't you do anything for us to have a baby? The one we so desperately want?"

I smile. *The one you want, not me.*

He goes downstairs for a smoke. I wait until I hear him humming in the kitchen before getting off the bed and quietly padding across the floor to the bathroom, using the shower to get it all out.

And then I stand, naked, and look myself over in the mirror. The bruise around my eye is fading, and the swelling has gone down, but it's a yellowy green now. I look so much older than twenty-three. The blond hair extensions I'm wearing are for Rob; he said he loves long hair, that he'd pay for me to get them. He did the first time, but I've been paying for them ever since, just to please him. They make my head itch, especially in this heat. My natural hair color is cardboard brown, but when he took me for extensions, he said I should try a lighter color, so I did. But the difference in my appearance runs deeper than that. I barely recognize the girl in the mirror.

What are you doing, Jade? What the fuck are you doing?

Rob's razor is sitting out, next to a bottle of shaving foam. I lift it, looking it over. I could do it, I think. When he's asleep, I could take the small blade out of the razor and press it to his throat, end all of this in a second.

I imagine it—the blood gushing out, hot and dark. How would I feel?

Relieved. I would feel relieved.

Other men drift into my mind now. Men from my past, men at the resort. The Pilates lech. Antoni, the way he always touched me without asking. I am so sick of being *used*.

I set the razor down, suddenly terrified at the thoughts that are wheeling around my brain.

But then, maybe this is the new Jade. And I'm not yet sure what she's capable of.

31

KATE

"No answer?" Camilla asks as Kate holds the phone to her ear.

Kate hangs up and stares at the phone. "He called me back but we got cut off. And now I can't get through." She sighs. "I'll try again later."

They head to the jetty, where they've arranged to meet Darcy for a double excursion—a trip to see manta rays, followed by a kayaking excursion to Emerald Island. Kate wasn't looking forward to either, but right now she can't wait to get out of the villa. Camilla is right—whoever sent those roses is probably on the other side of the world. Although, someone sick enough to send roses every year for over two decades is also sick enough to want to witness her reaction.

She forces herself to put it to the back of her mind for now. She must. It's Darcy's holiday, and she won't let anything ruin it.

"What did you get up to last night, anyway?" Camilla asks her, snapping her back into the present.

"Nothing much," she says. "Writing, mostly. What about you?"

Camilla breaks into a filthy laugh.

"What *didn't* I get up to?" she says. "I met up with Antoni."

"Antoni?" Kate says. "The man Rob wanted to beat up? *That* Antoni?"

"Mmmmhmmm."

"Well, that's a turn-up for the books," Kate says, noticing how unsettled Camilla appears. "I thought you loathed him."

"I *did*," Camilla says. "But then we got talking and one thing led to another, and . . . we were up all night."

"Playing chess?"

"Ha! I don't think I've heard of that position." She gives Kate a wink. "Do you know, I think there was a connection there. We talked for hours. I don't think I've ever met a man as *interesting*."

"Interesting? Meaning he's well endowed?" Kate asks, and Camilla laughs again.

The boat arrives, and they step on board, glad to be the only ones booked on the trip. The instructor is busy sorting out a box of gear, and they have the top of the boat to themselves.

"You seem a bit worried, though," Kate tells Camilla as the engines roar into life. "You sure everything went OK?"

Camilla pulls a puzzled face, too exaggerated to be convincing. "Absolutely. I just haven't seen him this morning, but I'm sure he's fine."

"I see," Kate says. She looks back at the jetty behind them, thinking about how to word it. She knows Camilla reacted to the roses, but there's something else, something beneath the fluster. But before she can speak, Darcy climbs onto the boat.

"What's all this about?" she asks, catching the conversation. "Who's fine?"

"Antoni," Kate tells her.

"I shagged him," Camilla says with a grin. "He was *amazing*."

"Antoni?" Darcy says with a laugh. "The guy Rob almost destroyed in the restaurant?"

"That one," Camilla says, taking a deep, satisfied breath. "Take note, ladies. You want the best sex of your life? Find ye a man who dances flamenco."

"That's clearly where I was going wrong," Darcy says, lying down on her stomach. "Flamenco. Noted."

"It's the hip flexibility," Camilla says. "And the stamina. It's been about twenty years since I've had someone who could shag all night."

"All night?" Darcy says. "I'm surprised you can walk this morning."

Camilla slaps her on the arm. "I'm not *that* old, you know."

"Aren't you tired?" Kate asks.

Camilla stifles a yawn with a fist. "Not at all."

"Are you planning to see him again?" Kate asks. She's immensely glad that Camilla is full of business this morning. Rapture beats off her in waves, a tonic for an otherwise gut-wrenching day.

"We were meant to have breakfast this morning, but—"

"But what?" Darcy says.

Camilla looks away, and Kate sees the worry return to her face. Her mouth is thin and tight. "He probably went off kayaking, actually," Camilla says, somewhat absent-mindedly. "He said he likes kayaking back and forth from the Emerald Island, like we're doing later. And it definitely didn't feel like a onetime thing."

"Maybe you'll bump into him, then," Kate says.

"Maybe," Camilla agrees.

The instructor appears at the top of the ladder, gesturing at them to come down. They put on their fins and snorkels. Kate's stomach curdles with an acidic fear; last time she did this, she got smashed on the head with an oar.

She looks out at the endless horizon. The resort is far behind them, and the expanse of blue sea spreads out like a clean cloth, no sign of any boats or people anywhere. Whoever sent those roses must think they can destroy her wherever she goes. And yet, for the first time since it happened, she is outside, her face in the sun. She hears Camilla laughing behind her, loudly announcing that the snorkel mask has caught in one of her hair extensions. Darcy's laughing, too. The sound is rousing, and Kate feels an old metal rise up inside her, a boldness.

She won't be cowed by it, she thinks. She won't be cowed by the roses, or by the anniversary. She refuses.

"Jump!" the instructor shouts then, encouraging her to plunge into the water. She's on the last rung of the ladder, warm water teasing at her finned feet. And then she sees them: a squadron of manta rays like black diamonds in the water, flapping their featherless wings.

"They won't bite," the instructor tells her with a smile, and he reaches down to touch one that nudges at the surface. It's enormous, the size of a dinner table, and Kate expects it to dart away. But it lets the instructor stroke it, its tail sticking out behind.

With a determined clench of her fist, she leans forward and jumps into the blue.

32

DARCY

NOW

They're on Emerald Island, having returned from the manta ray trip and kayaked across the lagoon. The white sand and fringe of palm trees are identical to those of Sapphire Island, which glances at them across the water.

The email from her lawyer first thing this morning has Darcy's stomach in knots. She didn't sleep well last night, either. Charlie's horrible WhatsApp, then this petition for full custody—it's all she can think about. She has spent a great deal of her life doing what corporates call "strategic planning," going to great lengths to ensure every part of her life is straightened out and shipshape, all the details the way she wants them. It was what made her so good at helping Jacob set up his company. She had zero experience in technology but taught herself, proving to be a fast learner. And it was Darcy who suggested that Jacob pivot to artificial intelligence; he'd wanted to go into gaming.

Her stomach plummets as she thinks of the phone call with Jacob. What is she returning home to? Three boys who prefer their father, and an ex-husband who never really loved her.

Did she love Jacob? She isn't sure. She thought she did. She performed it so well that she almost convinced herself. And the friends they shared, the friends who have been so very busy of late, who barely speak to her now. Life after divorce feels so terribly lonely.

And now Jacob's asking about Adrian Clifton. . . . It's not good at all that he is asking these things.

Perhaps it was a mistake to come all this way, she thinks. Leaving the country has made her situation more vulnerable. But then, it has to be this way.

Tell them, she thinks, glancing at Kate and Camilla as they head toward the buffet. *It has to be now.*

"I'm going for a walk," Camilla suddenly announces, stifling another yawn.

"You're not having something to eat?" Kate says.

"I'll grab something on the way back." Camilla is already heading off along the beach.

"I fancy a cold drink," Kate says, nodding at the restaurant.

Darcy slips her arm through Kate's. "I'll join you."

They sit at a table overlooking the lagoon, their own resort shimmering on the other side. She notices green parrots sitting on the tree branches close by, the light catching their beautiful feathers.

"Can I ask you something?" Kate says then.

"Yes."

"Do you remember I told you that someone has sent me roses every anniversary for the past twenty-two years?"

Darcy studies Kate's face, trying to focus on what she's saying. "I think so? Yes. Yes, I think you did."

"Someone sent roses to my villa this morning."

Darcy gasps, her attention now fully on her friend. "What, here? In the Maldives?"

Kate nods.

"Shit. Are you OK?"

"Well, no. Not really. I suppose I was actually looking forward to missing it this year. Being away from home . . ."

Darcy furrows her brow. Kate looks shell-shocked.

"So you think it's malicious?" Darcy asks. "Not one of the victims' families, perhaps?"

Kate frowns. "I don't think so. I think it's someone who resents the fact that I survived."

"What about your parents, trying to reach out to you?"

Kate bristles. "Definitely not my parents. The name of the sender is always an anagram of my birth name, Briony Conley. It's like a sick game."

"Oh my God," Darcy says. She squeezes Kate's hand. "It must have felt terrifying, all those years you received them. Especially if you think they were sent out of spite."

"It was," Kate whispers. "It felt like a shameful secret. I felt I deserved them."

She buries her face in her hands, and Darcy rubs her shoulder. "Oh, Kate," she says. "That is heartbreaking."

Darcy feels the words forming on her lips. *It has to be now*, she thinks. *Tell her.*

She opens her mouth to say it. She has prepared her reasoning. But even so, she knows this is both the most opportune and the worst time to tell Kate.

And so she switches gears, deciding instead to call attention to the thing that they're all ignoring. She needs to prepare Kate for the truth, lead into it a little better.

"Did you end up chatting with Jade last night?" she asks. "After dinner?"

Kate cocks her head. "Yes?"

Darcy clears her throat, trying to think of the best way to phrase it. "I was just wondering . . . you know, the skirmish in the restaurant last night. Between Rob and Antoni."

"What about it?"

"Camilla said that Rob was acting possessively toward Jade at the Pilates class," Darcy says. "So why didn't Jade, you know . . .?"

Kate cocks an eyebrow. "Why didn't Jade what?"

"I'm just thinking that . . . Oh, never mind."

"No, tell me," Kate says. Darcy tries to find the right words. She's making a total mess of it.

"OK. I'm probably wrong. But . . . I watched Jade last night. She was the one who approached Antoni at the restaurant, not the other way around."

"So?"

"Well, she knows Rob better than anyone, doesn't she? She had to have known what he would do if he saw her and Antoni chatting. And after what happened at the Pilates class . . ."

Kate stares at the ocean, her brow furrowed. "You think she deliberately wanted to get Rob worked up?"

"I've seen it before. Women who get off on pushing their man's buttons."

"Not a very feminist appraisal of the situation, though, is it?" Kate says. "Jade can talk to whomever she wants to."

"Kate, come on," Darcy says, folding her arms. "This is *me* talking. I agree with you a hundred percent. And, like I said, I'm probably wrong. I suppose going through a divorce has made me look at people differently."

Kate appears to be thinking now, mulling it over. "She did approach Antoni, didn't she?"

Darcy holds her in a long, regretful look. "I was just thinking how Jade seems to be this . . . you know . . . victim of violence, a beautiful young woman ensnared by a cruel, jealous man. But I'm wondering if it's really as simple as that. Maybe there's something more to it." She sighs sadly. "Things are never that black and white, are they?"

She watches Kate process this. "No," Kate admits finally, her eyes scanning the sea. "They're not."

"No sign of Antoni," a voice cuts in.

Darcy glances up to see Camilla looking pained, not like herself at all.

"Are you all right?" Kate asks, clearly thinking the same thing.

"He said he liked to kayak over here," Camilla says, pulling a chair from another table and sitting with them. "I thought I'd see him."

"I'm sure he's fine," Kate says.

"Have a drink," Darcy says. "This is meant to be a celebration, remember? A new start. We've only six days left. It'll fly by."

Camilla looks agitated, so Darcy rises and heads to the bar, returning a few minutes later with a tray of colorful drinks.

"Five drinks?" Kate says as Darcy sets the tray down on the table. "Are we expecting company?"

"I thought Camilla might need a little extra Dutch courage," Darcy says. "So I got a couple of extra Negronis. I'm sure we can manage those between us?"

"Cheers, love." Camilla raises her drink in a toast. They each lean forward, clinking their glasses.

"Sorry I've spoiled it a bit," Camilla says. "Antoni will probably turn up at dinner tonight with another girl on his arm and pretend he never met me."

"Oh, don't be silly," Darcy says. "He doesn't seem like the kind of man who would be that callous."

Camilla sips her drink. "Oh, it's not callous. It's just holiday sex."

"I think I should be the one apologizing," Kate says. "I had a panic attack the first day here."

"Don't apologize," Camilla says. "I got a shag out of it. Hey, maybe you can do it again and see if Darcy can get one, too."

Darcy gives a shrill laugh.

"Oh, come on," Camilla says. "What's a girls' holiday if there isn't sex involved?"

"Better?" Kate says, and Camilla rolls her eyes.

"I don't think I'm ready for that sort of thing," Darcy says, studying her drink. "I think it'll take a while before I feel ready to date again."

"Nonsense," Camilla says. "It's like . . . wild swimming."

"Wild swimming?" Kate repeats.

"You can't go in a toe at a time. You just have to jump straight in, otherwise you lose your nerve."

Darcy isn't convinced. "Oh, I doubt there are many single men out there eager to date a woman with three children."

"Who said anything about dating?" Camilla says. "I was talking about shagging."

"They're separate activities, are they?"

"Oh, mate, *completely*!"

"Kate," Darcy says, changing the subject. Sex isn't one of her priorities. She and Jacob had barely slept together in years. "How's your book going, lovely?"

"Ugh," Kate says.

"That bad, is it?"

"Haven't you heard?" Camilla tells Darcy, spilling some of her drink as she changes position. "Two things you never ask a writer—if they've written anything you should have heard of, and how their latest book is going."

"Can you back out of it?" Darcy asks.

"It's not that bad, honestly," Kate says. "It's just a bit *triggering*, as the kids say."

"Babe," Camilla says sympathetically, "that's shit. Why's it triggering?"

"I have to research psychopathic killers. The main character's one and I need to show how his brain works. It sounded interesting to begin with, but . . ." She trails off, fighting to keep her tone light.

"Ted Bundy," Camilla says. "Just make your character like him. Charming, attractive, evil. No more research needed."

"What makes a psychopath a psychopath?" Darcy asks, finishing her drink. She's feeling better now, the email and Charlie's WhatsApp message fading into the distance.

"They don't give a shit," Kate says. "But in all the wrong ways."

"I think I heard that Abraham Lincoln was a psychopath," Darcy adds.

"Abraham Lincoln?" Camilla exclaims. "But wasn't he all *for the people, of the people*, et cetera?"

Kate nods. "Yes, but that's the Jekyll and Hyde thing. They're not monsters *all* the time."

"So it's like a part-time job," Camilla surmises. "What about women? Why is it always men who are psychopaths?"

"The research only ever looked at males," Kate says. "Like autism. But they say one in a hundred people is a psychopath, so chances are you know one."

"I'm one," Camilla asserts, folding her arms, and Kate laughs. "I'm not kidding. Two days without Pilates and I'd knife a granny."

Darcy laughs hard, a head-thrown-back belly laugh. Kate joins her, and then Camilla. The glasses are empty, the sun is high, the trees shifting and glittering with colorful birds. Darcy reminds herself that she isn't lonely, not at all. She is here, in this beautiful place, with two of the finest women she has ever met.

And today, she will tell them the truth. Because she's been lying to them both all along.

IN DARCY'S VILLA, SHE ASKS them both to join her in the living room.

"Is something the matter?" Kate asks, sitting down in one of the armchairs. Darcy flinches, seeing how on edge Kate is. She sits down opposite, clasping her hands tightly together.

"Well . . . there was something I wanted to tell you both."

"What?" Camilla asks. She can't seem to bring herself to sit down.

Darcy hesitates before answering. "Adrian."

Kate looks puzzled. "Adrian Clifton?"

"We can do it later, or . . ."

Camilla glances from Kate back to Darcy. "Well, it sounds like something that can't wait, really. Why didn't you mention it earlier?"

Darcy bites her lip. "I didn't want to ruin the holiday, and then the trip today . . . and you seemed so caught up with finding Antoni. . . ."

"So?" Camilla says, folding her arms, shoulders high. "What did Adrian say?"

"He wants to meet with us all later," she says. "On Zoom. At nine o'clock London time."

"Tonight?" Camilla says, shocked. "Has something happened?"

Kate's mouth falls open. "Has there been a development in the investigation?"

"There has," Darcy says, folding her hands between her knees. "Adrian has found someone whom he believes was involved in the murders."

"Oh my God," Kate whispers.

"Who?" Camilla spits. "Fuck nine o'clock fucking London time, tell us now!"

Darcy retrieves her laptop from beside the sofa and sets it on the table in front of them. A few moments later, she opens an email from Adrian and clicks on an attachment. An image of a man pops up on the screen, taken from a height as he is getting out of a car.

"No." Camilla leans forward and squints at the image. "No fucking way," she says, her voice a low growl.

33

KATE

Kate watches Camilla dart into the kitchen and vomit loudly into the sink. Her own reaction to Darcy's land mine is less explosive—she feels her entire body grow numb, a creeping paralysis. She feels herself grow tiny, a speck on the armchair in which she sits, shrinking, shrinking. She can't speak, can't move.

Camilla returns, weeping into her hand, but instead of sitting down again she heads toward the door. Darcy lunges for her, firmly steering her back toward the sofa.

"Whoa there," Darcy says. "Let's not be too hasty. . . ."

"I'll kill him!" Camilla shrieks in her face. "Rob Marlowe from villa three killed my brother!"

Kate slowly feels herself return to her body, moving her fingers to check that the paralysis has left. Rob Marlowe, the brute who attacked Antoni in the restaurant. He's the man in the photograph. The man Adrian suspects as the second killer in the guesthouse.

She remembers what the psychologist taught her. *Focus on your breaths.* They feel very faint, her lungs like small balloons. Gradually, she is able to speak.

"When did Adrian send this to you?" she asks Darcy, her voice thin, high-pitched.

"Two and a half weeks ago," Darcy says, visibly rattled by Camilla's reaction.

"Two and a half weeks?" Camilla yells, and Kate reaches out to take her hand. Camilla pulls away as though she's been burned, but she manages to gather herself a little.

"Please," Darcy begs. "Let me explain. There's a good reason for it, I promise."

Camilla sits slowly, perched on the edge of the seat as though about to spring up again at any moment. Kate is still as a stone, her mind working hard to stay present. She can feel the fear nudging at her, her body aching to stiffen, lock her safely away from harm.

"Adrian sent this to me at the end of August," Darcy says, her tone earnest. "My reaction was like yours, Camilla. I wanted to go after him, hunt him down. Adrian talked me down. He said he still had information to gather and I needed to wait. But what he did know was that Rob was going on honeymoon to the Maldives. And I had wanted to book a divorce trip anyway, with the two of you. So when I heard he was coming here, I just . . . booked it. Just in case."

"In case of what?" Kate asks.

Darcy contemplates that. "When I saw the photo, I just knew," she says. "Adrian warned me not to do anything until he'd completed his investigation, but I just had this gut instinct that Rob Marlowe was the second killer. The missing piece of the puzzle."

"You didn't send it straight to the police?" Camilla asks, wiping tears away. Her face is streaked with mascara.

"After the mess they made of the investigation first time round?" Darcy says. "Obviously not."

"Let me get this straight," Camilla says, anger swelling in her voice. "You find the person who slaughtered my brother in cold blood, and then instead of—oh, I don't know—*ringing me and Kate* or calling the police, you book a holiday for the three of us to the same island he'll be on for his honeymoon."

Darcy holds her gaze, then looks away. Kate's anger subsides. She knows what a complicated emotion grief is. Oh, how she knows.

"Do you see what I'm struggling with?" Camilla asks no one in particular, gesticulating wildly. A vein pulses in the center of her forehead.

"I thought it was . . . an opportunity," Darcy says, bowing her head.

"Or fate, even. We're here, on a tiny island, away from our families. He's on his honeymoon. The last thing he'll be expecting is the three of us."

"Hold on," Kate says. "Expecting? The three of us?"

"I thought we could speak to him," Darcy whispers. "Look, OK. I misjudged this. But I knew if I told you this back in the UK you'd either want to wait for more evidence, or want to drive to his house and cut his balls off."

Camilla throws her head back and gives a wicked, unhinged laugh.

"At least here," Darcy continues, "he has nowhere to hide. We've got him cornered."

"When you say, 'speak to him,'" Kate asks Darcy, "what exactly did you have in mind?"

Darcy sighs and presses her hands to her cheeks. "I don't know. Find out the truth? This isn't exactly a normal situation, is it?"

"We could confront him," Camilla says, the wheels of her mind visibly turning. "The three of us."

Kate can't believe what she's hearing. "Have you failed to notice that the man is a tank?" she says. "And we're potentially talking about some-one capable of killing six people."

"His guard is down," Darcy repeats. "He's on his honeymoon. That's the beauty of all of this."

Kate feels sickened by this choice of words. "The *beauty*?" she says, her mind turning to Jade. This is terrible for Jade, too.

Darcy sighs. "I didn't mean that."

"I'm going to be honest with you, Darcy," Camilla says, wiping mas-cara off her face. "I'm so pissed off with you right now."

"I am too," Kate says. "Disappointed, really. Overwhelmed. I thought this was just a lovely trip to celebrate your new chapter. But that wasn't really the case, was it?"

"And today's the anniversary!" Camilla says, fresh tears brimming in her eyes. "The fucking anniversary! And now you tell us that we're really here to confront someone who *may* have killed my twin brother!"

She rises and starts to pace, exhaling loudly and shaking out her hands.

"I'm sorry," Darcy says, chastened. "I thought . . . God, I don't know what I was thinking. It made sense in the moment. . . ."

"Bullshit," Camilla says, turning. "You don't drop fifty grand on a trip to the Maldives without an idea of what you're doing."

Darcy sinks into her chair, presses her face into her hands, and sobs. "I'm sorry," she says again. "I shouldn't have said anything. I shouldn't have brought you here."

"What's done is done," Kate says quietly, resigning herself to it.

The silence in the room is thick as steel. Kate keeps a close eye on Camilla, aware that she's about a minute away from heading out to find Rob.

"Adrian's going to talk to us?" Kate asks Darcy. "Via Zoom, I take it? Or is he here, too?"

"Yeah, who else is on the island?" Camilla rejoins bitterly. "My ex-husbands? You going to tell me my mother-in-law is sipping a Manhattan in the Jacuzzi?"

"We're meeting Adrian on Zoom," Darcy says quietly. "And . . . if you like, I can book us a transfer to a different resort. Or a flight home, whichever you prefer."

Camilla gives a loud scoff, still on her feet.

"I think it would be best if we hear what Adrian has to say," Kate says. "For all we know, Rob is completely innocent!"

There's enough emotion swirling in the air just now. She thinks of Jade, of how an innocent newlywed could get caught in the crossfire of all this. But perhaps Kate's being naive, too trusting. Darcy had a point about the scene in the restaurant—Jade had approached Antoni, knowing that Rob was already riled.

Camilla turns and heads for the door.

"Camilla," Kate calls after her, a note of warning in her voice.

"I'm not going to kill Rob bloody Marlowe!" Camilla calls back. "I just need to clear my head."

34

JADE

NOW

"I'm off to the gym," Rob says, rising from his sun lounger. We're on the east side of the island, where the Emerald Resort sits in the near distance. The lagoon is like turquoise silk this afternoon, though the resort is quiet today. I think a lot of people went on some of the excursions—the kayak trip and the manta ray adventure. I'm relieved that we didn't bump into Antoni again. It gives me the ick, men creeping on me. And I scared myself a little, looking at the razor. I feel like I'm on the edge of something. Like I could snap at any moment.

Sex has calmed Rob down, but I know he could flare up again at the slightest thing. He turns and grins at me, flexing his biceps. He looks like a Greek god, his shoulders broad and his arms defined and tanned. He used to neglect his legs, but now they're sculpted from all the running, thick muscles running up from his knees to his hips, his calves ropy with veins.

He sees the blank expression on my face, and his eyes soften. "Jade?"

"Yeah?"

"What's wrong, babe?"

The tone of his voice is so tender, so like the old Rob, that my skin prickles. He steps forward and takes my hand. "You looked so sad for a moment."

I feel confused. Is he joking? I want to ask, *Have you forgotten that you pulled my hair yesterday? That you called me a whore for speaking to another man?* But instead I smile like I've just remembered I'm a millionaire and say, "It's nothing."

He grins, the softness in his eyes quickly vanishing. "Get some dinner. I want you in bed, naked, when I get back."

I watch him pad along the deck toward our villa to get changed before he heads to the gym. His training will take three hours. I saw the look on his face before. I have to do this. I have to obey.

And I have less than three hours to work out a form of contraception. A form that Rob won't discover.

I head to the island shop, trying not to look too suspicious as I browse the pharmacy aisle. They have condoms in all sizes and flavors, a few sex toys, but no caps or diaphragms. I'm concentrating so hard on all the different packages on display that I don't notice the sales assistant approach to pluck something from the shelf.

I watch her as she walks back to the front of the shop. She's an older woman, my mum's age, with an Australian accent.

I wait until the other customers have gone before approaching her.

"Excuse me," I say. "I don't suppose it's possible to get . . . the morning-after pill?"

I whisper it, and she pauses. "We don't have it in store," she says. "But I can see about ordering it in? It might take a couple of days."

I nod, eager, though the time frame isn't ideal.

"Can I take your name?" she asks, taking out a notebook and pen from the back of the till.

My face falls. "Why?"

"We'd have to ask a pharmacist to prescribe it," she says.

"Oh," I say, backing away. She calls after me, but I'm already walking off, making feeble excuses, my heart racing.

I can't risk Rob finding out. I need to find another way.

35

CAMILLA

NOW

She sits in the plunge pool in her villa sipping champagne, looking out at the Indian Ocean, feeling nothing but rage. Her therapist said that grief and anger were like siblings, meaning that they often overlapped. The wording was careless, but she thinks of Cameron now, and how sometimes she has felt that, if she became angry enough, she could bring him back to life. Nonsense, of course, but her anger has remained as obstinate, defying reality.

It's almost midnight.

The sun has bled out into the waves, and in the distance she can hear screams and laughter as some guests walk across a strip of hot coals near the pier. She feels like there's an earthquake inside her head. An ongoing, constant earthquake, the planet splitting right open.

It's the anniversary of the massacre, the actual day of it, and she's just learned that Hugh Fraser didn't act alone—exactly as she's suspected all this time.

And the second killer is possibly in the villa next to hers.

It is agonizing, waiting for the call with Adrian. She has spent the evening here on her balcony, staring out to sea and crying. She didn't dare go to the buffet for dinner, or leave the villa. If she bumped into Rob, there was no telling what she would do.

But Kate is right. They need to be patient, wait for Adrian to share his findings. She thinks of the dinner last night. The way Rob stormed across the restaurant with a face like thunder, fists ready to knock seven bells out of Antoni. And he probably would have, had the waiters not intervened.

Antoni is nowhere to be seen.

Camilla is given to acting on her gut instinct. And right now, her gut is saying that Rob Marlowe is the killer. Darcy knows it, too. They can examine their detective's evidence all day long, but she saw Rob's face contorted with anger, and she knows he hurts Jade. It makes sense.

Sometimes fate has a way of making things happen, of bringing impossible parts together. And now she knows that's why they're really here.

Her brother will have justice.

She is physically shaking, has already vomited several times, her face streaked with mascara and eyeliner from crying.

Her phone has been buzzing all night with messages of sympathy.

Thinking of you, Mum.

I hope you're OK, Camilla. I know today is the worst xo

We're holding you to the light xxx

But Camilla holds back from sharing this bombshell with them. *Not yet*, she thinks. Not until she hears it firsthand.

NOW IT'S TWO MINUTES TO one. Darcy and Kate are on the sofa next to her in her villa, candles lit, glasses of wine poured. Camilla's eyes are puffy and sore, but she's had a shower, has put on clean clothes and fresh makeup. She feels a little less untethered. She sets her laptop on the coffee table in front of them.

"Ready?" she asks them.

Kate raises her glass. "Ready."

Camilla clicks the Zoom link. The camera light flashes green. Adrian appears a few seconds later in his home office back in London.

"Evening, ladies," he says.

"We've all heard the news now," Kate says. "I think we're still trying to get our heads around it."

"What can you tell us about this man, Rob Marlowe?" Camilla says, wanting to cut straight to the chase.

"Tonight I'm going to give a comprehensive overview," Adrian says, "via PowerPoint presentation, if that's all right. I have some images to share."

"We appreciate that," Kate says. "Hopefully the Wi-Fi's OK—there's a bit of a time lag."

"Let me just share my screen."

The presentation pops up in the form of a slide featuring a mug shot of Rob. Camilla notes that it's dated three years ago. Her lip curls. How she hates this man. Already she is thinking of what she wants to do to him, the thought of him laying a finger on her brother dredging up her darkest memories.

She feels Kate squeeze her hand. "You all right?" Kate asks, and she nods, faking a smile.

No, she's not all right. Cameron's voice is loud in her head. She thinks of him as a little boy, how protective he was of her. How she'd wake sometimes and find him sleeping beside her. She thinks of the funeral. Of her mother falling to her knees.

"I'll tell you how I came across him," Adrian says, bringing up a slide with another photograph of Rob. It looks like a screenshot, perhaps a Facebook profile. "You'll remember that the owner of the guesthouse, Mike Rotzien, was involved in drugs, and there had been some trouble with his dealers right before the killings. Rob Marlowe was one of his dealers. I was able to access some of the interview reports from the original investigation. Marlowe's interview was the most interesting to me, because he was interviewed twice."

"Twice?" Camilla says, astonished.

"Why was he interviewed twice?" Kate asks.

"His DNA was found in the guesthouse," Adrian says, and Camilla takes a deep breath. "Now, Marlowe does have a previous address in Dover, but that doesn't explain why his DNA should turn up at a crime scene."

Kate and Darcy share looks.

"So what happened?"

"To cut a long story short—he was let go. He was able to prove that Rotzien was a client of his, and that was why his DNA was in the guesthouse."

"That'll be why they spent so long looking at Rotzien's drug background," Camilla hisses at Kate, referring to the meandering part of the investigation that upset Rotzien's family. He had been murdered, but the investigators had spent a long time portraying him as a possible collaborator.

"As I explained to Darcy," Adrian continued, "forensic science has moved ahead in leaps and bounds since 2001, but that also means that, back then, it was shockingly primitive."

"Why the fuck would they let someone go if their DNA was found at the scene of a massacre?" Camilla says, feeling anger flared up inside her.

"My educated guess would be that they felt they had their man," Adrian says. "Hugh Fraser denied that anyone else was involved. Rob Marlowe had an alibi, albeit a questionable one." Adrian shares a mug shot of a woman with bleached-blond hair and smeared red lipstick, her pupils glassy and dilated. Camilla reckons she must be a sex worker.

"But there is more evidence that persuades me to look again at Rob," Adrian continues. "He has a history of assault. A total of twelve earlier cases, four of which never made it to court. Five of the charges occurred in relation to drug dealing. He moved about a fair bit in his late teens. Was homeless for a while, spent time in Glasgow in this hostel."

Adrian next shares an image of a decrepit building, an address indicating a street in Motherwell. "Incidentally, there was a stabbing in a flat two streets away from this address the night before Marlowe fled for Cornwall. Police never found the killer."

Another image of an apartment appears on the screen, labeled with an address in Cornwall. "So, Marlowe moves to this place in the summer of 1999. No job, but manages to get himself an apartment. Most likely selling drugs at this point, which he returns to time and again." He shows them another image—a utility bill addressed to Rob Marlowe with the same Perranporth postcode, dated June 1999.

"Again, a stabbing. Drug dealer. Next day, Marlowe moves to Norfolk. In August 2001, he picks up a job as an apprentice for a plumbing company in Dover."

Another image: a utility bill dated August 2001 with Rob's name on it. Then a map, with a red arrow pointing at the Spinnaker Guesthouse, a blue arrow pointing at another venue.

"The blue arrow is Rob's apartment. As you can see, he's just over a mile away from the guesthouse. Interviewees mentioned that the guesthouse was known to drug dealers. My guess is Rob fell out with the owner over drugs. And then he took his revenge."

"How is Rob linked to Hugh Fraser?" Camilla asks. "And if Rob was involved, why wouldn't Fraser tell the police?"

Adrian clicks through to the next slide. The image makes Camilla's stomach drop. It is an old Polaroid photograph of a teenage Rob with his arm around Hugh's shoulders, the other hand giving a thumbs-up. Both grinning. They're in someone's house, faded floral curtains forming a background. His eyes turn to Hugh and his head tilts toward him, Rob's body language suggesting that, as a younger man, he was in thrall to Hugh.

"Oh my God," she hears Kate say with a whimper.

"Hugh had previously served time for sexual offenses against teenage girls," Adrian says. "My feeling is that he was also into teenage boys. Rob was nineteen at the time. They met while Rob was in foster care. The body language here is quite intimate. Rob was one of many boys that Hugh took under his wing, getting them to solicit other adolescents for him. Given that Hugh had been diagnosed with cancer, you could say he had nothing to gain by mentioning Rob to the police."

"So you're saying . . . they had a relationship?" Kate asks.

"I think that photo speaks volumes," Camilla says, taking her phone out to capture it. "And his DNA was in the fucking guesthouse."

"I'm sorry, I appreciate this can't be easy to take in," Adrian says. "I'm happy to meet again once you've had time to digest?"

"Thank you, Adrian," Darcy says.

"Yes, thank you," Camilla says in a hoarse voice.

The three of them sit in stunned silence for a moment.

"Can we chat, ladies?" Kate says finally. "Outside? I need air."

36

KATE

NOW

She stands by the remains of the fire walk, a strip of coals glowing gently underneath the worn top layer. Two resort staff members place a sign at the top, warning against the danger of injury while they head off to source buckets of water and rakes with which to sweep up the embers.

Kate takes a breath before stepping onto the coals. The heat is much less than she expected, but she keeps moving, glad of the chance to turn her mind away from the memories that have risen, viscous, swamp-like.

It strikes her that she forgot to mention to Adrian that she had tried calling him to find out if he could investigate the sender of the roses. She could have mentioned it during the call, but she was too distracted. . . . The email from Jacob sticks in her mind, the words *a software issue*. Perhaps Adrian has used Jacob's technology to find Rob. Perhaps she should call Jacob to get clarification.

For now, she needs to think carefully about everything she has learned. And what to do about it.

She jumps onto the sand, then turns to see Camilla tiptoeing across the coals, holding the hem of her dress up. Darcy is behind her, the two of them aglow in the red light of the small fires that shoot up between the coals in their wake.

Camilla lets out a scream that's somewhere between fear and joy, maybe both. A Bacchanalian scene, two Furies dancing on the souls of sinners.

The three women head away from the fire walk and the pier, far away from the people who sit near the bar, enjoying the voluptuous warmth of the night.

Kate checks her phone, noticing a new message from Jade:

I need a favor x

The sympathy she felt for Jade before is a little darkened by what Adrian has shared, and she tries to make space for it—Jade may not know about Rob's past, after all. She is young. She was barely a year old when the massacre happened.

Even so, she has a lot to process now. They all do.

She listens as Camilla talks on, repeating the details that Adrian shared, as though both she and Darcy weren't there. She's aware that Camilla needs to speak in order to grasp what she has learned, telling it to herself, whereas she and Darcy are introspective creatures, needing silence to plunge deep into their thoughts.

The anniversary is the turning point of Kate's year, has been since that terrible night, and as of an hour ago she has pitched into a new cycle.

Stunned, still, to have survived.

37

KATE

NOW

"How did you sleep?" Camilla asks. It's just after nine in the morning, and they're in the kitchen of Kate's villa as she makes a pot of tea.

"Not great," Kate says. "You?"

Camilla sighs. "Shit."

"Hello?" a voice calls. "Anyone in?"

Darcy's at the door, peering around it.

Camilla looks confused. "I closed that door, by the way."

"It's dodgy," Kate says. "They're meant to have fixed it."

Darcy steps into the kitchen, looking the others over. Kate sees that her eyes are puffy from crying, and her anger subsides.

"You all right?" Camilla asks after a long silence. Her arms are folded, and it's clear that she still hasn't forgiven Darcy for bringing them all here under false pretenses. But then, Darcy has offered to arrange a transfer to another resort. They could all go home, or try to make the most of their time here. *Impossible*, Kate thinks. Not even paradise is enjoyable after what Adrian has told them.

They take their tea through to the dining table, the mood strained. Kate has had Rafi bring a platter of fruit, croissants, and rolls for them to share, along with fresh juice and a jug of ice water filled with lemon slices, but it all sits untouched.

"So, then," Camilla says, "what do we all think?"

"I think we should go straight to the police," Kate says. "Let them deal with it."

Darcy nods. "That's one option."

"The local police won't do anything," Camilla says dismissively. "They don't have the authority. You know how it'll go. And even if we phone the police in the UK, there's no way they're going to fly out here on such scant evidence."

"So, what, then?" Darcy says. "Do we just pretend he's not who Adrian says he is?"

Camilla shakes her head. "God, no. After twenty-two years? After that shitshow they called an investigation?" She raises a hand to her mouth, emotion taking her by surprise. "No," she says, recovering. "I want to look him in the eye and ask him if he killed my brother."

"I want to do the same for Elijah," Darcy says sadly.

"So we just knock on the door of his honeymoon suite and say, 'Hello, can you tell us if you murdered six people, please?'" Kate says.

There's a long silence.

"We kidnap him," Camilla says. "That's what we do."

Kate laughs, but then realizes Camilla's serious.

"Kidnap him?"

Camilla nods grimly. "There's three of us," she says. "We can do it. Force him to tell us everything he knows."

"You're not serious," Kate says.

"Record it," Darcy tells Camilla, her eyes narrowed. "Send it to the police."

"Force him how?" Kate says, glancing from Darcy to Camilla. "The man could take on Mike Tyson with one arm tied behind his back."

"We protect ourselves," Camilla says with a dark look. "We take a knife." Kate looks even more horrified. "*Just in case*. And we use a code word in case one of us is in danger. 'Pineapple.'"

"'Pineapple'?" Darcy says, raising an eyebrow.

"This is madness," Kate says. "You can't seriously think we could do that." She watches them, reeling. Deep down, another voice is beginning to speak. The voice that has always felt there was something *wrong* about the investigation, that Fraser's confession felt too contrived, the investigation team too eager to congratulate themselves on solving the case.

Camilla and Darcy are already discussing the logistics of how they might approach Rob. Ply him with alcohol. Or perhaps not—it might decrease their chances of anything he says being taken seriously by the police. . . .

Kate can scarcely believe any of this is real. She stares at her cup of tea, realizing she can't stomach it.

Camilla turns to her. "Are you in?"

Kate blinks. "Am I in . . . what?"

"Are you willing to do this?" Camilla says, insistent. "We don't have much time left."

Kate looks at their faces. "This is crazy," she says finally. "You're talking about a kangaroo court."

Camilla rises to her feet, agitated. Kate feels torn, as though she's dissenting. As though she's a coward.

"Maybe *we* can do it, without Kate," Camilla tells Darcy. "Just the two of us."

"I'm sorry," Kate says, feeling ganged up on. "I just . . . it's too risky. . . ."

"This man murdered six defenseless people in their beds," Camilla hisses. "He murdered Elijah. He murdered Cameron."

"We don't know that," Kate says. She falters. "Innocent until proven otherwise, correct?"

Camilla rounds on Kate, her eyes flashing. "You have *no idea* what it's like—" She stops, a sob choking her.

"I know what you're saying," Kate says softly. "You're saying I don't have a right to an opinion, because I survived."

Camilla stares at her. "I'm *not* saying that," she says.

"I know your brother was murdered," Kate says, raising her eyes to Camilla's. She turns to Darcy. "And I know that you lost Elijah. And those poor people should never have died, any of them. But I was traumatized for *years* afterward. Within months I went from being a healthy twenty-four-year-old to a chronically ill agoraphobic."

"Oh, Kate . . ." Darcy says, reaching out to take her hand.

"I have been afraid for *twenty-two years*," Kate says, suddenly bursting into tears. Camilla sits, stunned, as she watches Kate weep, her head in her hands.

"But you lived," Camilla says coldly.

"Camilla," Darcy says, chiding.

Kate stops crying and looks up at her. "You're right," she says. Then, resigned: "I lived."

JADE

NOW

Kate still hasn't answered my text message.

I had a brain wave yesterday, after I spoke to the woman in the island shop. If the morning-after pill has to be prescribed, then I could ask Kate if she's willing to put her name on the prescription so Rob doesn't find out. I know it's a huge ask, but I'm hoping she'll understand.

Luckily, we have an excursion this morning, a snorkeling trip to see manta rays on the house reef, so Rob doesn't want sex. Still, I'm riddled with anxiety. Google tells me that the morning-after pill can work for three days after sex or five days, depending on which pill it is. No response yet from Kate. But every minute feels like a scythe swinging over my head.

I get dressed and tell him I'm going to check on Kate from villa two.

"Why?" he asks, incredulous.

"She's poorly," I tell him, lying. "I'm just making sure she's OK."

"Doesn't she have mates who can do that?"

I smile. "I'll not be long."

At Kate's villa I go to press the button but the door is already open, just an inch. I lift a hand to knock anyway. But then I hear raised voices.

"This is insane, Camilla. Do you actually hear yourself?"

It's Kate. She sounds proper stressed, like they're having a row. I should come back later.

But the clock is ticking.

Darcy says something, and although I can't make out the words, she sounds equally wound up. Shit. I can't. I'll text Kate again.

But just as I'm turning away, I hear Camilla say Rob's name. His full name.

". . . Rob Marlowe!"

Camilla sounds angry, and tearful. My heart stops in my chest. Did I hear that right? I step back toward the door, leaning against the gap.

". . . murdered," she says, her voice moving in and out of earshot. "I know he did it . . . that photo didn't come out of thin air!"

"Calm down, Camilla," Kate says, and Camilla snaps back, her voice growing louder.

"Don't fucking tell me to calm down!"

Now my heart is jackhammering in my chest. What the hell is going on?

I press my ear close to the open door. Something scuttles past, right over my foot and into the bushes behind me. I give a jump and emit a small noise of fright.

"Someone's at the door," I hear Kate say, and I freeze. But too late—Camilla pulls the door open and sees me standing there, both of us stricken with horror.

"I'm . . . I'm sorry," I stutter, stepping backward, my hands up. "I didn't mean . . ."

She glances to either side of me before grabbing my arm and pulling me inside, closing the door tightly and checking several times that it's locked.

INSIDE THE VILLA, I FOLLOW Camilla nervously into the dining room, where Kate and Darcy are sitting. There's food on the table and a teapot but everyone looks upset. The air in the room feels like lightning has just spiked through it.

"The lock on the door is faulty," Kate says, and I hear a catch in her voice. She's been crying. She turns to me. "How much did you hear, Jade?"

I shake my head, keeping my eyes on the apples on the table, glistening red. "Nothing," I say. "I didn't hear anything."

They don't believe me. I'm like a deer in headlights. Darcy gets up and approaches me, a smile on her face that looks weird, false. Shit.

"I was only coming by to ask . . ." I say, but Darcy speaks over me.

"Jade," she says quickly, "it's really important that you tell us exactly what you heard, because you might have formed the wrong impression. OK?"

I stare at her, my heart thumping loudly in my chest. "I . . . heard Camilla say Rob's name . . ."

"Was that all?" Darcy asks.

I swallow hard. "Yeah." The word *murdered* rings in my ears. Did I really hear that? It makes me break out in shivers. Darcy pours a glass of water from the jug on the table and hands it to me. "Why don't you have a seat?"

I stare at her stiffly. I really just want to go. I'm a bit afraid of these three. I'm afraid of what they might say next. But she points to a seat at the head of the table and I sit down, watching them as they do the same.

"Why were the three of you talking about Rob?" I ask gently. "Did something happen?"

Camilla turns to me, her eyes narrowed. "How long have you known him?"

"About three years."

"OK. And what do you know about his past?"

I blink, confused. "He went to school in Bromley, left at fifteen, got an apprenticeship in plumbing . . . He spent most of his childhood in foster care. He's close to his nan, though. And his mum left him some money when she died."

"Did he tell you what he did in Dover?" Camilla asks, her voice hardening.

"Dover?" I shake my head, confused. "No, I don't think so. When?"

"It was in 2001," Darcy says. "Before your time, I think."

"I was a year old in 2001," I say, looking at their faces.

"Remember I told you about what happened to me a long time ago?" Kate says. "At the guesthouse?"

I nod. Of course I remember. How could I forget it?

"We think Rob had something to do with it," Kate says, shifting in her chair. "Another man was charged with the murders, a man called Hugh Fraser. But there's new evidence. Evidence that implicates Rob, too."

"Rob? My Rob?" I say, her words landing like a kick in my stomach.

Camilla shows me a photograph on her phone. It's Rob, much younger, maybe even a teenager. And he's standing next to an older man in a way that makes the hairs on the back of my neck stand on end. He's kind of leaning into him, his hand on his stomach.

"Who is this man?" I ask.

Camilla hesitates before answering me. "That's Fraser."

I feel like someone is pressing very hard on my lungs. I look again, check the photograph. Rob's nana has some old photos of him on her walls and he looks just like this. But his body language . . . It looks like they're a couple.

"Six people?" I hear myself say.

"My twin brother was one of them," Camilla says, her eyes hard. "There were two girls, aged twenty-three and twenty-four. The owner of the guesthouse, a man in his sixties with grandchildren; a professor in his forties; Darcy's boyfriend, Elijah . . ."

I look over at Darcy, who nods to confirm it. "He had just turned nineteen."

"Rob's DNA was found inside the guesthouse," Kate says. "But the police let him go."

It feels like the floor has just dropped out from beneath me. All the lies Rob told, all the times I saw his face change into something . . . monstrous. I imagine him stabbing someone, the look in his eyes. The coldness I've seen there.

"What are you going to do?" I ask. My voice is barely a whisper.

I watch as they cast one another different looks. "We want to see if we can speak to Rob," Camilla says. "It's clear he had a relationship with Fraser, and that he lived near the guesthouse. Our detective thinks there was a possible motive, too. Does Rob have a history of selling drugs?"

I nod, my throat tight. "Yes. I know this. His nana's mentioned it in passing."

They trade looks again. "The guesthouse owner had a record of selling drugs, too. There might have been a dispute. And Fraser might have called in Rob to . . . sort him out."

"You must not say a word," Kate tells me. "Please. Not a word."

I nod. "I won't say anything, I promise. I mean, how can I? But . . . do you think he did it? I mean, the six murders. You really think it was Rob?"

Kate answers first. "We don't know, honestly," she says. "But this is the first time we're learning about Rob having been interviewed. And he clearly knew Fraser."

I press my hands to my face, wanting to cry. This is the most devastating thing ever. I'm married to a murderer. I want to be sick. And it's dangerous, unspeakably dangerous for them to approach him about it.

And he knows I'm friendly with Kate. He knows I'm here, in her villa. I'll get caught up in this. He'll think I had something to do with it.

Suddenly Camilla reaches across to me and grasps my hand. "You know Rob more than anyone," Camilla says. "Don't you?"

I nod, looking down at my engagement and wedding rings. Oh yes, I very much do know Rob. And I know what he will do if he finds out about this.

I lift my eyes to hers, realizing I have to steer this now. I have to be part of this, whether I want to or not.

"Let me help," I say.

39

DARCY

NOW

Darcy watches Jade carefully, tuning out the conversation between her, Kate, and Camilla to do some quick calculations in her mind.

How did Jade overhear their conversation about Rob? Darcy remembers closing the door to Kate's villa when she came in. Did she hear it click behind her? Kate said the door was acting up, owing to a digital fault. Or did she tell Jade to come along at this time? Only a fool would dismiss the timing of this as merely coincidental. Jade's tears seem real, and the bruise is genuine. And Rob—well, Darcy knows he's a bastard. She knows everything there is to know about Rob Marlowe.

But Jade? Darcy knows very little about Jade. That was an oversight. And it could cost them all dearly.

She thinks about Jacob's email. He knows about Adrian, and it continues to nag at her, the hows and whens . . . Did he find something on the computer? No, she thinks. She covered her tracks, she's sure of it.

Did someone tell him? If so, who?

Jade sits at the head of the dining table, her expression shifting through emotions. She seems genuine, but Darcy knows better than to trust appearances. There's no doubt this new addition to the mix poses a risk.

But Jade may also be useful.

Darcy watches Jade struggle to process it all, tears rolling down her cheeks. She asks questions, repeating many of them, as though her brain can't cope with the shock of it. Camilla and Kate tell her everything that Adrian shared with them: Rob's history of drugs and violence, the DNA, the questionable alibi. Fraser's history of abusing young girls and boys.

The truth is, Rob has constructed the reality Jade knows as his wife.

Almost twice her age, he lived a lifetime before Jade set eyes on him. And he wanted to keep it all from her.

Or maybe he didn't. Maybe Jade knows everything he did.

Could Jade be a Trojan horse, Darcy wonders now, sent in here to find out what they're planning?

40

CAMILLA

NOW

The resort is small enough to walk around in half an hour, less at a march, but there are many nooks and crannies that make it possible for two people not to bump into each other, if one or both of them is so inclined. As Camilla leaves Kate's villa, she decides to walk around the island, hoping to see Antoni. Darcy's bombshell pushed him from her mind for a few fraught hours, but now she's determined to make sure he's OK.

By the pool, she sees Antoni's nephew, Salvador, and a pretty teenage girl in a red bikini standing close by, and her heart lifts. She scans the bar behind them for Antoni. Then, not finding him, she approaches Salvador and gives a little wave. He is speaking to someone on his mobile phone, and gives her a funny look. She wonders if he doesn't recognize her.

"Hello again," she says. He lowers the phone.

"Is your uncle OK?" she asks.

Salvador says something in Spanish, the tone of his voice impassioned and urgent.

Panic shoots into her. Salvador is suddenly pleading with her, saying things she doesn't understand. The girl looks worried too, pressing a hand to her face as she glances around.

"Where is Antoni?" Camilla says. Quickly she lifts her phone and types the words into Google Translate. She holds it up, and Salvador glances at it, his dark brow furrowed. He gently takes the phone from her to type his response.

I don't know where he is

Camilla looks up at Salvador, seeing the worry etched on his face. Quickly she types back.

Is Antoni missing?

"*Sí*," he says. Then he types again.

Not seen since Saturday night

She gives a start. It's Monday afternoon. She last saw Antoni at around two or three on Sunday morning, before she fell asleep in a drunken, post-coital fog.

She squeezes Salvador's arm, turns and heads quickly to the resort office.

NURA IS SITTING AT HER desk and speaks before Camilla does. "We checked your deck," she says. "For blood? We found nothing there. We tried to reach you."

"I'm worried about a guest, actually," Camilla says. "Antoni Caballé. He was staying with his nephew in villa eighteen. I've not seen him all day, and his nephew says he's missing."

Nura nods. "Yes, Salvador has reported this. We are making inquiries."

Camilla notes that Nura doesn't look very concerned. "He did kayak across to the Emerald Resort sometimes," Camilla says.

Nura writes that down and throws her a smile. "I'll call them. Please don't worry."

Thirty-five hours. Antoni hasn't been seen by Camilla *or* his nephew for thirty-five hours.

41

CAMILLA

NOW

It's evening; tonight's excursion is a private boat trip for her, Darcy, and Kate to the sandbank in the middle of the ocean, which Camilla had prearranged before they'd even arrived. There, a rug will be laid out on the sand, a metal frame garnished with fairy lights surrounding them. Champagne on ice.

Kate had assumed they would cancel, asking if they should instead consider Darcy's offer of a transfer elsewhere, even just to Emerald Island. But Camilla said no. She wants to stay put until Antoni is found so she can keep an eye on Salvador. He seemed so much younger when she saw him before, so vulnerable in the face of a worrying situation.

"Come on, Camilla," Darcy calls from the boat, and Camilla gives one last look at the sand path behind her.

She can't shake the sick feeling in the pit of her stomach.

Her head throbs and a hot lump in her throat won't go away. God, it's so hard to think straight. How can she, knowing what she knows?

In the end, they had agreed to use this excursion to talk, away from Jade. Adrian's bombshell requires careful discussion; where better to do this than a tiny bar of sand in the middle of the Indian Ocean, the boat and crew several hundred feet offshore, and well away from Rob Marlowe himself?

The boat ride affords them a view of the sun setting over the ocean, a golden, liquid light, blush and apricot clouds clustered against the cerulean backdrop of sky. It's dark by the time they reach the sandbank, a silvery slice in the midst of warm navy sea, a canopy of bright stars glittering overhead.

The crew tell them to wait in the boat while they set up, laying out a large round rug, then three plump pillows for the women to sit on, before stringing up the lights.

They wait until the crew have retreated to the boat before taking their seats at the small table set with gilded champagne glasses and a small tray of petit fours.

"Shall we?" Darcy says, stepping onto the blanket and lowering herself onto one of the pillows. She looks tense, her jaw tight. Yes, Camilla thinks, they should have canceled tonight's excursion. It all feels wrong. And yet, they're here now. Resigned, she lifts a bottle of champagne, surreptitiously checking the bottom before pouring Kate and Darcy a glass.

No one drinks it.

The warm breeze settles across them like a blanket, the night sky thrumming with stars. It should be blissful, a moment to contemplate the beauty of the ocean. But instead, they think only about the dangers inside the dark.

"All right," Camilla says after a few moments. "What do we do about Jade?"

"Oh, it's time for business, is it?" Kate says, sitting upright.

"I think we need to discuss it," Camilla says. "Bit of a plot twist, wouldn't you say?"

"Indeed," Kate says. "A plot twist within a plot twist."

"Darcy?" Camilla says, noticing that she's fidgeting with the cushion, something bothering her.

"I'd like to know which of you told Jacob about Adrian," Darcy says after a moment.

Camilla stares at her, certain she's misheard. She looks from Darcy to Kate, then back to Darcy. "I'm sorry. Can you repeat that?"

"One of you told Jacob about Adrian," Darcy says. "I'd like to know who. Or maybe it was both of you?" There's a sharpness to her tone that cuts through the air, transforming the mood.

"You think me or Kate told Jacob about Adrian Clifton," Camilla repeats.

"Yes," Darcy says. "It's the only way he could have found out about him."

Camilla looks at Kate, who flicks her eyes at her quickly before returning her gaze to Darcy.

"Darcy, love," Kate says, gently. "I know this is all very stressful, but this is not the time to fling random accusations."

"I want the truth," Darcy says with a light laugh, turning to Kate. "And it seems that despite our pact to be completely honest, some of us are keeping secrets. Like you, Kate."

Kate looks astonished. "Me?"

Camilla watches Kate carefully, feeling her heart begin to race.

"I had a separate mobile phone that I used when I spoke to Adrian in case Jacob or one of the boys happened to check my personal phone," Darcy continues. "You know about it, don't you?"

Kate looks flustered. "I don't know what you're . . ."

"Did you give that number to Jacob?" Darcy presses.

Kate blinks furiously. She looks to Camilla for support. "Jacob gave that number to *me*," she protests, flustered now.

"So you *spoke* to him?" Darcy asks, shocked.

"Well, no, I —"

"And what did you tell him?"

"If you'll allow me to explain," Kate says, "I can tell you exactly what I said, and to whom."

"All right."

"But first," Kate says, straightening, "I have a few questions of my own. Seeing as tonight's turned into an interrogation."

Camilla rolls her eyes. "It's not an interrogation. . . ."

"What I'd also like to know," Darcy interjects, looking at Kate, then Camilla, "is whether Jade is someone we can trust. For all we know, she's putting on an act to protect her hubby."

Camilla picks up her glass and sips, her eyes on Kate. "I think you know the answer to that."

"Do I?" Kate asks.

Camilla shrugs. "You and Jade seem to be pretty friendly."

"Come on," Kate says reasonably. "You know you can trust me."

"But I don't," Camilla says simply. "It seems none of us can trust each other. Our friendship is based on an unspeakable tragedy, for crying out loud. We barely know each other."

"Of course we do . . ." Darcy counters, but Camilla shakes her head. She feels tears prick her eyes at the thought of how confusing and bitter this trip has become. Will they still be on speaking terms by the time they return home? She doesn't believe so.

And yet, so much more is at stake.

"We know each other's grief," Camilla says, her chest tightening. "But we don't *know* each other. And none of us should trust the other. Not with this information. The stakes are too high. When it comes down to it, we have to look out for ourselves."

"Well, then," Kate says, in a brittle, hurt tone. "Let's focus on the task at hand, shall we? The sooner we talk to Rob Marlowe, the sooner we can all get away from each other and get on with our lives."

Darcy shrugs. "OK, then. I guess neither of you wants to admit to telling Jacob about Adrian."

"I think neither of us *did* tell him about Adrian," Kate snaps, and Darcy smiles, not believing her.

Camilla sighs. Now that she's had time to think properly, she has new concerns of her own. It's all so complicated, so crazy. How can they really expect to get Rob to tell them anything at all? Even if he were to blurt out that he killed all those people, as if he ever would, they would still have to tell the police, and then trust that the police would act on it. The old Camilla—the one who hadn't experienced the justice system quite so thoroughly—would have believed that of course the police would leap to find out the truth, that if she went to them for help, she'd get it.

But she has learned that people get away with the most egregious crimes. In fact, the more brazen, the higher the chance they'll get off through some ridiculous technicality, a loophole, or via the kind of luck that should befall the good people of the world.

Instead, that kind of luck seems to gravitate to bastards like Rob Marlowe.

"I'm just going to say it," Camilla says. "I'll never forgive myself if we leave this island without at least trying to confront him."

"Despite the risk?" Kate asks. "Despite the likelihood of him attacking one of us, or all of us?"

"We have Jade, remember," Camilla says. "Perhaps she can persuade him to do things that we can't."

"We're putting Jade's life at risk," Kate says gravely. "That's what we're doing here."

"Her life is already at risk," Darcy says. "Domestic violence doesn't stop at a bruise."

"Well, if she manages to help us, he might get locked up," Camilla says. "She'll be safe as houses then."

"I don't think it works as simply as that," Kate says.

Darcy shrugs too. "It's something, isn't it?"

Camilla glances at Kate. The anger that has been brewing between them shifts to resentment. She has been wondering all day why Kate is so reluctant to confront Rob, after all she has been through. And now, she thinks she knows.

It has nothing to do with fear or grief, and she seems so very protective of Jade, a relative stranger.

She watches Kate quietly, wondering if the second killer hasn't been in front of her all this time.

42

KATE

She lets herself into the villa with a sigh, then checks to make sure the door is locked.

What was all that about? she thinks. Darcy's question at the sandbank—"Which one of you told Jacob about Adrian?" It was an impossible question, like asking, *How long have you been beating your wife?*

When did the three of them stop trusting each other?

When Darcy revealed the real reason for this trip, she thinks. That's when. Talk about an ulterior motive. She thinks she understands the reasoning behind Darcy's actions, how she was already raw after the long-drawn-out divorce battle, how she'd acted on impulse when Adrian told her about Rob. Darcy had just decided that this was where they had to go, because Rob was going to be here. But she hadn't thought beyond that, and now they're in a dilemma.

Still. It's all so much to take in. All three of them are emotionally battered.

She feels rattled by the evening, and not just because of what they're planning to do. They had felt like a team before, or at the very least they'd had a common interest. But something has changed. Darcy and Camilla believe she's too trusting of Jade. Camilla is determined to make Kate the outlier, and Kate wonders why. They're very different, that's for damn sure. Camilla looks down her nose at Kate, thinks she's weaker because she doesn't spend every second leading with her authentic core.

Or maybe it has to do with the massacre. Because she survived and Cameron didn't. Survivor resentment. The psychologist, Dr. Luxton, mentioned it years ago. Kate contacted Dr. Luxton when she first got in touch with Camilla and Darcy. She was the only person alive to know Kate had spoken to them; Kate wanted to know if there was anything she should expect, anything that might arise from their relationship that she ought to prepare for.

"Hopefully enough time and healing has happened to make this a good thing," Dr. Luxton said. "But you might find that they blame you for their loved ones' deaths. It's nothing personal if they do. It's just survivor resentment. Another facet of grief."

Ah, yes. Grief. The soundtrack of Kate's life, except the main person she has been grieving is herself.

She can barely remember being Briony. Who was she? She knows that Briony was thriving, steadily climbing her way out of a childhood and adolescence marred by poverty and toxic parenting. Kate's estranged from both her parents now, has no idea if they're living or dead. It's a good thing, though hard to explain to the kinds of folk who post things like "no one will ever love you more than your parents" on social media. Perhaps Kate wouldn't have been able to cut them off had the massacre not happened. Perhaps she would be living a different life, a lesser life.

But her memories are mostly vapors. The massacre has colonized the past, overshadowing all other events with the garishly Technicolor scenes of that night and the ones thereafter. Bright flashes that come to her with violence, even now.

For years, she thought she had raced out of the guesthouse after discovering the second body. In 2010, she started having flashbacks again. Her GP upped her meds, sent her to a psychotherapist. New memories emerged that contradicted the previous narrative—she had *attempted* to race out of the guesthouse after discovering the second body, but the door was jammed and she panicked, racing to the back exit, only to mistake the door to a bedroom for the one that led outside. She stumbled over two more bodies. Two of her fellow students, Bao and Chan-Juan, both postgraduates from China who were sharing a twin room.

During the trial, she kept hearing a strange twist on her situation: that she *survived*. The word confused her. Yes, she hadn't been murdered—but survived? Was this really what survival felt like? She was barely existing. She spent most of her twenties feeling like she was going out of her mind. But the fact that she had lived seemed to preclude her from an understanding of what it was like to be so traumatized that she hardly knew her own address, could only just function. Bizarre illnesses would visit her with vehemence, then depart, only to make way for a different condition, an alternative affliction. Severe psoriasis for a year, forming red crusts on her elbows and knees, all along her scalp. No family history of psoriasis. Stress, the doctors said.

And now the bloody menopause, creeping up on her, apparently years before it's meant to. She pours herself a glass of water from the tap and sips it thirstily. No point in feeling sorry for herself.

She did, after all, survive.

LATER THAT EVENING, SHE REALIZES that she hasn't responded to Jade's text. She needs to speak to her, follow up with her after the discussion with Darcy and Camilla.

She sends her a message.

"I'VE ONLY GOT A FEW minutes," Jade says, breathless, ten minutes later. She glances behind her, checking to make sure that the door to Kate's villa is closed.

"What was the favor?" Kate asks.

Jade looks reluctant to say. "I wanted to see if you might help me get the morning-after pill."

This wasn't at all what Kate was expecting. "Oh."

"It's not something I'd normally ask for, but I'm worried that if the prescription is in my name, Rob will find out."

Kate nods, understanding a little better. "I see. Can you get that here?"

"Yes, I've checked. Rob would go mad if he found out. He wants a baby so badly." She grows tearful. "But I can't. I can't. . . ."

Kate nods again, seeing Jade's face turn ashen. "We can put it in my name. Just tell me what I need to do."

Jade recovers and offers a smile. "Thank you."

"My offer still stands," Kate says. "I have two thousand pounds sitting in an account that you can take right now and go into hiding. I can ask my butler to arrange a seaplane. The girls and I will cover for you, send Rob on a wild-goose chase in the wrong direction. Buy you time."

Jade considers briefly, then shakes her head. "I can help you get what you need. I want to. Thank you, though."

She smiles, and Kate feels disappointed. It would be safer for Jade on all counts if she just got the hell away from here.

"We're thinking of confronting him tomorrow night," she says, still uneasy at the thought of it. "Darcy says the gym is the best place. No one uses it other than Rob, and no one can see in. And there's a disco on tomorrow night at the bar, so we figure most of the guests will be there."

She watches fear pulse behind Jade's eyes. "Tomorrow?"

"Yes. Is that all right?"

Jade bites her lip. "We're going on a scuba trip tomorrow morning. But we'll be back by then, I'm sure."

Kate takes a breath, scarcely believing what she has agreed to. "Camilla wants you to bring Rob there. Maybe you can . . . get him into a compromising position."

Jade's face drops. "Right."

"We'll make it look like you have nothing to do with it, OK?" Kate says. "We'll come in and take it from there."

"What if he suspects me?" Jade says, more to herself than to Kate.

"He won't," Kate says. "We'll make sure of it. With all three of us cornering him, he might just . . . slip up, reveal *something* that the police can follow up on. Camilla wants to record the meeting, just in case." She waits for Jade to object to it, to tell her how mad she sounds. But she doesn't. "I know it sounds desperate, but we won't get another chance like this."

"Fuck, this is all so dangerous," Jade says.

Kate nods. What is she doing? What is she actually doing, going along with this?

"What happens afterward?" Jade asks.

"We lock him inside."

Jade's eyes widen, and Kate waits for her to balk at the whole thing. But she doesn't, and so she continues.

"He won't be found until morning, when the gym opens. Darcy has arranged a seaplane to fly us all off the island straight after. You'll come too, back to the UK. You'll be safe."

She sees Jade take a deep breath and remembers how terrifying this must be for her.

"I give you my word," she tells the younger woman, squeezing her hand. "I won't let anything happen to you."

"All my stuff is at our house," Jade says, that deer-in-headlights look returning. "I'll have nothing, nowhere to live."

"You can stay with me, if you like," Kate says. "I'm in Carmarthenshire."

Jade smiles weakly, but when she lifts a hand to brush hair out of her face Kate notices that she's trembling.

"Are you all right?" she asks. "Please don't feel you have to do this. You can back out. . . ."

Jade shakes her head, determined. "No. You're right to speak to him here, in the Maldives. Back home you could lose him more easily, or you might not get away. And anyway, he has a ton of friends—pretty dodgy, some of them. They frighten me."

"Jesus," Kate says, imagining how connected Rob must be. She imagines he has networks in the underworld, long tentacles spread into dark places.

"Tomorrow night," she continues. "Eight o'clock. Bring him to the gym. You'll have ten minutes to get him . . . comfortable. At least make sure it's only the two of you in there. Then we'll come inside and take it from there."

Jade nods and turns for the door. "Thanks for trusting me," she says, and vanishes into the night.

43

JADE

NOW

Shit, what have I just agreed to?

I head back toward the villa, replaying the conversation in my mind. But I have to do better at acting like nothing is wrong. After Darcy and Camilla told me what they'd learned about Rob, he kept asking me what was bothering me. I ended up telling him I was feeling sick, and he was over the moon in case it meant I was pregnant, which made me feel worse.

I stop at the beach and look at the lights from the boats out at sea, trying to imagine what it would be like to be free of him. God, even the thought of it makes me feel like I can breathe easier. No more watching what I say, and how I say it, or how I look when I say it, or how I look when I say nothing at all.

And now that I know he might have killed all those people, I am extra conscious of how I am around him. Walking on eggshells, not even breathing too hard.

I dig my toes into the sand, fighting the urge to cry. He'll ask me why I've been crying and I'll have to lie again. He knows me too well.

The thing is, I'm probably crazy for trusting these women. I really like Kate, and a huge part of me believes she's for real. I believe that she'd really give me that money and put me up. But a voice in my head is also shouting at me. It's saying, *What the fuck, Jade? You don't even know these women's last names! You don't know anything about them! And yet you're offering to help them corner your husband?*

I decide to look it up on Google. *Spinnaker Guesthouse massacre.* Shit, there it is. No mention of Kate, Camilla, or Darcy, but I find a picture of one of the victims. Cameron, Camilla's brother. And a girl, about my age, called Briony Conley. She looks like Kate. No, she *is* Kate. The girl who survived.

I spend a long time reading through every news article I can find. There isn't a lot, but enough to prove it did happen. No mention of Rob, but I find loads on the killer, Hugh Fraser. His face isn't familiar, but suddenly I'm remembering a trip to the zoo with Rob and his step-nephew, Reece. We were looking at the elephants, and Rob asked me a strange question. "When does an elephant become a thousand wings?" I told him I didn't know. "In death," he said. "When it's eaten by flies."

I told him it was gross, and he said someone called Hugh had taught him that.

God. This is all actually real.

I'D HOPED ROB WOULD STILL be asleep, but he's in the living room of the villa wearing nothing but a towel around his waist, and as soon as I come inside he rushes up to me.

"Are you all right?" he says.

"Yeah," I say, a little taken aback. "Has something happened?"

"*Yeah*, something's happened," he says. "My wife went AWOL, that's what happened."

"Sorry," I say. "You were sleeping and Kate from villa two texted me."

"That frumpy old bitch?" He sneers. "What are you doing hanging out with her?"

"Don't be cruel, you." I laugh. "She just wanted some painkillers. . . ."

He wraps his arms around me, pulling me close. For a moment I drink in his smell, that deep, warm fragrance that used to make me feel safe. But then he takes me to bed, slowly pulling off my clothes, kissing me, and my mind flashes to the news articles I've just read. The faces of the victims. The way Camilla sat earlier, weeping over her dead brother.

A dead elephant, its corpse eaten by flies.

I want to ask him who Hugh Fraser was to him, but I dare not. He'll know why I'm asking. Rob is the most suspicious person I know. He thinks everyone is out to get him, is always looking over his shoulder.

And now I know why.

"JADE! GET UP. WE'RE GOING to miss the boat."

I stir.

"Jade!"

I sit up and look at my watch. It's light outside, but my watch says it's just past six in the morning. I've barely slept, waking every half-hour.

"You were tossing and turning all bloody night," Rob says angrily, pulling on his T-shirt. "Must have woken me up half a dozen times."

"I'm sorry," I say. My head is banging.

"Hurry *up*!" Rob shouts, stuffing a pair of trunks into his backpack. "We're going to the Ari Atoll, remember? To dive into the shipwreck?"

The memory of last night thuds back. Kate told me I need to bring Rob to the gym by eight this evening. "What time will we be back?" I ask him.

He shrugs. "Dunno. It's an all-day trip, I think."

"EVERYONE ABOARD?"

The boatman does a head count, then lifts a pen to sign off on the sheet next to me.

"Eight people. That's everyone."

He gives a thumbs-up to the crew member at the side of the boat, who casts off. The engine roars into life, and we're off.

Rob puts his arm around me, holding his phone up for a selfie. I lean my head on his shoulder and grin, the perfectly happy wife on her honeymoon. He edits the photo, then posts it to his Facebook page. He loves the adoration, the way he can curate a reality so different from the one we live. It makes me want to be sick.

"You want a drink?" he asks me, and I nod, surveying the cooler that

Farug, the diving instructor, has opened—bottles of Coke, iced coffee, and Fanta sitting on ice.

"I'll have an iced coffee," I say.

Rob gives me a look, the plucks out a Fanta and hands it to me.

"You should avoid caffeine," he says. "In case there's a bun in the oven."

He cracks open an iced coffee for himself and drinks it in front of me, smirking.

"Babe," he says, rubbing the back of his hand against my arm, "don't be sad. It'll be worth it. You'll see."

And there it is again: the desire inside me for the old Rob to return. I still carry it, even though I know it's so messed up. Half of me is certain that everything Kate, Camilla, and Darcy told me about him is true, that he's a cold-blooded killer. And the other half still loves him, would do anything for him.

The island shrinks behind us, eventually disappearing over the curve in the horizon. New islands appear in the distance, as though they've just popped out of nowhere. I look at the other people on the boat with us. Another couple, and one family with two teenage girls staring into their phones. They look so bored. I keep my eyes on the horizon, trying to work out an escape route. I'm electric with fear, my mind spinning. I might already be pregnant. I might be married to a murderer. If I try to escape, he'll kill me.

I find myself imagining where I would go, what I would do. Few women work on the islands, but the ones who do work in the massage centers. I could easily set up a nail salon on one of the islands. I bet they'd love that.

"What are you thinking about?" Rob asks, putting an arm tightly around me.

"Nothing," I lie.

He kisses the side of my head. "Not thinking of leaving me, are you?"

"Hardly," I say with a nervous laugh. "You've got me on a tight leash, haven't you?"

"Super tight," he says. Then, licking my ear: "Just the way I like it."

AFTER AN HOUR AND A half the boat comes to a stop in the middle of no-where, no islands in sight. No other boats, either. The water around us is neon blue and perfectly clear, as though I could step in and find it only comes up to my knees. For a moment, I wonder if we're lost. But then the crew begin pulling out plastic boxes from the storage cupboards, opening them to reveal dry suits, vests, and flippers. My heart begins to race. It looks so complicated, all the equipment and gear you have to wear. I've got my PADI license but we've only ever gone diving in an estuary back home.

I glance at Rob, suddenly panicked.

"It'll be fine," he says in a low voice. "It's easy. They'll show you what to do."

Farug lines up the equipment, lots of different devices and tubes. I watch as the others on the boat get suited up, hefting oxygen tanks onto their backs.

"This is your regulator," Farug says, handing me a device that looks like a hose. "And this is your gauge. You want to keep an eye on the pres-sure. Repeat after me: no bends."

Everyone repeats it. "No bends."

"It's when you surface too quickly," Rob tells me in a low voice, even though I know perfectly well what *bends* means. "It's fine. You'll be with me, remember?"

"The wreck is thirty feet down," Farug says. "So not too deep. Re-member your dive signals. Something is wrong is like this"—he moves his hand from side to side—"this means we're descending"—he gives a thumbs-down—"and this is the distress sign." He raises a hand to the side, makes a fist, and pumps his arm up and down. I try to remember it all.

"Now, make sure you all have a diving buddy."

Rob nods at me. "Diving buddies for life, eh, babe?"

The oxygen tank weighs a ton, and Farug straps a weighted belt around my waist. I feel like I'm going to sink to the bottom of the ocean. "That's the idea," he says, smiling.

Two teenage girls are the first to step off the boat into the rich blue water, shrieking with excitement. I was like them once. This kind of thing would have made me excited. I'd have embraced the challenge.

But I feel wary. Rob is being super nice to me. I should be relieved, but I'm not. I think he knows something. My blood runs cold.

What if he overheard them telling me about the massacre? What if there's something on my phone that lets him hear everything I do?

I watch how the others step out of the boat, one flippered foot stretched outward, then let themselves fall into the water. I'm shit scared but I do it anyway, sucking deeply on my oxygen as I let myself drop down, down, into the blue.

It's terrifying for about thirty seconds, until the oxygen kicks in and I realize I can breathe. The sound of it is weird, though, like Darth Vader. Bubbles everywhere. Rob appears in front of me, making the sign for *OK*, and I nod back at him, signing it. *OK*. Thank God. I haven't drowned.

He takes my hand and leads me down with the others into the depths, where the water is deliciously cold and a little hazy, transforming the world here into a dreamy realm of shadows and soft edges. I see a small shark flick away from us, too shy to stay close. There's a manta ray, too, about thirty feet from us, gliding through the clear water like a magic carpet. It's insanely beautiful, and I start to relax. I'm glad I came to see this.

It's a whole other world down here. For a moment, it feels as though I can pretend the last twenty-four hours never happened. That everything is all right.

The shipwreck comes into sight as we descend, a ghostly spectacle revealing its parts like an echo. There's the shadow of a mast, then the curve of the bow. I feel my heart pound as Rob pulls me forward, as I kick my flippers, pushing myself alongside him. The wreck is so much bigger than I'd imagined, about a hundred and fifty feet long. It's well preserved, too, the round windows filled with fish, coral swaying delicately from the deck.

Farug is ahead, signaling us to come to him. I let go of Rob's hand and swim ahead, more confident now.

Farug is suspended above the deck, pointing down. I see it: the ship's wheel, still intact, thick wooden spokes garlanded by seaweed. It's sad and amazing in equal measure, something so magnificent suspended here, colonized by new ecosystems. So many types of coral grow here, and I recognize some of the fish from the chart at the kayak hut. I see nudibranchs and pipefish nestled in its corners. Moray eels weave through the railings of the deck, lionfish and fusiliers bustling in the stern, a few large jellyfish suspended in the blue, their tentacles dangling down in delicate twists.

Farug signals again, and we follow him up to the boat's stern, where several reef sharks have appeared. He makes the OK sign, which means it's safe, though I'm quickly on guard. These sharks don't seem as shy as the ones I saw earlier, moving so close to me I can see a round eye sliding back and forth, cold and fearless.

Suddenly, I feel a jolt at my back, as though something has caught me. Bubbles begin to spiral upward next to me, and when I take a breath I realize I can't. I pull the breathing tube from my mouth and reinsert it, my lungs already aching, but it doesn't work. Something is wrong, and I can't see Rob. I start to flail, the bubbles making it too hard to see.

I can't tell which way is up or down. My weight belt has made it impossible to tell.

I feel something grab my arm, pulling me. A shark, I think, feeling the tug of it, and I try to yank my arm back.

But the grip is too strong. My lungs are burning, and I claw at my throat, desperate for air. I gulp back seawater and the fringes of my vision go blurry.

Everything goes dark.

44

CAMILLA

NOW

She's woken by a clamor.

At first, she thinks it's a bat. Those things make the most godawful racket. She'd never have guessed that bats are the loudest bloody creatures on the planet until she came to the Maldives, but they really are, particularly in the middle of the night.

She pulls a pillow over her head and tries to go back to sleep. A few moments later, there's shouting, several voices outside. She hears footsteps racing along the wooden causeway, and the sound she heard before grows louder. A man's voice, wailing.

Camilla sits upright, all her senses on high alert.

Something is really wrong.

She gets out of bed quickly, throwing on the linen dressing robe provided by the resort.

Outside, it's a cloudy day, a canopy of glaring white making her squint across the wooden causeway. She sees the Italian family, the one with the cute four-year-old, standing outside Jade's villa. They're all in their pajamas, staring at something behind the house.

"What's going on?" Camilla asks the woman.

"It is . . . a person in trouble," she says, in hesitant English. "In the water."

Camilla steps forward a little, trying to see behind the row of shrubs at the side of Jade's villa. Her stomach drops. What if something has happened to Jade? Perhaps she was wrong to doubt her.

But it's not Jade—it's Salvador, Antoni's nephew, farther up the causeway. He's wearing only his boxer shorts, his face red from crying. Two police officers are trying to coax him to come with them, but his hands are raking high in his hair and he's pacing, as though he doesn't know what to do with himself. He looks devastated.

Camilla finds herself running toward him. "Salvador!" she calls. "Salvador! Where is Antoni? Where is he?"

He's weeping and shouting in Spanish. A police officer tells her to step back—they need to bring Salvador to the main office.

"What happened?" she asks, but the officer shakes his head.

"His uncle has been found dead," a voice says behind her, and she spins around to face another guest, a woman with a Spanish accent. "They found him this morning in the sea, close to the sister resort." She nods at Emerald Island in the distance.

"Antoni's dead?" she says, the ground beneath her suddenly tilting.

"His nephew was shouting 'drowned,'" the woman says. "But—"

"Drowned?" she whispers, and the woman leans in.

"Well, they haven't confirmed it." She turns her eyes to two men standing at the edge of the causeway. "But they found the body, and one of them said his throat was cut."

Camilla stares at the woman, blood roaring in her ears, wondering if this isn't real, if she's just in the grip of a nightmare.

45

KATE

Kate:

You need to come over here. C is in bits. Antoni's been found dead.

Darcy:

Antoni?? The guy she slept with??

Kate opens the door a minute later to Darcy, who rushes in.

"The police are out there," Darcy says, breathless and wide-eyed.

Kate turns to Camilla, who is on the floor of the living room, knees drawn up to her chest, her face tucked between them.

"Oh God," Darcy says, pressing a hand to her mouth. She moves gently toward Camilla, sitting on the floor next to her, wrapping an arm around her shoulder. Camilla turns into her, pressing her head against Darcy's shoulder.

"They found his body this morning at the Emerald Island Resort," Kate says with a sigh. "His nephew is distraught."

"I should have made more of a fuss," Camilla says weakly, lifting her head. "I should have fucking *made* them go look for him."

Darcy looks to Kate for an explanation.

"She says she found blood on the deck beneath the dining area."

Darcy widens her eyes. "Blood?"

"I doubted myself," Camilla says bitterly. "It was the anniversary; I was all over the place. But I saw it. Right when Antoni went missing."

Kate feels the air in the room contract.

"How did he die?" Darcy asks. "Did he drown?"

"There's a rumour that his throat had been cut."

They share looks of horror.

"Where are Jade and Rob?" Darcy says. "I didn't see them in the crowd outside."

"They were on a scuba trip this morning. I doubt they're back yet."

KATE LEAVES CAMILLA AND DARCY in the villa while she goes to find out what she can. The crowd outside has dispersed. She walks to the restaurant, which has just opened for breakfast. Inside, the staff seem harried, some of the managers glancing around as they speak into walkie-talkies. The guests seem unsettled, too; word is spreading, and as she passes through the buffet room she hears snippets of conversation: *A body in the lagoon . . . drowned? . . . maybe, but . . .*

She pours herself a coffee and sits at a table with a view of the restaurant, close to the group of resort staff who are chatting quietly, their faces drawn. An Irish man at the table next to her makes a phone call.

"Hi, yeah . . . we'd like to arrange a transfer to another resort as soon as possible, please? Well, a body's just been pulled out of the lagoon, and someone said he'd been stabbed and frankly that makes snorkelling here a little less appealing. Yeah, I'll hold . . ."

Kate feels her body start to shake. There's a grim familiarity to all of this, to the knowledge that she spent the night sleeping in the same vicinity as a dead body. She fixes her eyes on the cup on the table, pressing her feet down into the sand, counting her breaths. The roses burn bright in her mind.

Outside, the sky is darkening, the glorious mornings of the previous week replaced with a stormy sky and restless sea. Quickly, the drips of rain that pock the sand turn into a deluge. Water slides off the roof in thick ropes, the windows blur and the sand path dissolves into puddles.

Just as Kate gets up to leave, the resort manager, Nura, steps forward into the center of the restaurant and claps her hands loudly, calling for attention.

"Everyone! Excuse me!" she calls. It's a few seconds until the tables fall quiet.

"As you all know, one of our guests has sadly met with a tragic event this morning. We've been told that the detectives are on their way and will be seeking to speak with guests from both the Sapphire Island Resort and the Emerald Island Resort. All excursions and seaplanes will be canceled, effective immediately, until this is finalized. If you are due to depart in the next forty-eight hours, please come and see me after breakfast in my office. Thank you."

The crowd erupts in anger and frustration. The Irish man seated next to Kate bangs the table with his fist, and she jumps. Nura is already besieged by guests demanding that they be allowed to catch their flights home, that she tell them what the hell is going on.

Kate turns her head to the window, her eyes searching for the horizon. She remembers running down the stairs of the guesthouse, the sight of the front door at the bottom. Safety.

She thinks again of Jade, of the way she approached Antoni that day in the restaurant. The way she appeared to glance back to check if Rob was watching.

46

JADE

NOW

I come to on the floor of the boat. My vision is blurred and I'm choking and gasping, rolled over on my side. Everyone is crowded around me, and Rob and Farug are kneeling over me, saying my name over and over.

Rob claps his hands to his face and I see tears of relief in his eyes. "Oh, thank God," he's saying. "Thank God!"

One of the other guests is standing behind him, a hand on his shoulder in support. My throat burns, and there's an awful chemical taste in my mouth. Everyone is clapping and cheering. Farug shines a torch into my eyes, then presses two fingers against my neck to check my pulse.

"Are you OK?" he says.

I attempt a nod, but I feel like I've been hit by a truck. Everything comes back to me in a rush—the majestic shipwreck under the water, the sharks, struggling to breathe.

Rob leans over me again, weeping openly now. "Jade, darling," he says, touching my face. "Oh my God. I thought I'd lost you."

One of the crew brings me a bottle of water, and Rob helps me sit up. I notice they've removed the oxygen tank and equipment, and someone has cut off the dry suit—it's lying in bits around me.

"It's shock," Farug says. "Can we get a blanket for her?"

I know it must be ninety degrees, given that the sun is still blazing, but I'm suddenly freezing cold. I can't stop shaking. The crew find an emergency blanket and wrap it around me, and Rob sits on the floor beside me and holds me tight. He presses his forehead against mine.

"Deep breaths," he murmurs. "Nice and slow."

He sounds just like the old Rob. I think of the first night we made love. He'd taken me to an amazing hotel in London. I fell in love with him that night.

"God, Jade," he whispers as the boat heads back to the resort. "I don't know what I'd do if I lost you."

He kisses my cheek. I'm breathing easier now. The other guests are opening bottles of beer, talking about the shipwreck. I feel bad for ruining the trip for everyone. It was meant to be several hours long, but we were only down there for about twenty minutes.

"You know I adore you," Rob whispers in my ear.

I soften. Maybe it is possible that he never killed anyone. Maybe Kate and the others made a mistake, maybe their detective had the wrong guy. Rob is *not* an evil person. The wedding put a lot of pressure on him. He has a lot to prove to his nana, and his brother. That's why we had the big wedding. But I know he loves me.

"I know you do," I whisper back. "I adore you too."

The boat speeds up, the wind in our faces. I feel the warmth returning, my lungs no longer burning.

"Do you, though?" Rob says, kissing my face.

I stiffen. "I do," I say. "You know I do."

His tone sharpens. "You've been spending a lot of time with other people during our honeymoon. During our fucking *honeymoon*, Jade. Did our wedding slip out of that pretty little head? I think you forgot, silly girl. And you needed a reminder. That you're *my wife*."

He laughs lightly and strokes my hair. I look around, desperate for escape. His arm around me tightens, as though he senses me wanting to bolt.

"Today was just a little mishap," he whispers gently into my ear. "Your tubes got disconnected from the oxygen tank. But I pulled you back up. I saved you, babe. I saved you because I love you. And you're my wife now. Just remember that, OK?"

My heart plummets into my stomach. I want to be sick. I feel dizzy.

And slowly, it dawns on me what he's actually saying—he pulled out the tubes that connected to my oxygen tank. It wasn't my lack of experience at all. Rob did it deliberately, to teach me a lesson.

That he can take away my life if I step out of line.

47

DARCY

NOW

Darcy and Kate are taking turns walking around the island to find out what's happening. Camilla is particularly worried about Salvador, and earlier Darcy spent fifteen minutes typing a lengthy message into Google Translate so she could communicate with Salvador once she found him: making an offer of help, should he need it, if only to call his parents or to arrange a flight home. "He's only eighteen," Camilla told her through tears. "He'll be beside himself, having to deal with this on his own."

There may be legal implications for Salvador, too, police to deal with. . . . Poor boy. A terrible end to a magical holiday.

Darcy heads to the restaurant, then to the main office. She hears Salvador before she sees him, sobbing in front of the resort manager's desk.

Nura glances up at Darcy.

"Hello, can I help you?"

"I'm Darcy," she says, smiling. "Look, my friends and I had spoken with Antoni before . . ." She trails off, and Nura rises from her desk to follow her outside, where they can talk out of earshot.

"We're worried about Salvador," Darcy says, glancing back inside. "I just wanted to see if there was anything we can do."

"His parents are on their way," Nura says. "We're in touch with the Spanish embassy."

"Can I pass a message to him?" Darcy asks, and Nura nods. Darcy hands her her phone with the Google translation.

"You can show it to him," Nura says, and she follows her into the office.

Inside, Darcy crouches down next to Salvador and shows him the translated message. He looks over it, his face red from crying, then raises his eyes to hers. "Thank you," he says.

She heads back outside, fresh drips of rain hitting her skin. The weather matches the atmosphere of the resort, she thinks. The whole place is in turmoil. A few guests file along the causeway with suitcases, apparently prepared to argue their way onto a seaplane. The rest of them seem to have crammed into the bar, brought together by drama and fear. Some are already drunk, shouting about their rights.

She approaches a table of four women drinking iced coffees, English accents drifting through the air.

"Hi," she says with a smile. "I don't suppose you've heard anything about all of this?"

The woman with a long blond plait leans forward, her voice low. "I heard someone say that the guy who drowned was kayaking over to Emerald Island every day. Apparently, he was buying weed, then smoking it over here. The Maldives have super-strict drug laws."

"God," Darcy says, shaking her head in dismay.

The woman shrugs. "No idea if there's any truth in it. The police are already here, apparently, though there's another team bringing sniffer dogs."

The woman next to her raises a hand to her mouth, whispering, "Our butler wondered if his drug dealer on Emerald Island killed him."

Darcy squirms, unsettled. Her mind turns to Rob, to how he'll respond when they approach him . . . A ripple of fear passes through her. It's risky. But time is running out.

She decides to pick up a few snacks to take back to the villa. Important to eat, now, to keep up her strength. Camilla hasn't eaten, refuses to drink anything. Darcy takes a few bread rolls, some skewers of grilled fish.

As she makes her way back to Kate's villa, she sees a boat pulling into the harbor. It's having a tough time, given how rough the seas are; a guest is hanging over the side, vomiting. She's about to turn away on to the sand path when she sees Jade, wrapped in a towel, Rob at her side. Jade looks up, catching sight of her.

Darcy stands behind a palm tree, waiting for them to disembark. It takes a while for the guests to file off, and when she sees Jade and Rob she follows after them, keeping her head down. Rob has his arm tightly around Jade and is walking with her as though she's about to fall apart.

"Excuse me?"

She turns to see a staff member behind her, one of the crew from the boat that has just docked. His name badge reads FARUG, and he's wearing a towel around his waist and a dry T-shirt.

"You are Darcy, yes?"

She nods, confused. "Yes?"

He hands her what looks like a piece of rubbish, his eyes moving to the line of people behind them. It's the wrapper of a Fanta bottle, folded into a small square. She unfolds it and finds something scribbled inside.

R tried to kill me

She stares at it for a moment, then calls after Farug, who has started to head off.

"Hello? Excuse me?"

He turns.

"Yes?"

"Who gave you this note?" she asks.

"A lady named Jade," he says.

"Did something happen?" she asks. "They were on a scuba trip, isn't that right?"

"She had a bit of a scare," he says. "The tube on the oxygen tank came loose while she was thirty feet down. She's fine now."

"Thanks," Darcy says, watching Jade disappear with Rob toward their villa.

"WE HAVE A PROBLEM," DARCY tells Camilla and Kate when she returns to Kate's villa. She hands Kate the piece of paper.

"What is this?" Kate asks, unfolding it.

"One of the staff passed it to me," she says. "It's from Jade. There was an incident on the scuba trip. Apparently, her oxygen tank developed a 'fault' while she was thirty feet underwater." She uses finger quotes for *fault*.

Camilla and Kate share a horrified look. "Do you think he found out about the plan for tonight?" Kate asks.

"I think he's a killer, is what I think." Darcy feels electrified by this news, her whole body charged with adrenaline.

"First Antoni, now this," Camilla says, pressing a hand to her mouth.

"Antoni was found on Emerald Island," Kate says.

"The tide could have pulled him out there," Camilla says. "But Rob did it. I'll bet you anything. He hated Antoni."

"What do we do then?" Darcy says.

She glances at Kate, who lowers her eyes, then turns to Camilla.

"I say we kill him," Camilla says. "He's clearly dangerous. And he deserves it."

"You can't say someone deserves to be killed," Kate mutters.

"Yes, I can," Camilla snaps back, eyes blazing. "I fucking can, all right? And I can say someone didn't deserve to be killed, like Antoni. And my brother. And Elijah. And everyone else who was slaughtered that night—"

"All right!" Kate says, raising her voice. "Let me rephrase that: it is dangerous to say that someone deserves to be killed. It is dangerous because you are making a moral judgment that can result in death, even if it's hypothetical."

Camilla leans into Kate's face. "I can say whatever the fuck I like—"

Darcy steps between them. "Ladies! Cut it out! This is getting us nowhere!" She eyes them in turn, her hands held up to separate them. "We're all dealing with this, OK? It is stressful and emotional and once the job is done we can all take our stances on moral judgments to our separate corners, but right now, we need to be a *team*."

Kate takes a deep breath and steps back. Darcy can see she's trembling, mentally exhausted. Camilla is rigid, poised for a fight, her hands held by her sides in tight fists. As a group, they're at breaking point.

"If we are not careful," Darcy says quietly, "Rob will escape, slip away out of sight again. We might not be able to find him. And everything we've hoped for will vanish."

"And more people will die," Camilla adds, her face in a scowl. "We are *lucky* that Jade didn't die today. And if we'd acted sooner, instead of pissing about discussing it, Antoni would probably be alive too." She glares at Kate. "We all of us have to live with that now. We could have prevented Antoni's death."

"We have no proof that Rob killed Antoni," Kate says. "We don't even know for sure if he was murdered."

Camilla scoffs angrily. "*Rob* killed him. And he's going to kill Jade, and us, and God knows who else if we don't stop him."

"We have a right to at least ask Rob about Antoni, see how he reacts," Darcy says, trying to straighten out the facts. "Agreed? We all saw how Rob attacked him, twice, and now Antoni is dead."

Camilla wells up. "Yes. We owe that to Antoni."

Darcy thinks quickly. "And perhaps, if we don't waste any more time, we might prevent Rob from killing anyone else. But we definitely need Jade's help. We'll need to make sure she's still up for it."

"She's probably too scared," Camilla says. "God knows I would be if my husband tried to kill me on my honeymoon."

"I don't have Jade's number," Darcy says. "Can I use your phone, Kate?"

"Sure."

Darcy takes Kate's phone, her thumb hovering over the letters on the screen as she plans a message in her mind.

"What are you doing?" Camilla asks.

Darcy begins to type.

Hello! Hope you enjoyed scuba diving! Gym tonight? Xx

She clicks on Jade's name, then sends the message. Camilla and Kate gather close to her, watching for a response.

"He might have taken her phone off her," Camilla says.

Darcy frowns. "We could slip a note under her door?"

"They'll have a butler," Kate says. "Safer to pass a note through him."

The phone makes a small *ding*.

Scuba was great! Yes to gym, be good to catch up. 8pm? xx

The three of them exhale at the same time. Darcy glances at Camilla, then Kate, who flicks her eyes up, cautiously.

"She's in."

48

KATE

NOW

She sits on a sun lounger by the edge of the sea, the bar to her right and the outdoor pool behind her. The weather has turned again, the evening sun shining brightly despite bruise-black clouds gathering on the horizon. Thunder and lightning are forecast for tonight.

Police are chatting with the resort staff outside the restaurant, and in the distance more police boats are arriving at Emerald Island. The resort is divided now into guests who are clearly trying to tune out the police presence and make the most of their stay, and the guests who are pissed at having their expensive, once-in-a-lifetime holiday interrupted by a corpse. Usually, the outdoor pool is occupied by half a dozen guests, but now it is as bustling as a Roman bath. The bar is heaving, too, the quiet of the last week replaced now with laughter and partying. Kate watches the scene mildly, aware of the strange effects that mortality can create in otherwise dull individuals. Experiencing a death, especially a traumatic death, can prompt a sudden rashness.

Often, the experience is not easy to see. Right now, she's afraid for her life.

The uneasiness she felt about confronting Rob Marlowe is quietly modulating into recognition that she may not leave this place alive. She's worried for her cats, and her garden, but after the list of things that may or may not be attended to in the event of her death is a question: has it all been worth it? She is almost half a century old; not quite old enough to write off a dramatic life change, an overhaul. What would she change, if she gets the chance to survive all of this?

She would like to have someone in her life again, she thinks. To come home at night to another human being, give them a kiss, share a meal. And a bed. To wake up in the middle of the night not to the sound of a cat purring, but to a person. To hear the words *I love you*, to feel them rest inside her.

She watches two police officers walk along the beach, both in distinctive blue uniforms, the gold-edged crests of their authority beaming at their breasts. Two women have also been moving through the crowd in the bar, chatting with the guests informally—plainclothes detectives, Kate thinks, pleased that they're women.

One of them approaches her. She's about thirty-five, her black hair pulled back into a neat bun, a white shirt and black trousers. A wedding ring. She smiles at Kate.

"Hello," she says. "I'm Detective Sergeant Rasheed. I'd like to chat with you for a moment, if that's OK?"

Kate takes off her sunglasses and fixes her kimono across her cleavage, quickly conscious of how she looks. "Of course. Pull up a chair."

Detective Sergeant Rasheed moves a sun lounger a little closer and sits on the edge.

"Better weather now, no?" she says, raising a hand to block out the sun from her eyes.

"It definitely is," Kate says. "Though I quite liked the rain. It was refreshing."

"Have you been on the island long?"

"Since Thursday," Kate says, and Detective Sergeant Rasheed pulls out a notebook and writes this down.

"And your name?"

"Kate Miller," she says. "I'm English, though I live in Wales."

"In the UK," Detective Sergeant Rasheed says. "You'll know that one of the guests sadly passed away recently. Antoni Caballé. You knew him?"

Kate frowns. "I chatted with him the first day after I arrived. He seemed to be a nice man."

"Can I ask what you talked about?"

"I believe we talked about the reason he was here. To celebrate with his nephew, Salvador, who was planning to go to university. He said he was a widower. He also mentioned that he liked to kayak out to Emerald Island. He told me I should rent a glass-bottomed kayak as the water was so clear."

Detective Sergeant Rasheed takes an interest in that, nodding and writing it down. "Do you think he might have kayaked across?"

"I'm afraid I have no idea."

"Did he mention anyone here on the island?" she says. "Any people he was planning to see?"

Kate feels a tightness in her chest. She doesn't want to mention Camilla. And the truth is, Antoni didn't mention that. But sooner or later, the police will discover that he slept with Camilla the night before he died. That she was one of the last people to see him alive.

"No, he didn't," she says. "I had a panic attack on the boat, so our conversation was mostly about how I was feeling after that."

"I'm sorry you had a panic attack. Do you know what caused it?"

More tightness in her chest. "No," she says, smiling. "Just one of those things."

The detective nods, writing this down. Kate opens her mouth, seized by an urge to spill all her suspicions about Rob to the detective. The words almost tumble from her lips, unbidden. *We think Rob might also have killed six people twenty-two years ago*. But an inner voice says that the detective won't believe her, that her admission will be taken for something else—a signal that she is implicated, somehow, and so she stops.

"Was he murdered?" she asks. "Antoni?"

"I'm afraid I'm not able to share such information," the detective says. Camilla's words ring in Kate's ears. *The police will do nothing*.

"We may decide to interview you again," Detective Sergeant Rasheed says. "Which villa are you staying in?"

"Villa two," Kate says. "I'm glad to help."

Detective Sergeant Rasheed smiles, rising to her feet. Kate watches as she heads back to the bar. What happens, she thinks, if they decide Camilla's a suspect?

As she watches Detective Sergeant Rasheed approach another group of guests, she sees Rob, with his familiar swagger, heading to the bar. Not a care in the world. *He will care*, she thinks, eyeing him coolly. *He will care tonight.*

WHEN SHE RETURNS TO HER villa, the door is open.

Kate steps inside, glancing around, jumping a little when someone appears in the kitchen.

"Good day," Rafi says. "I'm just replenishing your minibar. I hope I didn't frighten you."

"It's fine," Kate tells him, slipping off her sandals. "I spoke to Detective Sergeant Rasheed just now," she adds. "I suppose they're interviewing the staff, as well as the guests."

He nods. "Yes. Even the staff who are not here. So far, it seems nobody saw anything suspicious. Maybe he slipped and banged his head."

"Maybe," she says, catching sight of something in the living room—the bouquet of roses she dumped in the waste bin has reappeared, arranged in a tall white vase. She stiffens.

"Rafi?" she calls. "I don't mean to be a pain, but could I ask you to take these roses away?"

He steps out of the kitchen and glances at the arrangement. "Ah, apologies. I thought you would want them on display. I will remove them, this is no problem."

He crosses the living room and lifts the vase with gloved hands. "You are allergic?" he asks.

Kate nods. It's much simpler than giving him the full backstory.

"I don't know why she didn't give them to you herself," Rafi says as he heads into the kitchen. "Sending them all the way from Malé! Must have been very expensive."

Kate stares after him. "Who sent them from Malé, Rafi?"

"Malé?" Rafi says, brightening. "I believe there was a problem with the florist on Malé. They closed down very suddenly, but we did not want to disappoint our guests."

She narrows her eyes, trying to follow. "So . . . you provided the roses?"

"My brother-in-law was happy to assist. But we had to retake payment from the customer and extend apologies from the other florist. And roses, of course, are difficult to keep fresh in this climate. It took a while to fetch them for you. But we managed in the end. I was pleased to deliver your beautiful roses personally."

"Thank you," she says. "But I mean, who paid for them? Originally? Did the florist pass on that information?"

Her meaning dawns on him. "Oh, I see. Yes, the payment had to be diverted to the resort, so we contacted the bank to check the details. I believe it was your friend from villa six. Miss Darcy."

49

CHARLIE

THREE MONTHS AGO

"Come on, Charlie!" he heard his mum call. "Time to go."

He had packed all his clothes, his underwear, his spare shoes, but he couldn't find his anxiety teddy, Sherlock. He was panicking—if he asked his mum she'd probably tell him not to bring Sherlock, he didn't need him. He got down on his hands and knees and looked again under his bed. There was Sherlock, a ball of black fuzz behind the wooden bedpost.

And then he was waving goodbye to Marsha, sitting in the front seat of his mum's car as they headed off to the hotel in Manchester. A whole weekend away to help him prepare for his role in the school production of *The BFG*. It was a big deal, since he was playing the titular character, the giant. He wouldn't be onstage but would be voicing the giant behind the scenes through a voice-altering microphone designed to make him sound grumbly and giant-like. His drama teacher, Ms. Ellis, had assured him that this was still acting. In fact, she'd told him it could be even harder than acting on the stage because he had to perform his character entirely through his voice, while a big puppet got jerked about to look like the BFG.

They went to see *Frozen: The Musical* at the Opera House, then *The Lion King* at the Lowry, then *Wicked*, which was kind of scary. After each show they got food and talked about the performance, and then they came back to the hotel when it was dark and went to bed. His mum fell asleep quickly, but Charlie lay there, frustrated.

The next day of his weekend trip with Mum was Sunday, and they went to see *Life of Pi*, which he didn't really understand, and then they went to a fancy place to eat when he just wanted McDonald's. He was tired and sick of sitting in dark theaters now.

The waiter at the fancy restaurant came to take their order.

"I'll have the salmon," his mum said. "Charlie, what do you fancy?"

He kept his eyes on the table. "McDonald's."

"We serve burgers," the waiter said. "Plain, or we can add cheese?"

Charlie shook his head. "I want McDonald's."

"You can't have McDonald's," his mum said testily. She glanced up at the waiter. "He'll have a plain burger."

"I bet Oscar's mum would have taken him to McDonald's," Charlie said, loud enough for the waiter to hear. He saw his mum's face redden. *Good*, he thought.

They didn't speak for the rest of the meal.

He walked back to the hotel in silence, feeling a little remorseful about how he had embarrassed his mother. In the room, his mum passed him his swimming kit. "Come on," she said. "Let's go to the pool."

Charlie was a poor swimmer, but he felt bad after being so disrespectful in the restaurant. They went down to the large pool in the basement of the hotel, the water warm and smooth. No one else around.

His mum stepped into the water, and he plucked up a pool noodle to help him float.

"Come on, Charlie," she called, swimming to the deep end. "Let's practise your swimming."

He took the pool noodle with him, eager to please her, and although he didn't want to tell her he was sorry, he wanted to make her proud. In the pool he felt the bottom slip away from his toes, too far for him to stand, the pool noodle helping him stay afloat.

It happened so quickly. His mother had a look in her eye that he had seen only a few times before, a look that made him uneasy. And then, with a quick tug, the pool noodle was gone, and a sudden panic flooded through him as he realized he was sinking. He arched his neck, trying desperately to breathe. From the corner of his eye he could see his mother treading water a few feet away, smiling at him.

Why wasn't she helping?

It seemed to last hours, the sinking. He felt himself slip beneath the surface, his lungs burning. Everything was dark, his vision strangely clouded by fear, his arms thrashing.

Just as he was beginning to pass out, he felt a hand in his, and with a sharp tug he was out of the pool, his head banging against the tiles.

"Charlie!" his mum exclaimed. "Charlie, are you all right?"

He vomited water, and he saw several other guests were rushing through the doors toward him.

"Is he OK?" someone asked, and he heard his mum say he'd attempted a handstand underwater and it had gone wrong.

She had lied.

50

JACOB

NOW

The doorbell rings. Before answering, he glances at his reflection in the hall mirror, fixing his silvered hair, then checking his shirt. An old habit. There are no lipstick marks this time. Even so, he's nervous, and with good reason—Dembe is coming to meet his children. She's also here to help with the software issue, which remains very much an issue. But he finds his main source of nerves is his sons. Charlie, mostly, given how obstinate he's been of late.

Though what Charlie told him today about Darcy, about the kind of mother she has been to their sons behind Jacob's back . . . He feels like he's woken up in a maze, drunk and with a head injury. Nothing makes sense anymore. Charlie is twelve, and clearly the divorce has messed him up. Jacob is struggling to work out what's true and what is lies.

"Good evening, handsome," Dembe says at the door, kissing him on both cheeks before pecking him lightly on the lips. She's still in work clothes, looks delicious in a white silk shirt and beige slacks, thick gold hoop earrings and sheepskin mules. She notices how nervous he looks and touches his face.

"It's dinner, not a trial," she says.

"I know." He tries to look unbothered, sweat gathering between his shoulder blades.

Dembe gives him the same smile that reeled him in at the Tech Entrepreneurs summer party in June and he takes her hand. "Come on in."

Upstairs, Ben and Ed are fighting, their voices spilling down the stairway.

"Boys!" he calls. "Come down, please!"

Dembe's eyes fall on the row of framed photographs on the hall table. "That your ex-wife?" she asks, clocking the photo of the five of them in Disney World, posing in front of the pink castle. Shit, he forgot about that one. He let the boys have a hand in decorating, especially when it came to photos.

"Sorry," he says, placing it face down.

"No, I want to see," she says, lifting it up and inspecting it while Jacob squirms. "Oh, she's pretty. Different than I expected."

"What did you expect?" he asks, not knowing what else to say.

Dembe squints at it. "I feel like I recognize her."

"Boys!" he calls. "Our guest has arrived!"

Ben and Ed thunder down the stairs and race into the room. "Hello, Our Guest," Ben says, appraising Dembe.

"This is Dembe," Jacob says. "Dembe, this is—"

"But you said Our Guest has arrived," Ed interjects saucily.

"Oh, I prefer Dembe," Dembe says with a wink. "Which one are you, then? Ben or Ed?"

"Ben," Ben says, at the same time that Ed announces his own.

"This is Charlie," Jacob says, nodding at the sullen figure lurking behind his brothers.

"Hello, Charlie," Dembe says, leaning forward and extending a hand. Charlie takes it, blushing, and mumbles a "Hello."

"Charlie's twelve," Jacob says, explaining his embarrassment.

"You've mentioned," Dembe says with a bright smile. She notices something on Charlie's T-shirt. "Is that a *FNaF* badge?"

"A what badge?" Jacob asks.

"It is." Charlie beams.

Dembe grins at Jacob. "Jasmine's into *FNaF*, too, so I recognized it."

"What's *FNaF*?" Jacob says.

"I've got all the books," Charlie says, opening up, to Jacob's amazement. "Does Jasmine like Freddy Fazbear? He's my favorite."

"I *think* so . . ." Dembe says with a smile.

"We can continue this over dinner," Jacob says, glancing at Dembe.

"Dembe needs to help me with an urgent work matter and then we'll order takeout. OK?"

"Pizza?" Ed asks.

"Indian?" Ben pitches.

"Pizza and Indian," Jacob says. "Only if you're quiet."

IN THE STUDY, DEMBE SITS at his desk while he turns on the computer.

"I owe you," he tells her.

"No, you don't," she says. "I haven't found anything yet."

She clicks through to the review log of the Shelley program, and he explains all over again how his assistant, Sam, was able to find three usernames of people who had accessed the program. He emailed two of them, but a third, a man named Adrian Clifton, remains outstanding. He doesn't want word of this to get to Kabir, but the investment meeting is in two days' time and he still can't find the hole.

"I think Darcy has hired this guy," he says. "I think she's trying to fuck me over."

Dembe glances at him. "Why?"

He grimaces. "She's like that."

"So you reckon she hired a tech specialist to hack into it, but you've managed to get the email addresses of her mates?" Dembe gives him a look. "Not a very good specialist, then."

He runs a hand through his hair, exhausted from trying to work it out. "Can you find anything?"

"Not yet." She clicks out of the review log and enters the program with a sigh. "I'm not really the one you should be asking. Kabir would be able to find it."

"I'd prefer not to freak him out just yet," he says. "Let's give it a go ourselves. And if we can't find anything, I'll ring him. OK?"

She nods. Then, spotting an old family photograph on the bookcase opposite, she looks at him, puzzled.

"What?" he says.

She rises from her chair and crosses the room to the photograph. *Shit*, he thinks. Another one with Darcy in it. Dembe pulls out her phone and taps on the photograph app. "Jasmine's birthday party," she says.

He blinks, not following. "What about it?"

Dembe begins swiping through images of her daughter's eighteenth birthday party on the HMS *Belfast*.

He's exasperated. "We're running out of time—"

Dembe shushes him, continuing to scroll through. "I have this weird thing for faces," she says. "And I *swear* I saw her. . . ."

"Saw who?"

She stops and holds up her phone. "There," she says, triumphant.

He starts to complain, seeing only Jasmine and her friends smiling at a dinner table. But then, behind Jasmine, he sees her, lit up by the flash. It's Darcy. He zooms in until the image is pixelated. Either it's a doppelgänger or it's his ex-wife.

"I saw her," Dembe says. "I remember wondering what she was doing at the party. It was invite-only."

"How did she get in, then?"

Dembe shrugs. "I've no idea. I thought she was a teacher."

Jacob stares again, noticing the necklace at Darcy's throat. It's the one he bought her years ago. And the dress—he recognizes it, too. It's *her*.

"Fucking creepy," Dembe says. "Is your ex-wife stalking me?"

"I haven't even told her about you," he says quietly. He's trying to work it out, the gap between what he sees and what he knows. Her presence at Jasmine's party can't be an accident. He recalls the date of it, two weeks ago. . . . Darcy had asked him to have the boys a day early. He can't make any sense of it.

Just then, there's a noise from the doorway. He turns, spotting Charlie there.

"Are you talking about Mum?" he says.

"For fuck's sake," Jacob says. He catches the pained look on Charlie's face, his words hanging in the air like knives, the disgust in Dembe's expression.

Charlie turns on his heel and storms out of the room. A beat. Jacob glances at Dembe before striding after him. On the stairs, he grips Charlie's shoulders.

"I'm sorry," he says, suddenly mortified by his own behavior, his own callousness. "I didn't mean . . . I should haven't said that. OK?"

Charlie stares, his blue eyes wide, questioning. "Did Mum do something bad?"

Jacob falters. "What?" He studies Charlie's face. It's been a long while since he was this close to his oldest boy, but now he can see the slight twitch at the corner of Charlie's mouth, a repetitive tug. A tic. When did it start? He can't think.

He lets go of Charlie's shoulders and sits down with him on the stairs. His impulse is to barrage him with questions, but instead he sits quietly, an arm around his son's shoulders. He forces himself to listen. Not to question, just *listen*.

After a couple of minutes, Charlie says, "There's something else I need to tell you. About Mum."

Jacob nods, tries to stay calm. "OK."

"Our shed, back at Mum's," Charlie says. "I found something there."

"What did you find?" he asks gently. He feels sick as he turns to his son and watches as Charlie's eyes seem to roll slightly back in his head as he closes them tight shut, scrunching up his face. He waits, panicked, until Charlie opens his mouth and whispers:

"You're not going to like it."

51

CAMILLA

NOW

Camilla walks, harried, to Kate's villa. Her nerves are shot. She's probably having a full-blown nervous breakdown, her thoughts flinging in every direction.

She spoke to Detective Sergeant Rasheed earlier. She told her about the spat between Rob and Antoni during her Pilates class, detailing the way Rob crashed the class halfway through and made a point of harassing Antoni. And she told her about sleeping with Antoni the night before he went missing. All of that was true. But she embellished a little. She said that Antoni had told her he'd be leaving early to go kayaking. He said he enjoyed kayaking to Emerald Island and that he'd be heading off at dawn.

She probably shouldn't have lied. No, not probably—*definitely*. It was a moment of panic. She worried that the police might consider her a suspect, given that she was the last person to see him alive. What if the police find out she was lying, and decide that it implicates her in Antoni's death? She has no idea how the Maldivian justice system works, or what kind of penalties they impose for these things, but given that it's illegal to drink in public she's fairly sure murder is considered a pretty serious offense.

Fuck.

The only thing standing between her and being detained is the question about the time of Antoni's death. That will take a while to determine.

She takes a deep breath before entering Kate's villa. She could do without this, whatever it is Kate wants her for. Probably another bloody argument about her poor morals.

"I'm here," she calls from the hallway. "What do you want?"

Kate appears from the kitchen, carrying a pot of tea as bloody usual. Camilla hates tea but Kate doesn't seem to believe her. "Come and sit down," Kate says. Then, glancing behind her: "And lock the door."

Camilla is as curious as she is flustered. She watches for a moment as Kate pours two cups of tea.

"Where's Darcy?" Kate asks.

"She went swimming. What's going on?" Camilla says, watching as Kate sits down in the armchair opposite.

"Something's been bothering me," Kate says after a moment of contemplation.

"Oh, *same*," Camilla says sarcastically. "I have to say I've been feeling a bit *bothered* today myself."

Kate is silent, staring into the distance.

"Go on," Camilla says testily. "What's this all about?"

"Darcy sent me the roses."

Camilla widens her eyes. "Fuck off," Camilla says. "No, she didn't."

Kate sips her tea. "My butler said that Darcy sent them."

Camilla stares. "Does he have proof?"

"Why would he say she sent them if she didn't?"

Camilla looks away, visibly trying to reconcile this with the Darcy she knows. "It's probably some sort of computer error," she says. "Or he got mixed up. There's no way the butler can be sure."

"What if she did send them?" Kate says quietly. "Who else knew I was here?"

"You said you'd been getting them for twenty years," Camilla says, an icy feeling creeping over her shoulders. "You're saying . . . what, that Darcy resented you surviving when Elijah didn't?"

"Possibly," Kate says. "I phoned Jacob."

Camilla laughs. "Are you fucking kidding me?"

"Why not?" Kate says, her gaze firm. "Have you ever actually spoken to Jacob?"

"No," Camilla says, incredulous.

"We've heard plenty about him from Darcy," Kate continues. "And I thought, if he's going to drag me into this, if he's going to stoop so low as to contact me while I'm on a bloody holiday in the Maldives, I'm going to have words. So I did."

Camilla is baffled, but she can see that Kate is upset; her cheeks are flushed and that spot on her chest, the one that flares up when she talks about the massacre, is red raw today.

"And what did he say?"

"He asked if I recognized a mobile number."

"What mobile number?"

Kate sighs. "He said that his son, Charlie, had found a secret phone belonging to Darcy. He took photos of the calls made on his own phone. Jacob went through the list of numbers on the handset and called a few of them."

"And who were they?" Camilla asks, as patiently as she can. "Members of the PTA? Potential babysitters?"

"He said most were plumbers," Kate says. "One of them was a nail salon, another was a brothel."

She eyes Camilla, who raises her eyebrows. "A brothel?" She's heard it all now. Darcy working as a prostitute on the side. Ha! "Is he saying Darcy's a sex worker?"

"I'm just telling you what he said, Camilla."

"Oh come *on*. Darcy told us that the number Jacob gave you was for a phone she used to speak to Adrian."

"So why was she calling sex workers from that phone?" Kate says, and Camilla rolls her eyes.

"I don't know. A wrong number?"

Kate rubs her face, seeming to struggle now with her own doubts. "Jacob said the reason he emailed you and me in the first place was because he discovered that someone was using his software."

Camilla thinks back to his message to her. "He thought *I* was using his software. He emailed me about it and I told him to fuck off."

Kate lifts an eyebrow. "Look, why don't we call Jacob together?" she says finally. "Maybe he can shed some light on the matter."

Camilla begins to stand, tired of this. "No," she says. "I'm not calling Darcy's ex while we're here celebrating her divorce!"

"Camilla, the roses were from Darcy," Kate says gently. "And if she sent them to me here, she's been sending them to me for *twenty-two years*. Doesn't that change things? Just a bit?"

Camilla hesitates. She doesn't have an answer for that.

She pulls out her phone with another sigh. "Fine. Let's call bloody Jacob."

52

JACOB

NOW

Jacob asks Dembe for another favor—to stay at his house with his children as he drives to Darcy's. It's a lot to ask, but it's only a mile away, and Dembe knows this is important.

He pulls up at the gates and enters the code, then heads up the driveway to the front of the house. For a moment, he wonders if he should check Darcy's computer in case she has Shelley downloaded on it. He was still living here when the program was developed, which is how she knows about it.

He heads straight to the old shed at the back of the garden, a space he hasn't frequented for as long as he can remember. He never had time or interest in gardening, and so the space is unfamiliar to him.

He is surprised to find the old door locked, but the key is where Charlie said it would be—under the birdhouse at the right-hand side.

The shed is about eight feet by ten, a rotting structure inherited from the previous owner that they never got around to replacing. He finds cobwebbed gardening tools, and a galvanized potting bench with empty plant pots and—bizarrely—a jar of toothbrushes on the shelves. He stands for a moment, feeling foolish. Most of the equipment looks like it hasn't left the shed in years, including an old, folded-up paddling pool that he vaguely recalls blowing up one summer for the boys. It is mossy with age, like most of the objects in here.

Casting a glance over the room, his eyes settle on a metal locker in the far corner. It looks new, and he wonders when it arrived here. He tries to imagine Darcy installing it, and for what purpose. There's more than enough storage space in the double garage—why carry such a heavy object out to the far corner of the garden?

It's locked; he feels around for a key, giving up with a loud curse when he touches a large spider and sends it galloping across the floor. He pries the metal doors open about an inch, then pulls again, feeling the metal give. Darcy will know he's been in here now, and he won't have a rational explanation. She'll probably set her lawyers on him. But fuck it. He lifts one of the old shovels and brings it crashing down on the lock, flinging the doors open.

A noise escapes his mouth, somewhere between a gasp and a groan. An icy shiver crawls up his arms, coming to rest in his stomach. Were it not for what Charlie told him, he wouldn't believe what he is seeing. He wouldn't believe it has anything to do with his ex-wife.

Inside the locker, settled in rows as neatly as priceless jewelry, are dozens of tiny skulls: those of birds, rodents, a small fox. He reaches inside, feeling nauseous, to lift a black scarf, and there he finds more: rib cages, femurs, wishbones, all cleaned and arranged with the precision of an archaeology display. The glass jar of small toothbrushes on the potting bench suddenly makes sense, as does a stainless-steel scalpel he finds glinting on the bottom shelf of the locker. And the smell he dismissed as wood rot . . .

A ringing sound makes him jump, catching his hand in the metal doors. He staggers backward, falling heavily to the floor.

His phone vibrates in his shirt pocket.

53

KATE

NOW

Kate feels sick with nerves as she waits for Jacob to pick up. Camilla stares at her, both of them wary. The call connects.

"Hello?"

The voice on the end of the line sounds weak and breathy. She wonders if she's misdialed.

"Is this Jacob?" she asks tentatively.

"Who is this?"

She puts him on speakerphone. "It's Kate Miller. And Camilla is here, too. Have I called at a bad time?"

"No." She listens as he coughs, his voice distant. "No, I can talk."

"OK. Look, Jacob, Camilla and I both have some questions about the emails you sent.

Particularly what you said about Darcy possibly hiring Adrian. Can you clarify?"

"Right," Jacob says. "Look, this is all a bit complicated, so I appreciate I might have come across as a bit of an arsehole—"

"You can say that again," Camilla snaps.

"There have been a few developments, shall we say, since last week. I found both your names on my software report, so my first thought was that you had both hacked into this new software package."

"Hack into software?" Camilla says. "I can barely cut and paste."

"Look, I'm a bit . . . out of sorts at the moment," he says. She can hear the sound of a door closing in the background. "Has Darcy mentioned anything about hiring Adrian to hack into my software program?"

"What software program, exactly?" Camilla says.

"It's called Shelley. It's an AI program." He pauses. "Artificial intelligence."

Camilla screws her face up. "I know what AI is," she says.

"Adrian is a private detective," Kate says. "Darcy did hire him, but it was nothing to do with software."

"Why would Darcy hire a private detective?"

"To investigate the Spinnaker killings," Camilla says. "You know, Elijah? Who was murdered?"

"What?"

Camilla rolls her eyes. Kate knows what she's thinking—Jacob is leading them up the garden path, trying to blame Darcy because she's here, in the Maldives, celebrating their divorce.

"How well do you know Darcy?" he asks.

"Quite well, I'd say," Camilla says acidly.

"Look, I'm not trying to ruin your holiday," Jacob says. "I have a very upset and frankly traumatized twelve-year-old here who no longer wants to live with his mother, and so I've been trying to piece things together. And based on what I've found . . . I think you should be careful."

Camilla and Kate share looks. *Traumatized twelve-year-old?*

"Can you tell us what happened?" Kate says.

"There was an incident a few months ago with Charlie, our oldest. He's only just told me, and I want to speak to Darcy more about it. Basically, she took him away for the weekend to Manchester, and then they went swimming in the hotel pool. Charlie can't really swim—long story—and when he found himself in the deep end of the pool Darcy wouldn't help him. Just watched him start to drown, basically."

Camilla and Kate share another look.

"Is he all right?" Kate asks, still trying to make sense of this.

"Yeah, he's fine," Jacob says. "He's fine *now*. But he doesn't want to live with his mother anymore. And I've just found a cabinet full of . . ."

He trails off, as though unable to get the words past his throat.

"Go on," Kate prompts, her heart racing.

He takes a loud, rallying breath, forcing the words out. "I've just found all these . . . animal skulls. In Darcy's garden shed."

A beat. Kate wonders if she heard him right. "Animal skulls?"

"Yeah."

"Fucking hell," Camilla says. "Are you sure? I mean, they're not Darcy's . . . are they?"

"Sounds like I'm making stuff up now, doesn't it?" Jacob continues. "Charlie saw her when he was playing in the garden. Saw her . . . cutting things up."

Kate feels her stomach turn. She can't reconcile herself to the thought of Darcy killing animals. Even so, the image of it is vile. And her son finding it. Poor Charlie.

"She has the cabinet locked up but somehow he found the key. Don't know how I'm supposed to make him OK after this. . . ."

Just then, there's a knock on the villa door, the sound of Darcy calling a cheery "Hello!" Kate gives a little jump, Darcy's voice colliding with her macabre mental images of animal skulls.

Quickly, Camilla ends the call. "You all right, love?" she says to Darcy.

Kate is glad that Camilla's here, with her devilish ability to switch gears, to reply brightly to Darcy despite what they've just heard. Kate, however, can't manage to stretch a fake smile on her face, and so she looks up at Darcy like a deer caught in headlights. And when she glances at the clock and notes the significance of the time—twenty-five minutes to eight—and the reason why Darcy is here, she realizes she is too stricken to react.

The plan to confront Rob suddenly feels like a runaway train: she's no longer sure if it's more dangerous to jump off or stay on board.

54

JADE

I'm trying to get my head around this plan. I've got to take Rob to the gym, make sure we're alone, and then Darcy, Kate, and Camilla will come in and question him about Antoni and the guesthouse killings.

Oh God. I feel sick at the thought of it. But what choice do I have? He tried to kill me. If I go to the police about it, he'll tell them I'm making it up. And what proof do I have?

I stare at the box of pills in my suitcase. Thirty-six acetaminophen. For a moment I think about taking them all. Would it be enough to kill me? Maybe, if I made sure nobody found out.

"Jade, baby," he shouts up the stairs. "What you doing up there?"

"Just getting ready for the gym," I answer, careful not to let my voice give me away. I set the box back. I'm not confident enough.

"The gym?"

"Yeah," I call back. "You joining me?"

I'm keeping it casual. This is my strength: my knowledge of Rob. I know him better than he thinks I do. I know him so well I can sense when he starts itching to hurt me.

But I didn't expect to almost drown.

And it's doubly unnerving to me that a man here *did* drown. The Spanish guy, Antoni, whom Rob exploded at in the restaurant. His body was found on one of the beaches at the Emerald Island Resort this morning. Rob was in bed with me all night. I didn't sleep very well and he was there the whole time.

The police have spoken to him about it, but they haven't arrested him.

He appears in the bedroom doorway.

I turn, then, my skin gleaming from the aftersun I just put on, giving him a good view of my naked body. His breathing slows, and I see he's hard.

"How are the lungs?" he asks. He lifts a hand and places the palm flat between my breasts. "After your little accident this morning?"

I smile. This is his thing, now. To inquire about the injuries he inflicts on me as though they happened by accident. As though he had nothing to do with it. I don't think I can find the words for what a mindfuck this is. It actually makes me wonder if I'm going mad. If I just *imagine* him hurting me.

"Oh, fine," I say, and it's the truth. My lungs are fine. But I feel sick to my stomach and weightless with terror, because I am certain this man is actually going to kill me one day.

"So, what do you say? Shall we go to the gym?"

He looks at me, skeptical. "*You* want to go to the gym?"

"I'm your wife," I say, the words almost making me sick. "You love the gym, so I love the gym."

He's looking interested now, his face softening again.

"You know I love you," he says. Then, lowering his hand to my stomach: "And I love our future babies."

I falter then, wanting so badly for these words to be true.

And in his eyes, I see they are. In Rob's own, sick way, they absolutely are.

55

CAMILLA

Camilla feels like she is in a trance as she heads across the sand with Kate and Darcy. Then she thinks of what Jacob told her and Kate on the phone about Darcy. Animal skulls. Ha! What next? This day couldn't get any weirder if it tried.

The sky is dark, the blare of the disco in full swing behind them. It's almost eight. The gym is visible ahead, a light shining through the windows. Jade is meeting them there.

As they approach it, she feels conflicted, suddenly reluctant to see this through. She had a funny feeling when Darcy came in just before, which is to be expected after what Jacob said. She felt sick at the thought of Darcy carving up small creatures, and right as she was flicking through the possibilities for the skulls—*a nature project? Paganism?*—Darcy threw her a look that chilled her blood. Flinty, that's what it was. Her eyes were flinty.

But Cameron's voice is back in her head, pleading for her help. She thinks of the blood she saw on the deck the morning after she slept with Antoni. Of course it was his blood. How could she have thought otherwise? She imagines Antoni waking in the middle of the night, going outside for a smoke. Rob climbing over the deck, silently slitting his throat.

Her hands form tight fists, and she resolves not to leave the gym until she finds out the truth, whatever that is. They gather by a tall palm tree set back a little from the path, about twenty feet from the gym.

"Are they inside?" Kate whispers.

"The lights are on," Darcy whispers back. She glances at the watch on her wrist. "One minute."

The animal skulls may not even have been Darcy's, Camilla thinks.

She wonders about the previous owners of the house. And Charlie . . . Oh God, what if they're his? Jacob would never want to face up to something like that, would he, not when the poor kid is already suffering so much after his parents' divorce.

"Now," Darcy says, stepping toward the gym door. Adrenaline floods through Camilla's body, and before she knows what she's doing, she's following her, the door of the gym swinging shut behind them while Kate keeps watch outside.

INSIDE, ROB IS SITTING ON the weight bench, head back, shorts pulled down. Jade is between his legs; she sees Camilla and leaps back, leaving Rob with his penis bobbing, his eyes half closed in pre-orgasm.

"Get out," Camilla barks at Jade, who shrinks back against a wall.

Rob sits up, grabbing at his shorts. "What the fuck is this?" He glares at Camilla, then Darcy, his eyes wild with confusion and anger.

"We have a few questions," Camilla says, holding her nerve. "About the Spinnaker Guesthouse killings."

Rob raises his eyebrows. His eyes fixed on Camilla, he slowly lifts a dumbbell from the rack next to him and holds it on his lap.

"Gym's busy," he says. "Come back later."

"Out!" Darcy yells at Jade, who scuttles quickly for the door, but pauses instead of racing out. Rob raises the dumbbell at Darcy as though to threaten her, or perhaps strike her. Suddenly Darcy reaches both her hands forward, pushing the dumbbell down onto Rob's lap. Camilla reacts quickly, seizing a nylon skipping rope from the floor, frantically wrapping it around his neck. *OK*, she thinks, *this is going a little faster than I planned*, but her anger is guiding her. Darcy moves away, the dumbbell clanging to the floor.

Quickly Camilla pulls out her phone and holds it close to his mouth, recording.

Rob strains against the rope, his hands clawing at his neck. He tries to reach for the dumbbell but it has rolled out of reach, his feet skidding on the floor, unable to gain purchase.

"Tell us," Darcy pants. "You were with Hugh Fraser on September the tenth at the Spinnaker Guesthouse."

Rob grimaces, his eyes sliding to Jade, cowering now in the corner, but Camilla tugs tighter on the rope, then loosens it slightly.

"You murdered six people in cold blood—say it."

"What the fuck?" Rob gasps.

Camilla tugs on the rope again. "Why did you do it? And now Antoni, too. Why?"

She sees Darcy putting her phone back in her pocket, and for a moment she slackens the rope, wondering what Darcy's going to do. She sees her reach inside the sleeve of her kimono, producing a long, thin steak knife.

"We can help you remember, if you like," Darcy says, tapping the blade against the tattoo on his neck, visible above the coils of the rope.

"Jade?" he calls out stiffly. "You all right, babe?"

"Yes," Jade says in a thin voice. "Oh God, Rob . . ."

Camilla doesn't hear the rest, and for one terrible moment she worries that Jade is going to intervene. Darcy quickly jabs the knife toward Jade.

"Stay there," she growls at Jade, who shrinks into herself. Then she turns it back to Rob, who flinches.

"The Spinnaker Guesthouse," Camilla repeats now, voices in her head screaming at her, asking her what she's doing. "Dover. September 2001. You were there, with Hugh Fraser."

"No, I wasn't." He strains, and she tightens the rope at his neck, making him squirm in pain.

"You killed six people. One of them was my twin brother. Tell me why I shouldn't kill you for what you did?"

"It wasn't me," he grunts. "Jade? Where are you?"

"Bullshit," Camilla says, but even to her own ears she doesn't sound convincing.

"You better let me go," he says, his voice hoarse, "or I'll rip your fuck-ing head . . ."

He doesn't finish his sentence. Before Camilla can stop her, Darcy swings round and plunges the knife into his shoulder, a look of complete fury on her face. Rob gives an animalistic scream, raising his eyes to Ca-milla's in shock. She stares back at him. Dark, glossy blood gushes down Rob's chest, covering the floor, her hands.

So much blood, stark against the white floor. Camilla watches as he slumps forward. The knife sits in his skin, glinting in the red mist.

She's frozen to the spot, the rope slackening in her hands. But then, from the corner, Jade begins to shriek.

Camilla looks up at Darcy, who watches Rob, her expression strangely blank.

"We need to get out of here," Darcy says.

56

CAMILLA

A moment later, Camilla bursts into the hot night, almost colliding with Kate, who still stands guard.

"Run!" she yells, as Darcy emerges too, dragging Jade behind her.

Techno music from the disco pumps through the air, black waves reflecting the neon lights as colorful ribbons.

Behind her, Camilla can hear Kate's feet pounding the sand, Darcy and Jade following. She runs along the beach, letting the tide wash away the blood from her footsteps. And just then, it starts to rain, a thunderous downpour, the sky a livid shade of purple.

At the door of Kate's villa, there's a moment when the three of them have to wait for Kate to find her key card. It's as bizarre as it is frightening, the mundanity of the wait in the rain to be let inside following on so swiftly from the execution of their prime suspect, naked, and only recently erect.

None of them speak until they're inside, and Kate has locked the door behind them.

"What the fuck was that!" Camilla shrieks at Darcy. They're standing in the living room, the air crackling with energy. Kate and Jade watch on, deeply panicked.

"Is he dead?" Jade asks in a terrified voice.

"He must be," Camilla says, trembling. "There was so much blood, so much blood. . . ."

"What are you saying?" Kate asks. "What happened?" She notices Camilla's bloodstained face and, for a moment, it looks as though her knees might give way from the shock of it. She reaches out to the wall to steady herself.

"He . . . he called out f-for me," Jade stammers, her body starting to shake from head to toe. "He asked if I was all right!"

"I left the knife behind," Darcy says, panting.

"The gym door's locked," Camilla says, glancing at Kate. "Isn't it?"

"I–I'm sorry, I panicked," Kate says fearfully. "You told me to run and I just bolted. . . ."

"For fuck's sake, Kate!" Darcy shouts. "You only had to guard the door!"

"Oh God!" Jade wails, prompting Darcy to shush her sharply.

"You want the whole island to hear?" Darcy hisses.

Jade wilts to the floor, clutching her knees to her chest. "You killed him," she says. "You killed him!"

"You weren't supposed to *stab* him," Camilla shouts at Darcy. "The police are right here on the island. Oh God, why did you stab him?"

"He was about to hurt you," Darcy says. "I had to!"

"Have you lost your fucking mind?" Camilla screams at Darcy.

"What *happened*?" Kate asks, looking from Darcy to Camilla, who has started to pace, her hands clutching at her hair.

"He didn't have a clue what we were on about," Camilla tells Kate, trembling. "He was just worried about Jade. . . ."

Darcy shakes her head. "He's a liar. He'd have said he was bloody Maggie Thatcher if it meant getting his chance to wring your neck."

"He. Didn't. Do it," Camilla says, punctuating the words with hand gestures, her voice shrill. She fixes Darcy with a wild stare. "We have no way to prove to anyone that we acted in self-defense."

"Throttling a man in a gym isn't self-defense," Darcy says. "He got what was coming to him."

"Throttling?" Camilla howls. "You stabbed him, Darcy!"

But Darcy sounds disbelieving now. "You were the one who said you wanted to kill Rob for murdering your brother." She turns to Jade. "And he nearly killed you, didn't he?"

Jade is still sobbing hysterically. "What have I done?" she whispers. "What have I done?"

"Just *words*, Darcy . . ." Camilla says.

"Pretty bloody serious words," Darcy snaps back. "This is not the time for gaslighting, Camilla."

"Gaslighting?" Camilla says, eyes blazing. "I had him by the throat! He was answering my fucking questions, Darcy!"

Kate helps Jade up from the floor and coaxes her into an armchair, covering her with a blanket.

"We need to go back," Darcy says, strong on her feet. "We need to get rid of the body."

"Where the fuck do we put a body?" Camilla cries.

"Be quiet," Darcy hisses. "We'll have to . . ." She looks over at Kate and Camilla.

"What?" Camilla asks. "We'll have to what?"

Darcy pulls her and Kate into a huddle, making sure Jade can't hear. "You know," she whispers. "Cut him up."

"Did you just say we'll have to cut him up?" Kate asks.

Darcy sighs. "Tell me you've got a better idea."

"I don't have a better idea," Kate says. "When I woke up this morning I had no idea I'd end the day deciding how best to hide a body."

"Oh, fuck off, Kate," Darcy snaps, taking a step back from the huddle. "You knew the risk."

The room falls silent. Kate looks at Camilla, and Camilla can read her face. Disbelief. Sheer disbelief. This isn't the Darcy they know.

A bleep on Camilla's phone makes her jump. She glances at it. A text from Jacob, the first line flashing beneath her screen notification. She reads it once, then again, trying to make sense of it.

Camilla, Adrian Clifton is Darcy. Same person.

SHE LOOKS UP, STUNNED. TIME seems to slow. She sees Jade in a ball in an armchair. Kate standing opposite, staring at her with anticipation. And

Darcy, her white kimono soaked with a man's blood. A moment passes, a terrible fear settling upon her.

"Who is Adrian?" she asks Darcy.

Darcy looks puzzled. "What?"

"Jacob says *you* are Adrian," Camilla says, her voice filled with uncertainty. "He's . . . saying Adrian isn't real, I think. . . ."

"Adrian isn't real?" Kate says. "What?"

Darcy turns her eyes to Camilla. "I told you Jacob will say *anything* to take the boys from me. Anything!"

Camilla sees something pass across Darcy's face—the same expression she saw in the gym, right after Darcy killed Rob. It was a look that Camilla had never seen on her until then. So fleeting an expression of blind rage that she might have questioned whether she saw it or not, until she sees it again now, disorientating in its callousness.

Camilla raises her hand to her face. Rob's blood is still warm on her body. Did he kill Antoni? She feels dizzy with uncertainty.

"Jacob knows you've been using his software," Camilla presses, glancing quickly at the rest of the message. "He says you created Adrian Clifton. That's why Jacob's been asking about someone using his software. . . ."

Kate gasps for breath. "What do you mean, Darcy *created* him?"

"Rob Marlowe got exactly what was coming to him," Darcy snaps.

"To answer your question, Katie baby," Camilla says, panting slightly. "It seems Adrian isn't a real person. That was Darcy, hiding behind some kind of AI witchcraft."

Kate reaches out to the doorframe to steady herself.

"Wait," Jade interjects from the armchair. "Are you saying Rob didn't kill those people?"

"What about Elijah?" Camilla hears herself ask Darcy, the room spinning a little. "Was he really your boyfriend?"

Darcy flicks her eyes at her, folded like shepherd's crooks with amusement. Camilla wants to scream. *He wasn't?* She has watched Darcy cry about Elijah, her first love. The boy she'd wanted to marry. She's listened to Darcy talk about the nightmares she'd had for years afterward. Sometimes she'd even felt bad for talking to Darcy about losing Cameron, because she and Cameron hadn't been on the best of terms, whereas Darcy adored Elijah as much as he adored her.

Except, Darcy had never loved Elijah Morrison, the chemical engineering student in room four.

It was a lie. Every last bit of it.

Cameron's voice drifts into her head, begging, pleading. A flash of the way she imagined him that night, a desperate young man clutching his phone. A killer approaching.

Darcy.

"You killed them all," Camilla says. "Didn't you?"

57

HUGH

SEPTEMBER 10, 2001

He lit another cigarette and opened the window of the guesthouse, blowing the smoke out into the cool night air. They were in a tiny room on the ground floor with a queen bed, booked under Hugh's name, of course. No mention of Darcy on the guest list. She was just nineteen, and he fifty-eight. He had learned the hard way not to attempt to pretend that they were father and daughter. It had backfired last time and now he was on the sex offender list.

He sucked on his cigarette, enjoying the breeze on his bare chest. His belly was a deflated football hanging over the waistband of his jeans. He had lost so much weight that he had developed tits, his nipples hanging on the ends of loose skin like joke Christmas decorations. Age and illness had stolen everything from him, but Darcy looked at him with eyes like hearts from the old *Tom and Jerry* cartoons. She saw him as the figurehead of a movement, the leader of a cult. The Cult of Hugh, she joked sometimes. He liked the sound of it.

But in this last chapter of his life, he felt disappointed. He'd wanted to be famous, hadn't achieved the accolades he deserved. Even his "kids," as he called them, didn't seem interested anymore. Not as devoted. They were children whom he'd taken under his wing, loyal followers who saw him as a father figure. They stole for him, mostly, so that he could pay his rent. His main kids, Rob and Harry, had been thick as thieves with him in the old days, even calling him Pop. But he saw very little of them these days.

"We should get an early night," Darcy said, glancing at the dark street outside. "We've got an early start. The ferry leaves at seven, so we need to get out of here by five. . . ."

He stretched out a gnarly hand. "Come here."

The streetlight outside lit up her face in a golden glow. She was like an angel: lustrous chestnut hair, brown eyes flecked with flame, bee-stung lips. She clasped his hand in hers and looked at him with a flicker of worry.

He sighed and flipped the rest of his cigarette into the street. "There's no easy way to say this," he said.

Darcy sat on the other side of the windowsill, opposite him, her knee touching his. "You can tell me," she said, her face open and asking.

"You're not going to like what I have to tell you," he said. "But I need you to do something for me."

She nodded. "OK."

"All right. Last week I went to see the doctor, and what he had to tell me wasn't very good."

A fold of concern appeared on her brow. "What did he say?"

"He said that the reason I've been unwell for a while is not indigestion, like I thought. He says I've got some tumors in my liver, and some in my spine."

Her mouth fell open. "What?"

"Cancer," he said. "I suppose I should have taken better care of myself. Got checked out sooner."

She shook her head, those young, unjaded eyes filling with tears. "If this is you trying to break up with me," she said quickly, "I don't care about the age difference. And I don't care that you lied about it. I understand why you did."

"I'm not trying to break up with you," he said.

"I love you," she said. "Please don't do this."

He touched her cheek with his hand. "I'm telling you the truth. The hard truth. They say I won't see my birthday."

She straightened, her face falling. "That's two months away."

"Yes. Yes, I know. Which is why we can't go to France."

"Swear to me," she said, petulant. "Swear you're dying."

"I swear it," he said, coughing into a fist. "I'd much rather be getting on a ferry with you than sitting here, I promise you."

"Why didn't you tell me sooner?"

"I only got the prognosis last week," he said, rubbing his face wearily.

"You're lying," Darcy said, her voice tight with anger, and he did a double take. She was a fiery one, he reminded himself of that. "You want to break up with me. You want to be with *him*."

"*Him?*" he said, bewildered.

She pouted. "You know who I mean."

"No, I don't."

"Rob," she said, her gaze darkening. "You want him instead of me."

Hugh gave an amused chuckle. So Darcy was jealous of *Rob*. It was true that Rob idolized Hugh, but they hadn't slept together. Rob was an errand boy. A kind of son, or nephew. Hugh had met him five years ago, when he was a lad of fourteen, got him selling drugs and recruiting the odd girl. For a reason he'd never quite understood, Darcy loathed Rob. They rarely spoke, but she looked daggers at him whenever he came into Hugh's home. But now he knew: she was jealous.

"I'm not lying to you, Darcy," he said.

She looked up at him, seeing the yellow hue in the corners of his eyes, the dots of sweat on his forehead. He could tell she didn't believe him.

"Nothing goes the way I want it to," she said after a while.

"That's not true."

"It is," she said. "I wanted this. I wanted us to move to France, get a house, keep chickens."

He laughed. "That sounds nice."

"And we'd grow vegetables in the garden. We'd get married, and you could stay home with the kids while I went to work."

"Very modern," he said. "A house husband."

"Exactly," she said. "And now it's all gone."

He got up, plucking his jacket from the bed.

"What are you doing?" she asked, wary.

He pulled out his wallet and opened it, removing a twenty-pound note. He handed it to her. "Look, I want you to go home," he said. "We've had a bit of fun together. But now you need to leave. Tell your parents you ran away with your nineteen-year-old boyfriend, like we discussed."

She blinked, confused. "I wrote it in my note to them. . . ."

"Good. But go back in the morning. You can get the coach from the bus station first thing. Tell them you decided to come home." Tears were brimming in her eyes again. "It's for the best. I don't know how long I've got left, do I?"

She nodded, tears spilling down her cheeks. She looked like her heart was breaking.

He put on his coat.

"Where are you going?" she said.

"I'll go and find us both some food. I could do with some fresh air."

"You want me to come?"

He shook his head. He needed some headspace, some quiet.

OUTSIDE, HE WALKED SLOWLY, TAKING his time and pausing at street corners to gather his strength. Yes, he was ill. Walking even short distances took it out of him. And he was getting sicker by the day.

He bought two cans of Coke and a pasta salad in a plastic box for Darcy. He headed back slowly, too, feeling scared for the first time in his life. What would death be like? He had often thought about suicide, had had many days since his youth when the urge to end it all had nagged at him. And yet, this felt frightening. He had no control over it, and the end could be painful. It could be humiliating.

THE AIR HELD A DIFFERENT quality when he returned to the guesthouse: a new smell, he thought, and a weight to it, like the aftermath of heavy storms.

He ducked his head into the reception area to check on the owner.

"Evening, Mike," he said.

No answer.

At first, Hugh thought Mike had fallen asleep on his chair behind the desk.

"Mike . . ." Hugh began, falling quiet when he noticed the red splash on Mike's polo shirt. He stepped forward.

Mike's throat had a wide gash in it, his head tilted to the side against the wall, his eyes staring, seeing nothing.

Hugh stumbled backward, then turned on his heel and rushed to his room at the back of the ground floor. "Darcy!" he yelled. "Darcy!"

There had been a robbery, he thought. In the time that he'd been out at the shop, someone had broken in.

When he reached the room, the rickety door was open. No sign of Darcy. His heart thumped in his mouth. Had they taken her?

He turned and headed upstairs, frantic with worry. He glanced up and saw that the door to room six was open. Blood rushed in his ears.

"Hello?" he called. "Are you all right in there?"

Hugh glanced in, then stepped inside the room, his knees weak. A man was lying on his bed, his mouth open, both hands covered with dark blood.

"Oh God," he said, staggering out of the room. Where was Darcy?

The door to the room opposite lay open, and he lunged into it, glancing quickly at the scene inside: a man, also still in bed, a smear of blood on the wall above him.

Hugh felt like he was watching himself from above, running from room to room.

A noise drew him to room four. Thank God. Darcy was in there, just inside the door. She had her back to him, facing a man with black hair who was emerging from the en suite. "Hey," the man said, reaching out to her. Then, seeing Hugh appear behind her, he gasped, reaching out to grab Darcy protectively. But she spun away from his grasp, swiping at him with a knife. It all happened so quickly—the knife Hugh saw flashing in Darcy's hand, the younger man's mobile phone that was suddenly flung into the air, crashing down on the old granite fireplace and splintering into pieces. The dark bloom of blood on the man's T-shirt, soaking the fabric and reddening the man's hands.

Nobody spoke, though the room felt to Hugh as though a peal of thunder had clapped above their heads, the smell of lightning in his nostrils. He watched as the man clutched the wound at his abdomen with a look of pained horror, blood beginning to pool in copious, startling amounts on the floor.

Amidst his confusion, Hugh recognized the knife that Darcy was holding. It was his knife, the hunting knife that Hugh always kept with him for protection. She must have dug it out of his suitcase to defend herself.

Hugh felt as though his veins had filled with iron, fixing him firmly to the spot. He was unable to speak or move, his eyes wide as he looked on at Darcy, young, sweet, slightly mad Darcy, stabbing the man a second time. The young man staggered backward, his face collapsed like he might cry. Hugh clapped his hands to his mouth, astonished, as the man sank to the ground.

Darcy dropped down to the ground next to him, and Hugh managed to flip the switch that had held him frozen to the spot in order to lower himself beside her.

"Darcy," he murmured, reeling. "Darcy."

The man was still groaning on the floor next to them, agonized, wordless pants. He had curled up in the fetal position, unable to move, a glossy puddle of blood next to him. A glance told Hugh that he was dying.

"Are you all right?" Hugh asked Darcy, looking her over. She had a dab of blood on her forehead, and her hands were covered with it. She was trembling, her teeth chattering.

"I don't know," she said, weakly. "I don't know. . . ."

"Did he hurt you?"

She shook her head. "No. I was just so . . . angry. . . ."

Hugh finally registered that she wasn't injured, that the blood wasn't hers. And the look on her face . . . he'd never seen it before. He suddenly felt very cold.

"Who killed all these people, Darcy? Where are they?"

She lifted her eyes to his. "I did," she said, meek as a lamb. "I killed them."

Hugh felt something inside him tighten, a revulsion and a curiosity from some deeper part of himself lacing together. The gears of his mind turned quickly, shifting in another direction. "Get washed," he said, pulling her to her feet. He stood over the man, who was still groaning.

The knife was still in Darcy's hand, and Hugh took it from her.

"Go," he said.

ONCE SHE'D GONE HE STOOD over the man. A strange thrill to look down at him, helpless, his eyes pleading. But there could be no witnesses, and it was probably kinder just to finish him off, Hugh reckoned. He slid the knife into the man's chest, once, twice.

With a rattling exhalation, the man fell still, his unblinking gaze on the stained ceiling.

Back in their room, Hugh turned on the shower and set out a change of clothes for Darcy. When she stripped down, he took her bloodstained T-shirt and jeans and bundled them into a plastic bag, then zipped them into her suitcase. A quick scan of the room to make sure all her belongings were packed up, her shampoo bottle, her toothbrush. All trace of her, gone. As if she had never been at the hotel.

Satisfied that the room was clear, he headed quickly down the hall and checked the guest list that he had signed when he checked in. Shit. There was one name left.

One more person to arrive tonight.

Briony Conley.

Car headlights shone outside.

He squinted nervously through the blinds and saw a taxi pulling up out front. Someone was getting out. A woman. The last guest. Quickly, Hugh shoved Mike's body into the storeroom behind the reception desk, moving the chair to hide the bloodstain on the wall.

A girl pushed open the door to the guesthouse. It was late, and she seemed unsure if anyone was in.

"Sorry," Briony Conley said. "The taxi took me to the wrong place."

Hugh smiled uneasily and turned the guest register around so she could locate her name.

She looked at him warily. *Shit*, he thought, his heart hammering in his chest. Did he have blood on his hands? He hadn't checked. What if she decided to make a run for it? He'd have to go after her and kill her too.

But she stayed put, stifling a yawn. He ticked her name off the list, handed her a key, then listened to her go upstairs to her room. If she noticed anything amiss, she was probably done for, he thought darkly. Maybe he should kill her and get it over with.

The girl shut her door, and all went quiet. Hugh's heart was hammering from the exertion. He badly needed a smoke. And then a long sleep.

Hugh waited a few moments before heading quietly to his room, where Darcy was getting dressed. *Good*, he thought with a sigh. She had showered all the blood away, her clean clothes showing no sign of the stabbings.

"I need you to go now," he said calmly, picking up her suitcase.

"What?" she said, panicked.

"You're going to go home. You're going to tell your parents that you changed your mind about your nineteen-year-old boyfriend. Got it?"

She started to protest, but he raised a finger to her lips.

"You will do as I say," he said. "There should be a night bus at two a.m. Go."

Her face folded. "But I love you," she said.

He kissed her on the forehead and made lavish promises that he had no intention of keeping. He would be in touch. He would see her again. The lies settled her, made her compliant, as lies typically make people.

And so, he sent her out into the night with her suitcase.

At the front window, he lit another cigarette with trembling hands as he watched her to make sure she headed in the direction of the bus station. Then, as curious as he was sickened, he headed upstairs, his stomach churning as he revisited the grisly scenes behind each of the bedroom doors.

No one had survived. All but one had been stabbed in their beds, sound asleep. A frenzied, furious, determined attack. No, not frenzied— Darcy would have had to have been as calculating and quiet as a tiger moving through grass.

His breaths heavy and his shirt soaked through with sweat, Hugh stood outside room three, listening to the sound of light snoring behind the door. The young woman who had checked in was oblivious to the carnage that surrounded her.

Picking up the hunting knife, he slung on his jacket and headed out into the night. He would wait until morning, once Darcy was far away, before turning himself in.

I don't know what came over me, officer. I blacked out, then found I'd killed them all.

I just lost it.

Yes, officer. I did it.

58

KATE

Kate feels the air around her sharpen with a terrible understanding.

Darcy is the one who sent the roses, and not just this time around.

She has been sending them from the very beginning, each and every year. She has been watching Kate, enjoying how each delivery of six roses on the anniversary of the massacre poured salt in that gaping wound all over again. Kate can't fathom it, the notion that her friend, with whom she has shared the most intimate parts of her grief, is the one to have played such a cruel, depraved game.

The one who wanted her to suffer for twenty-two years.

"You killed them," she tells Darcy, and her voice sounds far away. "All six of them."

Darcy's eyes flicker over each of the women in turn. Her posture has changed, her feet planted wide and her shoulders square. "So what if I did?" she says.

A harrowing scream rings out, a cry so piercing that Kate whips around, certain that someone has been wounded.

The source of the scream of is Camilla, and she is not wounded. But she is lunging at Darcy, her hands stretched out as though to claw her face. Kate grabs her, holding her back.

"You bitch!" Camilla screams, her countenance contorted with rage. "*You* killed Cameron! You . . ."

The tears come, then, a sudden slam of sorrow removing the fire of Camilla's anger. She drops to her knees on the rug, breaking into gulping, wordless sobs.

Kate watches Darcy as she gazes blankly at Camilla on the floor before her, dispassionate as granite.

"Rob did nothing," Jade says, her voice shrill with outrage. "He did nothing!"

"Are you joking?" Darcy scoffs. "Did nothing? He tried to kill you."

"But he *didn't* kill those people," Jade cries. "You did!"

"You killed Antoni, too," Kate says. "Didn't you?"

Darcy shrugs, the carelessness in her manner making Kate wonder if this is actually Darcy, or if she didn't hear the question, or if she's on drugs.

"Why?" she hears herself say. "Why, Darcy?"

"Because I could," Darcy says with a prim smile. As though Kate has asked her about a cake recipe or a cleaning tip instead of murder.

Kate recoils at the strangeness of the woman in front of her. It's as though someone has scooped Darcy out of her body and replaced her with someone—or something—else. Even her posture is different, both legs straight and wide, her head held high. As though she's proud of herself.

"Did . . . did you care?" Kate asks, tripping over her words. She can't process it, can't bring the two facts together. The killings, and Darcy. How can those two things be related? "You saw us cry about the people we loved. Cameron. Professor Berry. You saw Salvador crying about his uncle. How could you do it, Darcy? How *could* you?"

With a sickening realization, she sees just how muted Darcy's reaction is. How the corners of her lips have turned in a snarl, the lines of her face seemingly sharper, craven. Jade and Camilla are looking on, all of them drawn in by this pulling back of the curtain, revealing a sole performer. Darcy Levitt, visibly basking in the spotlight of their horror.

"No," Darcy says flatly. "I really didn't give a shit."

Kate watches Jade's face fall, then Camilla's. With a sinking feeling in her chest, she suspects that this is a moment of triumph for Darcy. It makes no sense, but there it is—like a tiger emerging from camouflage, revealing itself in all its fearsome, savage glory. Oh God. She sees it now:

Darcy wants this moment, has craved it for some time. She has been waiting for the perfect moment to show them what she has done. What she
is capable of.

A noise at the door interrupts Darcy's glory. Through the shadows
a bloodied figure emerges, a flash of metal, an arm held out to one side.

Rob.

59

KATE

NOW

Kate freezes in horror as Rob staggers inside, bloodied, filmed with sweat, drunk with fury. He's unsteady on his feet, heading into the living room and knocking over a lamp as he swipes at Camilla with a knife. He misses, but Darcy crashes into his side, sending him flying, the knife hitting the floor. Darcy scrambles to get it, but he kicks out at her legs, and with a scream she falls forward, hitting the coffee table.

Rob turns to Kate, then, and she realizes she can't run, can't move, her whole body turned to stone. She holds up her hands.

"No," she pleads. "No!"

His gaze shifts, and from the corner of her eye she sees Jade, cowering and weeping by the sofa. Rob moves toward her unevenly. Blood is striped across his torso, a horrible gash in his shoulder from where Darcy stabbed him. *This can't be happening*, Kate thinks. *It's like something out of a horror movie.*

"You bitch," he growls at Jade. "You were working with them the whole time, weren't you? I should rip your fucking head off."

He grabs Jade by the hair, pulling her head roughly down to her knees, the other hand gripping her by the throat. Kate can hear Jade gag as he squeezes, hard. She wants to rush to her aid, but she can't. Her legs won't budge, and she feels helpless, pinned to the spot.

"Get off her!" she cries. Quickly, Camilla lifts the dolphin sculpture from the side table and throws herself toward Rob, bringing it down hard on his head. The pieces shatter to the floor, but he barely seems to notice. Rob lets go of Jade but catches Camilla with a heavy slam to the face, knocking her to the ground.

She doesn't get up. Kate raises her hands to her mouth with a tortured cry. Camilla is unmoving, completely silent. Kate is certain she's dead.

The knife, she thinks. The knife is on the ground, close to Darcy, but now Darcy is crouching for it and Kate remains utterly paralyzed.

Rob pauses, standing over Jade, panting. "I trusted you," he says, his voice strangely pained.

"Please, Rob," Jade whimpers. "I didn't . . . I didn't . . ."

He scowls at her in disgust. "I should have known you were nothing but a—"

He doesn't finish the sentence. With a scream, Darcy raises her hands high and sinks the knife into his back, a plume of blood shooting toward the ceiling fan. Rob manages to turn toward her with a deep groan, his face slack. But in one swift, precise movement, Darcy pulls the knife out, then sweeps it across Rob's neck, right across his tattoo.

His eyes widen, and he staggers backward, gagging. Blood bubbles out from a deep cut, his face full of surprise as he drops to his knees and keels forward.

The room lists for Kate, seeming to reel from the violence.

Darcy is standing over Rob, the knife in her hand. Camilla is on the ground, too, a few feet away, not moving. Jade is on her knees by the doorway of the dining area, holding her throat and gulping back air.

Kate approaches Darcy slowly. "Darcy?" she says, holding her hands up. "Put the knife down."

Darcy nods, lowering it.

"Jade?" Kate says, her eyes never leaving Darcy. "How are you, lovely?"

"I'm fine," Jade croaks.

"That's good," Kate says. "Let's keep it that way. Eh, Darcy?"

Darcy doesn't move. The knife is still in her grasp, her lace kimono soaked with Rob's blood. Her eyes hold a sudden cruelty, and she smiles at Kate. A smile that is at once familiar and sinister.

"I'll give you a five-second head start," Darcy says, the blade twitching in her hand.

It takes a beat too long for Kate to register Darcy's meaning. She can't be serious.

"One," Darcy says in a low voice. "Two."

"Jade, run!" Kate shouts then, and Jade dashes into the kitchen, locking the door behind her. Darcy's blocking the front door, and Kate knows that the entrance to the ground-floor deck is locked. There is no exit from this floor. No way out.

Quickly, she takes to the stairs, racing up to the main bedroom.

"Three," Darcy calls after her.

Kate's heart is clanging in her chest. She hasn't a second to spare. With a fresh spike of dread, she realizes that her phone is downstairs.

"Four."

She hears Darcy's feet on the stairs as she dives into the bedroom. The en suite, she thinks. It's the only door with a lock.

She darts into it, slamming the bathroom door shut behind her—too late.

"Five."

In moments, Darcy is there, kicking in the door and barreling after her.

Kate backs up against the shower door, flailing around the room for a weapon. Her hand falls on her open toiletries bag and she clutches at the small scissors she uses to tame split ends.

"They look blunt as spoons, those scissors," Darcy says with a smile. "You thinking of making a paper chain, Kate?"

In one swift motion, Darcy snatches the scissors from Kate. Kate's reaction is reflexive—she reaches back, and although she misses and makes Darcy lose her grip on the knife. It drops to the tiled floor with a metallic clang, and Kate kicks it quickly, sending it skittering under the bathtub.

"You bitch!" Darcy yells, punching her solidly in the face. The blow sends white lights shooting behind Kate's eyes, and she falls to the floor.

And then Darcy's on top of her, pinning her arms to her sides. Hot vomit explodes out of Kate's mouth as Darcy straddles her. Kate is still hacking and choking when she feels the sharp end of scissors against her tongue, Darcy pressing down

Oh God, she thinks, her mind turning to her cats at home. To her lovely armchair and her books. *This is how I die.*

"You couldn't leave it be, could you?" Darcy snarls, staring down with a menacing grin. Kate can sense a shift in Darcy's mood, something primal turning gears—she's lifting the scissors, just an inch, preparing for a last, fatal press of the blades into the back of Kate's throat.

Quickly, Kate bites down on the blades, a horrible scraping sound as she tries to keep them from slicing her tongue off. She shoves against Darcy with all her might, but there's no moving her, those terrible hazel eyes burning with malice.

Kate closes her eyes, a single tear sliding down her face.

60

JADE

NOW

I unlock the kitchen door with trembling hands and open it slowly, peering gingerly through an inch-wide gap. Rob is still on the floor. I watch him carefully, nervous in case he might spring up at any moment, arms swinging. But there's no movement. No rise and fall of his chest.

I step outside, inching toward him. He's lying on his left side, his arms sprawled awkwardly on the floor beside him, the long rug between the kitchen and living room darkening with his blood. Camilla is on the ground behind me, not moving.

I can't believe what's happened.

He looks like something out of a horror movie, stark naked and streaked with blood. I kneel down carefully, looking at his face. His mouth is open a little, and his eyes are, too, staring straight ahead. I move my hand in front of them. He doesn't blink.

He's gone.

I feel numb, and at the same time I want to fall to my knees and sob my eyes out. But beneath both feelings is an undeniable sense of relief, sweeping through me like a calm sea breeze.

Upstairs there's a scream, and a thud. *Kate*, I think. Darcy's lost it. I'm terrified, but I have to help Kate.

I head up the stairs, shit scared. This feels like a dream, not real. Oh God. Where are they? Blood streaks across the wooden floor of the bedroom, leading to the en suite.

Inside, Kate is on the floor, Darcy straddling her, kind of crouched over, and I wonder for a moment if Darcy is performing heart compressions, trying to help her.

"You bitch," she growls, and my heart races.

I could try to reason with Darcy. And had I never experienced Rob's abuse, that's exactly what I would have done. I would still be the sort of person who believes that everyone is reasonable to *some* degree, that most issues between people can be resolved over a cuppa and a chat. I would still believe that what I'm seeing is the result of an argument gone too far, that I could simply ask Darcy to get off Kate and separate them while I mitigated both sides, eventually bringing each to see the other's perspective.

But that isn't who I am.

I reach for the curtain tie by the window, move lightly on my feet toward Darcy and loop the cord over her neck.

"Let her go," I shout, pulling the rope as tight as I can.

The scissors fall from Darcy's hands. Kate rolls over and vomits on the floor, gasping for air.

Suddenly, my head is yanked down, and I see Darcy with a fistful of my hair, pulling with all her might. She forces me to my knees, then plunges her elbow into my nose, hard.

The pain is blinding. An arc of bright-red blood shoots into the air, and I hear myself scream.

Darcy grabs the scissors from the floor and lunges at me. I rock back, and she misses. Then, holding on to the shower door, she pulls herself to her feet.

"Please," I say. "Don't do this, Darcy."

She grins, and for a moment I think she'll relent. I still can't work out what's going on. I see her swipe at me with the scissors, but something snags at her neck, making her gag.

Kate is standing behind her. She's picked up the curtain tie that I dropped, and is yanking it around Darcy's neck. But Darcy kicks backward, catching Kate's knee. Kate looks like she's going to fall, and the scissors are on the floor, close enough for Darcy to grasp.

I've never hit another person in my life, but before I really understand what I'm doing I'm swinging all my weight behind a punch, landing it hard in Darcy's belly, making her fold forward against the curtain tie around her neck.

"No you don't!" Kate shouts, but Darcy is crazy strong, kicking out again. I feel her hands reach for my hair again, her nails in my scalp.

Then her grip loosens, and she finally falls still.

I can feel myself going into shock, like I'm leaving my body. None of this feels real. None of it.

Kate looks down at me on the floor.

She's a mess, vomit all down the front of her dress and in her hair, the bottom half soaked with urine and blood from my nose. Her front teeth are chipped, and her lips bloodied. But on her face is something close to relief.

"It's over," she says.

61

CAMILLA

Camilla comes to, finding herself on the floor. Her head is throbbing, and when she raises a hand to the part that hurts most, her fingers are met with blood. Her jaw aches, and she reckons it's dislocated. Her ears ring. She feels nauseous, too, until she recalls what happened, and she starts.

Rob was here, and he had a knife . . . and Darcy . . . She confessed to killing Cam, and everyone in the guesthouse, and Antoni.

Quickly, she scrambles to her feet, still unsteady and woozy but afraid that Darcy or Rob will come at her again. Her eyes fall on a shape on the floor close to the kitchen. It's Rob, and he very much looks like he's dead.

She looks back across the floor, at the pieces of the sculpture scattered across the tiles. She remembers bringing that down on Rob's head before he clocked her in the jaw and she cracked her head against the corner of the sideboard. There are long smears of blood on the floor, too. And a phone, lying on the floor by the sideboard where she fell.

It's Camilla's phone. Kate sees that the camera app is still open, a red "recording" notification flashing on the upper part of the screen. It's been recording for nine minutes. The visual is just the floor, but the audio will have captured more.

Quickly she presses STOP, then clicks on the recording above. It's the video from the gym. She deletes it.

Then she straightens, listening hard for a moment. There's a sound coming from somewhere, a drumming of feet. It stops, and she hears a knock on the door.

She can see the door is already ajar from when Rob burst inside. "Come in," she calls.

Two resort staff members enter the villa, looking spooked and apologetic at once. It's Rafi, Kate's butler, and Nura, the resort manager.

"We received a call from one of the guests," Rafi says carefully. "They said someone was in distress, that there was screaming." He looks her over. She's covered in blood. "I think we need to take you to hospital," he says.

There's a noise upstairs, and she glances up to see Kate and Jade standing on the upper landing, both bloodied, as though they've just climbed out of a den of lions.

Nura steps forward, noticing Rob's body on the floor. She mutters something Camilla doesn't understand, a noise of shock. Quickly, she bends and checks Rob's pulse, then shakes her head at Rafi. "He's dead."

"We've locked Darcy in the bathroom upstairs," Kate says grimly, emerging into the living room. "We were caught in the crossfire, you might say."

Camilla glances at Kate, then slumps down dramatically into a chair. "Oh, thank God you came!" she tells Nura and Rafi. "We were afraid for our lives!"

62

JADE

TEN HOURS LATER

"Mrs. Marlowe?"

I look up to see a woman at the door of the hospital room. "I'm Detective Sergeant Rasheed," she says. "Are you OK to talk just now?"

I nod and sit up a little in the small bed. "Yes," I say. "Have a seat."

Detective Sergeant Rasheed shuts the door quietly behind her before sitting down in the plastic chair to the left of me. I'm in the main hospital on Malé, being treated for a skull fracture, a broken nose, and shock. Kate, Camilla, and I flew here last night on a seaplane. I have twenty different cuts and bruises, but I feel lucky. There were many times over the past week when I thought I wouldn't live to see the morning.

They flew Darcy to the hospital in a separate plane. I was surprised when they said she was alive. I thought Kate had killed her on the floor of the bathroom.

"I've spoken with Kate Miller and Camilla Papaki," Detective Sergeant Rasheed says, taking out a notebook. "I wanted to find out from you what happened. It seems there was friction between your husband and your friend Darcy Levitt?"

I nod. "Yes. I'm not fully sure what happened."

"Did they know each other prior to coming to Sapphire Island?"

I shake my head, then hesitate. "Not that I'm aware of. But Rob was complaining about Darcy all the time. She really got his back up. And then, next thing I know, we're in the gym, and Darcy comes charging in with a knife. She stabbed him."

"You were having sex in the gym?"

I nod tearfully. "We were on our honeymoon. And I'd had a bad experience during a trip that morning so we were . . . I guess, trying to put it behind us."

Detective Sergeant Rasheed writes this down.

"The diving instructor, Farug, said you went on a scuba trip."

I nod. "That's right."

"He said he was worried about you. He had some concerns that Rob was violent with you. And the nurses here told us that some of the bruising they found on your body was not caused by the attack last night. That there were older injuries."

I flick my eyes nervously at her. How much of the truth can I tell her without her implicating me in all of this?

"Yes," I say quietly. "I hadn't told anyone. I was on my honeymoon. It felt like a shameful thing to admit. That your new husband is abusive."

"I understand," she says, touching my arm. I can tell she pities me.

"Tell me what happened right after Darcy stabbed Rob."

"I remember we chased Darcy into the villa, trying to get the knife off her."

I watch her write this down. "How did she get into Kate's villa? Did she have the key card?"

I hesitate. "I believe so."

"So . . . you left Rob back at the gym?"

"I was in shock," I say. "I just . . . ran."

She seems to get this. "And then what happened?"

"Then Darcy admitted that she killed a guest, Antoni. I think there's a phone recording of her saying it. And Rob came after us. He burst into the villa and attacked Darcy, but she . . . she killed him." I lift a hand to my mouth, tears spilling down my face. "I saw her slit his throat. I saw him die."

She reaches out and rests a hand on my arm. "I'm so sorry," she says. "We'll have you back to England very soon, with your family. This must be incredibly difficult."

"I can't believe I'm a widow," I say bitterly, wiping my face. I'm not pretending fully. I'm relieved and devastated all at once. Maybe it'll take years to process what's happened. I adored Rob once. I was the happiest girl alive. And then he turned into someone I didn't recognize.

"Even though he treated me badly," I tell the detective, looking her straight in the eye, "I loved him. Everyone always said how lucky I was to have him. You can ask them yourself."

63

DARCY

NOW

That day in London, after meeting Camilla and Kate in person, Darcy drove home, feeling rattled by their meeting. Her instincts had been correct—they'd both mentioned that they had doubts about the trial, about Hugh having an accomplice. In September, she had spotted a tabloid article about the Spinnaker killings, marking the twenty-first anniversary. The journalist, Motsi Sibanda, was now digging around internet forums, asking questions about Hugh's past. She had even spoken to Camilla, and Darcy had seen the skepticism on Kate's face when she admitted that the journalist hadn't contacted her.

She'd always suspected it might all open up again, new questions about the investigation stirred up. She had found the Facebook page set up for the victims' families. She'd made friends with the woman, Camilla, who had set it up, told her she was the girlfriend of one of the victims. She'd doctored a photograph of them together.

But it wasn't enough. Camilla was making a lot of noise about her doubts on the handling of the investigation, and many others agreed with her. Motsi Sibanda was pressing forward with a big tabloid piece, maybe even a documentary, and a book.

If Darcy didn't act quickly, they'd get the case reopened, and the police would find things to connect her to the massacre. And, almost worse, she would lose her reputation. The persona she had meticulously put together, the artistry of which she was infinitely proud, would be sullied, torn to shreds.

People would look at her as a criminal instead of a dedicated mother. All her darkness, out in the open.

She felt cornered. And an old itch began to nag, begging to be scratched. If the shit was going to hit the fan, she was going to go out with a bang. The gossip surrounding her divorce had made her want to claw her own skin off. She would take her power back, steer the narrative. Tell them who she *really* was. Catch the fear in their eyes and savor it.

The day she received the divorce certificate, a Friend Suggestion popped up on Facebook. Rob Marlowe, a profile picture of a tiger. She tended to use a fake Facebook profile to snoop about, and so she friended him. Rob had aged well. The jeans, the artfully shaved beard, the gold chain necklace—all of it screamed, *I'm still twenty-five, honest!* when she knew he was the same age as she. Many of his posts were about weight-lifting and marathons, and he posted numerous selfies of that familiar, cocky smirk. And the tiger tattoo on his neck.

She knew Rob from her life before Jacob. He had been one of Hugh's boys, one of his favorites. Hugh talked about Rob like a son, though she suspected sex was involved. She had only met him a handful of times, all those years ago, but he had treated her like something he pulled off the sole of his shoe.

The fuck you looking at?

Who's the slut, Hugh?

As she clicked through his photographs, a plan unfurled darkly in her mind.

She kept an eye on him via social media, and sourced a burner phone to make calls to his employer, to associates, using her pleasant, middle-class voice and fluid conversational style to wheedle out useful information: appointments, off-the-cuff character observations, mentions of other people he dealt with.

No, he's got a big plumbing job in Little Portugal on Thursday. You know what he's like, always last minute. Ask Ronnie, he'll know.

She took photographs as "evidence" to show Camilla and Kate, seamlessly integrating them with false details from the night of the massacre. She would curate her story and position him within it, make him what she wanted him to be.

With Jacob's AI software, she was able to create a puppet, an avatar, who was capable of following a script. "Adrian" could respond to questions via Zoom, as long as she provided enough information for him to supply answers. It was the perfect ruse. Despite having tried out the software a dozen times to ensure it didn't fail her, she was nervous in case it glitched on the Zoom call with Darcy and Camilla. But it didn't. It was perfect.

And then, a recorded PowerPoint presentation with fake evidence that they could all watch together in the villa, stirring them up to think Rob had been involved in the killings. She could hardly believe she had gotten away with it. No wonder Jacob had kept certain aspects of his software development under wraps.

Jacob had never suspected she would bother using the software, so why conceal it from her? He probably didn't even realize she'd kept the old log-ins from when she did his development bids. Potential clients were asked to sign confidentiality agreements before the full suite of products was made available, and he took injunctions against journalists who managed to wheel details out in the press.

Because if someone could create an avatar like Adrian, capable of holding a virtual conference call . . . in the wrong hands, it could be very dangerous indeed.

But when it came to it, she couldn't just use the software to frame Rob. She had to kill him. It was a wonderful feeling, too delicious to resist.

And to find something that felt so good in a world that taught only pain—well, why would you ever stop?

PART THREE

PART THREE

64

KATE

NOW

BRITISH WOMAN KILLS TWO IN MALDIVES

September 25, 2023

A woman from Richmond Park has been charged with the murder of two men at the Sapphire Island Resort & Spa in the Noonu Atoll of the Maldives on September 12. Darcy Levitt, a mother of three, allegedly murdered Antoni Caballé (59) within several days of arriving at the island to celebrate her divorce. Levitt also killed Robert Marlowe (41) from Stockwell in a separate knife attack.

Police are currently investigating claims that Levitt was responsible for a string of murders in a Dover guesthouse in September 2001, in which six people were killed in a frenzied knife attack. Convicted pedophile Hugh Fraser, then aged 58, was charged with the murders and died in prison in 2001.

Kate's cottage is small but charming, set aglow by honey-brown September sunlight. There's a red carpet throughout, a woodburning stove, a comfortable velvet sofa, wooden beams exposed in the ceiling. A bookcase groans under the weight of Kate's many books arranged haphazardly on the shelves, an eclectic range of ornaments and houseplants. The walls are covered in framed pictures of every genre: modern scribbles, still-life oil paintings, large posters advertising readings by famous writers. A dining table is also covered in books, and the place smells a little of cats.

The Maldives was beautiful, but in weather like this, she craves nothing more than her own back garden, a pot of freshly brewed tea, and a good book. A cat or two stretching lazily in the background.

She has a broken collarbone, a few chipped teeth, and a very strained jaw, but she feels content. The truth always comes out, she thinks. Even if it takes decades and bloodshed and injustice. The truth will always work its way to the surface.

The police in the UK want to speak to them as well, and it may well come out that Darcy duped her and Camilla into going to the Maldives to confront Rob, that Darcy utilized her husband's software to create a bogus private detective, and to doctor photographs of herself with Elijah, whom she'd never even met. That she created photographs of Rob—fake mug shots, Photoshopped portraits of him meeting up with Hugh Fraser. It seemed she wanted to make Rob the fall guy for the killings.

Kate is astonished at the lengths Darcy went to, and equally shocked by the tools that made it possible. By the fact that they believed it all so easily.

Darcy's still alive. She was unconscious for some time, and then unable to move due to what turned out to be a set of broken ribs.

Kate is certain that Darcy is a psychopath.

The day after Kate landed at Sapphire Island, she witnessed something so fleeting that it really should have made little impression. Before the dolphin cruise, she popped into the buffet for a light dinner. She had only just stepped inside when she saw a guest slip on wet floor tiles, about twenty feet from where she was standing. The place was almost empty, but Darcy was standing opposite the woman, holding a food tray. Kate watched as Darcy, instead of rushing to the woman's aid, stood and looked on as the woman gasped and grabbed her ankle. It must only have been half a minute or so before another guest came and helped the woman to her feet, and *then* Darcy leaped into action, setting her tray aside and bending to help her up.

At the time, she'd told herself that Darcy must have been distracted, or jet-lagged. That was why she had hesitated. But it stayed with her. The fact that Darcy had simply stared, blankly, as the woman fell to the floor, a slight reversal in her step indicating that she was about to turn away.

She probably *was* jet-lagged. Too jet-lagged to put her mask into place fast enough.

Not every psychopath is a killer, that much Kate knows. Perhaps there was something traumatic in Darcy's past that had generated the desire to inflict pain. No one could be that screwed up, that cruel, without something making them that way.

Could they?

Why, she wonders now, did Darcy wait so long to kill again? Or did she wait? Were there other murders throughout the years? Why not kill Jacob, whom she bitterly resented?

She runs her tongue gently along the chips in her front teeth, remembering with a shiver the look in Darcy's eyes when she had tried to kill her.

It was like looking at an open flame.

A YEAR LATER

65

KATE

Tonight is the vigil, held on the twenty-third anniversary of the killings in a beautiful chapel in Somerset.

Kate stands in her bedroom at the Airbnb, looking over the outfit she has picked, a green linen dress nipped in at the waist by a thick tan belt. Black, kitten-heeled ankle boots, small gold hoop earrings, and red lipstick. It's an outfit she would never have dared to have worn a year ago, but she had some persuasion from Camilla, backed up by Jade, and she's glad she relented. Her hair has been cut short, all the old brown lopped off, her silver brought to a fine shine with some kind of witchcraft in a purple shampoo bottle. Her teeth were broken after Darcy's attack, and it took some getting used to veneers—but she has straight white teeth for the first time in her life, and she doesn't give a shit if they're fake.

She stands for a moment longer, mentally telling the voices in her head to shut up. No, she doesn't owe anyone "pretty." No, she isn't mutton dressed as lamb, and no, she isn't kidding herself that she's the type of person who wears makeup. She can if she bloody well wants. And *this* Kate wants to.

She received a WhatsApp from Jade this morning, apologizing again for not being able to make the vigil tonight. She attached some photographs of Vietnam, where she's currently traveling. She looks different from the girl Kate met in the Maldives. Her hair is brown and cut to her shoulders, and she wears no makeup. She looks happier, like someone who has seen the ocean for the first time.

Secretly, Kate is celebrating a bit of news, too—yesterday her agent sold her first book, penned as herself. Well, almost. She's publishing this one as Briony Conley. A name she hasn't gone by in over twenty years. It feels like an old sweater she's dredged up from the depths of her wardrobe, surprised and delighted to find it still fits, that the colors haven't faded. The book is about deception, and about a protagonist, Jane, who almost sells her soul to the devil. The endeavor costs her dearly, but it makes Jane wake up to who she is.

There's a bottle of champagne waiting at home, which she'll chill in an ice bucket and enjoy by the fire tomorrow night. She might light a candle for Briony, and for Professor Berry, who held a dear place in her heart for many years. After all, he was the first person to really encourage her in life. When she was in her third year of an undergraduate degree, still feeling like an imposter, he invited her into his office and asked if she had plans to pursue a master's degree in archaeology. She blushed; she hadn't considered it at all. He said she should, and that he'd help her prepare a scholarship application.

The scholarship application was successful.

After the massacre, she couldn't return to her studies. She couldn't return to many things—physically couldn't. And she has no desire to resurrect those old dreams now.

But she feels a flicker of warmth inside whenever she thinks of that day in Professor Berry's office, of the way his words persuaded her that she was capable of more than she thought.

A brief word of encouragement, but one that has lived inside her all these years, waiting to flower.

THE CHAPEL IS WARM INSIDE, lilies lining the pews to symbolize new beginnings. Many have come out for the vigil, many more than expected. Church volunteers are busily arranging extra rows of folding chairs at the back to accommodate the crowd. Some journalists are here, too. Kate's interview with Motsi ran across two pages in *The Guardian*, and the case exploded into the media after that. Motsi is in discussions with TV producers about a possible multi-episode documentary.

Talk about a delayed response—but what a response! Darcy's murder charge, her marriage to a successful software engineer, and the revelation of the real murderer behind the Spinnaker killings made for a great story, and plenty of journalists wanted to dive deep into that night in 2001. Others wanted to explore Darcy's life, intrigued by what might have led the daughter of a decorated navy lieutenant to become a serial killer. The trial is about to begin. By offering a new way of thinking about #MeToo and toxic masculinity, Darcy's story also reframes discourses on catfishing, grooming, and the dangers of artificial intelligence.

And the renewed media interest in the massacre shows no sign of slowing.

Camilla arrives, her daughter, Natasha, following behind. She's wearing a black Westwood corset dress beneath a Prada trench, her hair tied up in a neat bun, gold hoop earrings the size of dinner plates.

A tray of votive candles burns brightly at the altar, and Natasha places a photograph of her uncle Cameron among the others that are already arranged, held in place by clips behind the candles.

"Jacob's here," Camilla whispers to Kate.

And there he is—the man she'd thought was a bully, a bastard, slipping in through the rear door of the church. He's wearing a suit, is accompanied by a woman. No sign of the boys. Of course not. Not for this.

She watches as he takes a seat at the very back, away from everyone. She catches his eye and he nods. He has earned her respect, for sure. Coming here poses a risk—not everyone will be sympathetic to him. But the fact that he has come regardless shows that he recognizes the impact of Darcy's actions on these people. And, perhaps, on his own children.

"Are you all right?" Camilla asks, squeezing her hand, and she nods. It feels good to be here. Emotional, too, and the horror of the massacre will never, ever fade. But there is a rightness about the vigil. A remembering of the ones they lost that night.

The minister rises and says a prayer. Kate usually hates these kinds of things, but it surprises her how the venue, with its old stone walls and saints embedded in stained-glass windows, the votive candles and even the prayer, feels appropriate for this service. You don't have to believe in God to believe in sanctity and the idea of a higher order; the tragedy that the victims' families met with, coupled with the media silence and the bungled justice system, deserves just this kind of vigil, held with reverence and love.

THEY'RE IN A PUB ACROSS the road from the chapel, both on their third drink since the vigil.

"I see the yassification of Kate Miller is coming along nicely," Camilla says.

Kate tugs at the neckline of her dress. "I had a little assistance in the clothing department."

"And what in the Tan France have you done to your hair?"

"I had it cut," Kate says, touching it. "The stylist showed me how to gel it. It's stiff enough to dig a ditch."

"I mean the color."

"Oh. Well, they dyed the brown bits gray to match the roots."

"It's gorgeous," Camilla exclaims. "Especially with the red lippy. I look like a jump-scare next to you."

"Don't be silly."

"Maybe I should try going gray. . . . Did I tell you I was thinking of getting a tattoo?"

"Oh?"

"Natasha wants to do it. A guitar, to remind me of Cameron."

"That's sweet."

Camilla cocks an eyebrow and looks Kate over. "You have a healthy glow about you, too. Kind of . . . smug. Like you've won the lottery, or had a *really* good shag."

Kate's eyes twinkle, and Camilla gasps. "You shagged someone? Oh my God, finally! Who?"

"Her name's Sasha," Kate says. "I met her on the plane home from the Maldives, actually. She runs her own ethical textile business."

"And it's going well?" Camilla says. "Don't answer that, actually. I can see how well it's going. Bloody hell. Talk about a glow-up."

Kate chuckles, realizing how much she enjoys shocking Camilla. "I'll let you in on another secret—I've been doing your workouts."

Camilla's eyes grow wide with astonishment. "What, online? You've been following my Instagram?" Kate nods, and she throws her arms up in a "hallelujah" gesture.

She tells Camilla that it's the first time in decades that she's been able to stick to an exercise plan for more than a week. She's had fibromyalgia flare-ups, but instead of quitting, she's gotten straight back into her exercising when she's started to feel better. The first time she did it she was utterly exhausted, ashamed of how unfit she was. She could barely lift her legs off the ground. But she's proud of herself, and not a little surprised. Not only has she stuck to it, but she can see a difference: she's stronger, able to do more repetitions than when she started, and her core—dare she say it—feels like it's actually bloody working.

"Can I ask you a question?" Camilla says, returning with her round of drinks.

"That *is* a question," Kate says, lifting her Negroni.

Camilla sits down and considers her words. "I don't know how to deal with it," she says hesitatingly. "The guilt. I mean, I said I wanted to kill *you-know-who*."

Kate nods. She knows Camilla means Rob.

"But it wasn't right," Camilla says, softening. "Even if he had killed my brother, and all those people . . . Even if he was the real killer. It wasn't right, was it?"

"Almost doing a deal with the devil is not the same as signing the deal with blood," Kate says slowly.

"Are you saying that just because I said I'd kill him, ultimately I didn't kill him, so it's OK?" Camilla says.

"I'm saying that sometimes a lesson can be learned by having your mettle tested," Kate says. "It's not easy to confront the shadowy parts of your character, or to learn that your moral fiber is full of holes. But . . ."

She looks away, thinking. "Well, I can only speak for myself. I won't make excuses for what happened in the Maldives. But I've realized that I hadn't been living. I'd made decisions after the massacre that cost me dearly. And without regretting too much, I wasn't living life as fully as I could be."

Camilla reaches out and takes her hand. "I'm really, really glad I met you. And I count you as one of my dearest friends. If that's all right."

Kate cocks her head. "Are you in danger of turning sentimental, Camilla?"

Camilla smiles, her eyes brimming. "I blame you," she says. "Rubbing off on me."

"Fuck off," Kate says, and Camilla laughs.

66

CHARLIE

NOW

"You don't have to do this if you don't want to," his dad is saying. "I'm just giving you the option."

Charlie sits at the dining table in front of a blank piece of paper. His dad sets a pen beside it before heading back into the living room, where Dembe is sitting. Charlie knows why his dad is suggesting this—the family counselor suggested at their last meeting that it might be good for Charlie to write to his mother.

He still can't believe any of it is real. He feels numb. Dad takes Ben and Ed to visit her, but Charlie refuses to go. He looks at himself in the mirror sometimes in case he can see it—the part of him that's like her. He doesn't look like her, but 50 percent of his DNA comes from his mum. It terrifies him. He can think about nothing else. The other day he was at his grandparents', sitting on the swing, and the neighbor's cat came up to him, purring. It was a beautiful cat with blue eyes and white fur.

"That's Snowball," his grandma said. "I think he likes you. You want to stroke him?"

The cat arched its spine as his grandma ran her hand along its fluffy back. He reached out to stroke it, then froze. What if he harmed the cat and didn't mean to?

Quickly, he got to his feet and dashed inside, racing all the way to the bathroom. There, he locked the door behind him and fell to his knees.

He hadn't cried when his dad sat him down and gently told him that Mummy had been arrested in the Maldives. And even when the kids at school WhatsApped him screenshots of his mum's murder charge, he didn't break down. But in the bathroom, he cried so loudly that his grandma knocked on the door and called his father when he wouldn't open it. And when they asked what was wrong, he was too terrified to bring the words to his lips: *What if I'm a killer?*

He looks down at the piece of paper. What would he write? That he still dreams about drowning? About the skeletons he found in the shed?

He doesn't know what to say. He doesn't have the words for what he feels.

He gets up and goes to his room, then comes down to the living room, where his father and Dembe are sitting.

"I want to send this," he says, handing his dad an A4 sheet.

"What is it?" Dembe asks. "A certificate?"

"It is," Jacob says, looking it over. It's Charlie's swimming club certificate, his name emblazoned there, STAGE 4 printed in heraldic red. It means he can swim eleven yards without a floating aid, even in the deep end. It took so much effort, so many tears, but he finally managed to get himself back in the water after that terrible day. And he learned to swim.

"Well played, son," his dad is telling him. "Well bloody played."

67

DARCY

NOW

She sits in her cell at HMP Bronzefield, knees drawn up to her chest as she reads.

She's reading the works of William Blake, and when she gets a chance to use the computers, she'll print out some of the poems she likes best. In her knitting classes she is working on a collection of knitted tigers to gift to premature babies at the local hospital, and she would like to accompany each toy with a copy of the poem that inspired them.

The workshop leader, Heather, is deeply impressed by Darcy's plans for the toys. It makes Darcy beam with pride. It doesn't matter at all that she's in HMP Bronzefield, that she has swapped her school-run uniform of floral day dresses for a drab prison uniform of gray sweatpants and matching T-shirt. She's found a way to shine still, and, for now, that is making her happy.

She doesn't receive much mail, but today a certificate arrived. She grimaced a little when she saw it, felt an urge to rip it up. But now, she folds it, inserting it in her copy of William Blake as a bookmark. A keepsake.

This new life in prison has made Darcy aware of the moment she realized she had a special power that made her different from everyone else. A power that set her apart from all the rules.

She was a child of four or five, walking through a street in the Cotswolds with her father. He must have been on leave from the navy, and she isn't sure where her mother was in this memory, but the one thing that stays bright in her mind is the garden she admired while they walked. A beautiful garden at the front of an equally beautiful cottage. A patch of beautiful sunflowers grew there, and she told her father she wanted them.

"On you go," he said, and she ran into the garden and plucked them all, taking them back to him.

"Good girl," he told her. "You see what you want and you take it."

She knew then that a wildness crouched inside her, indiscriminate, volatile, and without remorse: tenderness twinned with ferocity, indifference met by brutality.

Only one thing has ever mattered to Darcy: her father's approval. He had told her that she was Queen Darcy, indefatigable, unsurpassable, unequaled. She sensed that they were twin souls, that he had the same coldness at his heart, the same incapacity to feel things that other people mentioned: shame, empathy, love. She wondered, too, if her father had struggled with his own coldness the way she did, if he had had to seek out his own ways of finding satisfaction, or a sense of achievement. Darcy marveled at and sometimes envied people who seemed to experience joy in things like meeting friends for coffee, or caring for relatives, or reading a book. Darcy never read, because every character seemed ridiculous. She couldn't relate, couldn't empathize, and she could not for the life of her figure out why anyone would *want* to care for someone, and take pleasure in it, without wanting praise and acclaim. Sometimes it drove her mad, the lack of happiness. The vast, icy space where her heart should be.

But then, she found a way to experience delight: the rodents and birds she trapped in her garden. She relished slicing them up in her potting shed, inspecting their beautiful structures. Feeling the life leave them in her palm.

That was how she discovered excitement, or pleasure, though it was never as gorgeous as the moments after the killings in the guesthouse. As she listened to the stillness afterward, it was as though a blissful, heady nimbus had gathered around her, a burning exuberance leaping in her heart. Perhaps the same elation that other people found in baking a birthday cake for a friend.

How did that wildness get there in the first place? Was it germinated in grief, her profound sense of loss after her father's death? Was it nurtured by her mother's scorn? Or was it there from the moment of her conception, its blazing stripes rippling inside her DNA?

Who can say?

Darcy had worried about losing her reputation, her dignity. That fear had kept her in check for many years. It had pinioned her to the role of wife and mother, kept her from unleashing her impulses on people who crossed her over the years, and on people who did nothing, but whom she found herself daydreaming about killing. Her father would have wanted her to be a loyal wife, and so she was. Until now. She reasons that he would still be proud of her. *You see what you want and you take it.*

In prison, she is known for being a vicious, ice-cold killer, and so she is left alone. She has a little fan club, too, a group of fawning women who all clamor to do her bidding.

So, it's not at all as she feared—quite the opposite. She is finally stepping out of the shadows and telling the world, *This is who I am.*

Look at me if you dare.

[[ACKNOWLEDGMENTS TK]]

[[ABOUT THE AUTHOR TK]]

[[AVID CREDITS PAGE TK]]